THE LAST RENDEZVOUS

A TALE OF HIGH ADVENTURE AND TRAGEDY IN THE FINAL DAYS WHEN MOUNTAIN MEN REIGNED SUPREME

by

Bonnie Jo Hunt

and

Lawrence J. Hunt

... We have now to deal with another race — small and feeble when our fathers first met them but now great and overbearing. Strangely enough they have a mind to till the soil and the love of possession is a disease with them.

Sitting Bull, Lakota

A Lone Wolf Clan Book, Vol. III

Mitakuye oyasin
(We all are related)

Wicahpi Win
(Star Woman)

Bonnie Jo Hunt
Lawrence J Hunt

Copyright 1998 by Bonnie Jo Hunt and Lawrence J. Hunt
All Rights Reserved

Library of Congress Catalog Number: 99-93133
International Standard Book Number 1-928800-02-5 (Vol. III)

A special thank you to our fine editorial staff for their detailed and tireless efforts to make this book right.

Published by Mad Bear Press
6636 Mossman Place NE
Albuquerque, NM 87110

The authors wish to express their deepest appreciation to all who support ARTISTS OF INDIAN AMERICA, INC. (A.I.A.) in its work with Indian youth. All proceeds from the sale of THE LAST RENDEZVOUS go to further the work of A.I.A. For information concerning A.I.A. contact Mad Bear Press. Contributions to A.I.A. are tax deductible and most gratefully received.

Cover art work is adapted from "Trappers' Rendezvous," painted on the Green River in 1838 by A. J. Miller. Back cover photo is through courtesy of Ohosis Lumheefeegy, Cree Nation.

Printed in the United States of America by
First Impression, Inc., Albuquerque, NM

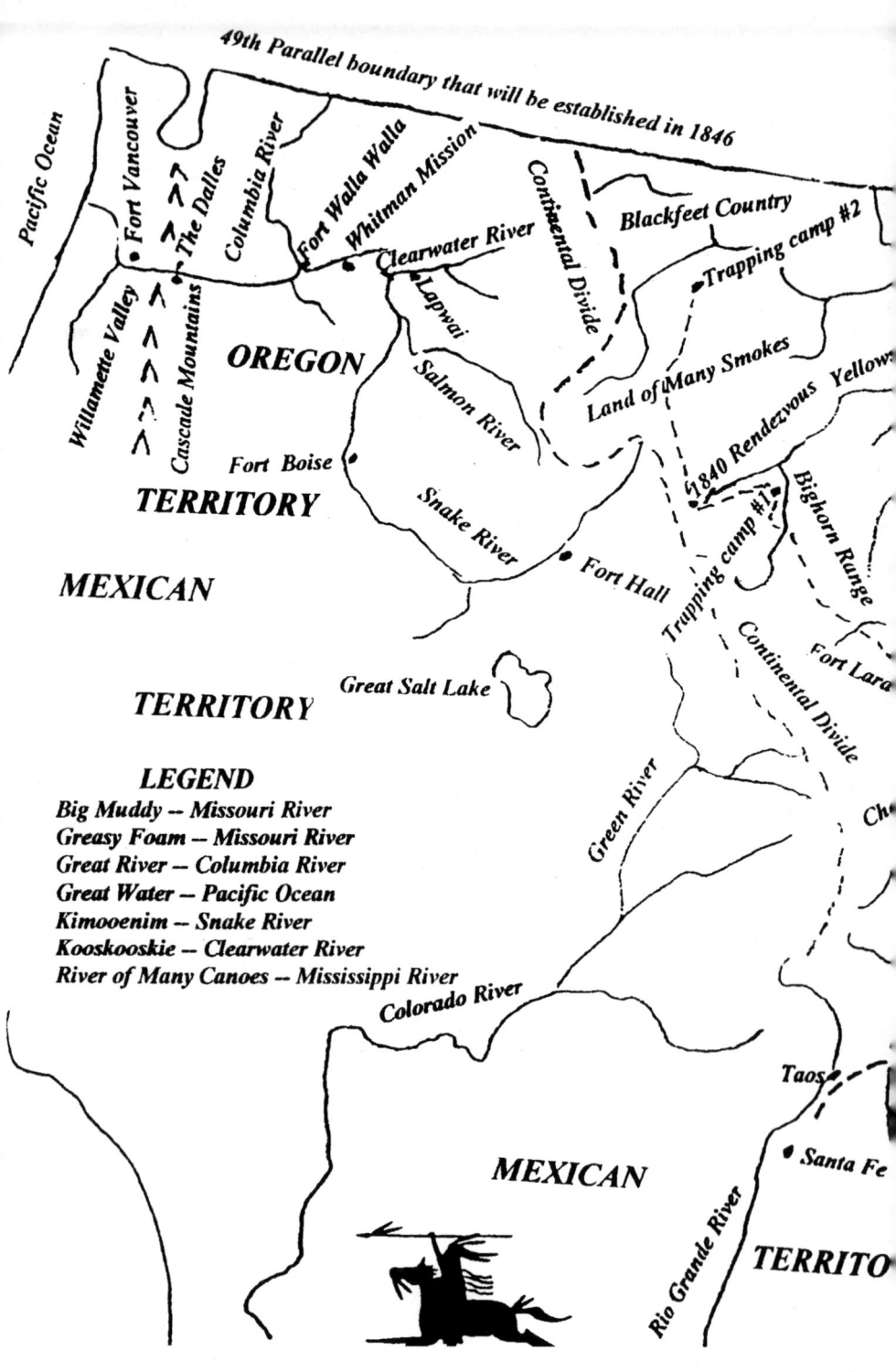

THE WESTERN FRONTIER 1840, YEAR OF THE LAST RENDEZVOUS

THE LAST RENDEZVOUS

HISTORICAL NOTE

There is a time coming when many things will change. The buffalo will disappear and another animal will take its place, a slick animal with a long tail and split hoofs.

Sweet Medicine, Cheyenne

The decade of the 1830's saw the decline of the mountain man. Beaver pelts were no longer in great demand. The beaver hat, the fashion that stimulated western exploration and made the mountain man, was out of vogue. A little worm in the Far East was the culprit. Silk top hats now took the sartorial fancy of gentlemen in the east and abroad. Buffalo robes replaced beaver pelts as the commercial product of the west. In 1839 some 90,000 buffalo hides passed over western fur trader counters. They were made into coats, carriage blankets and used as rugs, wall decorations and ornamental frills on a variety of modish apparel.

Many mountain men felt as did the Indian; the bison was a gift of the Creator. Every ounce of the shaggy animal's carcass served a purpose. To kill for hides and tongues, leaving the meat for prairie scavengers, was a crime against Mother Earth. If the mountain man did not turn to buffalo hunting, what was he to do? Some, like Joe Meek and William "Red" Craig, took up homesteads to try their hand at farming. Others resisted the tide of change and searched for trapping bonanzas in lands previously believed too dangerous to exploit.

Beginning in 1825 mountain men and traders from the east met each summer at pre-determined locations. At these meetings called rendezvous the trappers, isolated all winter in the mountains, went on colossal binges, traded their pelts and purchased sufficient supplies to last them through the next trapping season. In 1840 on the Green River near Horse Creek, the last rendezvous took place. What follows is an account of the declining days of the picturesque mountain man who accepted Indian people for what they were, married into their families and adopted their way of life.

THE LAST RENDEZVOUS

I

We always had plenty: our children never cried from hunger, neither were our people in want.

Black Hawk, Sauk/Fox

It was the Season of Tall Grass. The weather had been unduly warm. Already the hills above Lapwai Valley were turning brown. The water level in the rushing Kooskooskie had reached its peak and was on its way down. Early every morning women and children took to the hillsides to harvest the succulent kouse root. Others descended on creek banks where shoots of berry bushes were laden with fruit. The first run of eels and salmon was at its height. Fishermen outfitted with spears, nets, hooks and canoes, crowded fishing sites. In the village open space strips of meat were laid on drying racks. In pole corrals horsemen branded and gelded colts, in preparation to drive the herds to pasture in high mountain meadows.

Mother Earth's bounty was as great as any in memory, but the Lapwai band of Nimpau was troubled. In previous years they came together to offer the first fruits of every harvest to Father Sun who gave light and warmth to bring plants forth and make every living thing grow. The offerings were then buried beneath the surface of Mother Earth to give thanks for the nourishing valleys, streams and mountains. These ceremonies had been handed down from one generation to another — their origins lost in the depths of time.

These were spiritual occasions. It was the holy period when people reflected on the good life they led. These were times when people felt uplifted, as if they had risen nearer to the level of the Great Mysterious, the all powerful one who ruled the universe, who could take all good things from them with the snap of a finger. The all seeing and all knowing Creator could take away the warmth of Father Sun, make lakes and streams run dry, change grassy plains and forests into deserts and let all living creatures starve and die. The wondrous Being who brought them on Mother Earth, could destroy them in the blink of an eye.

The people recognized the power the Unseen and Eternal could unleash: the freezing storms that turned thick tree trunks so brittle they snapped from their own weight, lightening bolts that hurtled through space quicker than bullets fired from the white man's gun, wildfire that raced through treetops faster than horses could run, devastating floods that swept boulders aside like grains of sand. Yes, they knew the power of this miraculous spirit that held everything in its place. Yet, they did not fear the Almighty One. Everyone watching and listening to the messages of Mother Earth would understand and be forewarned. The Creator's voice came from everywhere. It was the whisper of the breeze in the grass and trees, the cry of the loon and call of the killdeer. It was the rippling of water in the fast moving stream, the light of the stars and moon. These messages were most meaningful in the still and quiet -- a forest glade at first morning light, on a windless mountain top or in the deep of night when all creatures of the forest slept. This was when the Creator and earthlings were one -- when the earthling felt exalted and humbled at the same moment.

These ceremonies honoring the Great Mysterious were an important part of the people's lives. Not only did these solemn occasions give people time to pause and reflect on the good their Creator provided; they were times of gayety, giving people an opportunity to dress in their finery, forget and set aside slights and previous differences. On these festive occasions lovers' quarrels were patched over, new romances started and friendships formed that would last for lifetimes. Now these ceremonies had been condemned. The missionaries, who were determined to civilize the heathen savages, said they were sinful paganistic practices offensive to the Christian God.

"I am the Lord thy God, which hath brought thee out of bondage. Thou shalt have no other gods before Me," Missionary Spalding thundered from his pulpit. "These are God's very words. He meant them for you. He meant them for me. He meant them for every human on earth. Thou shalt not bow down thyself to them, serve them for I, the Lord thy God, am a jealous God . . . ." The missionary paused, his shiny white forehead beaded with perspiration. Impatiently, he waited for the bewildered translator to catch up.

It was in 1836 when Reverend Henry Spalding began in his words, "to civilize the heathen Redskins." He never asked the people about their thoughts or expectations. Instead, immediately upon his arrival, Spalding assumed the role of feudal lord. The people, with the vision of learning the pathway to the white man's Great Spirit land called heaven, did everything they could to please him. They treated the missionary and his entourage as honored guests. They offered these teachers of the Great Spirit Book the best land on which to build their mission. When Spalding said the mission lodges should be built of logs they went far up the Kooskooskie to fell trees and float the logs down the river. Even talkative Hallalhotsoot, called Lawyer, and warrior Rotten Belly, whose evil smelling wound emitted an odor like the scent bag of a skunk, labored like slaves, taking on backbreaking tasks they never would have attempted on their own.

The people's thirst for knowledge of the Great Spirit Book did not go unquenched for long. Hardly were the foundations of the mission buildings laid before Missionary Spalding called the Lapwai villagers together before an outdoor pulpit. He spoke to them of the many things they had to do to be saved. Not once did he utter words that took into account their own spiritual beliefs or practices. It was his way -- God's way, there was no other pathway to this spiritual place called heaven. If they did not accept this, not a single member of them would enter the gates of heaven. He especially condemned the ceremonies honoring Father Sun and Mother Earth. The people were stunned; they could not believe their ears. These were sacred ceremonies they and their forefathers had observed since the beginning of time.

Like a dark cloud covering the sun, Spalding's sermon cast a shadow of confusion over the village of Lapwai. Around lodge fires people questioned themselves: should they cling to tradition or should they cast tradition aside and follow the path of Missionary Spalding? Some said yes; more said no. As a result the people continued the thanksgiving rituals but did so quietly and out of the missionary's sight. Spalding kept watch and discovered them. He vowed to stop these paganistic practices once and for all. Then another, even more sinful matter came to his attention. A single man and a married woman were living openly in sin. Raven Wing, the only daughter of former Lapwai band leader, Lone Wolf, had deserted her lawful husband. She had taken up with the Hudson's Bay trapper, Francois.

Spalding had a special abhorrence for adultery and fornication. Born out of wedlock, abandoned as a baby, and growing up with the name bastard ringing in his ears, he saw himself as a victim of these sins. Thoughts of his shameful beginnings were always with him, prickling him like a hair shirt. He called the villagers together. The crowd was so large it overflowed the mission square. "Thou shall not commit adultery! It is a commandment of God! Thou shall not covet thy neighbor's house, thou shalt not covet thy neighbor's wife, nor his manservant, nor his maidservant, nor his ox, nor his ass, nor anything that is thy neighbor's." Spalding shouted, glowering at his flock who stared blankly back. The mysteries of the Great Spirit Book were hard to comprehend. What were these strange words, "covet" — "adultery?" What were these strange creatures — ox, ass, manservant and maidservant?

Missionary Spalding, sensing their consternation, could see his sermon was not sinking in. "Aagh!" he thought, "what a cruel hand fate has dealt me. Why should I put up with this ignorant lot?" Spalding took a deep breath. God had called him to succor to the needs of these aborigines. He could not fail; he would not fail. In a more normal tone of voice he continued his harangue.

"Folks, serious sin is present in Lapwai Valley. There are two people in our midst who are making a mockery of the teachings of God. If we do not cast them out, God in all of His fury will come down and take us to task." Spalding's voice rose to its former earsplitting crescendo. "The way of the wicked is an abomination to the Lord . . . ." The people patiently waited for the sermon to end. Everyone knew of the couple who lived in the log cabin. Lone Wolf's daughter was a bit wild. No one was especially surprised when she ran away from her mountain man mate. He was a Boston, not one of

THE LAST RENDEZVOUS 7

their kind. Nor were they alarmed when Raven Wing returned after an absence of two years with the trapper called Francois and a third child. But the teacher of the Great Spirit Book had spoken. The couple were floating downstream into the fiery lake of hell. They must be rescued from this horrendous fate.

    That night the faithful surrounded the log cabin lodge where the sinful pair lived. They shouted insults, threatened to burn the place down, then showered the wooden structure with stones, arrows and spears. The assault achieved the result missionary Spalding demanded. Francois, the Hudson's Bay trapper, slipped out of the cabin under the cover of darkness, saddled a horse and galloped away, leaving Raven Wing and her three children behind — the youngest not five months old.

THE LAST RENDEZVOUS

II

*If you do bad things, your children will
follow you and do the same.*

In-The-Middle, Apache

Lapwai Valley was quiet. Dark-winged swallows swooped and dipped above the pasture grounds in the never-ending effort to satisfy their insatiable appetites. Except for the graceful swallows, the air was unusually clear and bright. The first rays of Father Sun bathed a distant hilltop. Gradually, the line of sunshine descended to bring patches of color to rocky outcroppings that studded the western bluffs. From somewhere came the melodious call of the meadowlark.

Raven Wing, her black hair tousled, uttered a sigh. It was a new day. The valley was at peace. The terrible ordeal was over — a night she would never forget. The most painful part was that she had caused it. Her man, Francois, had been against returning to Lapwai but she had insisted. She promised him again and again there was no danger, the missionary man would see that no harm came to them. They would be welcomed. Did not the teachers of The Great Spirit Book say Christian people were to love even their enemies? Had not the Long Robe at Fort Vancouver read to them from the Great Spirit Book, "Come unto me, the Lord your God is gracious and merciful. He will not turn his face from you if you return unto him." She had savored these words, repeating them over and over to herself. "Aagh!" Raven Wing thought bitterly. How little she understood these people who knew the mysteries of the book called Bible. Their tongues said things their hearts did not feel.

Raven Wing glanced at the circle of family members who had gathered to give her comfort. Her blue-eyed firstborn, Buffalo Boy, lay dozing beside his younger brother, Young Wolf. Buffalo Boy and Francois had never gotten along. He was probably glad the quick tempered man was gone. Beside her two sons sat her mother, Quiet Woman, softly crooning to baby Little Bird. Kind, tender Quiet

Woman lived for the children. If she had any thoughts about Francois, she kept them hidden.

The usually energetic, talkative Running Turtle, Raven Wing's younger brother, slouched against the porch railing, watching a family of wasps build a nest. He had more interest in insects than he did her. She glanced at her graying father, Lone Wolf, and slender older brother, Vision Seeker. They could have attempted to help her man but did not lift a hand. Vision Seeker and Francois almost hated each other. Feeling ran so high between them Vision Seeker had once taken a knife and sliced off nearly half of Francois' ear.

Lone Wolf, who sat cross-legged, his back against the cabin wall, raised his head. Like an animal testing for a predator's scent, he thrust his big nose into the soft breeze and sniffed. The result pleased him. He got to his feet and turned to the east. "The spirits of darkness are gone. The air is fresh. The evil of the night has passed. Let us thank Father Sun for this new day."

Vision Seeker and the two boys came to stand by Lone Wolf. Together, they repeated an age-old prayer of greeting to Father Sun. Without the warmth and light Father Sun provided, life on Mother Earth could not survive. Afterwards, the parents and brothers lifted their hands in gestures of farewell and drifted away, Quiet Woman giving the sleeping baby a parting pat. Vision Seeker lingered. He knew the distress his sister suffered. He wanted to ease her burden but what could he say? He had no liking for the man, Francois, but the manner in which he was forced to leave Lapwai was wrong. The behavior of the villagers shocked him. The emotion that drove them was as fierce and unpredictable as a wild prairie fire. It came to life without warning, roared into violence on the force of its own energy and was out of control before one knew what had happened. When would this smoldering emotion flare up again?

"Aagh!" Vision Seeker muttered to himself. It was like a bad dream. After Missionary Spalding delivered his acrimonious sermon, the mob gathered. Two loud-voiced youths came first. They shouted threats and threw rocks. Another group arrived, armed with clubs and spears. A noisy party of boys and dogs came next. Before long it seemed the entire village was on hand. What had possessed them? Before the coming of the missionaries the people would not have acted this way. They would not have approved of the couple's actions but never would they have resorted to violence.

Vision Seeker left the cabin. He passed Weasel Face's lodge. Except for fitful snoring, the Lapwai band leader's abode was quiet. Little did he care about last night's trouble; he was a missionary convert. Vision Seeker circled around to walk among the locust trees that bordered the mission house. A thin trail of smoke filtered up to hover above the roof. The tantalizing aroma of frying bacon hung in the air. As usual, the tireless missionary woman, Eliza Spalding, was cooking the morning meal. Soon she would awaken her husband and the day's mission activities would begin.

Did these people know what they were doing? Did they realize the change they had made in the lives of Lapwai villagers? Had they ever experienced a life of freedom, away from the strict laws of the church? How he would like to take the missionary couple to buffalo country, let them live in the fresh open air with a sky so blue and broad they could see forever. Perhaps then they would understand what the Nimpau had given up because of them.

Vision Seeker wandered on to the pasture, his thoughts glum. His parents were not well. They still grieved over the loss of Many Horses, their first son, who froze to death during a sudden winter storm. Raven Wing, their only daughter, caused them great worry. Vision Seeker inwardly groaned. Since he could remember, Raven Wing had acted more like an untamed animal than a rational being. She was irresponsible to the point of rebelling against her own good fortune. She had a good mate who gave her everything, yet she discarded him for a devious man who treated her worse than the scruffiest camp dog. What could he or anyone else do for her? She did not listen to a single word of advice. Yet, she was family, and had three sons. Who would provide the guidance and companionship they needed in the early stages of their young lives? Buffalo Boy, the eldest, needed special attention. He was as skittish as an unbroken colt.

Vision Seeker roped a horse and rode into the hills, leaving the fertile valley behind. High above the valley where few people ventured, Vision Seeker dismounted. Often he came here to watch over the herd. From this vantage point he had a clear view of Reverend Spalding's mission. He could see the students file into the building that housed the mission school. On quiet days he could hear Teacher Eliza Spalding's sparrowlike voice call the roll and explain the lessons. He wondered what it would be like to sit much of the day in the stuffy, nearly windowless classroom, listening to that high-pitched voice in the heat of summer and the cold of winter. He shuddered at the thought. Schools were against the laws of Mother Earth. They knew no seasons.

From his hillside lookout Vision Seeker could see Missionary Spalding's faithful flock plant and till the patches of ground allocated to each farmer. It was Spalding's belief the Nimpau would never become Christians until they settled down and gave up their nomadic way of life. To support this theory, he ordered plows and hoes and spent hours instructing the fledgling tillers of the soil.

The sight of the farming activity was almost more than Vision Seeker could bare. Hunters and warriors he respected marched out every morning with hoes over their shoulders to chop at weeds and scrabble in the dirt like crows searching for worms. Had these men forgotten the wondrous sight of wave after wave of waist high buffalo grass stretching to the horizon or the joy of riding full bent alongside a thundering herd of bison? Did ever they long to make camp under a canopy of stars so bright the light hurt one's eyes?

Like a humming bird going from flower to flower, Vision Seeker's thoughts flitted from one thing to another, always returning to Missionary Spalding. Vision Seeker scowled. Why was it the missionary had such a hold over the Nimpau? He spoke high-minded words but his actions did not match the words. "Thou shalt not covet anything that is thy neighbor's," Spalding told the people, yet took for himself whatever he wished as though all of Mother Earth was his for the taking. When he arrived in Lapwai he chose one of the most choice plots of land in the valley on which to build his mission.

Here springs of clear cold water gushed to the surface the year-round. It was a pleasant place where children loved to play and people liked to rest on hot summer days. Horses and wild animals, too, came here to drink and graze. Missionary Spalding had the area fenced off. Those who formerly used and enjoyed the pleasant spot were forced to go elsewhere.

Even with all of its attractions, Spalding soon soured on the mission site. He decided the flat land near the mouth of Lapwai Creek where the stream entered the swift and dangerous Kooskooskie, was a more satisfactory mission location. Local residents raised objections but Missionary Spalding stubbornly refused to listen. The land was needed for a great group of buildings that would be the center of all mission activity in the region, he claimed.

Moodily, Vision Seeker watched the village come to life. Like groundhogs emerging from burrows, lodge occupants appeared, blinking in the bright sunlight, clumping around still half-asleep. In the old days they would have been up to greet Father Sun. Not any more. Prayers to Father Sun were condemned. Vision Seeker eyed the mission compound. Missionary Spalding had eaten breakfast and limped out to inspect the millrace he was having his flock build. Days previously, he had fallen off his horse, badly injuring himself. His ribs were broken and a knee sprained. The injuries did not stop him from forging ahead with the development of the new mission site. On the banks of the millrace he had plans for a gristmill and sawmill. He was anxious to get the job done.

The thunder of galloping hoofbeats pounding up the Kooskooskie Trail caught Vision Seeker's attention. A horseman appeared closely followed by the men who guarded the entrance to the valley. A crowd quickly gathered in the mission square. Tall, gangly Weasel Face, leader of the Lapwai band, ran out to wave his long spidery arms. Students streamed from the schoolhouse followed by spare, wispy-haired Eliza Spalding. Vision Seeker recognized the rider. He was a member of Doctor Whitman's Cayuse mission at Waiilatpu, one hundred twenty miles to the west. It was obvious he brought urgent news. Trouble had been brewing among the Cayuse.

Perhaps it had taken a turn for the worse.

Vision Seeker swung into the saddle and rode down the slope toward the village. He chose a path that took him by Raven Wing's log cabin. He wanted to make certain she was all right. Suddenly the horse shied. Sounds of a struggle came from a patch of weeds. "Ah-hoh!" Vision Seeker uttered in surprise. It was Buffalo Boy, his face a mask of dirt and blood. The boy he faced was even more disheveled. They rammed at each other like rutting bull elk. The intensity of the encounter shocked Vision Seeker. Buffalo Boy, always quiet and unassuming, was flailing away like a person gone berserk. His opponent was his friend, Spotted Badger.

Vision Seeker's first thought was to separate the combatants. Buffalo Boy's nose dripped blood; one eye was nearly closed. He fought with a grimness that made Vision Seeker hesitate. He was about to deal with a boy who, over the past two years, had suffered through the worst kind of traumas. For months his mother and the man she had taken up with had lived like fugitives, always on the move, always looking over their shoulders, always wondering whether or not they would have anywhere to sleep, anything to eat. The healthy, happy boy who left Lapwai returned a moody starveling. Yet, here he was, fighting like a demon.

The two boys were evenly matched and getting tired. They leaned on each other, huffing like two wind-blown colts. He expected one or the other to drop. Instead of calling it quits, they seemed to gain new strength. Spotted Badger drew back his fist and planted it in Buffalo Boy's face. Buffalo Boy seized the arm and gave it a twist. Spotted Badger howled. Down they went, rolling over and over, kicking up puffs of dust. A village dog, excited by the commotion, came barking up the trail. It was Spotted Badger's pet. The dog snarled and snapped at Buffalo Boy. Vision Seeker pulled the dog away by the scruff of the neck. This time he did not hesitate. He let go of the dog and seized each boy by the collar and held them apart. A fresh flow of blood gushed from Buffalo Boy's nose. Spotted Badger's arm hung limp. With his good arm he picked up his pet and ran down the trail, looking hatefully over his shoulder as he went.

Vision Seeker brushed Buffalo Boy's dusty clothes and attempted to wipe the blood from his face. "What is this all about? I thought Spotted Badger was a friend."

The slender ten year old youth looked away. His lower lip quivered. For a moment Vision Seeker thought he might cry, then he pulled himself together. "I hate him and everyone in Lapwai Valley. I wish we never had come back."

Vision Seeker took his nephew by the hand and led him to a grassy spot where he sat him down. For a while they rested in silence. Vision Seeker knew what had happened. Spotted Badger had repeated village gossip. Buffalo Boy would not stand for it. He had defended his mother's honor. The talk came from Spalding's scathing sermon. The missionary denounced what he called "that wanton woman." He pointed a finger in the direction of the log cabin. "In Biblical times a woman taken in adultery would be stoned to death."

Finally Buffalo Boy spoke. Vision Seeker could tell he was near tears. "If father were only here . . . ." Vision Seeker winced. It was a call for help from one who had lost his way and did not know which way to turn.

THE LAST RENDEZVOUS

III

*The perverse in heart are an abomination to the Lord.
But the blameless in their walk are His delight.*

Book of Proverbs

On the far side of the continent a youth of seventeen years was also anxious to have a father again. His mother died giving life to him and his twin sister. Their grandparents had reared them and now they were in failing health. Their greatest wish was to see their only son, the twins' father, before the Grim Reaper came for them. They begged the youth to find him. The search was launched with high expectations. Family, neighbors and church congregation gave the youth a big send-off. From the bleak shores of the North Atlantic, down the turnpike to Philadelphia and west to the banks of the Allegheny, he journeyed. Dan, the old gray horse, gave out just beyond the city of Pittsburgh.

The youth, whose name was Joe, pulled the saddle from the lame animal's back. He patted the old gray neck and tried to swallow the lump in his throat. To abandon his friend was more than he could bear. Dan had been part of the family since he could remember. It was Dan who gave him his first horseback ride. It was Dan who waited each afternoon at the corral gate to greet him with a joyful whinny when he returned from school. Dan was the last link with his New England home. Joe watched the animal limp away to munch on a patch of grass. The horse lifted his head, and flicked his tail at a deer fly. The big soft eyes glanced at Joe as if to say, "It is all right; this is as good a place as any to die."

Joe choked down the lump in his throat. If he had a gun he probably should shoot the poor animal, but that would be like killing one of the family. It was best just to say farewell, old friend; it was a good life. He wiped away the mist that clouded his eyes and threw the saddle over his shoulder. At a crossroads he came upon a few shanties. A snuff-snorting, shifty-eyed man forking manure from a pole corral, offered Joe a dollar for the saddle.

"It's worth a mite more. But what kin I do? I'm barely able ta keep the wolf from the door as 'tis," the man whined. Inside the dirt-floored building three small white, peaked faces stared out, their eyes round as saucers. A scowling slattern wearing a dirty apron, loomed up behind them. A furry brown puppy with a white patch on its forehead, lolled out a pink tongue and wagged its tail, the only token of friendliness in sight.

"Hard times, is it?" Joe asked. It was almost as painful to part with the saddle as it was with old Dan. His grandfather had given it to him on his sixth birthday. He took the dollar and shoved it in a pocket. It would be foolish to lug the saddle any farther and he couldn't afford a horse. The important thing was to keep moving. He had to find his father before snow hit the high mountains.

"Yep, this Van Buren depression's hit us hard." The shifty-eyed man's complaining whine became more pronounced. "Everybody's pickin' up an' goin' west, hopin' fer the best, I guess. From the looks of yuh, that's what yer doin'."

"Yep, Dad traps beaver out west. I'm planning to find him."

"Yuh've a fur piece ta travel. Maybeso, yuh kin snag onta a keelboat goin' down the Ohiyo. They mosey but beats walkin'. Then they's steam packets, a mite faster. Down Cincy way you'll see stern-wheelers. I'm told some're outfitted like fancy hotels: featherbeds, fancy food, gamblin', dancin', drinkin' . . . Travelin' preacher calls 'em sin boats. Claims the hurrahin's somethin' scandalous, don't really git goin' 'til wee hours of the mornin'. Then there's fights, knifin's an' sech. Many a coon, nakkid as a jaybird an' dead as a mackerel, is found on the river banks. Yep, tain't a fittin' place fer God fearin' folk. I'd give 'em a pass, if I was you."

The slender youth slung his carpetbag over his shoulder. "Thanks for your advice. I had best be on the road."

The man lugged the saddle inside. "If times come normal, kin easy git ten, fifteen dollars fer this," he told the slattern whose right cheek bulged with chewing tobacco. "Thet poor coot. Talked so perlite I could hardly keep a straight face. So green, it's a wonder cheat grass ain't sproutin' outta his ears. Says he's goin' west ta find his beaver trappin' pa. Hell! He'll be lucky ta find his way across thet next row of hills."

"Yuh should've asked him in," the slattern scolded. "Whilst yuh was feedin' him corn squeezin's I could've gone through the carpetbag. Could've held some coin. Us'ns might as well gits it afore folks on the river pick the poor soul clean."

"Shut up, woman. Don'tcha hev no decency? I took disadvantage enuff as 'tis."

Unaware of the domestic crisis he left behind, the young man continued on his way. When he came to the Ohio River he remembered the shifty-eyed man's advice. He started looking for keelboats. His feet were sore. A soft spot in the sole of his boot told him it was about to wear through. At a place called Crow's Landing he came upon a keelboat pulled up to the river bank. A bearded man in a torn canvas coat was seated on a log. A tin of coffee simmered over coals of a nearly dead fire. Alongside the man two youngsters huddled together, warming their small hands. Like twin fledglings in a nest, their faces turned toward the stranger. Joe half expected them to open their mouths to be fed. They shyly watched him approach, sliding close to the man in the torn coat. They both were walleyed.

"Pa! Pa! Someun's here," one of them said, tugging on the man's tattered sleeve.

"Shut up!" a sharp female voice ordered. "What's the matter? Yuh think yer father's blind?" From under a shelter on the flat-bottomed keelboat a female emerged, her hair the color and consistency of soiled straw. She came down a plank and walked barefooted across the muddy bank. At each step mud spouted up between her toes. She stopped by the nearly dead fire, with hands on hips. Her spindly arms were mottled with puffy insect bites. Through rents in her soiled, long skirts, flies buzzed around scabby sores. They appeared so inflamed and painful, Joe glanced away.

"Why don'tcha talk ta the young fella?" The strident voice carried across the water. A flock of mudhens swimming along the far river bank took flight.

The man glanced up. His pale eyes had a filmy appearance as if peering through smoked glass. "Woman! Don't stand there. Git the young man a spare cup."

The woman took a battered tin object, sloshed it in a pail of water and wiped it with the tail of her soiled skirt. She poured from the steaming can only to drop it and curse. She sucked on a burned finger and slapped the two little girls who tittered. Like beaten pups, they whimpered and slid behind their father's back.

"Easy, ol' girl," the man chided. "They thought yuh was funnin'." He took the can that served as a cup from her and handed it to the guest. "Name's Ben Cook." He motioned for the young man to sit on the log.

"Joe, Joe Jennings." The youth sniffed the coffee doubtfully.

"Won't kill yuh. Put hair on yer chest. Yuh goin' down river?" the man asked.

Joe nodded. "St. Louis."

"St. Looey! We'uns are headin' thet way, too." His smoky eyes studied the youth. "The missus an' I was jest sayin' we need a strong young fella ta hep out, paddlin' an' steerin' an' the like. Since yer goin' our way maybeso yuh'd like a ride. Board an' room, sech as it is, all the way ta St. Looey. What do yuh say?"

The young man took a sip of coffee. The surface was oily, the taste bitter. It was all he could do to keep from spitting it out. Bravely, he swallowed and studied the keelboat. It was no more than a high-hulled scow with a tiller in the stern. The deck was jammed with household items and farm equipment: boxes, barrels, sacks and an old steamer trunk. Farther forward he could see a plow, a harrow, horse collars and harnesses. He knew nothing about river boating but it did not look like much of a craft. Yet, he'd had his fill of walking and there was a long, long way to go. "Sounds like a good idea," he finally said. "When do we start?"

Drifting, poling and paddling, they made it down the muddy river. Day after day the flat-bottomed scow zigged and zagged its way through and around snags and sand bars. Joe and the straw-haired woman took turns manning the tiller. The old man's eyesight was so bad he could not distinguish one side of the river from the other. They lived on beans, bacon and coffee, the children crying half the time from stomachaches.

They drifted past farms, villages, stretches of thick forest and an occasional landing dock where stacks of cordwood awaited to fire the boilers of steamers. They poled and paddled by Quincy, Marysville and into the outskirts of Cincinnati. Here a roustabout on shore answered Ben Cook's call for help. He came in a rowboat and took their line, rowed back to the dock and fastened it to a capstan. As they poled toward shore, the roustabout rolled in the slack line. Finally, he snubbed the rope tightly around an iron cleat. The unwieldy craft was safely secured to the wharf. With an assist from the roustabout, Ben Cook and his wife clambered up a makeshift ladder to the dock. The kind helper waited wistfully for a tip. Ben Cook reached in his pocket but his wife pulled him away.

"We're buyin' groceries. Thet's enuff business ta leave in one place," she snapped in her shrill, scratchy voice.

The roustabout backed off and watched them walk toward town. He glanced at Joe and shook his head. "Yuh look like a decent sort. What're yuh doin' with this trash, anyway?"

Joe was left to guard the boat and keep watch on the two walleyed girls who howled and screamed, furious and frightened they had been left behind. Everyone within earshot stopped to stare. Joe would have liked to crack their heads together. Finally, the wails turned to erratic sniffles as a stern-wheeler came thrashing alongside. A surge of water rocked the keelboat, bouncing cooking utensils from a makeshift cupboard. Black smoke jutted from the steamer's twin smokestacks, momentarily blocking out the sun. Its whistles screamed and bells jingled. A boatman on the stern-wheeler's bow threw a line ashore, another line snaked out from the stern. The paddles of the riverboat churned the river water into muddy foam. Gradually, the stern-wheeler inched up to the bustling wharf. The passenger plank went out and a uniformed officer led a parade of young women ashore. Clothed in full skirts, wide-brimmed hats and carrying fancy parasols, the ladies tripped along to an awaiting carriage. The display of finery sent the walleyed girls squealing with delight.

"Look it! Look it! Thet woman's hair's the color of a brass spittoon," one girl excitedly announced.

Joe found the holiday gaiety and bustling activity as absorbing as did the girls. After the passengers filed off, a loading platform was thrust out from the dock. A line of black-skinned workers began to carry freight aboard, trotting single file up the narrow gangway with sacks of grain, carcasses of beef, tubs of butter, kegs of beer, baskets of produce and crates of chickens. Coming off were crates, boxes, barrels and luggage that were loaded onto drayage wagons drawn by shaggy-legged horses.

Gradually, the turmoil ceased. The freight was aboard. The drayage wagons drawn by the shaggy horses lumbered from view. Only a few men remained on the wharf sweeping up the debris, mostly horse manure. Like a giant sleeping monster, the steamboat idly hissed, waiting for its masters to send it on its way. The two girls, remembering their parents had abandoned them, went back to howling.

#

Beyond Cincinnati river traffic became heavy. Besides packets and stern-wheelers, more and more keelboats appeared. Occasionally giant rafts of logs or sawn timbers glided along, taking up wide sections of the river. To keep from colliding with the varied river craft, constant vigilance was required, especially at night. Long hours without sleep and dysentery from bad food and water, made them all creep around like apathetic zombies. At Keokuck Ben Cook said they would put in and rest up for a few nights. For once his sharp tongued wife did not argue.

The diminutive river port was overcrowded and surprisingly busy. A medium-sized stern-wheeler lay docked next to a giant, panting side-wheeler. Two small side-wheelers churned in to vie for a single dock space. One pilot cursed and shouted at the other. The captain of the boat nearest to the dock ran out of the wheelhouse to shake his fist. "Yuh dumbbell, heave to. We was here first." The strident voice carried across the river. Somewhere on the far shore came the hee-haw of a donkey.

"I guess yer right, yuh long-eared coot. I hear yer mother callin'," the captain of the second side-wheeler answered.

The two river craft came so close together a deck hand on the first side-wheeler jabbed a long pole through the pilot house window of the second, breaking the glass. "Now, what was it yuh was sayin'?" the first captain asked. "I couldn't hear yuh."

By the time the three day rest stop passed, four more keelboats arrived, packed with families fleeing President Van Buren's depression. The Smiths, Browns, Reynolds and Parsons came from one West Virginia community in the Kanawha Valley. The Cooks greeted them warmly. In some obscure way the Cooks and the Kanawha Valley families were interrelated by marriage. They spoke with a twang Joe could barely understand. Among the newcomers were a dozen young people, including four single females about his age. They all had the same suspicious, squinty, hungry expression. They spoke at once, their voices shrill and unpleasant. Joe was reminded of his Granddad Jennings' pigs squealing and pushing at the trough, clamoring to be fed. Their clothing hung on them like sacking, faded and tattered. Holes and tears revealed patches of bare skin, caked and scaly with dirt. When they came aboard Ben Cook's vessel they gave Joe a bold, speculative examination. One of the girls coyly chucked him under the chin with a grime crusted fist. "What're yuh doin' tonight, big boy? Maybeso, we could do somethin' excitin'."

A tall, spare women with bony, long arms jerked her away. "Yuh lost yer manners? Thet ain't the way ta go 'bout courtin'."

"What's this young buck doin' here, anyways?" Joe heard one of the men ask Ben Cook. "He don't look nor talk like us'ns."

"Jest along fer the ride," Ben explained. "Goin' west ta jine his pa. They's goin' beaver trappin'."

"Ah! Thet fella couldn't ketch cold, let alone a beaver."

Joe gritted his teeth. "Damn these ignorant country folk," he swore under his breath. They thought anyone from east of the Allegheny had no common sense. Seething, he went about his chores.

The night before they were scheduled to leave Keokuck, the four families gathered on Ben Cook's keelboat for a party. Over an open fire they roasted sausages wrapped in bacon scraps. The people from Kanawha provided demijohns of hard cider. The young people sat on the stern of the boat, drank cider out of tin cups and ate the sausage and bacon bits off roasting sticks. Joe sat alongside the young men, trying his best to be agreeable. Their talk was as rough as their looks. Every third word was profane. If Granny Jennings were here she would wash their mouths out with lye soap, he thought wryly.

The young men looked and acted much worse than their female counterparts. Stringy, dirty hair hung to their shoulders. Their facial features were pockmarked with blackheads as large as buckshot. Scraggly, spotty beards sprouted from their chins. Facial skin not covered by hair and blackheads, was pimply and sallow. Big, wide-spaced teeth, discolored and dripping with tobacco juice gave them the look of slavering hyenas. Their eyes were shifty and discolored with prominent protruding red veins. The narrow, squinty faces reminded Joe of giant-sized rodents except he could not think of a rodent as homely and unclean.

Joe had to admit, he did not look much better. After weeks on the road his hair had grown down over his ears. He could feel the beginnings of a scratchy beard. His clothes had faded and shrunk from sun and rain. But he had attempted to keep his body clean by nightly dips in the river. It was the unwashed, smelly bodies of his companions he couldn't stand. They were surrounded by water but not once had he seen any of them, including the Cooks, do more than swish their hands in the river and dash water on their faces.

"Hev another swig. Yer fallin' behind." A redheaded youth with a pointed sunburned nose shoved a demijohn at Joe. The sharp profile with unruly red hair standing on end, gave the youth the appearance of a barnyard rooster.

Joe tipped the jug and took a tentative sip. The smell and bitter taste nearly made him gag. He handed the jug on but Red Rooster was not satisfied. "What's the matter, Greenhorn? Too prissy ta drink with us'uns? It's time this city dude larned country manners." He seized the jug and shoved Joe flat. "Hold him," he ordered. "This coon's goin' ta drink or inta the river he goes."

Two youths held Joe on his back. Red Rooster tried to pry open his mouth. The grating of the demijohn on his teeth gave Joe the strength of three men. He jerked free of the two holding him. Leaping to his feet, he threw himself at the redhead, knocking him overboard, demijohn and all. Just as the remaining Kanawha youth pounced on him there came a desperate call from the river.

"Help! Help me! Fer keerist's sakes, I cain't swim."

"Throw him a rope," one of the girls shouted. The rest of the females ran to the side of the barge and began to scream.

"There ain't a damned rope to be had."

"Fer heaven's sakes!" Ben Cook shouted, running up from midship. "Git somebody down there who kin swim. Yuh cain't let the poor fella drown."

Nobody could swim. The youths turned on Joe. "Yuh no good eastern dude, it's yer fault." Again, the youth in the river shrieked for help. Joe evaded the threatening hands of his attackers and dove into the water. It was obvious no one else was about to go to the rescue. Before he could surface the redhead was upon him. They both went down, down until they struck bottom. Joe attempted to free himself. The clutching arms were like tentacles of an octopus. He struggled, but the arms squeezing him only tightened. He found himself in complete darkness, weird shiny lights blinding him. His heart pounded until he thought it would burst. With all the strength he could muster, he thrust a knee into Red Rooster's midriff. The tentacles released. Joe's arms were free. He grabbed the redhead by the coxcomb hair and shot to the surface, pulling the gasping, clawing Red Rooster behind him.

Someone had found a rope and tossed it down. Joe looped the end around Red Rooster's waist. His companions pulled him aboard the keelboat like a hooked fish. No one bothered to help Joe. He swam to shore. He was so weak and trembly he could hardly crawl up the bank. After recovering, he came aboard via the landing plank. When the redhead came to, he sat up and began to curse. Joe dried himself the best he could, then picked up his carpetbag and walked off the boat.

"Hey! Where yuh goin'?" Ben Cook demanded. "Come back heya. We hev a bargain."

Joe kept walking. To heck with them. From here on he would take a steam packet.

"Kin yuh beat thet? We took thet boy in, fed him, give him a home an' thet's all the thanks we git . . . ." The sloshing and swishing sounds of Joe's wet clothes drowned out the whiny, complaining voice of Mrs. Ben Cook.

Joe stopped to take off his shoes and wring out his socks. He felt miserable. He expected to find westerners heroic stalwarts like his father. So far the only people he had encountered were mean, foul creatures little better than the lowest of animals.

THE LAST RENDEZVOUS

IV

*When the messenger of death comes,
all matters cease.*
Chinese Proverb

A messenger arriving from anywhere always created excitement in Lapwai Valley. This was the way news came from the outside world. No messenger, however, aroused more interest than did the rider from the Cayuse mission at Waiilatpu. He rode past the village outposts without breaking stride. It was a breach of protocol that could not be ignored. The offended sentries galloped in pursuit. So fast did the intruder ride the sentries did not catch up until the horseman brought his lathered mount to a stop in front of the mission building where the Spaldings lived.

"Why go past like we are children playing games?" an outpost guard demanded.

"I bring urgent message," the rider replied.

"What are these important words you bring?"

"For ears of missionary man. No one else."

Threats were useless. The messenger remained adamant. He would tell the message to no one but Missionary Spalding. A quarrel erupted. Weasel Face hurried from his lodge to see what was going on. He also questioned the messenger but had no better luck than the guards. He stomped back and forth, mortified that his authority as leader of the Lapwai band was so rudely ignored.

Lone Wolf, also attracted by the commotion, quickly sized up the situation. Here was an opportunity to show arrogant Weasel Face how a proper leader of the Lapwai band should act. "Do not abuse our Cayuse brother," he admonished. "Did not the Creator make us all equal, to share in the gifts of Mother Earth alike? Why not then treat this man with respect. If he has instructions to speak only to Missionary Spalding, that is what he should do. Perhaps these are holy words not meant for unlearned ears."

Inside the mission house Reverend Spalding, who had already been out to inspect the gristmill and sawmill sites, returned to relieve his aching feet by removing his boots. Now he could not get them on. By the time he was properly shod, the quarrel in the yard was getting out of hand. Just as guards were leading the Cayuse horseman away, Spalding hobbled outside. He crutched up to stand by the messenger's mount. The Cayuse horseman still remained silent until Spalding waved Weasel Face and the spectators away. The Cayuse dismounted. In a voice barely above a whisper, the message was delivered. Missionary Spalding turned pale. For a moment onlookers thought he would fall in a faint. Walking quickly from the school, Eliza Spalding arrived. More conversation in low voices was exchanged. Mrs. Spalding hurried her husband inside the mission house. The boy who helped around the mission came out. "Hurry! Fetch Missionary Spalding's riding horses and three pack animals from the pasture," he ordered.

The villagers glanced at each other in dismay. It was plain to see the messenger brought bad news. But what was it that would cause the missionary to pack up and leave? Why weren't they told? They looked to the messenger who unsaddled his horse and staked it out to graze, then sat down with his back against a tree and methodically began to chew on a piece of dried meat taken from the pocket of his sweat stained shirt. The grim set of his face told the watchers he would not speak. He had performed his duty. It was now time to recover from his journey.

Lone Wolf returned to the long lodge that housed his many relatives. In the days when he was leader of the band this situation would not have happened. He would have had a boy take care of the visitor's horse, have invited him into his lodge for refreshments and had a smoke of friendship. Afterward the messenger would have told him the news. "Wagh!" Now it seemed no one had time for the old, pleasing ways. It was hurry up do this -- hurry up do that: the millrace, gristmill, sawmill and mission buildings must be completed.

Yet, Lone Wolf was as curious as any villager. What message did the Cayuse man bring? Why was it so secret only the ears of the missionary could receive it? The previous night's troubles already had people upset. Did the messenger bring word of more trouble? Did it have to do with Raven Wing? He had to get to the bottom of this.

"Where's Vision Seeker?" Lone Wolf demanded of youngest son, Running Turtle.

Running Turtle answered with a shrug.

"Find him," Lone Wolf ordered. "When something important happens he's always some place else."

On the hillside, trying to smooth things over after the Buffalo Boy - Spotted Badger fight, Vision Seeker had completely forgotten the arrival of the messenger. He was reluctant to leave his nephew. Buffalo Boy's battered eye was nearly closed. His nose was swollen and oozed blood. His upper lip was puffed as though stung by a wasp. One glance at her son would send Raven Wing into a frenzy, something neither she nor Buffalo Boy needed. Vision Seeker attempted to tidy up the lad as best he could. His precautions were unnecessary. Raven Wing already knew about the fight. Young Wolf, her second son, had banged into the lodge. "Buffalo Boy is in trouble! Spotted Badger is beating him to death!" he blurted.

"Aaah!" Raven Wing groaned. What calamity would befall her next? She was at her wits' end. Five month old baby Little Bird had suddenly developed a fever. She could not leave the sick child untended and she had no one to call on. Her friend, Small Goat, refused to speak to her. Her parents' lodge was too far away to ask them for help. When Vision Seeker and Buffalo Boy arrived she was near tears.

"Shame! Shame! Why do you make silly quarrels?" she scolded. Before she could say more Running Turtle came rushing up the trail from the village. He dropped on the porch steps, panting like an overheated dog. "Cayuse man comes with message," he informed Vision Seeker. "Father says you must come quick, talk with him — ask what words he brings."

"Oh!" Raven Wing drew in a sharp breath. Her man, Francois, had taken the trail to the Cayuse homeland. Had something befallen him? Buffalo Boy's face took on an expression of alarm. One eyelid began to twitch. His thoughts were also of Francois. Did the cruel man send word for Raven Wing to join him? If so, his mother was certain to obey. Francois had such a grip on her no matter what he asked she would do his bidding. Buffalo Boy put a hand up to keep his eyelid still. The twitching had started after a beating by Francois. Now, just the thought of the man made the eyelid jump.

Vision Seeker glanced away, his thoughts bleak. Things were worse than he thought. The lad who made such a good fight against Spotted Badger had suddenly fallen to pieces. What had happened? He had been all right until Running Turtle appeared.

"Ah-hoh!" The messenger's arrival frightened the lad. The rider had come from Waiilatpu, the direction Francois had taken. Buffalo Boy thought he brought news of the Hudson's Bay trapper. What suffering the boy must have endured to have such terrible fears. Vision Seeker held out his hand. "Why don't you come with me? Let us hear from his own lips what message the Cayuse man brings."

Lone Wolf impatiently had waited for Vision Seeker to arrive. He met him outside the long lodge. "What have you been doing? As the elder son you should take more interest in village affairs," Lone Wolf scolded. "Oh! Ha!" he exclaimed, noticing Buffalo Boy. "What has happened to you?" He glanced at Vision Seeker for an explanation. With his lips and chin Vision Seeker signaled a warning. Lone Wolf understood. He had been in a scrape; the reason for it would come out in good time. "Hmm!" he grunted. "A wasp or bee can do great damage. Perhaps on the morrow the pain will leave. Come," Lone Wolf ordered as he hurried them along the path to the mission buildings. Buffalo Boy, still uncertain as to what to expect, had to trot to keep up. In his unhurried gait, Vision Seeker silently followed, his mind occupied with Buffalo Boy's plight.

"Ah! When I had the chance I should have slit Francois' throat instead of slice off a piece of his ear," he said viciously to himself. "No one, not even one of Mother Earth's slightest creatures, should endure treatment like this."

In front of Missionary Spalding's house a crowd had gathered. People stood quietly talking. Someone whispered a member of the Waiilatpu mission had had an accident. Buffalo Boy breathed a sigh of relief. The news the messenger brought did not concern Francois.

Weasel Face and his sons arrived with the animals Spalding requested. The horses were bridled and saddled, ready to travel. The pack mares with halter ropes trailing, stood waiting patiently to receive their loads. Weasel Face, his narrow, long face aglow with importance, strode back and forth switching his pant leg with a rawhide quirt. Vision Seeker went up to question him.

"It is not a matter that concerns you," Weasel Face said. "You take after your father. You think you should know all. Tell your father to go back to his lodge. He can do no good here."

Vision Seeker stared at the band leader, his dark eyes as cold and hard as pellets of ice. "It is not your place to tell me what my father should or should not do."

"Come! Come!" Lone Wolf interrupted, speaking so loudly the crowd fell quiet. "My son has every right to question you. We all should know what this is about."

Weasel Face's cheeks and neck grew turkey gobbler red. He did not accept criticism well, especially when it came from members of the Lone Wolf clan. "Old man, this is none of your affair." Weasel Face motioned for his sons to lead the pack mares next to the mission house where crippled Missionary Spalding and his fragile, spare wife, Eliza, struggled with cases and bags. Overhearing the sharp exchange, Missionary Spalding came forward. He walked hunched over as if his broken ribs had caved in his chest.

"Yes, the people should know what has happened. The messenger from Cayuse country brings sad tidings. Little Alice Clarissa Whitman fell into the Walla Walla River and drowned. It is important we go to Waiilatpu and do what little we can to help our brethren during this trying time."

A hush fell over the crowd. Not long ago little Alice Clarissa and her parents had visited Lapwai. They remembered a bright-eyed, wild rose, cheeks with a dimple in each and a pert pink nose that turned up at the end. Her cheery treble voice reminded them of the cheep of a robin in early spring. She had romped around the mission grounds like a newborn colt testing its legs. Every mother in the village adored this lovely creature and would have spirited her to her lodge if she could. It was unbelievable the Creator had taken this beautiful being away.

"This is very bad news," Lone Wolf said to Vision Seeker. "It is only proper a member of the Lone Wolf clan journey to Waiilatpu. In bad times like these we stand by our friends. Medicine Man Whitman has done much for our people."

Vision Seeker agreed. His father was right. Doctor Marcus Whitman had worked hard to relieve the suffering of the Nimpau. Even at that moment Quiet Woman used the salve the good medicine man provided. Inflammation of the eyes plagued many members of the village. The medicine Marcus Whitman handed out so freely gave the sufferers welcome relief.

The pack mules were loaded. The missionary group came to mount up. Spalding attempted to sit the saddle but the pain of his injuries was too great. For a moment there was confusion. Missionary Spalding had to make the journey but how was he to manage it? Someone came up with the solution; he could travel by canoe down the Kooskooskie and into the Kimooenim and on to the Hudson's Bay trading post at Fort Walla Walla where he would disembark to make the short land trip to Whitman's mission by wagon. Edwin O. Hall, who just days before had arrived in Lapwai with the first printing press in the Northwest, volunteered to lead a group of riders ahead. They would ask to have the funeral of baby Alice Clarissa delayed until Reverend Spalding's river-journeying entourage arrived.

Vision Seeker made preparations to leave. Buffalo Boy watched, his face sad. "Can I go?" he wistfully asked.

Vision Seeker hesitated. The woebegone expression tugged at his heart. "All right. Get your pony. I am sure your mother will be glad to have you go."

When they arrived at the cabin and asked Raven Wing, she frowned. "I need my son here. He is the man of the house now. I will not let the missionaries take him away from me as they did Francois."

"Oh, Mamma!" Buffalo Boy uttered. He was already astride the patched black and white pony that his grandfather had given him. Because of its strange coloring, he called it Magpie.

Vision Seeker thoughtfully rubbed his chin. He did not want to irritate his sister and he did not want to leave Buffalo Boy behind. They both were in a bad state. In her present mood Raven Wing might do something desperate, perhaps pack up her family and run away again. "It would make Quiet Woman and Lone Wolf happy if you went to stay in the long lodge," he suggested to his sister.

"Do you tell me how to live?" Raven Wing snapped.

"Your presence in the long lodge would give Lone Wolf and Quiet Women great comfort. They suffered much while you were away."

In his quiet, kindly way, Vision Seeker persuaded Raven Wing to stay with her parents in the long lodge. Before she could change her mind, he helped her mount his horse. Buffalo Boy carried the feverish baby and Young Wolf, Raven Wing's second son, tagged along as they made the way down the trail to the village. Lone Wolf and Quiet Women welcomed their daughter and her family with open arms. The twenty families that occupied the long lodge, gathered around. Everyone wanted to comfort the sick baby who was softly crying. While the crowd was occupied, Vision Seeker motioned to Buffalo Boy. They mounted up and were away before anyone realized they were leaving.

For a long while the two riders were alone. Missionary Spalding and his wife had already departed by canoe. Missionary Hall, who led the horseback riders and was expected to hurry ahead, had disappeared down the Kooskooskie Trail that led toward Waiilatpu. As soon as they cleared the valley, Vision Seeker urged his mount into a lope. Buffalo Boy, on black and white Magpie, followed closely.

Buffalo Boy felt as though all of his troubles had been washed away. He took a deep breath. The air was fresh and clean. For the moment he could look back over the past two years without a twitch or a tremble. Actually, there had been some good times, especially during the first weeks after leaving Lapwai. Everybody was happy. They saw country rich with game. Francois allowed them to hunt and play as long as they liked. The nomadic life seemed just right.

Then came the long dreary days when Francois insisted they stop where he could carouse and gamble. There was nothing to do but sit and wait. More times than not, he returned in a surly mood, smelling of firewater. When things did not please him, he slapped and cursed, treating family members worse than unruly dogs. If Buffalo Boy and Young Wolf were asleep they were aroused and ordered into the darkness. One night they were forgotten and spent the night huddled in a clutch of brush. Only once did they attempt to creep back before they were called. The sounds they heard frightened them. What they saw made them sick. The man did unspeakable things to their mother. What hurt most was that she did not resist. Right then and there Buffalo Boy vowed one day to kill the cruel stranger who had taken the place of his Boston father.

Late in the day Vision Seeker and Buffalo Boy caught up with Missionary Hall and the other Lapwai riders. Weasel Face gave them a scornful glance and did not bother to greet them. Vision Seeker did not mind. He nodded to Missionary Hall and spoke to the others in his soft, thoughtful way. Near nightfall the riders made a stop to water and rest the horses. The men stretched their legs and chewed on dried meat. Before an hour was up they were back in the saddle. Dawn broke; still they kept riding. At midday Waiilatpu came into view. The tired horses and riders pulled up beside a pole corral. Missionary Hall dismounted and flipped open the lid of his silver-cased pocket watch.

"Not bad going," he chortled. "We covered the one hundred-twenty miles in exactly twenty-five hours."

Buffalo Boy barely heard him. A horse in the mission corral caught his eye. It was a Nimpau-bred Appaloosa gelding. He recognized the markings. "Aiiee!" he uttered so sharply Vision Seeker glanced up in surprise. Too terrified to explain, Buffalo Boy pointed.

THE LAST RENDEZVOUS

The horse was the one Francois rode when he fled from Lapwai Valley!

THE LAST RENDEZVOUS

V

A good man can't be corrupted by the tavern nor a bad one reformed by the synagogue.
Yiddish Proverb

The river port of St. Louis did not disappoint young Joe Jennings. The steam packet he had boarded after the frustrating keelboat journey chugged against the current, holding for a place to berth. All dock space was filled. Smaller craft also waiting, impatiently skittered about like skater bugs on a pond. The chugging vessels created a series of wakes leaving the waters roiled and choppy. A rowboat burdened with passengers, baggage and a dog, bobbed on the crest of a wave, then fell back into a trough. The dog leapt overboard. A passenger attempted to seize the dog, only to lose his balance and fall overboard himself. After rescuing the man the oarsmen turned and plowed toward shore to disappear midst the black pilings that supported the wharf.

The western river bank was also a picture of confusion. People ran hither and thither like ants taking cover from a storm. Huge horses with shaggy fetlocks pulled iron-tired wagons and carts that sent sparks flying on cobblestone streets. Sacks of grain, bales of cotton, stacks of lumber, even a pen of sheep and goats crowded the already chuck-full wharves. The livestock, supplies and raw materials awaited transport to factories, warehouses or buyers in distant cities, trading posts and farms.

St. Louis had a population of fifteen thousand but the industry and commerce of a city much larger. Everywhere the flow of riches and burgeoning growth was in evidence. North of the loaded wharves unwieldy looking flat-bottomed bateaux laden with buffalo hides, casks of salted buffalo tongues and bales of beaver pelts were lined up like dominoes, the bow of one rammed tight against the stern of the next. Log rafts lay grounded below a screeching sawmill that spewed lengths of lumber like kernels from a split sack of corn.

Columns of black and yellowish smoke spiraled skyward from a foundry, giving the overhead sky a somber, tarnished appearance.

Back from the levee were corrals of horses, mules, oxen and cattle. Beyond the corrals rolling stock of every kind were parked higgledy-piggledy along deep furrowed tracks. Heavy freighters, prairie schooners, Dearborn carriages, two-wheel mule killers, buckboards and two mud splattered stage coaches stood waiting for loads of freight and passengers. Everywhere there was construction. Carpenters, bricklayers, roofers and artisans of every trade labored at a hectic pace. It was obvious the Van Buren depression had not crippled St. Louis.

Pounding hammers, screeching saws, ringing bells, blowing whistles, shouted orders, boisterous laughter, explosive curses, calls of greeting and farewell bombarded the newcomer's ears. A marching band struck up a lively tune as a big stern-wheeler cast off and swung into the river. The steam packet took advantage of the open space and scuttled in to dock. Joe waved his hat and cheered. He had finally arrived. Now, in this anthill of activity, all he had to do was pick up his father's trail.

Only after he came ashore and was buffeted by the crowd, did Joe's confidence fade. He had a slip of paper with an address on it but how did one find it in all this confusion? He looked for a policeman but none was to be seen. He attempted to ask an officious looking gent. The man brushed him aside as though he were an annoying insect.

A street sign said Front Street. Every place seemed to be either a tavern or a grog shop. From their dark interiors came curses, laughter, the tinkle of banjos and jaunty rhythms of piano players. In front of each were motley groups of men. They were sitting, standing and still others were lying asleep or passed out, Joe could not tell which. Everything smacked of debauchery and gaiety.

Away from the bustling waterfront the city's inhabitants appeared more sedate. The limestone mansions of merchants made wealthy by the rich flow of commerce through the river port, gave off an aura of permanence and respectability. In the cosmopolitan business district, every race and class of folk walked the streets. From their lips came the melodious languages of Spanish, French and others not identifiable to Joe's untrained ear. The garments they wore were as varied as the people. Strolling side by side were businessmen dressed in broadcloth suits, gamblers in black frock coats, flashily dressed belles from the French quarter, uniformed steamboat officers, big men in fringed weather-worn buckskins and an occasional Indian wrapped in a blanket.

In the business district banks stood cheek to jowl with barbershops, mercantile establishments and haberdashers. An imposing building named Rocky Mountain House, rocking with merriment, attracted Joe's attention. He had once overheard his father mention this place. He stopped to size it up. The twang of a banjo, high pitched female voices, shouts and whoops of men enjoying gambling and drink, drifted to Joe's ears. He turned away, shuddering at the thought of what Granny said happened to people who frequented places such as this. He dug into his pocket and pulled out the slip of paper, the only address his father had left behind. Gimpy's Horse Emporium, was written in an almost illegible scrawl.

A youngster carrying a small wooden box, tugged on his sleeve. "Shine, mister? Best shine in town."

Joe looked down at his shoes and laughed. The leather was cracked and worn. The top of one toe poked through a hole. "Tell you what," Joe said. "I'll give you a couple of coppers if you'll take me to this place." He showed the paper to the boy.

"Mister, I ain't much fer letters an' numbers. What does it say?"

"Gimpy's Horse Emporium."

"I know about mercantile but em-em-por-ium? What kinda business is that?"

"I suppose they deal in horses."

"Maybeso, a horse corral? Ther's plenty of 'em in town. Emporium! Awful fancy way of sayin' horse barn." The youngster grabbed the piece of paper. "I'll ask me friend in the barbershop. He hears lots from gents goin' on whilst gettin' shaved an' trimmed."

The youngster quickly returned. "A fellow named Gimpy runs a stable near the waterfront. Shorty, the barber, thinks thet might be the place yuh want. Walk toward the river a couple of streets, then turn left. After a short ways yuh'll see a tall buildin' thet ain't been painted fer years. I'd take yuh but a fella wants a shine."

Joe thanked the boy and handed him a couple of coins. He turned down the narrow street the boy had pointed out. He mopped his face. The weather was sultry and hot. He felt faint. To conserve money, he had taken deck passage which meant days and nights spent on open deck. The days were not too bad but nights were terrible. Besides passengers jostling for space, hordes of mosquitoes tormented would-be sleepers from dusk until dawn. Joe felt as if he hadn't slept for a week. He walked along barely taking notice of his surroundings. A scattering of horses tethered to hitching posts stomped their feet and with their tails swatted flies. Somewhere in a room above the street a baby cried. Halfway down the block a blacksmith was shoeing a horse; smoke and heat poured from the forge. A wagon pulled up to unload a dozen barrels of flour at a bakery dock. The smell of fresh bread penetrated the street aroma of urine and horse manure. Joe's mouth watered. He hadn't eaten since morning.

Two streets down Joe turned to the left as the shine boy had instructed. He walked another three blocks and came to a high-pitched, dilapidated building that had the looks of a barn. A skinny old man with a red bandanna knotted around his throat was pitching hay. The polished tines of the fork gleamed in the sun's fading rays. Down each side of the stable was a line of horses. Through a back door Joe could see more horses and a dozen or more long-eared mules impatiently waiting to be fed.

"All right! Yuh dumbos, yer worse than a pen full of squealin' hogs," the man with the pitchfork grumbled. He walked through the barn and into the back corral with a noticeable limp. Joe followed, coming up so quietly the poor man jumped.

"Dad blast it! Don't yuh know better'n sneak up on a fella like thet? Yer lucky I didn't take a pitchfork ta yuh."

"Hello! I'm looking for Mr. Gimpy, owner of this establishment."

"Don't yuh smooth talk me. I ain't buyin' a thing. Cain't yuh see, I'm busier than a one-legged man at a butt kickin' spree."

Joe put down his carpetbag and picked up a spare fork. "I'll give you a hand."

"Yeah?" the querulous voice softened. "If'n yuh wanta help, git up in the loft an' pitch down some hay. These critters go through feed like a grasshopper plague."

For awhile there was only the sound of hay plopping on the ground and the munching of teeth, punctuated by satisfied snorts, stomping of hooves and swishing tails.

"There, I guess thet'll hold 'em fer a spell," Gimpy said. "The hell of it is, in the mornin' I havta do it all over again. Might as well be tied down to a barn full of milk cows. Say, where'd yuh larn ta handle a fork? Yuh act like a regular hay hand."

Gimpy leaned on the fork handle and studied the stranger. He liked what he saw. A slender youth in his late teens. Wide shoulders, narrow hips, a strong determined chin that was just beginning to sprout whiskers. When he got filled out he would be quite a man. Rather handsome bucko -- startling blue eyes, well-proportioned nose and fair skin, except where it was peeled from too much sun. He was polite, helpful and spoke pleasantly and respectfully — qualities seldom seen in young men any more.

"Reared on a farm," Joe explained. "Worked a lot of haying in the summers: mowing, raking, shocking, stacking. Forked it again in winter to feed the stock."

"Nuthin' like workin' a farm ta larn things. Yuh ain't lookin' fer a job? Sure could use an experienced hand."

"No, I'm looking for my pa, Nathaniel Jennings. Thought you might know him. When he left home there was a paper with your name on it, 'Gimpy's Horse Emporium.'"

"By gum! How long ago was thet?"

"Two years ago, haven't seen him since. Dad's not one to write; he sends money but never says where he is, just that he's working the trap lines catching beaver."

"Son, yer lookin' fer a needle in a haystack. Beaver country takes in all outdoors. As fer thet piece of paper — anyone could've writ them words. Cain't recall a gent with the handle of Jennings. Course, lotta folks don't go by their right names. What does yer pa look like, anyhow?"

After Joe described his father Gimpy uttered a sympathetic cluck. "Sounds like hundreds of men out here. Don't think yuh'll hev much luck findin' him in the city. Most beaver hunters're at the summer rendezvous. I betcha thet's where yer pa is. The past few summers they've been in Wind River country, a fer piece from here."

The young man looked so disappointed Gimpy tried to cheer him up. "There's one party of trappers in town. Those hungry critters in the side corral belong ta 'em. I wish they'd come an' git 'em quick. The hungry varmints hev stuffed enuff hay an' grain down their skinny necks ta make 'em sick. Anyways, I was thinkin' these boys might hev news of yer pa. If'n yuh wait aroun' a spell yuh could ask 'em."

"Dad mentioned Rocky Mountain House. Might he be there?"

Gimpy looked doubtful. "Most trappin' fellas don't bed down there, least not fer long. Yuh see, it's kinda a place where yuh hit town an' let yer hair down -- womin, likker an' sech. If yuh expect ta find yer pa in this burg, yer best bet is ta stay right here. Sooner or later every respectable traveler puts his horse up in this barn. Yuh kin pitch hay fer room an' board. Not a roomin' house in town kin match thet."

#

The St. Louis weather remained hot and muggy. The bustling, noisy activity that so impressed Joe at first, began to get on his nerves. He had remained at Gimpy's stable, pitching hay, mucking out, doing anything he could to help. Gimpy praised him, fed him, gave him a place to sleep and taught him many things about the care of horses and the management of the stable. Joe met and spoke with horsemen who rode in from all points of the compass. He asked everyone the same question. "Do you know a trapper by the name of

Nathaniel Jennings?"

"Nathaniel Jennings? Naw never heerd or seed a galoot with such a fancy moniker. Maybeso, yer lookin' in the wrong place. Sounds like a dude from the east," was a typical answer.

As the days rolled by Joe became increasingly uneasy. The terrible thought his travels had been in vain, haunted him. He had taken the old man's advice and waited for the appearance of the trapping brigade that housed its horses in the barn. He had the sneaking suspicion Gimpy encouraged him to stay on because he enjoyed his company and needed his hay pitching help.

A week passed. Still the trappers did not show. The confidence he felt when he left home was gone. Perhaps it was a mistake trying to find the big man he and his sister called Dad. After all, he had not been much of a father. He first went west when they were barely toddlers. He was absent nearly a dozen years. When he did return he only stayed a year, not long enough for the twins to get to know him. While he was home he spent little time with them. He walked around the farm like Tabby, the cat, stalking a bird. He seldom spoke. When he did it was slow and deliberate as if his thoughts were elsewhere. There were times when he did appear to take an interest, asked about their schooling or picked up a textbook and leafed through it. Then one day he was gone, left a note saying he was going back out west to work the trap lines. Only once since then had they heard from him, a scribbled note attached to a bank draft.

#

Somewhere a rooster crowed, then a mule hee-hawed. Gimpy pushed the squeaky barn door open and began to pump water into the horse trough. Joe, still half asleep, clambered down from the loft. Another day had come and gone and the brigade of trappers had not appeared. Working together, Gimpy and Joe forked hay and mucked out the stable. Not until the sun's rays began to filter through the tops of the cottonwoods that shaded the corral did they go in to feed themselves. Gimpy fried bacon and eggs on a potbellied stove. After he dished them up he spoke the first words uttered that morning.

"I tol' yuh these dumb critters was worse than a pen full of milk cows: feed 'em in the mornin'; feed 'em at noon; feed 'em at night. Yuh might as well hev a flock of kids, leastwise yuh kin train 'em ta do somethin' fer theirselves." He took a sip of coffee and spit on the floor. "Aah! Tastes like the bottom of a slop barrel. I guess I fergot ta throw out yestiday's grounds."

While a fresh pot of coffee brewed, Gimpy sat back and lit his pipe. "I know yuh been thinkin' I been takin advantage of yuh by keepin' yuh here but yuh see, I know this town an' the people an' yuh don't. Thar's crooks an' cutthroats thet kin take the skin off a tenderfoot in a minut. Anyways, now thet I see yuh got yer head screwed on pretty good, I think yer ready fer the Rocky Mountain House. By chance thar might be someun hangin' aroun' the place thet could hev a line on yer pa."

Joe was furious. Just as he suspected, the old fraud had been putting him on all the time. "Thanks for the room and board," he said stiffly. "Maybe I can pay you back some time." He walked out without looking back.

An hour later Joe stood in front of Rocky Mountain House. It was not yet mid-morning. Already the place rocked with the sounds of merrymaking. A man stumbled through the swinging doors, grinning to himself. He doffed his hat to a lady and nearly fell flat on his face. Joe hesitated. What would he do if he did find his father in there? What would he say or do? Perhaps it was best he did not find him. He turned to leave. A mountain of flesh layered over with buckskin blocked his way. He muttered an apology and stepped to one side. A big hand seized him by the arm and held him fast.

"Pilgrim! Don'tcha look where yer goin'?" A single beady eye peered out from under the brim of a hat, black and shiny from wear and dirt. The other eye was hidden beneath a black patch. A buckskin shirt lay over the human hulk in folds so bedaubed with grease it had the look of badly polished leather. Tangled hair fell to the creature's shoulders. Before Joe could resist, the one-eyed man thrust him through the swinging doors.

"Don't yuh know, it ain't perlite ta stand outside an gawk? Patrons don't like ta hev theirselves spied on. Suppose yer ol' woman was a teetotaler an' yuh wanted ta down a couple of slugs? Yuh see what I mean?"

Joe attempted to free himself. The big hand that gripped his arm tightened. It might as well have been in a vise.

"I guess yuh ain't accustomed ta sech high falutin' places an' don't know perzactly how ta act," the big man rumbled. "Jest stick with ol' Link. He'll larn yuh fast. First off yuh need a leetle courage." He propelled Joe up to a long polished bar. He slapped a meaty hand down with the crack of a rifle shot. The bartender abruptly turned around.

"Link! I don't want to tell you again. There's nothing on the house!"

Link leaned across the bar and glared at the bartender with his good eye. "I'll hev yuh know, we's payin' customers. Show the color of yer money, son. This galoot ain't too bright."

The bartender glanced at Joe and shook his head. "Young fellow, I hope you know what you're doing."

"Two whiskeys!" Link snapped. "We ain't here fer conversation."

The bartender slapped amber liquid into two glasses. "All right, let's see your coin."

Joe hesitated until Link jabbed two meaty fingers in his face. Begrudgingly, Joe plunked the dollar he got for the saddle on the bar.

"Mud in yer eye." Link tossed the drink down in one gulp, then fished inside a greasy shirt pocket to extract a long, thin black cheroot. Clamping it firmly in the wide space between his front teeth, he lit it from the flare of a whale oil lamp. His one eye studied Joe through the smoke. "Bottoms up! We ain't got started yit."

Joe took a tentative sip and grimaced. It was worse than Red Rooster's hard cider. Again he thought of Granny. Many times she had warned about the curse of demon liquor. She claimed when it got a grip on a person his brain dissolved bit by bit. Yet, here he

THE LAST RENDEZVOUS 43

stood, drink in hand, like an old saloon guzzler. Joe took a gulp and choked.

"Ho! Ho!" Link chortled. He took Joe's glass and downed what was left. "Now let's toddle back an' pay our respects ta the ladies."

Reluctantly, Joe followed the big man into a back room. A buxom woman and two younger females lounging on a sofa, glanced up. The buxom woman glowered at Link.

"I warned you, Link. No rough housing. These girls are not biddies at your fur trapper rendezvous."

"Melissa, we're on bona fide business. This here lad's larnin' the ways of the west. Now, who's better ta edify him in the matters of the flesh than Madam Melissa?"

The madam eyed Joe with a mixture of pity and interest. "Son, are you actually here on business?"

"I guess so," Joe said, still dazed by the turn of events. He felt the need to keep her talking. She was protection from the one-eyed monster.

"Let's visit first." Melissa brought a tray with several glasses and a bottle and set it down on a low table. She poured an ample amount of liquid into two glasses; in a third she poured a few drops. She handed the full glasses to Link and Joe. The third glass she kept for herself.

"Down the hatch!" Link toasted, tossing off his drink with a flick of the wrist. He smacked his lips and helped himself to another drink. "Come, young fella, watcha waitin' fer, the cows ta come home?"

Wishing to look good in Melissa's eyes, Joe took a swallow. The fiery liquid went up his nose, down his Sunday throat and somehow flooded into his eyes and nose. He gasped for air. When he finally sucked in a tortured breath, Melissa took him into an adjoining room. He was happy to hear the click of the lock as she turned the key in the door. For the time being he was safe from the terrible Link.

Melissa insisted he lay down. He sank onto a bed so soft it

seemed to fold around him. Satisfied he was all right, she went out, closing the door behind her. It was such a relief to be away from One-Eye Link, Joe laid back. Sleepless nights, worry over finding his father, the drinks, soft bed and quiet, combined to send him sound asleep. He awakened to find Melissa sitting beside the bed. Through nearly closed eyes, he studied her. An expression of tenderness had replaced the brittle, garish demeanor. She looked so pleasant and happy, Joe smiled.

"Playing 'possum, are you?" she brusquely asked.

Joe sat up so abruptly he felt dizzy. For a moment the madam's look of concern returned. "Son, you shouldn't be in places like this. You look like you had good upbringing. Go home. I'll bet your mother is worried sick."

"I don't have a mother," Joe blurted. He suddenly felt sorry for himself. Why had he gotten himself into this mess? It was the worst disaster yet. He should never have left home.

"Ah! Just like me to put my foot in it. But you can't stay here. Find a good boarding place and keep away from men like One-Eye Link. How are you fixed for dinero? Here's a dollar. Should see you through the night." Over his protest, she thrust a bill in his pocket. "Now, I'll let you out the back way." She opened a door and glanced up and down the street. "It's all clear. Do as I say, there's a good clean boarding house near the waterfront. Ma Harris is the proprietress." She gave him a motherly peck on the cheek then pushed him into the street, locking the door behind him.

Joe looked about, feeling lost. When he had entered the saloon it was broad daylight. The streets were filled with people, horses and carriages. Now, in the gloom of the night, the streets were nearly empty and frighteningly dark. He was tempted to beg Melissa to let him stay the night, but she had locked the door. She didn't want him underfoot. Heavy footsteps coming toward him, made the boardwalk creak. He pressed against the wall, waiting for the heavy treads to pass. A side street door opened. A shaft of light shot out, blinding him. He groped along the wall. The heavy tread came nearer. Joe started to run. He was too late. A huge hand spun him around. A blow sent his head reeling. His nose spurted blood. A big fist pummeled him, this time in the ribs. The pain doubled him up. A hand thrust its way into the pocket containing his purse. Desperately, Joe struck back. The side street door opened again. The light revealed a silhouette of the thief. Long black hair fell forward over a narrow forehead. Where there should have been an eye, there was a black hole.

    The thief gave him a final kick, and disappeared into the darkness. Joe struggled to his knees. His ribs felt as though they were crushed, his stomach and side ached. Blinded by pain, he stumbled off the boardwalk and fell sprawling into the dusty street. Four horsemen riding abreast, rounded the corner. Joe clawed his way toward the boardwalk. The pain was too much. He rolled over and put up his hands to ward off the flying hooves. Streaks of red and white danced before his eyes, then total blackness descended to bring relief.

THE LAST RENDEZVOUS

VI

Then came . . . missionaries who had houses to sleep in, and gardens planted, and who hesitated to sleep in the Indian's wigwam or eat of his wild meat. . . .

Ohiyesa, Santee

The Waiilatpu mission stood in a pleasant open space. A large adobe house was the first evidence of its presence to attract the visitor's eye. This was the residence of Marcus and Narcissa Whitman. A short distance away rose another adobe structure only slightly less imposing than the main house. Between the two houses was the blacksmith shop and a corral formed by a circle of wood slabs standing endwise secured by a frame of poles and posts. Beyond the second adobe house a millpond was taking shape to supply water for a gristmill which was still in the planning stage. In front of the mill site a garden was laid out. The warm weather had already brought forth waist-high rows of corn. Alongside the bright stalks of green, tendrils of peas and beans wound up stakes planted in the ground. Next came short rows of radishes, carrots, lettuce and other low-growing green vegetables. On the far side of the gristmill site lay a large area set aside for field crops. In uncultivated areas grew great clumps of coarse grasses, some higher than a man's head. The abundant coarse grass gave the location its name, Waiilatpu, which in the Cayuse language means "Place of The Rye Grass."

Just behind the mission compound rose a steep hill. In earlier days, before the coming of missionaries, from its summit native guards watched over their herds, spotted game and kept a sharp lookout for enemy raiders. From this vantage point the landscape could be surveyed in all four directions. On the western horizon dark rocky cliffs brooded over the Great River on its way to the sea. To the north, rolling hills stretched to the southern banks of the Kimooenim. To the east, sage-covered bluffs gave way to a purple backdrop of haze that cloaked the Blue Mountains -- homeland of the Nimpau. To the south, grassy plains faded into gray-purple foothills leading

THE LAST RENDEZVOUS

to rich pasture lands bordering the upper Walla Walla and Umatilla Rivers. The scene, with its brilliant canopy of blue overhead, displayed all the wondrous beauty of Mother Earth. It was hard to believe God took innocent baby Alice Clarissa away from a paradise like this.

The advanced party of Lapwai mourners led by Missionary Hall did what little they could to ease the burden of the grief-stricken Whitmans. Still, waiting for the arrival of the Spaldings and the day of burial, was a period of tension, especially for Buffalo Boy. The presence of Francois' horse kept him on edge. Was the cruel man somewhere nearby? The thought caused goose bumps to rise on Buffalo Boy's skin. Francois still would be furious over the treatment he received at the hands of Missionary Spalding's flock. He was a vindictive man who would not allow the least affront to go unanswered. In his present mood there was no telling what he might do if he should come upon the Spaldings traveling unprotected along the trail from Fort Walla Walla.

Vision Seeker was also uneasy. His fears were not so much for the safety of Missionary Spalding but for Buffalo Boy. The former Hudson's Bay trapper was like a trapped snake. He would strike out at anybody in the Lone Wolf clan. He had good reason to hate him, Vision Seeker. It was he who had sliced a good chunk from one of Francois' ears. The desire for revenge must burn like a hot coal in Francois' heart.

Vision Seeker, accompanied by Buffalo Boy, climbed the hill behind the mission and studied every square foot of the mission grounds. Their search was in vain. Vision Seeker was not surprised. It was futile to think Francois would be hanging around. It was not likely a man who fled one mission establishment would take refuge in another, but there was no doubt about it. He had been here. The horse he had ridden away from Lapwai was here in Waiilatpu.

The two Nimpau men returned to inspect the animals in the corral. Vision Seeker opened the gate and slowly walked toward Francois' mount, holding out his hand while uttering soft, coaxing words. The horse jerked its head up, snorted and shied away.

"Ah!" The poor creature has been treated badly," he muttered angrily. Its mouth was bloodied and torn. On its back an open saddle sore attracted a swarm of flies. From the way the horse favored a front leg it had a bruised frog, the pad that protected the underside of the hoof. "Aiiee!" The man was evil. Anyone who treated his mount this cruelly should not be allowed to live.

"Whatcha after, Injun?" A bearded, tobacco-chewing mission worker slouched up to lean against the side of the corral. From the way he spoke Vision Seeker knew he was a newcomer. None of Whitman's regular mission people would speak and act in such an officious, rude manner. Vision Seeker stopped his inspection and walked toward him.

"Are yuh deaf? I say again, whatcha doin' here? If yer thinkin' on thet hoss, it ain't fer trade ner sale." The bearded man loosed a flow of tobacco juice. The splattering liquid came within inches of Vision Seeker's moccasined foot.

Vision Seeker strode straight ahead as if unaware of the intended insult. He vaulted over the fence, landing directly in front of the bearded wrangler. Deliberately, he took the knife from the sheath at his belt. With a flip of his wrist, he sliced a chunk of wood from the fence and began methodically to whittle it to a point, the shavings falling at the bearded man's feet. Buffalo Boy held his breath. He had never seen his uncle like this. His face had the cold, threatening look of an approaching winter storm. The bearded man took a step backward until blocked by the fence. When he had the stick shaved to a fine point, Vision Seeker, rammed it into the top of the post inches from the man's bearded chin.

"Now, my good man," Vision Seeker said in perfect English. "How did you come by this animal." He pointed with the knife blade toward Francois' horse.

The bearded jaw dropped. Tobacco juice dribbled from the corner of the startled man's mouth. An English speaking Indian, one who spoke the king's English better than he did, left him flabbergasted. He swallowed his spit and nearly choked. "I swear, I got the animal fair an' square. Well, maybeso not so square. This guy busts in hiya like his tail was on fire. He pulls up on thet critter an' wants ta trade — tall, dark an' mean, acted like fer two cents he'd bite the head off a snake. I tell yuh, he was mad as a rabid skunk, wavin' a long-barreled gun. He picks out a nag an' switches saddles, swearin' an' carryin' on all the while. He ain't satisfied with one animal; he takes two. Opens the gate an' takes off, ridin' one critter an' leadin' the other. Thet's the gospel truth."

"Which way did he go?"

"Thataway." The man pointed a dirt crusted finger toward the Blue Mountains. "He went bustin' through the Cayuse herd, scatterin' critters from hell ta breakfast. A couple of herders took after him. Doubt if'n they caught him. Last I saw he was ten lengths in front, hightailin' it fer thet far range of hills."

Vision Seeker glanced at Buffalo Boy. They had the same thought. With the missionaries gone what would keep Francois from returning to Lapwai? He had two horses. He could cut out more from the Lone Wolf herd, pack up Raven Wing and the two youngsters and be miles away before anyone could stop him.

#

On the third day after setting out on the canoe trip from Lapwai, Missionary Spalding and his wife, Eliza, arrived at Fort Walla Walla. They spent the night with the fort factor, Pambrun. The next day they departed for Waiilatpu in a spring wagon. Near midmorning they arrived at Whitman's mission. The two missionary ladies fell into each other's arms. Finally, Narcissa Whitman, who had held up so well, broke down.

"Oh! How terrible it's been," she cried. "I keep telling myself it is God's will but inside I know it was all my fault. We had set the table for supper. I went to the garden to fetch some radishes and lettuce. When I came back Alice Clarissa was gone. I had the terrible feeling she was in great danger. Somehow it came to me exactly what she had done. Alice Clarissa saw the table was set. There was no water in the cups. She took the empty cups and went to the river to fill them. That has to be what happened. We found two cups on the river bank. No one else could have put them there. Oh! How unknowing we humans are. Tragedy awaits around every corner and we pretend it isn't there. We leave everything in the hands of God hoping He will keep us from harm. But we have to do our part. I let Him down. I leaned on Him too often. He took Alice Clarissa to teach me a lesson. Oh, the heartache — the guilt. How will I ever be able to live with myself again?"

Umtippe, the Cayuse who had discovered the drowned girl's body and pulled it from the river, was given the honor of carrying the tiny casket to the grave site. The missionaries followed, Reverend Spalding, leaning heavily on the arm of Eliza. The situation was almost more than he could manage. His thoughts kept reminding him of what could have been. A requirement of the Mission Board was that missionaries have wives as helpmates. He had asked Narcissa Prentiss, who later became Mrs. Marcus Whitman, to be his helpmate. She refused him. If Narcissa had accepted his proposal, this could have been their child. "Ah!" The pain that penetrated his heart was far greater than all the suffering endured from the fall off the horse.

At the side of the grave the funeral entourage stopped to line up on either side of the open pit. Umtippe placed the small coffin on the mound of freshly dug dirt. Reverend Spalding took his place at the head of the grave. To steady himself, he stood shoulder to shoulder close to his wife who held him by the crook of his arm. He opened the Bible. For a moment he stood silent, tears flowing down his cheeks. Through blurred eyes he read from the Book of Kings.

"Run now, I pray thee, to meet her, and say unto her, 'Is it well with thee? Is it well with thy husband? Is it well with the child?' And she answered, 'It is well.'"

In spite of an attempt to remain unmoved, Buffalo Boy found tears coming to his eyes. He had not known little Alice Clarissa nor had he met the Whitmans before, but the solemnity of the occasion, the grief-stricken missionaries and the stolid face of the Cayuse, Umtippe, made him weep. The scene and its sounds created an atmosphere of desolation and dejection. The sun was low, throwing lengthy, dark shadows across the mourners. A breeze blowing in from the river, made a keening moan as it passed through the tall grass and weeds. A lone crow in a tree kept cawing dolefully. A turkey buzzard circled high over the hilltop and from the Cayuse encampment a dog howled. It was as if all creatures and things of Mother Earth sorrowed over the loss of baby Alice Clarissa.

The drone of Missionary Spalding's voice ended. A hymn was sung, the haunting melancholy notes rising up to echo back from the hillside. Even impassive Vision Seeker was moved. He brushed a hand across his eyes and had difficulty in clearing his throat. Missionary Spalding intoned a prayer; Umtippe placed the coffin in the grave and Marcus Whitman sadly dropped a handful of soil into the burial pit. The mission folk replaced their hats and slowly began to move away. A group of Cayuse, who had watched from a respectful distance, came forward. The two groups made for the mission house yard where a beef roasted on a spit. Already the savory aroma filled the air. It was Whitmans' gift to the people who came to help, mourn and give solace during their painful hour of grief.

Marcus and Narcissa Whitman graciously accepted the condolences of the Lone Wolf Clan presented by Vision Seeker, but it was obvious their thoughts were elsewhere. Vision Seeker understood. In their minds they were following the path their daughter walked to the Great Beyond where she would abide for all eternity. After the brief meeting, Vision Seeker withdrew, marveling at the composure of the missionary couple. His respect for them grew. Their faith was real. They truly believed in their god and his power to comfort, welcome and make a home for those who were called to the other side. The Great Spirit who walked and talked with the Nimpau had that same power. Was the God called Christ and the Great Mysterious the same holy Being? Vision Seeker left the mission house in a quandry. He had always questioned the presence of this Christian God who created the universe, the stars, moon, Mother Earth and Father Sun . . . "Aiiee!" He had to quit thinking such thoughts. He did not want to become like arrogant Weasel Face, the devoted follower of Missionary Spalding.

The following day Vision Seeker and Buffalo Boy saddled their horses, preparing to leave. Although Missionary Hall, Weasel

Face and the other riders from Lapwai waited to return with the Spaldings, Vision Seeker saw no reason to do so. He felt a great need to get away and gather his thoughts. He could not erase the sight of the Whitmans from his mind. Behind the glow of their spiritual dedication an ominous shadow dark as a rain cloud hung above their heads. It was a vision. The death of baby Alice Clarissa would be followed by an even greater tragedy in the not too distant future.

As dusk began to fall Vision Seeker reined his mount off the trail toward a patch of bulrushes. From the base of the hillside a spring bubbled to the surface, the water clear and cold. A small stream carried the water to a pond where bulrushes grew in abundance. A flock of scolding red wing blackbirds rose up to defend their nests. "Be at peace," Vision Seeker said. "We will not harm you." He dismounted and motioned for Buffalo Boy to do the same.

After watering and staking out the horses, they sat on a grass covered knoll and ate the parcel of food Narcissa Whitman had kindly given them. The bread was unlike their own and the cheese something they had never before tasted but it was all consumed with relish. When finished eating, Vision Seeker laid back and pointed to the stars that began to light up Father Sky. First came the bright orb in the east. Then one by one twinkling dots emerged overhead. Finally the total sky took on a golden sheen. Over the distant hills slid the edge of a full moon. At first a thin, bright yellow arc appeared on the horizon, gradually it grew to the size and shape of a beaver mound rising above the level of a pond, then it became a golden ball almost as bright as Father Sun. For a long while they watched, entranced by the display Father Sky presented. Then an owl hooted and coyotes on the nearby hills answered.

"Ah!" Vision Seeker aroused himself. The magnificence of Father Sky had revived him. "Mother Earth's creatures are giving thanks to the Creator for the beauty that surrounds us and all the other good things that we receive. Perhaps animals and birds observe a religion much like ours and say prayers. They may do these things better than we, for do they not receive everything they need?"

Buffalo Boy shivered. The owl and coyotes spoke a different

message to him. The spooky hoot of the owl and lonely cry of the coyotes seemed to sound a warning. "Don't be misled by all this beauty. There are trying times ahead. Somewhere out there under the bright light of these same stars and moon is cruel, cunning Francois up to his same old evil deeds."

The next morning Vision Seeker awakened Buffalo Boy before dawn. They drank from the spring, chewed on a piece of dried meat, mounted up and were on the trail. They expected to arrive in Lapwai before dark. Again it was a silent ride. The magic of the night was gone. The reality of a new day was ahead. Vision Seeker did not feel like talking and Buffalo Boy worried over what he would find when he arrived home. His mother was as changeable as the weather. She could be bad-tempered and hateful or she could be loving and kind. Whatever her mood, he hoped she was there.

The barren hills that rose above the Kooskooskie came into view. In a short while the riders were on the ridge overlooking Lapwai Valley. The usually busy mission buildings appeared abandoned. To the right and east, smoke spiraled up to hang above the long lodge. Buffalo Boy urged Magpie forward until the pony was in a full lope. He rounded the mission grounds and came to a stop at Lapwai Creek. He hurriedly tethered Magpie and rushed into the long lodge. Lone Wolf and Quiet Woman, who were eating the evening meal, glanced up in surprise.

"Where is Mother?" Buffalo Boy asked. Before his grandparents could answer, he ran outside. Untethering Magpie, he mounted and urged the pony across the creek and up to the cabin. He dismounted in such a hurry he stumbled and skidded on his knees. Ignoring the painful scrapes, he dashed up the porch steps and pushed through the door. Raven Wing was sitting on the sleeping pallet rocking the baby.

"What is the matter?" she cried out. "Do you want to frighten us to death?"

Buffalo Boy threw his arms around her and held her tightly.

THE LAST RENDEZVOUS

VII

Do not boast about tomorrow, for you do not know what a day may bring forth.
Book of Proverbs

There were the sounds of horses snuffling and munching. A smokey lantern gave off a dim glow. Joe opened his eyes wider. It was hard to do. One eye was swollen and nearly closed. The shadowy face of Gimpy appeared. Joe struggled to sit up. Hadn't he and Gimpy quarreled and he had left the barn for good? Then the events of the day came back to him -- the meeting with the one-eyed monster, the kind madam, the pummeling . . . Joe reached into his back pocket and groaned. His purse was gone. He was flat broke.

Gimpy uttered a sympathetic grunt. "Rest easy, son. I've rubbed yuh down with horse liniment best I could. Thet should put yuh right. Sure does the animals good."

"How did I get here, anyway?" Joe asked weakly. His ribs pained him so he could hardly breathe.

"Thet band of trappers I been tellin' yuh 'bout stumbled over yuh in the street. First, thought yuh a fallen down drunk, then saw yuh was battered like an ol' milk bucket. Didn't know where else ta take yuh, so brung yuh here. They didja a good turn. Yuh was 'bout as lifeless as a froze snake. What kinda ruckus didja git yerself inta, anyways? Yuh look like yuh'd been caught in a buffalo stampede."

"I was waylaid, robbed of every cent," Joe confessed.

"I tol' yuh they was rowdies an' cutthroats up thar."

"It was only one rowdy, big as a house, wears a patch over one eye."

"Of course, yuh tangled with One-Eye Link," Gimpy said without hesitation.

"Yeah, I knew it was One-Eye Link," Joe said in disgust. "I should have been more careful."

"Yuh know ol' Link?"

"Sort of." Joe told of his adventures, realizing what a greenhorn he must appear.

The stable keeper shook his head. "I must say, yuh've been hurrahed by the best. What're yuh fixin' ta do now?"

"I have to get my stake back." He felt in his shirt pocket. He wasn't completely broke. He still had Melissa's two dollars which somehow escaped Link's grasping hands.

"Yuh'll play hell gettin' anythin' back from One-Eye Link. He's tough as a worn-out boot an' mean as sin. He lost thet eye wrestlin' a grizzly. They say the bar took one bite a ol' Link an' found the taste so rank he runned off inta the brush spittin' an' screechin'. Must've thought he was poisoned."

Late in the morning Joe was up, limping around. He attempted to fork hay but gave up and sat and watched Gimpy do the midday chores. Later, while Joe and Gimpy ate a late lunch, a stable customer knocked on the door.

"If yer ears're clean come in," Gimpy shouted.

The buckskin clad man who stepped into the cramped room was nearly as large as One-Eye Link. Instead of wearing greasy buckskins, the newcomer's dress was weathered and worn but neat and clean. A blue bandanna circled his neck. On his head jauntily perched a visored cap. From a wide belt hung a hatchet, a holstered pistol and a broad-bladed knife secured by a leather sheath. His leggings, hunting shirt and moccasins were decorated with porcupine quills and beadwork. From beneath sun bleached, almost white eyebrows, came the light of blue eyes that sparkled like rays of sun on Nantucket Sound. He took off the belt holding his weapons and hooked it on a wooden peg.

"Is this the lad we brought in last night?" he asked, giving Joe a quick glance.

"Yep, tells me jest afore yuh fellas picked him up he tangled with One-Eye Link," Gimpy reported. He scurried around to offer the visitor coffee in a battered cup.

The big man took a sip and nodded his thanks. "So young man, you received a rough introduction to St. Louis, did you? I'm

Buck Stone. May I ask your handle?"

"Joe, Joe Jennings."

"I can tell by your accent you come from New England. What's a young fellow like you doing getting mixed up with a rascal like One-Eye Link?"

"I was looking for my dad, Nathaniel Jennings. He's a trapper like you. Have you ever run into him?"

"Nathaniel Jennings? Know a Nathaniel Wyeth, but Jennings . . ." Buck shook his head. "Can't say as I have met him. How long has he been in the mountains?"

"Oh, years and years. He left my sister and me in care of our grandparents when we were babies. We only saw him once after that, came home a year and left. Sends money every summer. Drafts come from St. Louis. That's why I started my search here."

Buck Stone shook his head. "Mountain men like your father don't often frequent the city. They meet traders or teamsters at the summer rendezvous and send messages and money back to St. Louis with them. These letters and money are then forwarded east. Probably this is what your father does. Tell me about your run-in with this one-eyed varmint. We can't have newcomers like yourself beaten up and robbed. Gives the frontier a bad reputation."

Joe repeated the story, leaving out none of the embarrassing details. "I guess you must think I'm a real country yokel," he said ruefully at the end of his account.

Buck held up a broad hand. "More trail-wise folk than you have been taken in by the likes of One-Eye Link. If he had a mind to do so, the tiresome rascal could be a good trapper. Instead, he takes advantage of honest people like you. Hmm! Hanging around Rocky Mountain House, was he? Like as not, he'll still be in that part of town. In fact we should sniff around. If you are up to it, we'll mosey over there."

Buck took his knife from its sheath and tested the cutting edge of the blade, then began to sharpen it on a square of pumice stone. He took a horse hair from a saddle blanket and neatly sliced it in half. "I'd say it's just right for pole cat skinning."

Joe slowly got to his feet. He was not at all sure he wanted to take part in what was to follow. The expert way Buck handled the knife sent shivers racing up his spine. He hoped One-Eye Link was far away. Getting his money back was not worth killing for. He started to protest but the determined expression on the big trapper's face kept him silent.

Although it was still mid-afternoon, the saloon buzzed with activity. Around rows of circular tables sat men hunched over cards and stacks of brightly colored poker chips; gamblers, Joe decided. From their tired, droopy, disheveled appearance they had been plying their trade for hours. In a far corner a piano player pounded out a brassy tune. Along the bar a line of customers leaned on their elbows. Bartenders wearing white aprons, busily polished the counter between serving patrons. At a table Madam Melissa and one of her girls visited with two men in broadcloth suits.

Soundless in his moccasins, the big trapper padded up to the near end of the bar. "Before we go varmint hunting perhaps we should reconnoiter," he suggested, nodding to the nearest bartender.

"Evening, Buck," the bartender greeted. "What'll it be?"

"The usual and one for my partner." Buck turned to survey the crowd. He caught sight of Melissa. He gave a slight bow and a tip of his visored cap. "Let's join the ladies," he said, tossing a coin to the bartender.

As they approached, Melissa's smile of welcome turned to a look of concern. She put a hand to Joe's bruised cheek. "Oh dear! Did you get into trouble again?"

"He sure did," Buck said. "Link was waiting outside your rooms and lifted his purse."

"So, that's where the old billy goat got his roll!"

"Been spreading it around, has he?" Buck questioned.

"Yep, been with one or another of the girls half the night and most of the day. Can't get rid of him. Right now he's in number seven."

Buck turned to Joe. "Why don't we mosey back and say howdy?" He tipped his cap to Melissa. "I promise we won't mess things up badly." Buck gave Joe a nudge. "Drink up. No point in keeping the varmint waiting."

Joe took a sip of his untouched drink and shuddered. It didn't give him a bit of courage. It burned all the way down and his legs felt so weak he could hardly move his feet. Unsteadily, he followed Buck toward Melissa's back rooms. The big man opened the door and they stepped inside. Two girls lounging in the parlor started to get up. Buck put his fingers to his lips.

"Where's number seven?" he whispered. The girls pointed down a hall. Buck glanced at Joe. "Good! We've got him just where we want him, cornered in a cul-de-sac. His only escape is through this parlor. Now, if I was handling this shindig I'd slip into Link's room, heist his clothes and vamoose. I doubt he'll come out. A man does not like to run around naked. If he does come out I'll tickle him with old Betsy." Buck tapped the handle of the newly honed knife.

Joe's mouth was so dry he could not speak. His blood ran cold. Buck Stone expected him to do the dirty work. Old Link would eat him alive. But it was too late to turn back. If he did he would be the worst kind of coward. He took a step forward, then another and another until he faced the door of number seven. He listened. He could hear the growling sound of the one-eyed monster's voice. Cold goose bumps popped out on his skin. He glanced back. Buck was chatting with the girls. He could not believe his eyes. The big man had a smile on his face. He was enjoying himself. Joe gave the knob a twist. He shoved the door open and quickly stepped inside. A female voice squealed. Link cursed. Joe stumbled and nearly fell to his knees — the clothes! The big man's buckskins were piled in a heap on the floor. Joe scooped them up and dashed down the hall.

"Hey! What's goin' on?" One-Eye hollered. There was a thunderous crash. The bed had collapsed. Hurriedly, Joe dug through the buckskins. His hands shook so he could hardly find the grimy pockets. He came on his purse, half the thickness it had been.

"Left you a little flat, did he?" Buck had to raise his voice to be heard. The air was filled by the screams of the two girls and

Link's thunderous curses "To make up the difference let's keep One-Eye's duds." Gingerly, he picked up Link's clothes.

The door to number seven crashed open. Link stumbled out and thundered the length of the hall. "Come back here," he shouted. He shoved the screaming girls aside. His big hairy-backed hands reached for Joe. Joe ducked under his grasp and darted through the back doorway which Buck had alertly opened. Buck slammed it shut and turned the key in the lock. "Pretty good skunk hunt, don't you think?" he asked, placing Betsy back in her sheath.

#

The elation Joe Jennings experienced over recovering the stolen money and his triumph over One-Eye Link, quickly faded away. Buck Stone had been his last hope of finding his father. It was a cruel blow to hear the big trapper had never heard of Nathaniel Jennings. He had to look elsewhere but where did he start? The west was an enormous territory, much of it uncharted. Everyone said the most likely place to begin the search for his mountain man father was at the rendezvous where trappers and traders gathered each summer. Little good that advice did him. The next rendezvous was a year away. What would he do until then? He certainly didn't intend to stay pitching hay and manure in Gimpy's Horse Emporium.

"I've been thinking," Gimpy said the morning after the Rocky Mountain House episode. "If'n yer goin' ta find yer pa yuh'd best take up with Buck's brigade. Spend the winter in the mountains an' go ta the next rendezvous. Every beaver huntin' jasper'll be there. I kin scrounge up an old nag fer yuh an' there's an' extra saddle or two layin' aroun' hiya somewheres. If yuh like, I'll hev a word with Buck. He's a good man ta larn yuh the trappin' trade, thet's fer sure."

"Hmm!" Joe grunted. Living amongst strangers in the mountains for a winter didn't especially appeal.

Late in the morning Buck Stone appeared with two members of his brigade. The two newcomers were so different and odd, in spite of his gloom, Joe had to smile. They both wore fringed buckskins but that was where the resemblance ended. The one was tall and stringy, the other short and round. The tall man had the strangest face Joe had ever encountered; a long curved nose like the beak of an owl, hung over narrow lips. A black raven feather curled above a misshapen beaver hat made him appear even more like a gangly-legged stork. His sharp eyes were also strange, one blue and the other gray. "They call me Hawk Beak," he said. The hand he offered also caused Joe to suppress giggles. The long, thin fingers curled in yellowed, tobacco-stained claws were like the feet of a chicken.

The squat man's appearance was just as strange. A bushy beard fell to his chest, making him appear shorter than his actual height. He doffed a fur trimmed cap to reveal a head without a trace of hair. Heavy eyebrows shaded quick-moving eyes that seemed to take in everything at once. His round face and cheerful smile reminded Joe of Robin Hood's Friar Tuck. He was called Deacon Walton, the squat man announced. As a youth he had trained in a seminary, he proudly explained. "I ain't preached fer a spell but like ta keep in touch with the Scriptures. Don't know when yuh might havta say a blessin' or conduct a funeral."

The trappers gathered around the side corral and began to cut out their horses and mules. It took them a good while to settle the animals down. Joe did his best to help. If he was going into the mountains with Buck's brigade he reckoned he had to show he could do something beside fork hay. He made an unfortunate beginning. He looped a rope around a mule's neck but was unable to snub the animal to a post. The mule took off, scampering around and around the corral. With the rope caught around one wrist, Joe had no choice but to scramble after the mule. Faster and faster he had to run to keep up. The mule gave the rope a hard jerk, knocking him off his feet. For a ways he skated flat on his belly, plowing through horse dung and dust like a runaway sleigh. Deacon, who stood by hooting and shouting advice, finally came to the rescue.

"I'll show yuh how ta tame thet critter." In a surprisingly quick move, the fat man got another rope on the mule. Realizing it was defeated, the mule turned as docile as a tabby cat.

At lunch time the men crowded into Gimpy's back room. On the potbellied stove simmered a kettle of beans, corn and ham.

"Whatcha goin' to do with thet grub?" Hawk Beak asked, "throw it to the hogs?"

"Yep! Sooee! Sooee! Belly up ta the trough, yuh snout-nosed shoats." Gimpy, delighted with his role as host, bustled around the small room. From an old crate that had been nailed to the wall to serve as a cupboard, he extracted tin plates and utensils. With a tin cup serving as a dipper, Gimpy ladled out the simmering stew. His guests squatted wherever there was room. For a while the only sounds were the clatter of forks against plates and the grinding of teeth.

"Where yuh takin' the crew this year, Buck?" Gimpy finally spoke.

Buck set his tin plate aside and filled a short-stemmed pipe. "I'm thinking we should try a valley in the Bighorns."

"Thet country's dangerous!" Hawk Beak exclaimed. "Beaver're plentiful there 'cause no one lives long enough to catch 'em. They say some places are so fearful Injuns won't even go near 'em. Ghosts of dead warriors keep comin' outta caves, or somethin' like thet."

"Yep. That is what they say" Buck agreed. "People who believe in ghosts should stay away, that's for certain. But I was through there once; all I saw were beaver. Perhaps it's one of the last good beaver grounds in North America. Beaver pop out of the streams like salmon going home to spawn."

"How'd yuh come ta stumble onta it, anyways?" Gimpy asked.

"I learned about it from an old Crow man. According to this old Crow there is a special valley there that over generations has become a legend." Buck turned to address Joe. "You see, young man, my hobby is mythology. When I hear of an Indian myth or legend, I'm interested. Each tribe has its own version of how they came to be on Mother Earth and the way they are supposed to act while they abide here. I collect these legends like some people collect butterflies. Indian people interest me. In many ways they are like prankish children. They observe the rules and are peaceful as long as it suits them, then the men folk go on little sprees; they raid for a few horses, take a few prisoners for slaves, sometimes kill and scalp a few of the enemy. Afterwards, they come back to their village to receive scoldings from the womenfolk. They pay no attention. They count their coups and brag about all the devilish things they have done."

"Buck, yer off the subject," Deacon complained. "What about these beaver grounds?"

"There is a legend about this valley," Buck continued. "In ancient times a group of Crow were about to write on the canyon walls an account of some feat of daring. Along comes a band of Sioux, who either didn't like the story or were just up to devilment. They outnumbered the Crow, something like fifteen to one."

"Mighty soberin' odds," Gimpy observed.

"Now, the wise old Crow leader knew he was in a tight fix. His braves would have to fight like Billy-blue-blazes just to save their hair. So, he rides up on a hill where he could be seen by everyone, Sioux and Crow alike. He told his men that the Great Spirit would come to them on a white horse and give them strength to kill their enemies. Lo and behold, soon after he spoke there appeared a white horse carrying a rider with yellow hair and piercing eyes. He rode right up to the leader's side."

"Thet was no blinkin' Injun. More likely a dude dressed fer a New Orleans' ball," Hawk Beak scoffed.

"The Sioux, who watched, were stunned by the apparition," Buck continued. "Before they could collect themselves, the Crow charged down the hill straight at the Sioux. They killed a bunch and escaped unscathed. To this day the Sioux avoid this field of battle where the Crow shamed them. To the Crow it is sacred soil. Except for young men on vision quests, they stay away too. That's why game and beaver there are so plentiful. Least that's the way I see it."

"Humph!" Gimpy grunted skeptically. "The fellow thet told thet story 'bout the white horse an' yellow-haired Injun stretched the blanket a bit, I'm thinkin'."

While they debated the merits of Buck's suggested trapping

grounds, a large man wearing a wide-brimmed black hat and weathered buckskins appeared. He had to stoop to get through the door. He leaned a long, shiny-barreled rifle against the wall and sat down on the floor without saying a word. No one but Joe seemed to take notice of the stranger. They continued to discuss the Bighorn beaver bounties. The big man sat and politely listened.

Deacon finally turned to the new arrival. "So, yuh finally got yer special made Hawkin, didja? I 'spect yuh'll be challengin' Hawk Beak fer the marksman championship of the brigade?"

The newcomer shook his head. "No, I wouldn't want to show him up." He took off his wide-brimmed black hat to reveal a shock of equally black hair. He hooked the hat on a nail, sniffed the air and turned around. "Smells like you have been digging into a kettle of Gimpy's vittles. Anything left for a starving man?"

Joe drew in a sharp breath. He had grown a beard. His black hair was streaked with white but there was no doubt about it. This was his father! Or was it? The big man put down the spoon he had started to eat with and thrust out his hand. He introduced himself as Little Ned. They shook hands like strangers meeting for the first time. Joe's spontaneous words of greeting stuck in his throat. His father made it clear he did not wish to acknowledge him as kin.

THE LAST RENDEZVOUS

VIII

Observe, . . . silence is greater than speech. This is why we honor the animals, who are more silent than man, and we reverence the trees and rocks, where the Great Mystery lives undisturbed, in a peace that is never broken.

Ohiyesa, Santee Sioux

It was the night of the storyteller. It was his custom to call at the long lodge lodge every full moon to weave his tales. In olden days Storyteller had the same role as Schoolmaster for he taught the ways of the ancients — the life people lived before the coming of the horse. In those days the Nimpau were fishermen. They lived along the Kimooenim. Their homes were cave-like huts sunk deep in the river banks. The children loved the night of the storyteller, not only for the wondrous tales they would hear, but on these occasions extra wood was thrown on the fire, warming the damp cold air that permeated the lodges that lay half buried in Mother Earth.

Raven Wing, who had moved to the long lodge while her son, Buffalo Boy, was away in Waiilatpu, looked on Storyteller's coming with apprehension. Many of the villagers present would be the same ones who had made up the mob that drove her man, Francois, from the valley. Her first thought was to avoid the gathering — leave the long lodge and take to her log cabin but her parents would not hear of it.

"No! No!" Quiet Woman admonished. "Storytelling night is a night of peace. No one quarrels; no one is mean. Storytelling night is a magical time when everything is good."

The evening meal was hurriedly eaten; the cooking things were quickly cleaned and put away. Mats and buffalo robes were laid around the central lodge fire. People from nearby lodges brought additional robes and mats. Everyone smiled and greeted Raven Wing as if she was expected to be there. As Quiet Woman had insisted, this was a time when friendship and good will abounded.

THE LAST RENDEZVOUS

The long lodge grew quiet. The greeter, who waited outside, gave a thump on a drum announcing Storyteller's arrival. The children, who sat nearest the fire, held their breaths, their bright eyes on the doorway. Each one wanted to be the first to see Storyteller enter. Suddenly he was there, his features almost hidden in the shadows. The children jumped to their feet to make room for him by the fire. He came forward, an elderly man with a lone eagle feather thrust upright in his graying hair. His lined face, now bathed by the firelight, was a picture of peace and contentment.

For a moment Storyteller stood glancing over the crowd, then raised his hands in prayer. His lips moved but no words were heard. The people knew he was speaking to the Great Mysterious. He was giving thanks for the gift of the bright day that had passed and for the comfort the coming night would bring. He spoke to the Great Spirit of little Alice Clarissa who had died in far away Waiilatpu, asking that a special place be set aside for her in the Great Beyond. At the end of the prayer Storyteller dropped his hands to his side. His glance fell on the round face of a dark-eyed girl.

"Welcome, my little one, what story do you wish?" The voice of the storyteller was pleasant to the ear but carried to the far corners of the long lodge.

"Please, Storyteller, tell of Red Tail the Hunter," the girl shyly whispered.

"Ah! yes, that is a favorite of mine. It teaches us important things of life. Listen well and you will recognize what they are. We all know our friend, Red Tail Hawk, do we not?"

The answering chorus pleased Storyteller, he smiled his pleasure. "First we must honor our mother." He lowered himself to sit on bare floor, smoothed by hundreds of footsteps. With the nails of his thumbs he made twin marks in the earth, then carefully rubbed them out. He lifted his hands and passed them over his body.

The crowd murmured approval. The earth was their mother who nourished them and healed all their wounds. The tales Storyteller told would be in her honor.

"Red Tail the Hunter, we will call him," Storyteller began.

"Red Tail and his mate always build their nests in the tallest tree in the forest. They want to be where they can see everything that takes place. Creatures that make their homes among the trees call them sentinels of the forest. The wiliest of predators cannot evade their watchful eyes.

"Red Tail has a family of four fledglings. Every day he goes in search of food. Some days he flies to roost on a dead snag at the edge of the forest. There he sits, silently watching and waiting for his prey to appear. Then, with the quickness of a lightening flash he strikes, his sharp, curved talons capturing the prey that passes below his perch.

"But Red Tail is a soaring bird. He loves the freedom of being alone in space. He likes to hunt from high in the sky. In the mornings he floats silently above the treetops, barely moving a feather. Higher and higher he climbs, riding the air warmed by Father Sun. He goes into the clouds and drifts beyond until he is only a black dot, no larger than the eye of a beetle against Father Sky. All the while he is watching Mother Earth, waiting for prey. He sees the wolf leave his lair. He sees Brother Coyote sniff the tracks of a hare. He sees buffaloes, deer and elk graze in the meadows. He sees boys and girls from the village go out to play. He does not bother them. These are his friends. He watches over them.

"Suddenly, the tips of his wings quiver. The wings draw back. Like an arrow in flight, Red Tail makes the long dive to Mother Earth. The sharp, curved talons reach out for the head of a prairie dog that pops out of its hole. So swift and silent is Red Tail the victim does not see him coming. He snatches up Prairie Dog and hurries home. There he drops the catch in the nest beside his mate who tears it into bits to feed her fledgling children."

The little girl who asked for the story, involuntarily shivered. She had heard the story before but every telling made goose bumps rise on her skin. Storyteller, who had been watching her closely, put out a comforting hand. "Yes, Red Tail the Hunter does cruel things to keep his family alive. He is only following the plan of the Great Mysterious. The same Red Tail who kills and eats prairie dogs, mice, chipmunks and squirrels, also guards those who are his friends. One day while sitting on a dead limb overlooking an open space on the river bank, Red Tail watched children at play. After splashing in the water they ran to the bank. Unknown to the children, while they were in the river Brother Snake from the forest had slithered up to hide in the tall grass. He sensed he was in danger, believing he would be trampled. He coils himself to strike. A little girl running ahead of her playmates, came nearer and nearer. Brother Snake rose up to protect himself. The little girl suddenly saw his big head, weaving back and forth. It was too late. She could not stop running. She closed her eyes, waiting for the deadly strike, but she felt no sting of pain -- no bite of poisonous fangs. The child opened her eyes. Brother Snake was no longer in the grass. She looked up. There he was high above the treetops, dangling from Red Tail's sharp, curved claws."

The dark-eyed girl who asked for the story, jumped to her feet and ran to snuggle in the arms of her mother.

"Yes, little one. It is a frightening tale, but it is also a lesson. When you play, know where you are. Danger comes in many ways. Even in the friendly river and forest you must be on guard. Pay attention to all things that cover Mother Earth: animals, birds, insects, plants, trees, rocks and streams. Each of them is here for a purpose. We must study them, learn this purpose. When we know their purpose we will learn to respect them and be able to live in harmony with them. Remember! Each of them has as much right to enjoy the gifts of Mother Earth as do we. When we do harm to them, we also do harm to Mother Earth."

Storyteller paused. The children's eyes had become dulled. The young minds were overburdened. He clapped his hands.

"Red Tail the Hunter! What did we learn from him?"

"Red Tail is patient. He waits and waits," a youth answered.

"Red Tail is silent. Prey never hear him," another boy said.

"His sharp eyes see everything," a third boy offered.

"Good. Patience, silence and observance — this is Red Tail's message, qualities all of us should strive to acquire."

The storytelling took Raven Wing back to her childhood. Like the dark-eyed girl, she had sat entranced by Storyteller's charms. She often had heard the story of Red Tail the Hunter but only now, after bearing three children of her own, did she give serious thought to the message the story contained. How foolish she had been. She was always in trouble and no wonder. She had little patience and often spoke when silence would have served her far better. She gave herself credit for observance. She had a sharp eye and could read the thoughts and acts of others almost as well as all-seeing Vision Seeker.

Late into the night Raven Wing pondered, was the story of Red Tail the Hunter an omen, repeated tonight for her benefit? If she was ever to practice patience it was now. Her fate depended upon time. Francois had promised to return, but when? It could be days or it could be years. Then there was her Boston mate: now that she was back in the log cabin he had built especially for her, would he reappear? What if both men came back? What would happen then? They hated each other with a vengeance. "Aiiee!" All she could do was wait and see.

#

The missionary entourage that had set out for Waiilatpu to attend baby Alice Clarissa's funeral, returned to Lapwai. Business as usual soon resumed. Missionary Spalding went back to work on the mill sites and Eliza Spalding sent a messenger around the village announcing classes at the mission school were in session. Running Turtle rushed into the log cabin. "School! School! It's time for school! Buffalo Boy and Young Wolf must start. They can come with me." In his excitement Running Turtle stumbled on the top porch step and went sprawling.

The news had a mixed reception. Young Wolf clapped his hands. "Yes! Yes! School!" he exclaimed. Buffalo Boy remained silent. His mother read his thoughts. Spotted Badger and his other former friends attended the mission school. Buffalo Boy had no desire to face them. There would be more taunts and mean things said. He could not fight everybody.

"What good is school?" Raven Wing scoffed, bitterness over the way her man, Francois, was forced to flee welled up making her voice shrill. She suddenly thought of Storyteller's words. "If we watch and listen Mother Earth tells us everything we need to know. She sends birds north to announce the Season of First Grass and south before the snows of winter descend. She tells us when roots and berries are ready to harvest and sends white birds from the west to warn the salmon are coming home. When the bloom on the camas meadow withers we know it is time to dig the camas bulb. The Season of Falling Leaves tells us snow will soon cover the land. Ah! The foolish white man. He believes we have to go to school to learn how to live."

"There is so much more to learn than how to hunt, fish and gather food," Running Turtle insisted. "The missionary woman tells of many things we never have heard. She talks of lands beyond the seas where all people are black and another land where all people are yellow. She tells of great stone buildings called pyramids and of times when people were put in huge rings and fought big cats called lions and tigers. She tells of great wars where many warriors battled each other, some with guns as large as tree trunks that belched fire and steel, killing dozens at a time. Then there were wars of ships with wings that attacked each other on the deep great waters called oceans." Running Turtle paused to catch his breath.

Young Wolf gasped in admiration. He wanted Running Turtle to tell more but Raven Wing had heard enough. "Does learning these things help us to live or turn us into better people?"

"I do not know but the missionary woman teaches many things that come from the Great Spirit Book called Bible. She tells us about the God Jesus, who died for our sins. If we do as Jesus teaches we will go to a place called heaven where everyone lives forever and ever. Then we will be like one family, love one another . . ."

"Bagh! The Nimpau always lived together like a family. Before the missionaries came we did not make trouble for one another," Raven Wing retorted. "Do you not see what has happened? Our people quarrel and fight among ourselves. It is the missionaries who made us this way. They say our ways are bad -- we do bad things. Do you hear them say good words of our people? Never.

You should not do this . . . You should not do that. We are treated like naughty children. We do nothing right. They make us unhappy with ourselves."

Running Turtle did not give up recruiting his nephews for Eliza Spalding's classroom. At his urging, a few days later Eliza Spalding, herself, walked up the steps and politely knocked on the door. Raven Wing had seen her coming. She thrust Little Bird under the sleeping robes, quickly removed her worn buckskin dress and slipped into her wedding dress, decorated with porcupine quills and cut glass beads, smoothing it into place. She did not want her family disgraced. She greeted the missionary lady with a smile and a handshake as she had seen Redcoat ladies at Fort Vancouver do. Raven Wing made a place for her on the porch bench as she did not want the missionary woman to come inside and see how ill she kept her lodge.

Eliza Spalding acknowledged Raven Wing's greeting with a smile and sat down on the hard porch bench as if she were quite at home. She spoke the native language well and had taken care to learn the customs of the people. Unlike her husband, she was held in high regard by the villagers. She asked about the baby and commented on Raven Wing's two older sons.

Unaccustomed to making small talk, Raven Wing remained silent. She sat and stared at the flower garden. What did the missionary lady want? Not even Quiet Woman came merely to visit. Former old friends and acquaintances appeared occasionally but they did so out of curiosity so they could take home more gossip.

"I would like to have your two older sons come to the mission school," Eliza Spalding finally said. "I am sure they would enjoy it. There is so much in this world to learn. God has given us the calling to teach you. We want to do His will the best we can."

"Ah!" Raven Wing finally uttered. Of course, that was why the missionary lady had come with her ways as sweet as the comb in a honey tree. All the bitterness she felt came to the surface. The missionary people would not rest until they turned everybody into soft, ground-plowing Christians. She hated them all. She remembered well the people who called themselves Christians at Fort Vancouver. They spoke with forked tongues. The first day of the week they dressed themselves in their best clothes and went to chapel to hear how to avoid sin. They came home, had big dinners, read their Bibles and said loud prayers. The rest of the week they gambled, caroused and did as they pleased.

Raven Wing almost laughed in the missionary woman's face. She knew all about the ways of Christians. Her man, Francois, had taught her. He called himself a Catholic Christian. He knew all the strange signs and words of the Long Robes. When he passed a grave site or did something forbidden, he made the sign of the cross and mumbled words she did not understand. After doing evil he went to the chapel at Fort Vancouver and told a Long Robe who hid behind a curtain. Then, like other Christians, on the first day of the week he went to hear the Long Robe speak and dropped to his knees to take bread and wine that he said was the body and blood of Christ. How could anyone believe such a thing? For a few days he acted kind and humble, then he became his old cruel and violent self. What kind of religion was that? He wanted Young Wolf and Little Bird to have the Long Robes sprinkle water on their heads, baptized was what it was, he said. "Aiiee!" she uttered in such agony Eliza Spalding gave her a look of alarm.

"Are you not well? Perhaps this is not a good time to talk." Raven Wing watched her go. She felt like she would choke if the missionary woman said another word.

THE LAST RENDEZVOUS

IX

*Trouble is like strong medicine — too much
at a time is harmful.*

Yiddish Proverb

The sudden appearance of his son left Little Ned speechless. He could not believe his eyes. The callow youth he had left behind had turned into a rather handsome man with shoulders nearly as wide as his own. Although marred by recently received bruises on his cheeks and forehead, he had an open, intelligent face. The clear blue eyes met his own with a steady, direct gaze. Little Ned knew he should be proud of the boy. Instead, his first thought was to send his son packing. What business did he have tracking down his father as though he were a fugitive running from the law?

The big man took another spoonful of beans and tried to choke them down. He stared at the bottom of the nearly empty kettle and attempted to think his way out of the dilemma. He came west to lose himself. He had told no one his real name and never once discussed his origins. People accepted him for what they saw, a big man with shoulders as broad as an ax handle, a quiet person with modest demeanor who kept to himself but whose skills over the years earned him the reputation as one of the best trappers in the mountains.

Little Ned inwardly groaned. The secret he had guarded so diligently from his people back east was about to be exposed. At least, so far his son had sense enough to realize his presence was not wanted and kept his mouth shut, but for how long? He had to get him alone and order him back home. If Deacon, Hawk Beak or Buck should begin to blather about the days when they trapped the Northern Rockies... Little Ned shuddered. There was no doubt about it;

THE LAST RENDEZVOUS 73

he had to find an excuse to send his son back home.

Gimpy and Hawk Beak began to argue about the merits of mules versus horses as pack animals. Joe made no attempt to follow the conversation. His eyes were intent on the big man called Little Ned -- his father. He could see the man was in turmoil. What was the matter with him? After a long absence a father should be happy to see his only son. Joe attempted to swallow the lump in his throat. He felt betrayed. He had traveled months, suffering privation and every humbling indignity possible to find his father, and it was all for naught. The dreams that had kept him going were dashed. He was bursting with news: Granny and Granddad's declining health; Tildy approaching womanhood; the crop failures on the back forty; the new furniture factory built on the Boston Road; the new wing on the church; and the tragic loss of poor old Dan. His father was not interested. Joe brushed at his eyes. What was he to do?

Little Ned finished eating. He got to his feet and motioned for Joe to follow him outside. They walked to the corral where the horses and mules snuffled and snorted as they picked at what remained of their portions of hay.

"Why did you leave the folks?" Little Ned asked, his manner abrupt. "They're all right, aren't they?"

"The folks are poorly. They need you. The doctors say Granny will not last much longer. Then there's Tildy . . . " The stony expression on his father's face caused him to fall silent. He suddenly realized how little both Tildy and he knew their father. Never had they sat down and had a good heart to heart talk. Even when he was home he had been a stranger. Through the years they had placed him on a pedestal. He was a heroic figure, fighting Indians, evading mountain lions and grizzlies, taming the western wilderness so it would be safe for people to live.

The big man chewed on a splinter of wood and stared at the horses and mules. "They want me to return home, do they? It's out of the question. Don't you see, we're setting out on an important trapping expedition. This is our job, the way we make our living. It's like harvest time. When the grain is ripe, you reap it or all is lost."

That night, heartsick, Joe flopped down in the loft. The finding of his father, which he had looked forward to with such anticipation, had turned into the worst kind of nightmare. There was no love; there was no kinship. His father had more regard for his trapping life than he did his family. "Agh!" Joe turned over and tried to sleep.

The following day was busy with people coming and going. Buck Stone and the other trappers began to inventory their supplies and stow them away in packs. In the evening, they again crowded into Gimpy's back room to partake of a pot of stew. Gimpy kept chuckling to himself as he ladled out the food.

"What's ticklin' yer funny bone?" Deacon asked.

"A customer brung in news 'bout a bust-up at Rocky Mountain House. It's got the whole town in a tizzy." Gimpy stopped to guffaw so long his face grew red and tears ran down his cheeks. "Sakes alive! I never heerd such goin's-on in me life."

"Well, what is it?" Hawk Beak snapped. "Yuh gonna keep us on tenterhooks all night?"

"Seems while thet ornery one-eyed baboon, Link, was visitin' Madame Melissa's girls someun slipped in an' lifted his duds." Gimpy paused to guffaw.

"They must've been crazy drunk," Hawk Beak exclaimed. "There's not a soul in town thet can fill Link's buckskins."

"Yeah, sounds kinda silly but thet's what happened. Kin yuh 'magine, there's Link, big as a house an' bare as a picked bird, crashin' through a door an' inta the saloon, madder than a scalded dog. He wades through the card tables, sendin' poker chips, cards an' gamblers flyin'. A galoot holdin' a full house is fit ta be tied, hits ol' Link over the head with a bar stool. Don't faze him a whit. Link grabs Gus, the manager, an' nearly chokes him ta deeth — claims he's been robbed. No one kin reason with him. Sheriff Barnes an' deputies come runnin', swingin' billy clubs. 'Most everyone in the saloon joins forces tryin' ta wrestle him down, but he's slippery as a greased eel. Someun finally slugs him with a rifle barrel, knocks the poor gazebo cuckoo. Then they really hev a problem. How're they gonna git his carcass ta the jail house? He's as hard ta handle as a beached whale. A dock worker comes up with the idea of loadin' him onta one of those cotton drayin' carts. They hauls him away like a bale of cotton."

Gimpy stopped to wipe at his eyes. "Yuh kin 'magine the trouble they must've had when ol' Link come ta his senses. Wouldn't surprised me none if'n he didn't pull the jail down 'round his ears. He's strong as Samson, an' when mad, he's mean as a sore-nosed pig. When Link gets free there'll be the devil ta pay."

"Who was this crazy jokester thet stole his duds?" Hawk Beak asked. "Must've been someun with a grudge again' ol' Link."

Gimpy wagged his thumb toward Buck and Joe who sat in a corner spooning down Gimpy's stew. "They're the culprits. Look at 'em. They don't even care."

Deacon and Hawk hooted and laughed but Little Ned did not join in. He glumly shook his head. "One-Eye Link is about the worst enemy anyone can have," he said.

#

It was an hour before dawn when Buck Stone led his brigade of trappers away from the bustling city of St. Louis. They followed the well traveled trail west along the Missouri, the river Indians called the Big Muddy or Greasy Foam. Joe brought up the rear. Buck had invited him to join the brigade. At first he had hesitated, then decided why not? He had nothing to lose. If he returned home what could he tell the folks, that his own father had turned his back on him? If he went with Buck's brigade perhaps sooner or later he could win his father over. Anyway, it was worth a try.

To clear the city limits before people were up and the roadways clogged, Buck set a fast pace. The animals, especially the mules, had grown fat and lazy during the city stay. Surly and rambunctious, they kicked, crow hopped, and jerked their heads against the halter lines, keeping the riders watchful and annoyed. Joe, leading two pack animals, had his hands rubbed raw. The rough sisal rope kept slipping through his fingers as the truculent mules bobbed their heads down to nip at succulent grass that grew in bunches alongside the trail. Near mid-morning a mule broke loose and loped into a roadside patch of clover. The party of trappers had to stop while he caught it and brought it back, red-faced with embarrassment. The trappers quietly watched. He considered that a bad sign. They were judging his worth. For the moment he was not worth a hill of beans.

By noon he ached all over. He had not ridden a horse for weeks, not since he abandoned old Dan. The new buckskins he purchased with the last of his money, rubbed against his legs and backsides leaving him chaffed and raw. When Buck finally called a halt at the edge of a stream, he barely could dismount. He walked in a crouch like a crippled old man. His condition did not go unnoticed.

"I say," Hawk Beak observed. "Our new partner's lookin' kinda spavin-legged."

After a short break to slake their thirst, chew on a piece of stringy jerky and let the animals drink and graze, the trappers mounted up and continued their journey. The road was clogged with traffic traveling both ways. Two-wheel mule killers, heavy freighters drawn by three span of oxen, light wagons with single teams of mules and horses and mounted riders of various ages and shapes were on the move, the majority of them wending their way west. Most of the teamsters and horsemen said a friendly "howdy." There were others who eyed them coldly, silently examining them and their outfits. A particularly tough looking party of armed horsemen riding across country, turned up the trail to meet them head-on. Buck slid his rifle out of the boot. The rest of the trappers did likewise. Little Ned dropped back to ride alongside Joe.

"You can't be too careful in these parts," he said but did not explain. These were the first words his father had spoken all day. The dust and dirt did not encourage conversation. Ruts in the roadway were filled with powder that swept up in choking billows. They rode with bandannas covering their faces but the flimsy covering did little good. At the end of the day Joe's eyes, nose and mouth were filled with grit.

Near the city of Independence Buck announced they would

THE LAST RENDEZVOUS

stop for a spell. Independence was the last outpost where they could top off their supplies. They made camp near a semi-circle of heavy wagons, modified versions of the even heavier Conestoga.

"Big freighters takin' the Santa Fe Trail," Hawk Beak remarked. "I'll betcha they're loaded with Mexican dinero. Maybeso, they'd be interested in a hand of faro. Nuthin' I'd like better'n relieve 'em of some of those silver cartwheels they call pesos."

"The last time yuh tried ta best the Mexes yuh come back busted," Deacon said scornfully.

"Yeah, had an unlucky streak. Right now I feel hotter than a hornet's nest. I kin jest feel thet Mexican silver fillin' my pockets. This may be my last chance to strike it rich. Young Joe, why don't me an' yuh saunter over an' reconnoiter. Who knows, we might run inta some of those girls they call senoritas."

"Young Joe is not going anywhere," Little Ned said sharply. "He's staying right here to do the chores."

"Ah, thet's too bad. We could've had a whole bunch of fun but I guess yer right. Chores come first."

Dutifully, Joe removed the packs from the mules, unsaddled the horses, led them to water and then staked them out to graze. He resented Little Ned's bossiness. Was he going to order him around like a strict father, yet not acknowledge him as his own flesh and blood? If that was to be the case maybe it would have been better if he had returned home.

Joe's troublesome thoughts were soon dismissed. Here on the edge of the frontier there was too much excitement to allow niggling problems to dampen the joy of being alive. From the encirclement of freighters came the sound of music, the rippling but melancholy tunes of the Spanish. Joe edged nearer to get a better look at the party traveling the Santa Fe Trail. A dozen of the heavy wagons were arranged in the shape of a horseshoe. In the dusk their white canvas tops gleamed like the sails of a four mast schooner. The long wagon tongues all faced out, with eight sets of harnesses laid beside them ready for quick hitch-up and getaway. A crowd of people milled around in the half enclosed circle of wagons. Most of them were busily going about the business of preparing for the long trip to the Southwest. Some greased axles, others worked at tightening the iron wagon tires; a few braided riatas and others repaired harnesses. A group surrounded four men sitting in a circle. That was the faro game Hawk Beak was so anxious to join, Joe guessed.

It was the music that attracted Joe. It came from a trio with guitar, fiddle and some kind of wind instrument. In front of them two couples were dancing, flinging their arms and swinging with the rhythm. The music and the dancing couples drew Joe like a magnet. He hoped Hawk Beak would ask him again to visit the Santa Fe encampment. This time he would not let Little Ned put him off.

Joe walked nearer for a better view. The attire of the people was as varied as their activities. Many of the teamsters wore weathered buckskins. Silver buckled belts encircled their waists. Their flat-topped, wide-brimmed hats also flashed with silver. A couple of men wore coonskin caps and plain buckskins. Joe figured them to be scouts. Wool homespuns identified some as newcomers to the trail. A small group of men dressed in broadcloth sat watching the faro players. Joe decided they were traders, perhaps the caravan owners. Off to one side stood a small band of Indians clad in little more than arm bands and breechcloths.

The Santa Fe group was so fascinating Joe lost track of time. He returned to camp to find Deacon had already cooked the evening meal. The trappers were sitting down to eat. Joe was amazed to see they were all spruced up in their Sunday clothes. His father had on a string tie. Buck wore a new bandanna and had his unruly corn colored hair combed back from his forehead. He had trimmed his side whiskers and eyebrows, probably with old Betsy, his razor sharp knife, Joe decided. Hawk Beak and Deacon had changed into clean buckskins.

"We're off ta do a bit of last minute hurrahin'," Deacon explained. "I talked Hawk Beak outta the faro game but he ain't givin' up on havin' a last fling. Buck, Little Ned an' I gotta see he keeps outta trouble. We figured, since yuh done a good bit of hurrahin' in St. Louie, yuh might not mind watchin' over things."

THE LAST RENDEZVOUS

"Yep, we'd take it kindly if you would stand first guard," Buck added. "Shouldn't be any trouble, but keep alert. Someone along the trail may have taken a liking to our outfit. There were some Pawnee hanging about. They aren't dangerous but will lift the pockets off your pants if you don't watch them. Just send a slug whistling over their heads and they're sure to take off."

"If'n things git real serious, there's Buck's double-barreled scatter-gun," Hawk Beak added. "Blast off with both barrels. Thet'll put the fear of God in 'em."

Joe glanced at Little Ned. He didn't like the idea of being left alone but his father's face was impassive. He could almost read his thoughts. "Don't look to me for favors. You are out west now. You have to learn to make it on your own."

Joe watched the trappers ride away with an empty feeling in the pit of his stomach. He knew survival on the frontier meant protecting lives and property even if one had to kill. Was he up to that? He didn't know. He got out the old Henry Gimpy had found in a closet, a rifle left by someone who couldn't pay his feed bill. He made certain it had a proper load of ball and powder. Then, he looked to Buck's double-barreled scatter-gun. He checked the loads and propped it within easy reach.

For a long while Joe sat with the rifle across his knees, feeling lonely and homesick. How nice it would be to hear Tildy's voice and see her cheery smile. How heartwarming it would be to sit at the kitchen table across from Granddad and talk about the harvesting that would soon have to be done. He wouldn't even mind listening to Granny's shrill warnings about an early frost and the long winter ahead. He shook his head and tightened his grip on the Henry. He had to stop thinking about things like that.

A rustling noise came from where the mules and horses were tethered. Joe quietly got to his feet. The shadows played tricks with his eyes. He moved beyond the lean-to tent to stand in the darkness beneath the branches of a tree. From this vantage point he had a clear view of the entire campsite. If anyone approached he was certain to see them.

Along the road to Independence came the sounds of riders going and coming. From the shouts and off-key singing, it was obvious they were having a good time. Again a feeling of loneliness gripped Joe. What was he doing here in the wilderness when he could have remained snug and warm in his grandparents' New England home? Another group of horsemen cantered down Independence Road. Except for hoofbeats and creak of leather, they passed by silently. He thought of the hard-eyed riders they had met on the trail. Their searching gazes had inspected each pack, speculating on what it contained. They had eyed the animals in the same studied manner. Joe shivered. He would be no match for them. He quietly cocked the Henry and moved deeper into the shadows.

After what seemed like hours another boisterous group of horsemen passed, finally turning in at the Santa Fe freighters' camp. With his attention on the revelers he almost overlooked the stealthy approach of the intruder. Out of the corner of his eye, Joe caught sight of a tall figure flitting from the shadow of one tree to the next. He threw the Henry to his shoulder, tracking the intruder with the sights. Above the crouching figure's head curled a feather. Pawnee! He was going right for the tent. Joe pulled the trigger. The intruder gave a yell and collapsed. Joe felt sick to his stomach. He had shot too low. He had killed his first Indian man!

"Hold yer fire!" The voice sounded very much like that of Hawk Beak! From the clump of trees beyond the tent came a chorus of guffaws.

Joe could not believe his ears. His companions had tricked him. He was furious. "What is the matter with you people, are you trying to get yourselves killed?"

Little Ned came up and put his arm around Joe's shoulder. "Son, you did just right." Joe's anger faded. Did this mean his father accepted him? His spirits were quickly dashed. Little Ned turned away and went about laying out his bedroll. Deacon came to take his place.

"Yuh jest won yer spurs," the baldheaded man said with approval. "Ol' Hawk Beak likes ta test new men. I guess next time he'll be more keerful."

"Thet's fer certain." Hawk Beak sheepishly admitted. He held up his hat. The raven feather he wore there was gone. Only a stub remained.

THE LAST RENDEZVOUS

X

True Indian education was based on the development of individual qualities and recognition of rights.
   Luther Standing Bear, Lakota

Like a dark shroud, the sad aftermath of baby Alice Clarissa Whitman's death and burial hung over the valley. The little girl's visit to Lapwai had been like the visitation of an angel. The villagers who had adopted Christianity were especially stunned by her death. It confused and perplexed them. They watched over their own precious children with apprehension. If the Christian God took the blonde-headed angel away what would keep Him from taking their children, too?

The Lapwai villagers were not alone in their distress. Inside the mission house the members of the missionary family were silent and grim as they went about their duties. "How fragile, how mortal and how ignorant we are of the spiritual world we espouse," Eliza Spalding commented to her husband one evening.

Henry Spalding gave his wife a disconsolate glance and shook his head. "I wonder if we are doing God's will. We started on the Lord's work three years ago and look how little we have accomplished. We barely have made a mark on this community. People continue their sinful ways and remain away from our school and services. While we were away with Brother and Sister Whitman in Waiilatpu a party of young men traveled to buffalo country on a hunt, something I forbade them to do. No matter what I say or do these people continue to follow the old ways. We must work — we must pray. We must find a way to turn them from their sinful pursuits. Only then will God bless our efforts."

The following day the missionary couple believed their prayers had been heard. A party of missionaries from the Willamette Valley arrived. One of them was a tall gangly man named Jason Lee who had established a Methodist mission in the Willamette Valley.

A former Maine woodsman with little formal education, Jason Lee made up for his lack of book knowledge with religious zeal. He also firmly believed the Oregon missions had fallen short of expectations.

"We have to forget about the past and go forward," Jason Lee said to the missionary group gathered at the evening meal. "As Apostle Luke says, 'No man, having put his hand to the plow and looking back, is fit for the kingdom of God.' Let's keep these words of Brother Luke in mind. We will not look back. We will look forward. With the Lord's help we will civilize this land and make it part of the United States of America. Here is what I propose . . . ."

The gathering of missionaries created a stir among the villagers. What were these people of God up to was the question on everyone's tongue. As head man, Weasel Face welcomed the visitors and saw to the needs of their horses and pack mules. However, his attempt to take part in the discussions was thwarted. He had to admit to fellow villagers he had no more idea than they did what the gathering of missionaries was all about.

From his lookout point on the hillside Vision Seeker caught sight of Jason Lee's entourage entering Lapwai Valley. He recognized the leader at once. He had met Jason Lee at a mountain man rendezvous held at a place called Ham's Fork. He, along with fellow villagers, had gone to welcome Jason Lee who had promised to live with them and teach them the mysteries of the Great Spirit Book. Instead of keeping his promise, Lee informed the Nimpau delegation they were not civilized enough to receive the word of God. Vision Seeker, who had learned English under the tutelage of the Harvard College trained mountain man, Buck Stone, understood every word. He did not forget the bitter disappointment and chagrin his people endured. They were insulted. Missionary Lee said they were too dumb to learn the ways of the Great Spirit Book. But here was Weasel Face greeting the missionary, smiling and wriggling all over himself like a camp dog waiting to be tossed a meaty bone. "Bagh!" Vision Seeker muttered. There was something not good about these hairy-faced men dressed in black. He was reminded of a flock of crows gathering to pick through a pile of offal. Their presence did not bode well.

The next morning Jason Lee and his party departed but they left behind a newly energized Henry Spalding. Almost before Jason Lee and his party disappeared from view, the clang of the gong summoned workers to their assignments. Soon laborers were sawing, hammering and shoveling rocks and earth at the gristmill and sawmill with Missionary Spalding running from one site to the other overseeing the work.

Before he left, Jason Lee had laid out a plan to improve and expand Oregon missions. If the missionaries made a greater impact on the population and were more productive the US government could not refuse to give Oregon Territory military protection, he argued. Spalding was in complete agreement. He sat down and wrote a letter to the Mission Board asking for reinforcements. The list of people he sought was long: thirty more missionaries, thirty farmers, thirty schoolteachers, ten physicians and ten mechanics, all with their wives. In addition he ordered innumerable supplies, including a request for tons of iron and steel for a blacksmith shop. The iron was intended largely for the making of plows, hoes and other agricultural equipment.

Missionary Spalding proudly announced these requests to his flock. He wanted everyone to know of the big plans he had for Lapwai. He envisioned the valley as the center of industry, trade and education for the entire Oregon plateau. Faithful members of the tribe were impressed. Those who had grown wary of Spalding's intentions were doubtful. Already, due to the missionaries' presence, Lapwai Valley was overcrowded. Much of the land that had provided good pasture in the past was covered with buildings or fenced in for crops.

As one of Eliza Spalding's most dedicated students, Running Turtle was pleased with the plans for developing the mission. Bursting with the news, he ran home after school to inform his parents. They paid little heed to what he said. Lone Wolf smoked his pipe and stared into the fire. Things were moving too fast for him to comprehend. Quiet Woman also said nothing. Her thoughts were on her grandsons. What would become of them with bearded ones taking over the valley? To get sufficient food to live would they be forced to root and dig in Mother Earth like the grunting pigs Missionary Whitman kept trapped in a small corral at Waiilatpu?

Deflated by the manner in which the mission plans were received, Running Turtle hiked up the trail to Raven Wing's cabin. Perhaps his sister, who had mated with two Christian men, would understand. He arrived at the cabin to find Buffalo Boy and Young Wolf chasing a puppy around and around the garden. The flowers Raven Wing's Boston mate had planted and Running Turtle had tended so carefully, were lying flat. Running Turtle was furious.

"Stop that," he ordered. He seized the puppy and shooed the boys out of the flowers. "Look at what you have done!' He was so upset tears came to his eyes. Raven Wing came out the cabin door and onto the porch. She started to scold the boys but held her tongue. It was not their fault. She should have kept an eye on them. Ah, how badly she needed a man, someone who would take these rambunctious boys in hand.

To mollify Running Turtle, Raven Wing invited him to sit on the porch bench and handed him a basket of roasted camas bulbs. Running Turtle, always hungry, consumed them with relish and sadly eyed the plot of broken flowers. "What these boys need is something to do," he said. "They only will get into worse trouble if they are not kept busy. First Son is too old to be playing with puppies. When I was his age I was killing buffalo."

Raven Wing smiled to herself. When Running Turtle was Buffalo Boy's age he fancied himself a great warrior and hunter. He walked around with rodent skins tied to his belt to represent the scalps he had taken. He probably killed more rodents with his bow and arrows than any youth in the village. Yes, he had been in on a buffalo kill. Blinded by a snowstorm, a buffalo stumbled into the Lone Wolf lodge. Running Turtle stabbed at it with a lance and Many Horses, their dead brother, finished it off with a knife. Unfortunately, the days of buffalo hunting were over. Boys did not have that adventure to look forward to any more.

"If Buffalo Boy and Young Wolf went to school they would not have time to get into mischief," Running Turtle said with authority. He told of the missionaries' plan for enlarging the mission and expanding the school.

Raven Wing remained silent. She disagreed with him yet what Running Turtle said made sense. The boys needed something to do besides playing with puppies. If her Boston mate were present he would insist the boys attend school. He said it was important for the youth of the tribe to learn what he called the ABC's. This was one of the few things upon which they disagreed. "No! I will not send my sons to school," she said fiercely to herself. After speaking to the missionary woman as she had, it would make her look a fool. Besides, it was time Buffalo Boy went on a vision quest.

Running Turtle did not give up. The next day he was back with a book. "I want to show you the interesting things we learn at school," he said. "Every day we read stories and other things from books like this. I will read you a story about a foolish boy who kept playing tricks on his people." Running Turtle stumbled through an edited version of the Aesop fable, 'The Boy and the Wolf.' "You can see, by calling wolf, wolf all the time, when the wolf really did come no one believed the boy. The wolf ate up all the sheep."

"What a foolish story," Raven Wing scoffed. "You should listen to Storyteller. His stories are the ones you should learn and retell."

Buffalo Boy, who sat silently in a corner, enjoyed listening to the stories. He urged Running Turtle to read more from the talking paper. Running Turtle, miffed by Raven Wing's cutting remarks, refused. If they wanted to hear more stories they had to come to the mission school where they would learn to read stories for themselves.

#

Before the villagers could fully digest the news of Missionary Spalding's ambitious plans, tragedy struck Lapwai Valley. Remnants of the party of hunters that had trekked to buffalo country, straggled back empty-handed. They had crossed the mountains without mishap. On the plains bordering Sun River they came upon a herd of buffalo. They were so elated they threw caution to the winds. One buffalo after another fell to their arrows and bullets. While they were skinning and butchering the kills a band of Blackfeet rode over the ridge. The youthful hunters were trapped. They had set aside their bows and neglected to reload their rifles. They had to face the enemy with clubs, lances and knives. Only three of the party of twelve escaped. The tragedy left the Lapwai village distraught. Nine of their best young men had been lost. The fact their bodies were never recovered made the disaster worse. Their bodies would have been mutilated, their spirits left to wander restlessly through the buffalo grass that cloaked the Sun River hunting grounds.

Cries and piercing wails of grief filled the air. Farmers did not tend to crops. Work on the sawmill and gristmill came to a stop. Herders left horses to graze on their own. School had to close for lack of students. Missionary Spalding, unaware of what caused the anguish, angrily began to search out his absent workers. When told of the hunting party's hapless journey, he was furious. The people had disobeyed him. He ordered the survivor hunters whipped but he was thwarted. Yellow Panther, leader of the hunting party was badly wounded. The other two survivors ran away.

It took weeks for life in Lapwai Valley to get back to normal. Even then another band of young men kept the valley in turmoil. They organized a war party to wreak vengeance on the Blackfeet. Their fanatic behavior kept everyone on edge, none more so than Raven Wing. The thought that in a few years her sons would be old enough to engage in dangerous adventures like this made her blood run cold.

Almost every morning during the time school was closed, Running Turtle came to the cabin to repair the damaged flower garden. The puppy, thinking Running Turtle wanted to play, kept running into the garden, undoing all of his work. Running Turtle finally tied the pup to a post where it whined, howled and barked. To try and entertain the pup and keep him quiet, Buffalo Boy and Young Wolf raced up and down the porch steps. It made matters worse. The excited dog ran around in a circle, barking as loud as it could.

Inside the cabin baby Little Bird started to howl. Raven Wing stormed through the door.

"Untie the dog. Take it away. Go to the pasture. See to the horses. Do anything, but stop that noise!"

The very next morning Buffalo Boy and Young Wolf were enrolled in the mission school. Immediately after the camas harvest they would begin. "Anything is better than having to deal with two idle boys and a dog," Raven Wing explained to Quiet Woman who did not approve.

THE LAST RENDEZVOUS

XI

I have found out there ain't no surer way to find out whether you like people or hate them than to travel with them.

Samuel Clemens

One delay after another kept Buck Stone's brigade of trappers at the Independence, Missouri campsite. The morning after Joe Jennings successfully passed his guard duty stint, it began to rain. For an hour or more driving wind sent sheets of water skittering over the landscape. The downpour was so heavy the Santa Fe encampment faded from sight. Rivulets ran down slopes to form pools in low spots. The creek below camp became a raging torrent. The trappers and all of their belongings were drenched. At the height of the storm a mule slipped its halter and bolted. The last the trappers saw of it, it was hightailing down the Santa Fe Trail.

For Little Ned the delay was torture. On the trail he could distance himself from his son but confinement to camp found them sitting cheek to jowl. It was all he could do to keep from dropping his reserve and asking about the farm, his ailing parents, the nosy Abernathy neighbors and most of all, the apple of his eye, little Tildy. But the thought of her also brought him great sorrow. She was the picture of her mother. The sight of her almost tore his heart in two. He kept forgetting himself, calling her Grace, the name of her dead mother. Now, the presence of his son was nearly as bad. It brought back those days of wonderful happiness followed by that unbearable sorrow. Why couldn't he confess why he had to leave home and never return? How could he ever explain? "Agh!" Little Ned left the lean-to shelter to stomp around in the mud pretending to inspect the horses and mules. The men called to him, begging him to get in out of the rain. Only when sodden and chilled to the bone did he come in, ignoring the curious glances of his companions.

Little Ned almost had himself under control when out of the past came another demon to torture him. While packing for the trail a lone horseman cantered up the trail from the west. When he came abreast of the camp he abruptly pulled up.

"Ho! Is this Buck Stone's outfit?" he called out.

Buck stopped cinching on the girths of the pack mules. "Who in blazes is that?" he asked. The newcomer approached riding a pinto and leading a horse even more strikingly marked.

"I say," Deacon exclaimed. "Those're Injun ponies, maybeso, Cayuse. " Tarnation! Look who's come callin'."

Little Ned stopped packing to study the newcomer. His lips tightened and his eyes narrowed to slits. His face paled, then flushed red. He gripped the pack saddle so tightly his knuckles were white. Viciously, he jerked the new Hawkin from its protective sheath.

"What's the matter?" Deacon blurted. "Yuh've seen this bird afore. Why I 'member the time yuh . . ."

"Quite blithering! I'm not blind." Little Ned turned on Deacon so angrily the rotund trapper stumbled backward.

His father's vehemence stunned Joe. The presence of the newcomer had turned him into a wild man. Joe studied the horseman. He was as lean and tall as Hawk Beak. He wore faded, well worn buckskins that needed patching and cleaning. An elbow poked through a hole in a sleeve. His features were angular. His dark skin had the appearance of well worn leather, a half-blood of some kind, Joe decided. When he came near he could see his eyes were deep set, black as coal and bold. There was something else very strange about the newcomer. It was his left ear; nearly half of it was missing! After shaking hands, he and Buck walked up to the campsite.

"You know Hawk Beak, Deacon, Little Ned, and this is our new partner, Joe," Buck introduced.

Francois nodded. His gaze stopped on Little Ned. In a split second the coal black eyes became as hard as agates. Little Ned did not acknowledge the newcomer. He turned his back on him to check the load of his new rifle. Joe shivered. The morning sun was warm and bright but a chill penetrated to the very marrow of his bones.

The men went back to packing. The cheerful camaraderie that prevailed before the stranger appeared was gone. The pack animals sensed the change. One of Hawk Beak's mules refused to take the pack saddle and began to bite and kick. Hawk Beak caught a hoof in the shin and hopped around on one leg.

"Damn this spavin-legged hay burner, I'm goin' to eat it live." Hawk Beak clamped his teeth on the mule's long ear. The mule let out a pained snort and pawed the ground. With his jaws still clamped tight on the ear, Hawk Beak wrapped a blindfold around the mule's eyes. The mule backed away, then stood still. Hawk Beak quickly threw the pack on its back and strapped it tightly. "There, yuh miserable critter, try an' shake thet off."

Buck and the man called Francois moved away to squat and talk. With his mules saddled and packed, Little Ned leaned against a tree. Methodically, he began honing his long-bladed skinning knife, his eyes fixed on the stranger. Hawk Beak, finished with the obstreperous mule, snubbed it to a tree and sat down to inspect his injured shin and the loads of his pistols. Deacon hunkered down by his thin friend with his rifle across his knees. Joe watched in astonishment. What was there about this newcomer that turned his father into a surly bear and set them all to reaching for their weapons?

"Beats me why Buck gives this galoot the time of day. If yuh remember correctly, he left us high an' dry at the Green River rendezvous," Deacon observed.

"Yeah," Hawk Beak agreed. "We was shorthanded all season."

"Why don't Buck tell thet Canuck fish snapper ta shove off. Time's a wastin'. At this rate we'll never git ta the trappin' grounds," Deacon continued to grumble.

"Now, now," Hawk Beak cautioned. "Yuh must have charity in yer heart fer others even though they be followers of the Pope in Rome."

"Yeah," Deacon answered. "I guess we should be more forgivin'. Hath not God created us all equal?"

"God created the sidewinder, the viper, the adder, the asp and the hornet. That doesn't mean we must press them all to our bosom," Little Ned retorted, his eyes fixed balefully on the newcomer.

Joe could hardly contain himself. Why did this man cause so much dislike and hate? Besides leaving the brigade high and dry on Green River, what else had he done? He glanced around the circle of faces. The set expressions told him they did not want to talk about it. While Joe wrestled with the mystery, Buck and Francois finished their conversation and strolled up.

"Francois wants to join us," Buck announced. "I think we should take him along. Where we're going we can't have too many experienced hands."

Little Ned uttered an inaudible grunt but no other response was made. The trappers untied the mules, mounted their horses and, with Buck and Francois leading, started down the trail. Joe jogged along moodily, the high excitement with which he started the journey had paled. Suffering through the miserable weather, his precious new clothes dirty and stiff and now the threatening atmosphere that had descended, brought the realization home that the life the mountain men lived was not all one glorious adventure. The talk Little Ned had given him on the hardships of trapping expeditions was beginning to make sense. This was not a life for the fainthearted.

Late in the day Buck called a halt near a stream lined with willow trees. Thick pasture carpeted a meadow. A rabbit darted through the grass. Francois seized a pistol, snapping off a shot. The rabbit stopped in midair and dropped. A small band of geese squawked and flew up from behind a patch of brush. Francois dropped the pistol and reached for his rifle. Barely taking aim, he pulled the trigger. The lead honker's wings collapsed. The bird dropped like a rock, landing in a pile of feathers on the far bank.

"Golly!" Joe uttered, his mouth agape.

"Yuh bet, the guy kin shoot," Deacon said. "Thet's the main reason Buck brung him along."

Francois' kills supplied meat for the pot but they gave Joe little pleasure. As junior man it was his duty to skin and butcher the rabbit and pluck and draw the goose. When he finished there wasn't much left of either and he had blood and feathers all over his new clothes. To add to his chagrin, the trappers were critical.

"Hell, man, yuh've wasted enuff meat ta feed a pack of starvin' wolves," Deacon, who was in charge of the stew bucket, complained.

"I say, yuh've got more feathers on yuh than yuh took off the goose. Betcha if yuh flapped yer arms yuh could take off an' fly," Hawk Beak critically observed.

His father was no help. He looked at the mess Joe had made and sadly shook his head as if to say, "I don't know whether you are going to make it or not."

Joe ate his portion but each bite stuck in his craw. He was bruised, dirty, exhausted and defeated. He wished he had never left home. As soon as he could, he rolled up in his blankets, clothes and all. Almost before he closed his eyes, he was dead to the world.

Buck and Francois continued to lead the pack train northwest, toward the Platte. Here Buck hoped to run into a band of Cheyenne. "You see, they have had all winter to trap and all spring to hunt. They should be loaded with hides and pelts and ready to trade," Buck explained. Before the week was out they did run into Indians. They were Kiowas, a fierce looking lot that rode up fast to inspect the trappers' camp. They stopped some distance away, their haughty eyes surveying the mules and stack of packs.

Buck calmly gave orders to corral the stock and secure camp. The old timers were quick to act. They pulled the animals into a tight circle and stacked the packs to form a triangular breastwork, piled high enough to protect a man's body, yet still low enough to make ideal rests for gun barrels. The trappers checked the load in their rifles, laid out their hand guns, hand axes and knives to use in close combat. For such a slight group they presented a formidable foe. With everyone in place Buck nodded his approval.

"Guess it's time to have a little powwow," he said and, unarmed, stepped in front of the barricade to face the Kiowas whose horses danced nervously back and forth. Joe tensely gripped the old Henry. This was something else he had not given much thought — Indians on the warpath. Buck walked halfway to the Indian group and stopped. There ensued a bit of sign language and much guttural muttering.

"Wants us to pay passage," Hawk Beak interpreted, spitting in disgust. "This country ain't even theirs, belongs to the Pawnee."

Nevertheless, Buck appeared to make conciliatory signs. He returned to dig into a pack. "Let's not make trouble. I'll buy them off with a little tobacco."

After Buck parceled out handfuls of tobacco, the band of Indians rode away, scowling their displeasure. "You have to know when to be tight-fisted and when to be generous," Buck instructed Joe. "These Kiowas are young bucks who probably strayed away from the tribe to kick up their heels and pick up a few coups. If we'd not been alert they'd likely tried to lift our scalps and make off with everything we have. The way it is, they're frustrated but smart enough to see they won't get a thing without a good scrap."

On the North Platte the trappers ran into their first trading prospect. Near dusk several Indian horsemen rode into camp. They greeted Buck with obvious pleasure. Another mixture of guttural talk and sign language took place. Joe attempted to see and hear what was said but it made no sense to him.

"Our old Cheyenne friend, Little Antlers, has a camp nearby," Buck said after the Indians left. "They have invited us over to palaver and trade."

The next morning Francois and Hawk Beak rode out of camp to hunt for game. "It's always politic to bring sufficient food for a feast," Buck explained. "Nothing Indians like better than trade on a full stomach."

Late in the day Francois and Hawk Beak returned with three antelope carcasses draped over the backs of pack mules. Buck nodded approval. "That should do. Add a slab or two of bacon, a sack of beans and a few cans of molasses and we'll have them eating out of our hands."

"How about dispensing whiskey? The young bucks'll be certain to expect firewater," Francois said.

Joe glanced at the dark face in surprise. It was the first time Francois had said little more than "Howdy."

"There'll be no whiskey," Buck said sharply.

THE LAST RENDEZVOUS

Francois did not argue. Instead, he unsheathed a short shafted knife with a curved blade and began to hone it viciously. As they were packing up to leave Joe asked Hawk Beak why Francois felt they should offer the Indians liquor.

"Old timers claim they cain't make profitable trade with Injuns 'less they're feelin' no pain. Buck won't stand fer it. He says if yuh cain't trade on the up an' up yuh should go inta the bunco business. Trade ain't fitten an' proper 'less both parties walk away feelin' good 'bout theirselves."

The following morning Buck led the trappers along the trail to Little Antlers' camp. Joe was all eyes and ears. Except for a few wickiups set along the banks of eastern rivers, this would be his first view of an honest to goodness Indian camp. First they were greeted by youthful camp guards who solemnly saluted with outthrust clasped hands. "Peace! Our hands are empty," they said. Soon a dozen or more dogs appeared, tumbling over themselves, snarling and barking. Behind the dogs a group of happy-faced children shyly waited. Then, like turning a page in a picture book, the Indian encampment popped into view. Dozens of tipis loomed among a grove of scattered trees. The funnel shapes made by poles emerging above the tipi coverings resembled nesting places for giant birds. Joe noted the lodge entrances faced the same direction, east. "It's so they kin greet Father Sun. These people ain't lazy. They're up at the first light of dawn," Deacon explained. Tipi flaps lay open revealing the contents inside. There wasn't anything unusual: rolled bedding, cooking utensils, woven reed baskets and stacks of rawhide bags.

At the edge of camp the trappers stopped. Buck went ahead to parley; the others sat and watched. In the center of an open space several lodges stood apart, apparently empty. Clustered near them a group of villagers waited to greet the visitors. As Francois predicted, a body of young men appeared begging for whiskey.

"Do they expect us to hand them a jug to pass around?" Joe asked after Deacon and Hawk Beak had fended them off.

"Spect so," Hawk Beak answered. "Fer sure they wouldn't turn a jug down."

"How do the traders who give out whiskey manage?"

"They've made a science of it," Deacon answered. "Ta make certain Injuns stay sober enuff ta trade, they cut a gallon of alcohol with three or four gallons of water, an' ration 'em ta a cup. If thar ain't no cups they select a buck with an average size mouth as bartender. He takes a mouthful, spits inta the next mouth an' so on. The whiskey dispenser usually ain't honest. He sneaks a few dribbles here an' there, oft as not passes out afore everyone gets his share."

"Yeah, it's a fact," Hawk Beak agreed in response to Joe's look of disbelief. "Thet's the way 'tis. Ah! Here comes Buck. We're 'bout to settle in."

Joe went about his usual chores with Indians of all ages watching every move he made. He attempted to ignore them but it was hard to do. Eyes seemed to peer at him from every direction. As dusk fell and he prepared for bed, he attempted to clean his buckskins. He took off the hunting shirt to scrub away the worst dirt and stains. He looked up to see a pair of bright eyes watching. Thinking it was a bashful boy, Joe beckoned with a motion of his chin. Instead of a boy, a slender lass came forward. Her eyes, as soft and gentle as those of a doe, locked into his. She held out her hand and would have taken the shirt but he jerked it back.

"No! No!" he uttered sharply. With a hurt expression, the Indian maiden quickly withdrew to disappear.

"What's the matter with you, lad?" asked Francois, who had observed the by-play. "She wasn't going to steal your shirt. She just wanted to help you clean it. If you had let her, she would have taken your pantaloons too and maybe kept you company all night. You missed an opportunity, son."

Joe rolled up in a blanket and tried to sleep. Each time he closed his eyes the hurt look in the doe-like eyes of the Indian girl appeared. He rolled over and pounded the bag of meal that served as pillow. What was the matter with him? That was all he needed, to get mixed up with an Indian female. Even so, thoughts of the girl haunted him. It was dawn before he slept.

THE LAST RENDEZVOUS

XII

*Young Black Beaver lay basking in the sun, happily unaware of any danger
other than those which nature had fitted him to cope.*

Frank Conibear, trapper

When Joe awakened, it took him a moment to realize where he was. Camp dogs were barking, blue jays squawking, children of all ages hysterically shouting and women clapping hands while performing a little dance. The trappers had given the antelope carcasses to the people the evening before but had waited to present the other foodstuffs until morning: bacon, cornmeal, beans, hardtack and several cans of molasses. It was the sight of the molasses that created the excitement. The usually impassive faces of the womenfolk were wreathed with smiles of delight.

"Molasses always pleases," Deacon observed. "Guess it's 'cause they never had sugar, candy or sweets."

The obvious pleasure the villagers displayed reminded Joe of happy children at Christmas time. Were these the "red heathen — the pagan savages" Pastor Barclay preached about "whose natures needed taming and souls needed saving?"

Buck, who noticed Joe's fascination with the people, nodded his approval. "Treat them right and they're the best folks on God's green earth. Aren't these kids lovable? Sometimes I would like to take the whole batch of them and give them the advantages we know back east. Of course if we did they would hate it and wish they were home, and I don't blame them. The life they lead out here is mighty good."

Joe thought of the doe-eyed maiden who offered help he had so rudely rejected. He wished he could make amends. He searched the encampment but she was not in sight.

In the open space near the center of the village, the trappers spread out blankets and buffalo robes on which to lay out their wares.

An enticing array of knives, beads, small bells, mirrors, blankets, lengths of bright colored cloth and a variety of trinkets and doodads, were soon on display. The women and children exclaimed, giggled and pointed, as each new item appeared. Some children could not be constrained. A girl with long braids bobbing, dashed in to pick up a shiny beaded bracelet to show her mother. Her mother wagged a finger. Reluctantly, the little girl put it back but not before she slipped it on her wrist and hopped from one foot to the other with a beaming smile.

Finally satisfied with the display, Buck announced it was time to trade. For a moment order almost broke down. People pushed forward, pointing and shouting at the items desired. It was Francois who restored calm. With a few sharp words Joe did not understand, the French Canadian stopped the pushing and shoving.

The manner in which the tall, dark half-breed took control of the crowd amazed Joe. It was obvious he commanded respect. Why were Deacon, Hawk Beak and Little Ned so down on him? So far he had caused no trouble. He said little and kept to himself. Joe's thoughts were abruptly interrupted by Deacon.

"Wake up! This is no time ta go ta sleep. These people're thirstin' ta trade. Thet's what we come fer, so let's git after it."

Hesitant at first but with Deacon's help, Joe was soon immersed in the give and take of trade. Before long he could tell at a glance the difference between a prime pelt and a second. He quickly discovered he had a knack for sign language. To the amusement of the elders, the young females were attracted to him. One after another, they shyly sidled up. They wanted mirrors, beads, bells, colored cloth of every kind. The young maiden he wanted to see most did not appear. Again he searched for her in the crowd, but in vain.

After the feverish trading activity came feasting, followed by competitions and games. It was like a community picnic back home, Joe thought. The elders sat together to smoke and talk. The women cleaned up after the meal. A group of young men started a series of foot races. Others vied in feats of strength and skill: arm wrestling; lifting and tossing stone weights; and throwing tomahawks and knives.

Groups of less energetic young people gathered in circles to play the game of "hand." Joe was astonished to realize he knew the game. At home they called it "button-button — who has the button." Here a player took a pebble, shook it in his or her hands, then held out closed fists. The opposing player attempted to guess which hand contained the pebble. Onlookers made wagers on the outcome. When the hand chosen held the pebble, the winner's backers clapped and cried out in delight. When a player failed to guess correctly, they groaned in anguish.

"Kind of a silly game," Joe said.

"Don't look down yer nose at the game of hand, ol' hoss," Deacon cautioned. "When yuh've got yer favorite nag or bankroll ridin' on a guess, it gits mighty tense. I say, one of yer girlfriends is givin' yuh the eyeball. No! No! Over here. Now she's pretendin' ta be modest an' shy. Ah, she's as purty as a red heifer in a patch of clover."

Joe glanced toward a circle of girls who played hand as excitedly as did the men. A slender maiden had the pebble. Her opponent was agonizing over which hand held it. The slender girl's black hair glistened, gleaming like the shiny coat of a blackbird. The straight locks fell to her shoulders, almost hiding a tan face glowing with health. The dark, doe-like eyes glanced up. For a moment her eyes met his. It was the girl who had wanted to clean his hunting shirt. A sensation unlike any he ever had known gripped him. He quickly glanced away. What was the matter with him? He was acting like an infatuated schoolboy.

The following morning Little Antlers and a host of villagers came to see Buck and his trappers off. A band of young men rode alongside, gaily demonstrating their horsemanship. Near the edge of the village a group of women watched. Among them was the slender maiden with the doe-like eyes and shiny black hair. She raised her hand in a gesture of farewell. Joe acknowledged it with a doff of his cap. For the rest of the day he berated himself. He didn't even have sense enough to find out her name.

The days grew shorter and campsites more frequent. There

was a touch of fall in the air. Each evening the trappers went to sleep to the mournful serenade of coyotes and wolves. In the mornings they awakened to find a touch of frost on the grass. The mountains ahead grew higher and brighter. Game became more plentiful. Small herds of elk and deer watching from grassy meadows, could be seen along game trails.

Francois started leaving camp at night. Scouting ahead, Buck explained. Occasionally, distant gunfire could be heard. In the morning there would be a turkey, opossum, once a small deer, lying by the dead fire, game that Francois had killed on his nocturnal jaunts. When they entered hostile territory Francois discarded the noisy, long-barreled Hawkin for the silent bow and arrow. The flow of game for the stew pot continued unabated. Since Joe had to skin, pluck and butcher the game, he was appalled at the amount Francois brought in. The tall dark man intrigued him. The trapper never talked about himself but Joe learned Francois was a French Canadian who for years trapped for Hudson's Bay. Once before he joined Buck's brigade only to abruptly desert the trappers at the Green River rendezvous in '34 or was it '35? Where Francois had gone after that or what he had done was a mysterious blank. For that matter, Joe knew little of the background of any of his companions, including that of his own father.

One morning Joe, still half asleep, glanced across the valley and blinked in amazement. Directly opposite the camp was a herd of woolly beasts. "Buffalo!" he shouted. Then felt chagrined. Everyone else was up and going about breaking camp as usual. The presence of the buffalo herd did not excite them at all.

After several days of buffalo sightings, Buck made early camp. "I say it's time we take advantage of these buffalo and make meat," he announced. "It could be a long hard winter."

For Joe, the stopover was an experience he would never forget. Before the hunt Little Ned took him aside. "When you hunt buffalo it's important to follow a few rules," he instructed. "The first thing to remember is to get as close as possible before rousing the herd. Since we're after meat, don't go for the biggest critter you see. Young cows are best. When you shoot, aim between the shoulders. If you hit them right the lead goes down into the heart and lungs. That'll finish them every time."

Joe watched the others prepare. They all checked the rifle loads. Besides their rifles, Francois, Hawk Beak and Buck carried a brace of pistols and the usual hatchets and knives. They made certain saddle cinches were tight and mounted up. The horses, sensing something unusual, danced and jerked their heads, impatient to be off. After brief instructions Buck started up a ravine that led toward the herd. Joe marveled how near they came before the first shaggy beast noticed them and began to run.

"After 'em!" Hawk Beak shouted. The riders kicked their horses into a full gallop.

Little Ned let the others take the lead. He wanted to keep an eye on his son. During a buffalo run anything could happen. A horse could shy or be gored. A saddle cinch could break, pitching a rider into the path of a thousand hooves. A maddened bull could go on the rampage, knocking horse and rider down.

The herd began to move. Close behind rode Francois, his attention fixed on a pair of young cows. Little Ned raised his Hawkin. He would take one of the cows. Instead of a cow, the hated dark-faced trapper passed across his sights. A terrifying thought came to his mind. "What a perfect time to make that despicable hound pay for all the dirt he's done. It will look like a hunting accident." Little Ned held his breath, his finger tightened on the trigger. Francois' mount abruptly veered into a cloud of dust obscuring the target. Little Ned lowered the Hawkin. Perspiration poured down his face. He had come within an eyelash of committing cold-blooded murder.

Joe raced alongside the galloping bodies. The entire pack of animals was now on a dead run. The noise was fearful, like the roll of thunder before a summer storm. The trampling hooves sent up a cloud of dust so thick Joe barely could distinguish one body from another. There was one smaller than the rest, surely a cow. He urged his mount forward, guiding it with his knees. He raised the rifle. He could not miss the broad back. Still, he hesitated. It seemed cruel to take this wild creature's short life. Yet, every year on the farm he helped kill and butcher calves, pigs and some years, a lamb. This was no different, he told himself. He rode close and fired almost point blank into the bobbing back. The bullet struck far from the shoulder but the cow bellowed and stumbled. Hawk Beak, riding nearby, dispatched her with a pistol shot between the eyes.

The riders pulled up to examine their kills. "Yuh done good," Hawk Beak said to Joe. "I've seen greenhorns on the first hunt fire inta a herd an' not graze a whisker."

Joe looked at his kill with mixed feelings. He was pleased he hadn't failed, yet saddened at taking the life of this noble animal of the plains. Hawk Beak had no such inhibitions. He callously kicked the carcass. "Now thet yuh shot her, yuh gotta gut her."

Uncertain of how to proceed, Joe watched Francois whose kill had fallen nearby. The half-breed rolled the carcass on its belly, the legs splayed out to nearly hold the body upright. Francois ran his skinning knife the length of the dead animal's back. With swift deft strokes, he peeled the hide down until it fell to make a blanket on either side of the carcass. Expertly, Francois sliced the meat away to lay it in neat piles on the freshly removed hide. With a hand ax, Francois chopped through the rib cage to sort through the viscera, selecting items to keep and those to leave behind for prairie scavengers. The skeletal bones he tossed aside. Francois then took the ends of the hide and lapped them over the meat leaving a neat package protected from dirt and flies.

"He sure can butcher," Joe marveled.

"He's got to be good for something," Deacon said sourly.

"He's always sharpening that curved knife but never uses it," Joe observed.

"He's used it plenty. Thet's his scalpin' tool."

That evening, after a feast of roasted buffalo tongues, the trappers began to preserve what remained of the hunt. They sliced the meat in long strips and laid them over a network of poles fastened together with rawhide thongs. As the camp greenhorn, stretching, scraping and treating the smelly buffalo hides fell to Joe.

"Yuh should've been kinder ta thet Cheyenne, lass," Deacon

said. "If yuh'd brung her along she'd be doin' the job fer yuh."

"Ugh!" Joe grunted. If he had brought her along he wouldn't have her slaving on green buffalo hides. How could anyone ask a delicate beauty like her to cover herself with grease, blood and gore like this? The very thought made him sick to his stomach.

When Buck reckoned each man had added sufficient meat to his pack, they renewed the trek northward, up and across the North Platte. At Fort Laramie they stopped long enough to ship the pelts and hides they obtained in trade from the Cheyenne down river to St. Louis. The money they brought would be held for the trappers until they returned. Upon leaving Fort Laramie they traveled northwest, toward the range of mountains called the Bighorns.

"This is dangerous country," Buck told Joe one day. "These lands are the crossroads of the northern tribes. The Piegan, Crow, Blackfeet, Sioux and God only knows who else, fight over this piece of ground. I don't know exactly why. The place is hot as Hades in the summer, cold as Billy-blue-blazes in winter and wind slices through here that'd peel the hide off a rhino."

A few days later Little Ned and Joe, riding ahead of the column, came upon beaver signs. Little Ned dismounted and motioned for Joe to do the same. The big trapper wet a finger to test the wind direction.

"These critters have an uncanny sense of smell," he quietly explained. "A whiff of man'll scatter them like spooked quail."

Little Ned tethered the horses in a grove and led the way up the slope to the crest of a ridge. At the summit they stopped to look down on a mountain meadow surrounded by cottonwoods and quaking aspen. Through the length of the valley ran a stream. Joe was enchanted. The view was like a landscape painting. The green fields of grass, the rows of white tree trunks, a small hill topped by red volcanic rock, all set against a background of snowcapped mountains, made him gasp. No wonder mountain men like his father risked their lives to enjoy wondrous views like these.

The two trappers moved forward to cross a smooth path that followed the contour of the hill to disappear into a stand of white-barked aspens. From the aspen grove came the sound of unusual activity. Down the path four squat, reddish-brown animals nudged a short log. The log rolled a few feet and stopped. The beavers, scrambling after it, gave it another push. It rolled a few feet farther. The beavers were upon it again. Down the slope the animals and log went until they passed from view. Joe had never seen anything like it. The little animals were almost human.

Instead of watching the beavers, Little Ned covertly studied his son. It was good to see him take pleasure in Mother Earth's creatures. There were so many enjoyments like this fathers and sons should share. Suddenly it seemed important to him to bring his two families together. It would be hard to do but not impossible. Soon he would know this eastern son well enough to confide in him. Give him a little more experience and he would understand how it all happened. But it was really up to Little Ned to clean the slate. First on the list was Francois. "Ah!" he inwardly groaned. Why hadn't he pulled the trigger when he had the damned fellow in his sights during the buffalo hunt?

At the bottom of the hill a team of beaver pushed their burdens into the water and floated them across to a dam which blocked the slow moving stream. Another team of beaver came swimming toward the dam. Like a string of tugboats pulling barges, they were hauling loads of dirt on their broad flat tails.

"Mortar for the dam," Little Ned explained.

Joe watched in awe. These little animals worked together like people. The two teams, the one with the logs and the other with the mud, converged on the dam. In a flurry of activity, dirt and logs were placed on the face of the dam, the dexterous tails of the beaver pounding them in place.

"Golly!" Joe exclaimed. "It must have taken more than a year to build that dam."

"Many years," Little Ned corrected. He pointed up stream. There's the sentinel. When danger approaches he'll sound a warning."

In the smooth water that formed a small lake behind the dam

a miniature island of land remained. On it sat an old gray beaver. It appeared he was overseeing the project. From time to time he shifted his position, his head following the activity. Suddenly, he plunged into the lake; his flat tail slapped the water, creating a sound like a pistol shot. Every beaver vanished as though a magic wand made them disappear.

"Dammit," Little Ned grumbled. "Our noisy companions have arrived."

Overjoyed by the abundance of beaver, the party of trappers set about establishing permanent winter quarters. With considerable deliberation, Buck examined the rise and fall of the land. When storms blew in from the north they could expect several feet of snow, he said. Protective rocks and trees were needed to break the wind and forestall drifting snow. The living quarters should have a southern exposure to gain the warming benefits of the sun. They needed sufficient wood to fuel fires and provide building material and they needed to be near running water.

Buck finally settled on a protected draw that ended in a cul-de-sac but was open to the south with easy access to the trapping grounds. Its only fault was that it faced a canyon wall where ancient Indians had chiseled petroglyphs in the sandstone cliff. When the sun's rays struck them just right, lines of warriors appeared to gallop directly toward the campsite.

"Kinda spooky, ain't it?" Hawk Beak said.

Joe silently agreed. Francois also did not appear comfortable with the location. When passing the cliff he furtively made the sign of the cross. Buck and Deacon took the cliff drawings for granted. They were just part of the rugged landscape.

"This'll do fine," Buck said. "Home is where you make it."

Anticipating a long season, the trappers constructed sturdy quarters. Buffalo hides were draped over a slanted network of heavy aspen poles held in place by thick posts. Next to the living area another shelter was erected to provide protection while preparing the pelts and storing them through the winter.

When everything was finished to Buck's satisfaction, he called the men together. "There are several matters we must decide. How are we to divvy up the chores? The bothersome business of cooking and keeping the camp clean must be done. Then there's the feeding and care of the horses and mules. It's important they be kept in good condition. Who knows when and how fast we may be forced to leave. It's quiet and peaceful now but that could quickly change. To be on the safe side we'd best keep guard. Then there's the matter of sharing the catch. Do we do as usual, put the pelts into a common pot and divvy them up at the end of the season?"

Allotting camp duties and looking after the livestock were easily decided, but when it came to sharing the catch an impasse arose.

"I don't mean to share with any greenhorn," Francois said, glancing pointedly at Joe.

Joe felt his face glow with embarrassment. To be singled out as the weak member of the party hurt, and coming from Francois, whom he had come to respect, made the blow doubly hard to take.

"Oh, so you're too good to share in a common pot, are you," Little Ned glowered at Francois. "That's fine with me. In fact Young Joe and I will be partners. You'll see. We'll take more beaver than the rest of you put together."

"All right," Buck said. "No need to fuss. Each man will tally his own catch."

Joe felt chagrined at the way the meeting ended but also he was pleased. He and his father would be partners on the trap line, a dream come true. Perhaps his journey west would turn out well after all. In his mind's eye he could see his father and himself returning home after a successful trapping season. Ready money in their pockets and dressed in fringed buckskins, trimmed with porcupine quills and beads, they would set Pastor Barclay's congregation on its ear.

THE LAST RENDEZVOUS

XIII

Brother! You have got our country, but are not satisfied. You want to force your religion upon us.

Red Jacket, Seneca

While Buck Stone's brigade prepared for the winter, far to the west, Lapwai villagers were similarly involved. The feel of autumn was in the air. Locust leaves had turned yellow and were starting to fall. Hillsides surrounding the valley were bare and brown. Formations of geese were heard honking their way south. Lapwai Creek had fallen to a trickle. There was hardly sufficient water in the millrun to operate the gristmill. Almost instinctively, villagers began to make ready for the camas harvest. Weasel Face, the band leader, met with the elders. They agreed the time had come to harvest the camas bulbs. One bright crisp morning all but the elderly and infirm took to the trail that led to the camas meadows.

Realizing his flock of worshipers and workers was leaving, Missionary Spalding cornered his disciples and asked them to use their influence to stop the exodus. With all able bodied villagers gone, work on the mission compound and classes in the schoolroom would come to a halt. It was no use to ask the people to stay, Spalding's disciples said. The trek to the camas grounds to dig bulbs was as much of their nature as it was for salmon to spawn. The camas harvest was essential. The camas bulb had been a staple food of the tribe since the Nimpau first appeared on Mother Earth.

Missionary Spalding watched his flock leave with bitterness in his heart. He had left a comfortable home to dedicate his life to these ignorant people who had never heard of the wonderful rewards that lay in store in heaven above. His efforts to get the nomadic people to settle down and become civilized had gone for naught. Every year it had been the same. Like lemmings heading for the sea, everyone able made the journey to dig for camas bulbs. There was no turning them back. He had believed his grandiose plans to enlarge the mission, making it the center of social, religious and economic life on the Columbia Plateau, would bring a change. It did not. Even so, he rode alongside the column pleading with his faithful to come to their senses. Finally Weasel Face promised he would lead the people back in time to celebrate the Sabbath, six days hence.

At first Raven Wing dreaded the thought of making the journey. Villagers still avoided her. No one except members of her own family came to the cabin. She was as isolated and friendless as she had been in Fort Vancouver where she had spent the last two years. At least there she had a man who, after a fashion, supported her. Instead of the ordeal Raven Wing anticipated, however, everything went well. Vision Seeker and Running Turtle helped her collect the necessities, loaded them on pack horses and brought a gentle mare for her to ride. Quiet Woman helped with the baby. Raven Wing found herself looking on with barely anything to do.

The trail ride was also undemanding. Relieved of the baby, traveling along the forest lined trail with the blue sky overhead, Raven Wing found herself taking pleasure in her surroundings. It was like a festive occasion. Everyone was in a happy mood. People who had not spoken to her in months, greeted her and made her feel welcome. Even some she recognized as having had a hand in forcing Francois to flee, gave kind glances, nodded and smiled. Buffalo Boy and Young Wolf rode the almost identical ponies their grandfather gifted each of them after their two year absence from Lapwai. Lone Wolf was in his glory. He regaled his grandsons with stories of his youth, pointing out sites where he had made elk and deer kills and where he once encountered a family of grizzlies, the papa bear providing the paws for his bear claw necklace, of which he was so proud.

At midday the column stopped in a grassy clearing beside a musical creek. Overhead a soft breeze made the trees sigh. Blue jays, annoyed by the intrusion, flitted from one limb to another, scolding sharply. Chipmunks and squirrels flicked their tails and scampered to safety as camp dogs ran up to sniff and yelp. In the shadows of a nearby glen the white tails of two deer flashed as the startled animals darted away. A covey of grouse took off in a flurry of beating wings. Youngsters spied a porcupine nibbling on the bark of a tree and urged it along to protect their dogs from its dangerous quills. Quiet Woman sat by the creek to feed the baby. Grandfather Lone Wolf and his grandsons followed a trail of bees into the woods in search of honey. Raven Wing rested her back against a fallen tree. She looked around and smiled. It was the first time in years she truly had time to appreciate the sights and sounds of Mother Earth.

The camp on the camas meadows was just as pleasant. The Lone Wolf family shared an open-sided shelter set in a fringe of trees. Here again they were surrounded by creatures of Mother Earth. Two cottontail rabbits scampered out of the high grass. A flock of magpies chattered from a dead pine and circling hawks patrolled the cobalt blue sky. Swallows dipped and sailed over the meadows. Meadowlarks welcomed the newcomers with melodious song. Every night a coyote chorus lulled them to sleep. Raven Wing wished the camas harvest could go on forever. It was almost as if a magic wand had waved her troubles away. When she thought of the two men with whom she had lived, she dwelt on the pleasant aspects of the time they had spent together, especially the way they looked at her. Francois' dark bold eyes consumed her with his fierce love. The Boston man, who did everything he could to make life pleasant for her, admired her with his eyes as blue and clear as the autumn sky overhead. She could not help wondering where the two men were and what they were doing. Did they think of her? "Aiiee!" What did it matter? Each one had every reason never to see her again.

The morning after their arrival on the camas grounds, the Lapwai band members went to work. It, too, was a joy for Raven Wing. With the warm sun on their backs, the women and children gathered in groups to dig the camas bulbs. The digging tools were sharp curved sticks. Those new to the camas grounds collected the sticks in the nearby woods. Old timers who had been on many camas digs, brought their own, smooth from previous diggings, some with fancy carved handles. Other veteran diggers had elk or deer horn fitted over the blunt end of the sticks to protect their hands.

The work was not difficult but did require a certain degree of skill. On either side of the dried remains of the tuberous camas plant the sharp sticks were thrust into the ground. With a deft movement of the wrists, upward pressure was applied to the sticks. When properly done the loamy soil opened up to expose the camas bulbs that were hidden just below the surface. The bulbs were tossed into piles where teams of children cleaned them, put them in reed baskets and carried them back to camp.

At first, forcing the sticks into the soil made Raven Wing's hands sore. Then a worker offered rawhide coverings for her hands. The act of kindness was like the first rays of Father Sun on a spring day, bringing brightness to the shadows that darkened her heart. She glanced at her fellow workers, their hands busy, their eyes intent. A warm feeling of kinship surged through her body. It was like the old days. Lapwai people were still kind and good. It was those missionaries and their religion that had turned them hateful and unkind.

Digging the camas bulbs was only the start of camas harvest work. After sufficient bulbs had been harvested, pits were dug to roast them and ready them for winter storage. Raven Wing had forgotten how it was done. Quiet Woman clucked impatiently.

"You should have learned this as a girl," she scolded. "But you had no time. You were always riding or playing games with the boys. Now watch what I do. First we dig our pit."

When Running Turtle had dug a pit sufficiently deep and round to satisfy Quiet Woman, she had him gather stones which she placed in the bottom. She then built a fire. When the stones were hot, she poured water over them. Before the steam could escape she threw in handfuls of grass and then a layer of leaves. After that came the bulbs; more than two full baskets were stacked on top of the leaves. The layer of bulbs was then covered with a protective cloth. After the cloth came another layer of grass and then a bit of dirt. Finally, a fire was built on top of the pit and left burning all night. The next day the baked bulbs were removed from the pit and laid out to dry in the sun or made into loaves which were steamed again before being dried and stored away for winter use.

The camas harvest was not all work. Especially in the afternoons, the people enjoyed themselves. Lazing in the sun, mothers watched their youngsters play tag among the trees. Elders gathered in groups to smoke and talk. Young maidens worked with beads and quills, casting shy glances at young males who showed off by racing, wrestling, playing tricks on one another or doing silly things like walking on their hands. The harvesters, who came from all parts of the tribal homeland, went from campfire to campfire visiting, laughing, joking -- enjoying the opportunity of renewing old friendships or making new ones. A few, like Raven Wing, merely sat idle, glad to be relieved of the responsibilities that weighed on them at home.

Tribal leaders sat on a hillside to smoke and discuss tribal matters: Tamootsin from Alpowa, Tuekakas from Wallowa, Flint Necklace from Aston, Tackensuatis and Hallalhotsoot, the man the Red Coats called Lawyer, from Kamiah; all took part. Vision Seeker, who spoke little but listened to every word, sat with the leaders. His silent reserve and ability to see into the future made him welcome. Everyone wanted his views on what lay ahead. But they were disappointed. If he had seen signs or received visions lately, he kept them to himself.

Vision Seeker did not like these meetings. Now that Lone Wolf had lost his position as leader of the Lapwai band, he found the matters they discussed boring. Vision Seeker only attended because he felt the Lone Wolf Clan should be represented. He seldom, if ever, spoke because each time he did the arrogant Weasel Face found a way to belittle what he said. Also, he found the meetings a waste of time. Even though the council might reach a decision, there was no obligation on band leaders to adopt it. Only under threatening circumstances did the meetings produce any good.

The discussions covered a wide range of subjects. A good deal of time was spent deliberating over Missionary Spalding's ambitious plans for the mission. Some leaders thought them good. Others opposed them. The appearance of two Catholic priests in the region assumed great significance. The Long Robes had visited Fort Walla Walla where they met with Young Chief of the Cayuse. It was said one of Young Chief's children was baptized by the Long Robes.

Those who witnessed the event reported on the splendid garments the priest wore, the magnificent altar trappings and the seriousness with which the ceremony was conducted.

"The language and ways of these Long Robes is strange," said Red Wolfe, a friend of Young Chief. "Their teachings on ways to reach the Great Spirit land called heaven, are different from those of Missionary Spalding. Is their teaching better? Some say yes, some say no. The Long Robes are happy to baptize our people. Their words are kind. They do not whip. When one is bad he tells the bad things he has done and is forgiven. We should think much about this. There is much good about the Long Robes. They do not force us to plow and scrape Mother Earth. We can return to live as our forefathers did."

"We should not talk about things like these," Weasel Face, Missionary Spalding's disciple, said. "It gets us all mixed up. It only makes for trouble." He got up and stalked away. He did not want to hear more of this dangerous talk.

"Why is Weasel Face out of sorts?" Lone Wolf asked Vision Seeker that evening. "He acts like a spoiled child."

"The Long Robes have him upset. He is afraid they may come to Lapwai and teach our people of their ways. This would anger Missionary Spalding who would then make big trouble for Weasel Face."

"Hmmp!" Lone Wolf uttered a grunt of disgust. Since Weasel Face had become Missionary Spalding's right hand man he could not stand the sight of him -- executing Spalding's orders; whipping people; mouthing Spalding's sermons; and carrying tales back to the missionary. It pleased Lone Wolf to hear Weasel Face, the arrogant braggart, could be chasing a false religion. The Long Robes had a spiritual look about them. Perhaps they were the ones to follow. They walked quietly, talked softly, often making signs with their hands. This was the way to speak of the true god — not shout and rave as Missionary Spalding did. He shook his fist, pointed his finger, made threatening gestures . . . "Ah!" What did the Great Creator think of such behavior?

Lone Wolf thoughtfully walked away from camp and into the darkened camas field. He glanced up at the brilliant canopy of stars. The brightness and nearness of the twinkling lights made him feel small and humble. They knew the mysteries of life for they had seen everything that had happened on Mother Earth since the beginning of time. Vision Seeker said his most powerful signs came from the stars. Vision Seeker believed each star was the light of a lodge. The occupants of the lodges were spirits of those who had gone to the other side. These spirits watched over each person who lived. When they saw a person they liked, they sent a shooting star down to invite him to their lodge.

"Aiiee!" Looking skyward had given him a crick in the neck. Was this a sign? Did the sky people have their eyes on him? Were his parents and son looking down? Ah! He wished he knew. He walked farther from camp and threw back his head and shouted. "Speak! Tell what you see from the other side."

Lone Wolf stared at the twinkling blanket so long his eyes blurred and his head whirled until he staggered and fell to his knees. Vision Seeker, disturbed by his father's strange behavior, had been watching. He came and helped his father to his feet. Lone Wolf steadied himself and shook his son's arm away.

"I have not lost my strength nor my senses," Lone Wolf said. He trudged back toward camp, his thoughts bitter. Why had he acted the fool? He was like a coyote howling at the moon. He had sought wisdom from the stars but if they spoke, their words had evaded him. It all started with this talk about religion that had everyone so confused. If people could only agree on one way of worshipping the Great Creator it would make life so much easier. Toupin, the interpreter at Fort Walla Walla, said the Long Robes had the only true religion. Did Toupin speak the truth? Had Missionaries Spalding, Gray, Smith and the others deceived them? "Ah!" Lone Wolf groaned. There were so many gods -- so many ways to worship them -- so many paths to the Great Beyond -- so many things he did not understand . . . He dropped on his sleeping pallet and pulled a blanket over his head, blanking out the twinkling dots of light that seemed to mock him.

The days passed pleasantly. The beautiful weather held. The harvest was plentiful. Many baskets bulged with roasted camas bulbs and cakes. When the last bulb had been harvested there came the traditional ceremony of thanksgiving. The followers of Missionary Spalding were somewhat uneasy. The Reverend had condemned activities like this as paganistic. However, there was little chance he would find out. He was miles away at the mission compound. The people joined together to pay tribute to Mother Earth and Father Sun for giving life to the plants. The four directions were honored for bringing the seasons to pass that allowed the plants to grow and ripen. When the ceremony was completed, the harvest was over except for a celebrating feast and a day of fun and games.

Young men organized a hunt with the intention of bringing back carcasses of deer and elk. Boys set snares for squirrels and rabbits. Others went to the creek to fish. When the game was brought in women gathered in groups to prepare the feast. Pots were filled and fire pits deepened. Wood was collected and fires built. The aroma of roasting meat and simmering stews soon filled the pine scented air.

While the women prepared the food, the men laid out a race course. They decided on a course that stretched from the fringe of the trees on one edge of the camas meadow to the creek bank on the opposite side. Almost every horseman had an animal he wanted to run. There was not room on the course for them all. Organizers decided eliminating races should be run in the morning. The winners of these races would then race again in the afternoon.

Lone Wolf insisted the two older grandsons enter in the youth race, riding the almost identical ponies he had given them. Vision Seeker looked on doubtfully. Buffalo Boy's pony, which he had named Magpie, ran as swift as the wind. Young Wolf's pony was much slower. If Buffalo Boy's Magpie won and Young Wolf's pony lost, would it cause a quarrel? Young Wolf liked to think he had the best of everything.

Several races were run and then came the youth race. The

officials called the racers to the starting line. The horses jostled for space. Spotted Badger reined his mount to the forefront, making Buffalo Boy's pony step aside. The racing judge signaled for the race to start. The horses leaped forward. Magpie was left behind. Buffalo Boy furiously urged his pony forward. Magpie edged even with Young Wolf's mount but Spotted Badger, the rider Buffalo Boy wanted most to beat, was a full length in the lead. Buffalo Boy kicked Magpie in the ribs and gave him a swat with his hand. The pony responded. The two horses crossed the finish line nose to nose. Spotted Badger shouted he had won. The judge said they crossed the finish line at the same time. Many of the spectators had placed wagers on the race and began to protest. Weasel Face galloped up, waving his arms. "Stop! Stop! Missionary Spalding has come! Missionary Spalding is here!"

Weasel Face's announcement was ignored. Riders and spectators milled back and forth. "They must race again," someone shouted. Spalding, his hat askew, the tails of his frock coat flapping in the wind, rode into the melee. Above his dark beard, the usually pale flesh had a purplish hue.

"Sinners! Blasphemers! Desecrators! You and you and you!" He singled out the racers and the gamblers. "You have broken the Fourth Commandment. 'Remember the Sabbath, to keep it holy.' Everyone that defiles the Sabbath shall surely be put to death." His wild eyes swept the crowd that had gathered. He spotted Weasel Face. "You lied. You said you would have the people back in Lapwai in time for Sunday worship. Shame! Shame is upon you!"

THE LAST RENDEZVOUS

XIV

Man is like pepper: not until you chew him do you know his heat.
Hausa Proverb

  For the mountain man, the first day of a trapping season was always a time of excitement. Establishing a new trap line was like opening a mysterious present on Christmas morning. No one knew what to expect. Would there be adequate sites to set the traps? Would predators slink in and steal the catch? Would the wily beaver get wise and change its habits? This time the valley which Buck Stone selected was in the heart of Crow country. That meant there was always the threat of hostiles. As usual, the season was a new challenge, testing trappers' courage, skill and equipment.
  For Joe the prospect of working a trap line was especially exciting. His hopes were high. He and his father were partners. They would spend hours in each other's company. Perhaps Little Ned would drop the reserve that kept them apart. Before the day, week, month or season was over, surely they would form the warm companionship that all fathers and sons should enjoy. He wanted to call him Dad and be called Son. He had barely slept the night before thinking of the many things his father and he would say and do.
  The trappers were up early. They breakfasted on coffee and soggy pan bread. No one complained. They were anxious to get started placing their traps. Little Ned and Joe finished eating and left camp first. Until late in the morning they went from one beaver sign to another. Joe could not imagine what his father had in mind.
  "Let the others have these sites," Little Ned finally said. "I like to go after two year olds. About this time of year beaver mothers chase their two year old sons and daughters from the lodge. They're making ready for the new generation of kits that is about to arrive. The two year olds now have to build new homes, mate and start families of their own. I like to catch these critters while they are still childless. The cry of an orphaned kit breaks my heart."

THE LAST RENDEZVOUS

The isolated and rigorous work suited Joe. He followed every move his father made and listened to every word he said. Joe wanted to learn everything he could. Little Ned said they would trap more beaver than the others put together. He did not want to let his father down. He wanted them to have a season so great they could go back home in style.

The first few days were hard work: wading in cold water, setting traps, skinning carcasses, stretching and shaping pelts. The grueling chores were tiresome and endless. It was all Joe could do to keep up. Whenever he lagged Little Ned snapped at him as he would a slow moving pack mule. Then, as he managed to become proficient and the stack of beaver pelts began to rise, Little Ned became almost confidential, making quips and telling interesting stories. One day, in a loquacious mood, Little Ned stopped in an open space where they sat down to rest in the warm sun. While chewing on pieces of dried buffalo meat, Little Ned began to talk. "Beavers are very much like humans. They live together, work together, and protect their families. Some Indian people honor the beaver, won't trap them or disturb their lodges. Many, many years in the past they believed they were beavers themselves."

Little Ned went on to relate the Indian legend about the feud between the beaver and the porcupine. To get the best of the beaver the porcupine carried him to the top of a tall tree and left him there believing he would starve. Instead, the resourceful beaver escaped by gnawing away the tree from the top downward.

Joe gloried in these sessions. It was clear his father regarded him with affection but something kept him from declaring his parental love. Then there were days when Little Ned barely uttered a word. It was usually after a tiff with Francois. He went about the business of setting traps, skinning and shaping pelts with an intensity that kept Joe silent and apprehensive. What secret demons brought on these frightening moods?

Whether Little Ned was talkative or quiet, the beaver pelts continued to mount as did the catches of the other trappers. The trapping successes continued all fall and winter. The valley seemed to have a special magic that brought good fortune. Not a threat of hostile Indians, no disastrous storms, and pasture for the livestock and firewood were in ample supply. Even so, the trappers were wary. They stood guard at night and made it a practice not to shoot firearms, a rule Buck insisted on for fear noise could attract unwelcome visitors. At regular intervals Francois left camp to go hunting with bow and arrow, usually returning with small game: rabbits, grouse, ducks and turkeys. These extras were a welcome change and extended the stores of dried meat.

The camp was not completely free of mishaps. A mountain lion got in among the animals and badly clawed a pack mule. By the time Hawk Beak, who had been standing guard, arrived, the mule's jugular nearly had been severed. Blood was everywhere. The smell of it sent the other animals into a panic. The only thing Hawk Beak could do was put the poor mule out of its misery and calm the living animals before more damage was done.

"This is rotten luck," Buck said after the mountain cat attack, "We can't afford to lose any animals. The way our catch is piling up we'll be short of transport as it is."

The only other dark aspect of the season came late in the winter when a heavy snowfall kept the trappers imprisoned. Inactivity was an enemy. Buck fared best. He buried himself in his books of mythology. Hawk Beak and Deacon snapped and barked at each other like quarrelsome dogs. Joe worked on the pelts, taking pleasure in counting each one and estimating the price it would bring. According to his calculations, the partners' harvest of pelts would bring a thousand or more dollars. This amount would take them home with plenty left over.

It was the grim wall of silence between Little Ned and Francois that got under everyone's skin. They sat at the work table hour after hour scraping and shaping pelts without uttering a word. The work space vibrated with tension. It was like watching two surly dogs just waiting for an opportunity to attack each other. Only their respect for Buck kept them under control.

To avoid the tension, Joe frequently took his Henry and plowed a path along the base of the petroglyph walled canyon that opened up on the trappers' camp. In places protected from the wind there was little snow. During these explorations Joe studied the Indian writings, trying to decipher their meanings. Some of the more interesting petroglyphs he sketched on parchment. In the evenings he discussed them with Buck who also had taken a great interest in the native artistry. Buck interpreted most of them as accounts of successes: a good hunt with many downed buffalo, a victorious raid with numerous horses and slaves taken, or a triumphant war party returning with great loads of plunder.

During one of their discussions Buck took out a journal. "These are the notes I've jotted down on Indian beliefs and behavior," he said. "When I get a sufficient number I plan to get them into print. Hopefully, they will be of value to students who have an interest in our aborigine brethren."

He leafed through the pages, stopping now and then to study the contents. "Here we are. On my first trip here I wrote this about the petroglyph canyon. 'It appears to be a monument commemorating historic events. Instead of erecting statues like the Greeks and Romans, these people honor their heroes by chiseling their deeds on canyon walls.'"

Buck closed the journal and scratched his head. "I guess you might say this canyon is sort of an outdoor hall of heroes. I expect that's why vision seekers come to this place. They believe spirits of dead heroes inhabit the canyon. They hope these spirits will speak to them, give them visions that'll assure them of accomplishing great deeds. It's rather mystic but don't Christians do much the same? They go to church to pray before Christ on the cross and say rosaries to statues of the Virgin Mary in hopes of receiving spiritual blessings. It goes to show, whatever the color of our skin or our walk of life, on the inside we are pretty much the same."

Joe looked at Buck Stone with new respect. This man was not an ordinary trapper. He was a deep thinker. His thoughts were beyond the average man's comprehension. He was a teacher -- a philosopher. Why did he isolate himself in the wilds of these western mountains?

One day the tension between Little Ned and Francois reached a fever pitch. They sat at the work table scraping, rubbing — putting the finishing touches on prime pelts. In getting up to put away a pelt, Little Ned accidentally bumped the table. The movement jarred Francois' arm. His knife blade slipped to cut through the thin skin of a pelt, ruining it. With a movement the onlookers could hardly see, Francois sent his broad bladed knife whistling across the narrow room. Its sharp point nailed the pelt that Little Ned held to the center post. For a long moment the watching trappers barely breathed. The acrid smell of fear seemed to permeate the room.

Buck was the first to react. He walked up and calmly pulled the still quivering knife from the post. "Sometimes these dad burned toothpicks have a way of slipping out of a man's hand," he said, tossing the knife back to Francois. That was all that was said. The older trappers returned to what they were doing as if nothing unusual had occurred.

The near disaster left Joe weak. He picked up his Henry and trudged through the snow to the petroglyph canyon. In a short while Deacon followed. When they were well away from camp, Joe turned to Deacon. "This can't go on. Somebody will get killed. What's it all about, anyway? Why do they hate each other so?"

Deacon sighed. "Ah! Goes back a long ways. Let me see, must've started a dozen years ago. 'Twas at the Bear Lake rendezvous. They both had their eye on the same Injun lass, right purty handful she was. Little Ned won her hand. He an' the gal got hitched. They had some kids, a couple of boys. Don't know perxactly what went wrong. Me thinks Francois broke it up somehow."

Joe stopped dead in his tracks. He stared at Deacon in disbelief, his father married to an Indian! And they had children! "I don't believe it!" he said with such fervor Deacon glanced up in surprise.

"Yep, it's true," Deacon said. "I should know. I had a hand in it, kinda egged poor ol' Ned on. At the time thought 'twas best, a woman'd do him good."

Joe's heart seemed to have forgotten how to function. Was

the fat man telling the truth? He had no reason to lie. Joe blindly stumbled up the trail. It was like a bad dream. His father had an Indian family! No wonder he never came home. No wonder he did not want him around. No wonder he had those silent spells. No wonder he hated Francois.

"Why did Buck bring Francois along? He must have known Little Ned and Francois hated each other."

"I've pondered over it meself," Deacon admitted. "Buck's the kinda fellow who thinks the best of everybody. I reckon he didn't know how bad things was between these two. Then, of course, Buck owed Francois. The Canuck saved his life. 'Twas at the Battle of Pierre's Hole while fightin' the Gros Ventre, a mean bunch if there ever was one. Buck's gun misfired. An enemy warrior was on top of him, reachin' fer his hair. Francois shot the Injun full in the face, nearly blasted his head away. Yuh don't fergit chaps who save yer hide in close scrapes like thet."

Joe leaned against the petroglyph cliff. He was dumbfounded. He barely heard a word Deacon uttered. He had been a fool. He should never have left home. How could he ever tell Tildy . . . and what could he possibly tell the old folks?

"Yep," Deacon said, unaware of the effect of his words, "thet's at the bottom of the hate. Thet scrap of a lass. Right purty piece. Raven Wing's her name. 'Member the first day Little Ned set eyes on her. We ran inta her pa's huntin' party in buffalo country along Sun River. Lone Wolf's her ol' man's name. He wanted ta trade. We laid out our goods. Little Ned had an elk skin dress he fussed over, puttin' on porcupine quills, beads an' the like. Raven Wing took a fancy ta it. Well, one thing led ta another . . . ."

Joe turned away. He couldn't stand to hear more. Deacon thought he was returning to camp. "I don't think we should go back jest yet. Let things cool off. Anyways, yuh might as well hev the rest of the story. After the trappin' season Buck invited Lone Wolf an' his huntin' party ta ride with us ta the Bear Lake rendezvous. This Raven Wing had an older brother, Many Horses he was called. Whilst we was meanderin' aroun' the rendezvous a Blackfeet war party came, raised hell with a bunch of trappers, stealin' their mules an' pelts. We all rode hell bent out, whoopin' an' shootin'. A few careless galoots got theirselves killed. Anyways, in the fracas an ignorant idiot took Many Horses fer an enemy warrior. Shot him, then lifted his scalp. The lad lived but what a mess he was. The medicine man couldn't do nothin' fer him. I doctored him best I could. He was a miserable sight but he lived. We felt guilty as hell. Lone Wolf and his gang wouldn't hev been at the rendezvous if Buck hadn't invited 'em. Anyways, when 'twas all over we wanted ta make amends. That was when Little Ned took the elk skin dress an' handed it ta Raven Wing as kinda peace offering. Ol' Lone Wolf, her pa, thought Little Ned had come courtin', wanted ta bargain fer his daughter's hand. Before he knew what hit him, Little Ned found hisself wed, Injun style."

Joe felt sick to his stomach. Ah! He could not bear to think about it. The shame would surely kill Granny. Pastor Barclay would be appalled. The Abernathies next door would be in their glory spreading the foul news.

But the more immediate problem was how they were going to get through the winter. How could he stand by and see hate consume his father? He had to do something about it. The way things were going either Little Ned or Francois was sure to commit murder.

"Maybeso, it's safe ta go back now," Deacon said. It was Joe's turn to be reluctant. He was not yet ready to face either Francois or his father.

"I don't like it. Them sitting there silent as monastery monks makes my skin crawl. Each minute I expect one of them to explode."

Deacon nodded. "It's like havin' a couple of mad hornets loose in a closed wigwam. Maybeso, Buck figured by gettin' the two together they'd bury the hatchet. As he likes ta tell, under the skin everybody's the same. Well, I kin tell yuh if these galoots bury the hatchet, it'll be in each other's skulls."

THE LAST RENDEZVOUS

XV

We found there were too many kinds of religion among white men for us to understand, . . . scarcely any two white men agreed which was the right one to learn.

Plenty Coups, Crow

The camas harvesters had returned to their homes but the happiness and good will the people experienced at the camas fields was gone. The bad taste left by Missionary Spalding's interruption of the traditional camas harvest that supplied a vital portion of their winter food needs lingered on. Even the missionary's staunch disciple, Weasel Face, was subdued. For days he kept to his lodge. Then, the weather turned bad. Snow clouds scudded overhead. Fog hung over the Kooskooskie; slowly it drifted up Lapwai Valley, enveloping the village in its cold, clammy grip.

The people sat in their lodges and stewed. What hurt most was that they felt falsely accused. They had not deliberately violated God's law. Camas harvests went on until they were completed. One did not count the days. It was against the people's nature to say they had to do this or do that by such and such a date. When they launched on a journey, a hunt or a harvest they did not worry over how long it would take. Time was a gift the Great Spirit had bestowed on them to enjoy and use as they wished.

Vision Seeker, who saw how deeply the villagers were hurt, attempted to heal the rift between the missionary and the Lapwai villagers. He approached the missionary at one of the mill sites. Speaking in his quiet thoughtful manner, he explained the importance of the camas harvest. Missionary Spalding was enraged. Did one of these aborigines have the affront to criticize him? Who was this person who spoke like an educated man? Ah, yes, one of the Lone Wolf clan -- a brother to that woman caught in adultery.

"Do not tell me about the importance of harvests and such things," Spalding spluttered. "The Lord's work comes first."

The first day of school was a curious experience for the boys. Young Wolf, who had looked forward to this day with great anticipation, could not contain himself; everything was so new and different. He examined the pictures and maps that hung from the walls. The daily lesson printed on the blackboard fascinated him. "Black talking paper!" he exclaimed.

Buffalo Boy took little interest in his surroundings. If it hadn't been for Running Turtle's urgings, he would have turned tail and fled. At the camas grounds, in his wrath, Missionary Spalding had singled him out as one of the sinners who desecrated the Sabbath. He never would forget the terrifying words, "Everyone that defiles the Sabbath shall surely be put to death!" He had no desire to encounter Reverend Spalding ever again.

The initial classroom hours were trying. Since the brothers were new, they were shuffled from one place to another. It was all done in Eliza Spalding's friendly way. She merely was trying to discover at which class level the new students belonged. Since they both knew the rudiments of the ABC's and numbers learned from their Boston father, they were more advanced than many of the others. Buffalo Boy finally found himself placed in the same class as Spotted Badger. His old friend turned enemy was aghast.

"You do not belong here," he practically had shouted. Buffalo Boy could barely concentrate on the lessons and made one blunder after another. He knew when he left the classroom Spotted Badger would be laying for him. Gradually, he forgot about the threat that awaited and recited with confidence. He did so well the teacher praised him, turning the scowl on Spotted Badger's face a shade darker. At the end of the day Buffalo Boy left school walking on air. The fight with Spotted Badger never occurred because the bully was kept after school and given a stern lecture on classroom behavior.

Except for the glowering presence of Spotted Badger, Buffalo Boy began to enjoy the classroom sessions. Unlike her husband, Eliza Spalding had empathy for the two fatherless boys. She immediately noticed the brothers were not readily accepted by the other students, mainly because Spotted Badger belittled them and insisted the other students follow his example. Eliza Spalding approached the matter carefully. She knew how cruel youngsters could be away from the classroom where she had no control. To keep the students' minds on their studies, she challenged them to excel. They were assigned homework. Those who turned in the best results were awarded gold stars. Once Eliza Spalding had the program started, the results were even better than she expected. Almost from her first teaching day she discovered a major trait of the Nimpau was the desire to out perform their peers. Before long Buffalo Boy and Young Wolf were reading at home. To impress each other and their mother, they read out loud, their voices rising to a clashing crescendo that made the dog howl and the baby cry. Raven Wing was furious. The main reason she agreed to send them to school was to get them out of the house so she could enjoy peace and quiet.

Gradually, ill feeling in the village against Missionary Spalding died away. Weasel Face emerged from his lodge to resume his place as Spalding's right-hand man. It was rumored the missionary group finally planned to accept natives as members of the new church. Weasel Face had hopes of being one of the chosen. Instead, on November 17, 1839, Spalding selected Tuekakas of the Wallowa band of Nez Perce, to whom he gave the Biblical name, Joseph. Toomotsin from the Alpowa band, who was given the name Timothy, was also one of those chosen. Spalding baptized the two Nimpau along with a mountain man, James Conner. The occasion was conducted with great ceremony.

"What a glorious day this is," Spalding rejoiced. "The souls of two Red brethren and a mountain man transgressor are delivered into the fold of Christ."

Lapwai villagers were incensed. Why did the missionary have to select outsiders to become the first native members of the church? The people of Lapwai had made the greatest sacrifices; they gave up their land and slaved to build the mission. Were they to be held in disfavor forever because of the camas harvest affair? Weasel Face, particularly, walked around the village bitterly voicing complaints. If Missionary Spalding knew of his disciple's unhappiness, he paid no heed. On the following Sabbath he baptized Timothy's two sons and Joseph's son and three daughters. This was too much for Weasel Face. Momentarily, he forgot his enmity with Lone Wolf. He stopped his longtime foe at the pasture grounds and poured out his problems.

"Missionary Spalding's actions are not good," he complained. "He is not true to his friends."

Lone Wolf uttered a sympathetic grunt. He suddenly felt sorry for his old rival. The way he groveled before Missionary Spalding and carried out his every whim, Weasel Face deserved to be rewarded. Lone Wolf also recognized there was a bright side to the situation. If Weasel Face, the leader of the Lapwai band, turned against the missionary, the chances of driving the Reverend and his bearded crowd from the valley were better than ever.

As the Season of Falling Leaves turned to the Season of Falling Snow, the attention of the Lapwai villagers was taken up with moving the herds into the protected lowlands where bunch grass remained and green willow groves were in abundance. The brown hills received a dusting of snow. Ice appeared on the edges of the creek and a thin film of ice began to form on the millpond. Buffalo Boy's and Young Wolf's moccasined feet were nearly frozen by the long walk to school. They did not mind; the drive to excel in their studies had taken over their lives.

For the most part the Season of Falling Snow passed easily. The harvests had been plentiful, fishing was good and an early snowfall brought herds of deer and elk into the valley where sharp-eyed hunters awaited. The fresh meat was shared among the lodges; everyone, including Raven Wing's family, received a portion. Except for caring for the horses and collecting wood and water, most villagers remained comfortably indoors. Women worked deer, elk and buffalo hides into supple leather from which they made moccasins, dress garments and articles for the lodge and trail. Men fashioned bridles, halters, plaited lengths of grass rope, knotted fish nets and carved saddles from green cottonwood logs.

The Season of Melting Snow and the Season of New Grass that followed, brought a flood of activity. Farmers began to work their plots of ground. Herds were moved to new pasture fields. Hunters followed the game into the hills to make a few last kills. High water started the wheels of the gristmill churning. People from all over the valley came to have corn and wheat ground into flour. Flights of geese, on their way north, swooped down to pick at the fields and spend nights honking and whistling. Early in the mornings they continued their journey, taking off in a flutter of wings, sailing over the high north ridge of the Kooskooskie to disappear into the misty clouds that were a common sight at this season of year.

One bright afternoon appeared a party of travelers — Flatheads on their way to the Chinook trading center on the Great River near the place hairy faces called The Dalles. They were welcomed and stayed the night. One of the travelers was an old friend of the Lone Wolf family. At one time Many Horses, Lone Wolf's first son who was now on the other side, favored the daughter of this Flathead friend. The Lone Wolf family had made a special trip over the mountains to the Flathead homeland to bargain for her. Nothing had come of the pending match. Instead of Many Horses, the daughter had taken a Delaware man from the east for a mate. Her choice still rankled Lone Wolf. Nevertheless, he greeted the Flathead man warmly and invited him into the long lodge to talk and smoke.

"Your mission is large," the Flathead visitor observed.

Lone Wolf did not particularly want to talk about the mission but the Flathead did. "We will soon have a mission," the visitor said.

"If you wish it; that is good."

"Yes, the Long Robes are coming to live in our midst. A Father DeSmet will come the Season of Tall Grass."

"Father, huh!" Lone Wolf grunted.

"Yes, the Long Robes call each other father. It is because we are ignorant of the Christian ways and we will learn from them like children do from their fathers."

Late into the night Lone Wolf and his Flathead friend talked about the hairy faces' Great Spirit Book and the teachers who came to explain the mysteries it held. After the visitor left, Lone Wolf sat by the fire and stared into the coals. This religion business was so confusing. The Long Robes called Catholic, Black Robes called Anglicans and those with no robes at all called Presbyterians, worshipped the same God but did it in different ways. Who was right? Were any of them right? If they could not agree on the proper way to worship God, what made them insist the Indian way was wrong?

"Aiiee!" Lone Wolf groaned. He still had not forgiven Missionary Spalding for forcing the father of his baby grandson, Little Bird, to leave the valley. Why should the missionary be concerned if Raven Wing exchanged one mate for another? In these troubled times it was important to have at least one man in every lodge.

Late into the night Lone Wolf sat alone smoking his pipe. "Ah!" he finally muttered. Everything was falling apart. Why had he and his people been so foolish? They had hungered so for the Great Spirit Book and its teachers that they sent four emissaries to the big village called St. Louis to plead for them. From the start the effort was doomed. Not a single man returned. Two bodies lay in the ground on the banks of the River of Many Canoes. The other two passed to the Great Beyond on the way home. Why did these bad things happen? Did the white man's god read their hearts -- that the Nimpau desired the Great Spirit Book and its teachers for the power and prestige they believed they would bring the tribe? Did the white man's god see this as evil and punish them?

"Ah!" They were punished, all right. They had welcomed Missionary Spalding into their midst and let him do anything he wished. In the drive to turn them into Christians he made warriors powerless and without spirit. He took away the buffalo hunt and the trading trips, and now he wanted to stop the camas harvests and trade away their horses for cattle. What was to become of his people if they lost their means of transport and squatted in one place like a flock of old women too weak to manage lodge work or pack for the trail?

If the Great Creator wanted people to remain in one place he would have made Mother Earth stand still. The animals, the birds, the bees and fish in the lakes and streams all moved from place to place. They followed the warmth of the sun to where plants and flowers grew. They searched out valleys and high meadows where grass was green and tall. In their season the animals went to hillsides where roots grew and berries ripened. They traveled across lakes and up rivers in search of proper places to mate, feed and make their nests. Was it not proper for man to follow the same paths as other creatures of Mother Earth?

Lone Wolf sighed so deeply Quiet Woman gave him a look of alarm. Why did her man act so strangely? He should be giving instructions to his grandsons, seeing to it they learned to make their way in life. Then she remembered Buffalo Boy and Young Wolf were in the missionary woman's schoolroom taking their lessons. When they got home all they did was read books and chatter about what they had learned.

Quiet Woman picked up the reed basket she was weaving and also sighed. Her thoughts followed a similar path to those of Lone Wolf. What had become of the old days when all people had to worry about was collecting food and preparing it for winter? Now one had to spend day after day learning the ways of the hairy faces' talking paper. What were they to do with this knowledge? It did not bring meat from the hunting grounds, fish from the river, berries and roots from the mountainsides or camas bulbs from the meadows. If the people did not wake up and change their ways they would lose their skills — wander around as helpless and worthless as toothless coyotes.

Quiet Woman still worried over the matter when Raven Wing brought her youngest son to visit. Little Bird, named because he puckered his lips to a point like the beak of a fledgling bird at feeding time, held out his arms to his grandmother. Before Quiet Woman could take the baby, Grandfather Lone Wolf jumped up from his place beside the fire. He seized Little Bird and carried him outside. He wanted this little man all to himself.

After Lone Wolf left, Quiet Woman voiced her worries to her daughter. "What is to become of us?" she asked. "Our young people sit all day listening to the missionary woman. Are they to become like the cricket that sits rubbing its legs together making noises to please itself? What do we live on next winter when the Season of Deep Snow comes and the stores of food are not there? Will we freeze and die like birds that have their feathers clipped and cannot fly to the lands of summer?"

As Quiet Woman poured out her fears, Raven Wing could not believe her ears. She had never heard such a flow of thoughts coming from her mother's lips. All through the years she and her brothers believed Quiet Woman had no more of a mind than the pack mares she loaded and unloaded. Yet, here she spoke words that one could expect only from a deep thinker like Vision Seeker.

Quiet Woman's words made such an impression on Raven Wing she did not sleep that night. The following morning, when her two older sons started to get ready to leave for school, she ordered them to stay. From that day on they were to forget the study of books. They would learn from the rocks, streams, birds and animals like their forefathers had done.

THE LAST RENDEZVOUS

XVI

> *I have a rendezvous with Death*
> *At some disputed barricade.*
>
> <small>Alan Seeger</small>

Warm Chinook winds began to strip away the snow and ice which coated the Bighorn region. Like bears coming out of hibernation, the trappers emerged from their dripping shelter to wade in the slush and breathe great gulps of clean fresh air. Gratefully, they went back to the streams and ponds to add to their already bountiful beaver pelt harvest.

Yet, the good weather brought little joy to Joe Jennings. Living and working alongside Little Ned had become torture. Every waking moment he thought of his father's Indian family. It was almost impossible to accept the fact he had dusky-skinned half brothers. He attempted to picture what they looked like. The images always appeared in the shape of the fierce looking Kiowas they encountered in Pawnee country. How could his father get mixed up with such savages? How could he! He ate with them! He slept with them! He gave them the attention that should have gone to his New England twins. Tildy, Granny and Granddad never must know. They never would understand.

The high point of the spring came one bright May morning. Little Ned struggled into camp lugging the carcass of a seventy pound albino beaver. Its pelt glistened as white as freshly fallen snow. Even Francois rushed up to inspect this rarest of species.

"I ain't never seed one afore. It's the catch of a lifetime," Hawk Beak declared.

"I'll give you a dozen prime pelts for it," Francois offered surprisingly.

"Nothing doing," Little Ned retorted. "This is too special to trade or sell."

For days the major topic of conversation was Little Ned's fabulous white pelt. Almost every evening Little Ned would inspect it for flaws. Hawk Beak and Francois insisted they see the place the catch was made. "Can't tell, might be another un hangin' about," Hawk Beak said hopefully. "Maybeso, a twin."

Little Ned's good fortune was followed by bad. The partners' traps yielded fewer and fewer beaver until one day Joe and Little Ned found every one sprung, but empty. Grim-faced, Little Ned strode back and forth searching for signs of intruders.

"I'd swear it's the work of some two-legged varmint," he said. "These traps have been dependable all winter. It's nonsense to believe they would fail all at once. Yet, let's not jump to conclusions. First we'll try a new set."

It took much of the morning to pick up the traps and locate suitable new trap sites. "Now," Little Ned said when they finished, "if these are empty in the morning we'll know for certain someone is doing us mischief."

Angry and disappointed, the partners walked back to camp and reported the news to Buck, who took it seriously. The other trappers did not. They had made their normal day's catch.

"After trappin' the white beaver yuh gotta expect a turn of luck," Hawk Beak said.

"Shouldn't wonder but what the white beaver's like a queen bee. When it disappears the whole colony picks up an' leaves," Deacon observed.

"Quit prattling about something you don't know a thing about," Little Ned snapped. "I'm telling you straight. Someone is up to mischief. Those traps did not spring by themselves."

"Maybeso, Indians are about," Francois said, to everyone's surprise. These were the most words he had uttered since offering to trade for the white beaver pelt.

Whether or not someone threatened the trap lines, Buck did not take the matter lightly. He doubled the guard and ordered a breastwork built around the living quarters. After helping with the fortifications, Little Ned walked from camp to disappear near the petroglyph cliff.

"Let him go," Deacon advised Joe. "He needs ta do a bit of

thinkin'. When he don't catch beaver he's like a sore-nosed bear, nothin' pleases him."

In spite of Deacon's warning, after an hour or so, Joe followed the big man. More than anything else he wanted to hear from his father's own lips the story of his Indian family. Where were they? Why wasn't he with them? Had he abandoned them like he had his New England twins? What he wished for most was to hear the story was not true. Joe found Little Ned sitting on a boulder whetstoning his skinning knife.

"Sit awhile, partner," Little Ned invited. "I've been thinking on the sprung traps. It wasn't something an Indian would do. He doesn't much like trapping but wouldn't stoop to a trick like that. It was someone who knows the trap lines and who is just as clever in the woods as an Indian."

Joe pondered over the thought. "You mean . . .?"

"I mean that beaver-toothed Canuck. It's just the type of mischief he'd do."

"He wouldn't dare. Buck would run him out of camp."

"That Canuck is capable of anything. I know him from way back. For a long time I couldn't understand why he joined us. I've finally figured it out. He's got to prove he's the better man. That's why he sprung our traps. We've out-trapped him every which way. Our taking the white beaver pelt was the last straw."

Joe sat silent. He wanted to blurt out that he knew all about the reason for the ill-feeling between Little Ned and Francois and the existence of the Indian family. He couldn't bring himself to do it. "What do you plan to do?" he finally asked.

"I don't know, but soon he's certain to slip up. When he does, we'll have a showdown, you can bet your life on that."

Made uncomfortable by Little Ned's vehemence, Joe got to his feet. "I thought a white pelt was supposed to bring good luck. Deacon says the Indians believe so. This one seems to bring bad luck."

"It'll be plenty bad for that Canuck."

That night Joe stood late guard. The hours crawled by with

agonizing slowness. To add to his misery, Joe's thoughts were grim. The adventure he had looked forward to with such excitement had turned into a bitter experience. As soon as the trapping season was over he would make an excuse and return home. He groaned. Even that prospect made him cringe. What would he say to the folks, especially Granny? She had her mind set on seeing her family together again. "Ah," he groaned again, this time so loudly a night bird fluttered out of a tree and sailed away.

Just as the sun began to brighten the eastern sky, Little Ned rolled out of the blankets. He quietly adjusted his clothes, picked up his Hawken and buckled on his belt with knives and hatchet attached. He walked softly over to where Joe stood guard. For a moment he stopped to thoughtfully study the sky. A checkerboard of clouds streaked with crimson spread from east to west.

"I reckon the weather may change. As Great Granddad Captain Jennings, liked to say, 'Mackerel sky and mares' tails make lofty ships carry low sails.' Yep, he was quite an old boy. I always wondered what happened to him. He sailed away one day and never returned. Some say he fled from Grandma. When he was home she ruled him with an iron hand -- couldn't stand his rough and ready seafaring ways -- made him keep his cuspidors outdoors. The poor fellow couldn't even smoke inside his own home. Well, I'm going to the trap line." He unexpectedly gave Joe a friendly tap on the shoulder, the first real show of physical affection he had shown since they met in St. Louis.

"Shouldn't I go with you?" Joe asked.

"No, stay on guard. If there's trouble, I'll give a holler."

Joe continued his pacing. He had a feeling of elation. For once Little Ned truly acted like a father. He had spoken of old Cap Jennings, who was hardly ever mentioned at home. Some said the old captain had made his money slaving, others thought him a privateer. Mrs. Abernathy once let it slip that he had a terrible thirst for drink. What was the true story? Now that Little Ned was talking to him like a father, he might find out. All of a sudden he seemed to know his father better. Perhaps Little Ned inherited his wandering nature from Cap Jennings. It was in his blood to travel to the far ends of the earth seeking riches and adventure. Like his grandfather, Little Ned did not feel comfortable at home. That would explain why he stayed away. Perhaps he felt more at ease with his Indian family. They were a part of his adventuresome life. After all, it would not be hard to become infatuated with a dark-eyed Indian lass.

Joe shifted his rifle from one shoulder to the other. Affection for his father welled up in his heart. Poor man, he had led a lonely life. It was only natural he should fall in love with a beautiful Indian woman. His thoughts flashed back to the trading stop at the Cheyenne village. Yes, he could understand his father. That Cheyenne maiden had gotten under his own skin like no female ever had. He could envision the dark wing of hair, the soft doe-like eyes. She was truly one in a million. Any man with gumption would be a fool not to fall for someone as lovely as that Cheyenne girl.

A crash came from the animal shelter. Joe cocked his rifle and ran toward the corral. For a moment he studied the mules. Buck said they were the best sentries of all. Their ears always shot forward in the direction danger threatened. They acted normal. He counted them. None were missing. The noise had been caused by an altercation between a mule and a horse, he decided. The mule had crowded the horse against the rails. The crowded animal took a nip out of the mule. The mule answered with a kick that shattered the bottom fence rail. The rest of the animals drowsed, methodically switching their tails against the ever present mosquitoes.

The noise aroused Deacon. He got up, groaned and glanced at the sky, his bushy beard a tangled mess. He pulled up his suspenders and started rustling among the pots and pans. "Get up, yuh lazy heads," he ordered. Francois rose and stretched, studying each bedroll, carefully noting who was up and about. He took his bow and quiver of arrows and strode for the trap lines. Hawk Beak was the last to rise. He groaned. "Wonder what day 'tis, maybeso Saturday. Think of what city folk're doin', probably havin' a mornin' glass of champagne, gittin' ready fer a big day on the town."

"Hah! Yuh wouldn't know a glass of champagne if it was

poured down yer skinny neck," Deacon scoffed.

There was another commotion among the horses and mules. This time they milled about, making the corral railings sway and creak. "Hey!" Hawk Beak ran to quiet them down.

A movement near the canyon wall caught Joe's eye. Rays of the early morning sun flickering through the trees made the warriors carved into the sandstone cliff seem to gallop straight toward him. Joe had the uncanny feeling someone was there, someone had moved through the shadows along the base of the wall. He cocked the rifle and walked forward. The sun's rays rose above the treetops, bathing the petroglyph cliff with light. The line of horsemen stood transfixed. Joe released the hammer on the Henry and walked slowly back to camp. He needed sleep. His tired mind was playing tricks.

Buck squatted down by the fire and helped himself to a cup of coffee. "I've been thinking maybe there's an ill wind blowing our way. Perhaps we've overstayed our luck. If the Indians take a notion they don't want us poaching on their land, we could find ourselves trapped. Where's Little Ned? He's the one who got me to thinking."

Joe explained Little Ned's early departure for the trap line.

"Dammit all, he shouldn't be by himself."

Joe glanced at Buck in surprise. It was most unusual to hear him swear.

"I guess he'll be all right," Buck said as an afterthought. "Other than this odd business about the traps, there have been no danger signs."

Francois returned with a sack full of fresh skins. He was later than usual, which irked Deacon, who had saved breakfast for him. Francois paid no attention to Deacon's grumbling. He hummed a tune as he washed up and ate with unusual gusto. His good humor and Little Ned's absence put Joe's nerves on edge. There was something wrong. Little Ned should not have been gone so long. He berated himself. Buck was right. If there were poachers around, Little Ned should not be alone. Joe picked up his Henry and started toward the trap line. The big man was nowhere to be seen. Then Joe remembered, they had reset the traps farther upstream.

To keep from polluting the banks with his scent, Joe braved the icy cold water. He waded around one clump of bushes and then another. He felt unusually edgy. Everything was so still. He approached each clump of bushes with his heart in his mouth. He could see an Indian behind each one. Then he did see a movement and stopped, his heart thumping wildly. He cocked the Henry and began to breathe again. It was only a flicker hopping from one tree trunk to another.

He waded farther, crossing a miniature waterfall where the boulders were slick with slime and moss. He slipped and nearly fell. He righted himself and took a better grip on the Henry, then gasped. A cry like a wounded animal might make escaped his inner being. On the bank lay Little Ned! Between his shoulder blades was an arrow, the feathered shaft sticking straight up. Little Ned's black hat lay alongside his body. For a moment Joe thought he would faint. Where the shock of black hair had been glistened a circle of blood and gore. His father was dead and had been scalped.

THE LAST RENDEZVOUS

XVII

We believe that the Spirit of God is not breathed into humans alone, but that the whole created universe shares in the immortal perfection of its Maker.

Ohiyesa, Santee

Raven Wing's decision to withdraw her sons from school came at a bad time. It was early spring. There was little to do. The ground was wet and muddy. The streams were dangerously high. Since the drowning of little Alice Clarissa Whitman, village mothers were frightened to have their youngsters go near the rushing waters. Hunters were angry and sullen. They were forced to cancel a buffalo hunt that would have brought much desired meat and hides. The previous year's disastrous excursion into Blackfeet country and the way his flock had disobeyed him at the camas harvest had irked Missionary Spalding to the point that he issued an ultimatum: only a few people at a time were allowed to leave Lapwai without his approval. When weather permitted, he kept all able-bodied men dredging the millrace.

As soon as the ground dried and the streams ceased to overflow their banks, Buffalo Boy and Young Wolf spent afternoons riding their patched black and white ponies into the barren hills and up the trail that bordered the Kooskooskie. They pretended to be warriors and hunters. Some days they made raids on enemy lands, capturing horses and slaves and plundering villages. Other times they followed the game trails in hopes of spotting deer and elk.

The excitement of these make-believe adventures soon palled for Buffalo Boy. Every morning he enviously watched as the village came to life and his former classmates dashed out of their lodges and hurried to school. Spotted Badger, in particular, annoyed him. The school bully often made a detour by the cabin to shout taunts. "Yah! Yah! Dumbhead, the classroom is much better without you."

More and more Buffalo Boy found his footsteps taking him

to the schoolyard where he paused to listen to Eliza Spalding conduct her classes. "Why do I do this," he wondered. Gradually, it dawned on him. He missed school. He wanted to be back in the classroom. He missed the books. He missed reading aloud at home. He even missed some of his classmates.

Lone Wolf and Quiet Woman watched their daughter struggle to cope with her growing sons. Lone Wolf approved of the older sons riding in the hills. It was when they tired of it that he thought he should take a hand in their upbringing. One morning he walked up to Raven Wing's cabin. He stopped on the porch, shocked by the commotion inside. Most lodges were quiet at this time of day but this was bedlam. He pushed the door open. His daughter was scolding her older sons. Baby Little Bird added to the confusion by scrambling around on hands and knees, pulling at everything he could lay his small hands on. The cabin occupants fell silent at the presence of Lone Wolf. The boys were half afraid of the tall, austere man with the big nose. Raven Wing could not imagine what brought her father unannounced into her lodge. Only Little Bird didn't see anything unusual. He crawled up to the big moccasined feet. His tiny hands clutched at his grandfather's leg. Lone Wolf picked him up and set him on his shoulder.

"Ah, my big man, you will soon need a pony to ride." He carried the boy outside and bounced him up and down as they jogged down the porch steps. Baffled by his sudden appearance, Buffalo Boy and Young Wolf followed. At the bottom porch step Lone Wolf stopped and sat down. He motioned for his grandsons to sit beside him.

"You boys should not make trouble for your mother. Buffalo Boy, I think it time you went on your vision quest. Most youth of your age have gone into the mountains and returned with *Wyakin*, the spirit that guides them through life."

"Yes! Yes," Young Wolf shouted. "I want to make vision quest, Grandfather."

Lone Wolf glanced at the lad. It was said he was not the Boston man's son but had been fathered by the tall, dark Francois.

From the looks of the boy's swarthy skin and deep, dark eyes, that could be so. "Your time will come," he said. "It is best the older son go first. Now, how shall we do this? I think we should talk to Vision Seeker. He will counsel you. He has been on many vision quests."

The idea of going on a vision quest did not please Buffalo Boy. Wandering around in the mountains for days waiting for a vision to appear seemed foolish and a terrible trial. In one of his serious talks with his Boston father, the big man said a person's guiding spirit came from within, not from without. It was the goodness or badness one had within one's self that guided him through life. After his father told him about the spirit that dwelled inside, he had searched for it. When Francois had turned mean often he looked to it for help. But it never made itself known. The spirit inside was as mysterious and elusive as *Wyakin* who lay unseen in the mountains, lakes, woods or streams.

However, Buffalo Boy did as his grandfather suggested. He sought out Vision Seeker, finding him at his usual lookout point overlooking the valley. When questioned about the impending vision quest, Vision Seeker hesitated. It was easy to see this was not Buffalo Boy's idea. He was undoubtedly doing it to please Raven Wing.

"Ah!" Vision Seeker uttered to himself. The poor boy was going through a troubling time. On his mother's whim he was sent to the mission school. Just as he was beginning to feel comfortable in the classroom, she had another whim and removed him from school. Now, Raven Wing wished to undo the influence of the mission school. She was going to force her son into the traditional Indian mold. She would begin by sending him on a vision quest.

Vision Seeker studied the distant horizon. He suddenly felt inadequate. A father should be the one to counsel a son. How he wished the Boston man would return. Mothers could do so much, but when it came to learning the ways of warrior, hunter and leader of men, there was no replacement for the wisdom of a father.

Buffalo Boy tugged at his arm. "Lone Wolf says you will counsel me on the ways of the vision quest."

"Ah, yes," Vision Seeker glanced at the earnest blue eyes

that set the boy apart from other village youth. What could he say? Finding *Wyakin* was not a simple task, impossible for a person who did not believe. Oftentimes those who did believe spent days in the mountains without food and water before the spirit came to them. There was no point in sending the lad on a vision quest if he was not mentally prepared. For those who really believed, receiving *Wyakin* was one of the most powerful spiritual experiences they would ever have, so powerful it changed a person's entire being, but what would it do for Buffalo Boy? Probably it would be another unpleasant experience to add to all the others the lad had endured in his short life. Yet, Vision Seeker could think of no way out. Raven Wing and Lone Wolf would nag at the boy until he did as they wished. Sooner or later he would have to make a vision quest. The best thing to do was to make the ordeal as pleasant as possible.

"Are you ready to spend a few nights in the mountains?" Vision Seeker asked.

Buffalo Boy shrugged.

"It is something you must do. Let us start first thing in the morning. Dress warmly and bring a sleeping robe. It will be cold."

The ride to the mountains was made in silence. In his mind Vision Seeker rehearsed what he should say and do. Buffalo Boy was too apprehensive to converse. Near nightfall they stopped. Together they made camp, started a small fire and cooked a meal. Although he was supposed to fast, Buffalo Boy ate his fill. After eating, to keep buzzing insects away, Vision Seeker threw greenery on the fire to create a smudge. When they were comfortably settled, Vision Seeker spoke.

"People say I do not have *Wyakin*. They believe I search for *Wyakin*. That's why they call me Vision Seeker. The people are wrong. I have many *Wyakins*. Some see me through a season; some stay a moon or two. Most of them come to me during the night, others appear in the first light of morning and depart when Father Sun disappears. My *Wyakins* come from dreams and visions. Some are helpful, others distress me. Some bring messages I understand, others speak of things I do not know. Some lead me to do good, others lead me to do bad."

"Ah!" Buffalo Boy exclaimed. "This is much like missionary talk of the Devil and God. The Devil has bad angels who lead people into hell. God has good angels who guide people to heaven."

"Yes, you do not have to go into the mountains to find these guiding spirits. They are all around you. Wherever you are they enter your mind and heart and walk by your side. A thoughtful mind and quiet heart is what attracts *Wyakin*. It is important to listen carefully to the messages Mother Earth sends. She speaks in many different ways. One must listen to the quack of the duck, the cry of the loon, the howl of the wolf, the whisper of the grass and trees. They all send messages. The wise man seeks to understand these messages. The unwise never take the time to listen or understand. They blunder blindly along life's trail without enjoying beauty, heeding warnings or taking advantage of the bounty Mother Earth provides. Your guardian spirit will help you find and enjoy all these good things if you will let it show you how."

Vision Seeker paused. He not only had to make Buffalo Boy believe in *Wyakin*, he had to make him feel *Wyakin*. Most important of all, he had to make Raven Wing believe her son had received *Wyakin*. If he didn't she would send him into the mountains again and again until he was successful or invented a lie.

"In the morning you will go deep into the mountains," Vision Seeker instructed. "You will listen to the sounds of Mother Earth. You will look at the beauty that surrounds you. Fix everything you see and hear in your mind just as carefully as you would if you were putting them down on talking paper. If you do this well *Wyakin* will come to you."

Buffalo Boy's eyes clouded. "I do not know if I can do this. Everything is mixed up in my head."

"I understand how you feel. I have searched for *Wyakin* many times and have always been troubled. I am troubled now. I see signs I do not understand. They come to me when I awaken and come to me when I sleep. You cannot imagine how I am tortured. Since before your birth there is one particular vision which continually walks by my side. In the darkness of night it resembles a ghost. In the bright light of day it becomes a shadow. It follows wherever I go. This is something I have revealed to no one. It came to me again last night. This time you were present." Vision Seeker fell quiet. How could he make this boy understand what he did not understand himself? "Ah!" There was so much he did not understand. The vision of his Boston brother continued to bother him. The last time they were together the big man disappeared into the mist and never reappeared. It was surely a sign but what did it mean -- that he was soon to pass to the other side?

"The name of your oldest uncle is never spoken in our lodges," Vision Seeker continued. "He is now in the Great Beyond. Yet, he comes to me day after day and night after night. He appears riding a great white horse. He emerges out of Father Sky, breaking through the clouds as if they are not there. In his hair are two feathers, one pure white, the other white, tipped with red. In these visions he holds the feathers out as if to give them away. In last night's vision he offered each feather, one at a time, not to me, but to you." Vision Seeker paused. The fog that always clouded the vision dropped away.

"Ah-hoh!" Vision Seeker exclaimed. "I see everything clearly. Why did I not see it before? In your veins flow the blood of a Boston and the blood of your Nimpau ancestors. The white feather stands for the blood of your father, the red tipped one represents the blood of your mother. Why did your uncle's spirit offer the choice of feathers to you? It is the same message he has been trying to tell me, that I had to chose between following the way of the hairy faces or the way of our people. Can one follow both paths? No, and that is what Missionary Spalding keeps telling us. A Christian has no choice. They must follow the way of the hairy faced ones' God. Your uncle's spirit is now telling you to make your choice. You can follow the ways of your father or go the way of our people, the Nimpau."

Buffalo Boy remained silent. The revelation of the mystic uncle who came riding out of the clouds wearing two feathers, was beyond his imagination. He glanced at Vision Seeker in suspicion. Did he and Raven Wing conspire to make him believe this story and accept *Wyakin*? His mother would do almost anything to make him follow in the footsteps of his Nimpau ancestors.

Vision Seeker sensed Buffalo Boy's confused thoughts. From his saddle bags he removed the soft rawhide pouch which contained the two feathers his brother, Many Horses, always wore in his hair. He secretly had kept them through the years. No one, not even Lone Wolf, knew of their existence. He built up the fire and took the feathers from the pouch. Buffalo Boy held his breath. These were the feathers of the vision, the feathers of his uncle who had passed to the other side. He gazed at them in awe. The pure white feather gave off a luminous glow; the tip of the other was the color of fresh blood. When Vision Seeker held them up, like live things, the feathers swayed and twisted in the breeze. Vision Seeker replaced them in the pouch and handed it to Buffalo Boy.

"These are yours. They are sacred items which should never be defiled. They will guide and protect you wherever you go. Now, it is time for sleep." While Buffalo Boy laid out his sleeping robe, Vision Seeker mixed a potion made of dried berries and roots. He insisted Buffalo Boy drink it. As Vision Seeker planned, its soothing properties sent Buffalo Boy into a deep sleep.

That night Buffalo Boy had a dream. Two feathers floated down from Father Sky on a cloud. They stood upright like humans and spoke to him in a language he did not understand. They started talking peacefully, then began to quarrel and shout so violently he awakened. It was still dark. He glanced around for Vision Seeker. He was not there. He searched for the pouch that held the feathers. It was not there either. He shivered. It was just a nightmare. He lay back, trying to recall the talk with Vision Seeker. The talk and nightmare became confused. Had Vision Seeker been there or was that also a dream? As the rays of Father Sun appeared Buffalo Boy stood to repeat the prayer of greeting. Afterward, he began to roll up the sleeping robe and there was the rawhide pouch. The two feathers were inside, one stark white, the other white tipped with red.

Buffalo Boy remained in the mountains one more day and night. On the third evening he entered the log cabin lodge. "I have

Wyakin and a new name. From now on I shall be called Two Feathers, Michael Two Feathers," he announced to Raven Wing.

Raven Wing gave him a scornful look. She had never liked the name Michael, the name her Boston mate had given their firstborn. "Michael Two Feathers! Don't play games with me. You have not been in the mountains long enough to find *Wyakin*. Besides no *Wyakin* would give anyone the name Two Feathers."

The more Buffalo Boy insisted he had *Wyakin*, the more Raven Wing became incensed. The spirit of an animal, fish, bird, tree or plant should have spoken to her son, not two feathers which quarreled and shouted. What kind of *Wyakin* was that? Was Two Feathers a name that would command respect in the tribe? Raven Wing was certain it would only bring scorn. "Your *Wyakin* is not good. You must go on another vision quest," was her ultimatum.

Michael had intended to keep the two feathers hidden. They were sacred. He did not want Young Wolf or Little Bird to touch them, but he drew them from the rawhide protective covering them and handed them to his mother. To his astonishment Raven Wing uttered a shriek. She seized the feathers and ran down the trail for the long lodge, screaming and shouting all the way.

Michael hesitated, then slowly followed. When he arrived at the long lodge Lone Wolf stood outside. In his hand he held the two feathers. His usual stoic expression was transformed into a look of awe.

"Never has a young man returned from a vision quest with more powerful medicine than this," he said, his voice hushed with emotion. "These feathers truly come from the Great Spirit Land." He clasped Michael in his arms. "You have been favored by the gods. They sent you a very special *Wyakin*. The spirit of my son has been chosen to guard you and guide you through this journey we call life."

THE LAST RENDEZVOUS

XVIII

*Men heap together the mistakes of their lives,
and create a monster which they call Destiny . . . .*
John O. Hobbes

Buck Stone's depleted brigade of trappers gathered on the creek bank to lift their dead companion and lay his body across a pack mule. The mournful funeral column slowly and sadly plodded toward camp. Joe blindly stumbled along behind. His mind was numb. He could not accept the sudden death. Mere hours ago Little Ned had spoken to him, reminiscing about Cap Jennings, their seafaring ancestor who had sailed away and never come home. Joe uttered a low moan. He should have gone with his father. His presence might have saved his life. Joe lifted an arm to hide his streaming eyes. It was no use. He could not hold back the terrible gnawing grief. He choked on the lump in his throat and openly sobbed.

The trappers chopped a crude hole in the hard clay soil. After wrapping the body in a buffalo robe, they lowered it into the shallow grave at the foot of the petroglyph cliff. They looked to Buck for the signal to proceed. For a long moment the leader of the brigade stood by the open pit. He had known Little Ned for more than a dozen years. He never knew him to have a dishonest thought or do a dishonorable deed. Over the years, except for discussing matters of travel and trapping, they had said little to each other. Yet he knew he always could depend on Little Ned. He was a true-blue friend. Buck attempted to clear the lump in his throat. "Deacon, you know the Bible best. Kindly say a few appropriate words," he said, trying to keep his voice steady.

Deacon crushed his fur cap in both hands and bowed his head. In a voice filled with emotion, he clearly enunciated words from the Book of Psalms: "Yea, though I walk through the valley of the shadow of death, I will fear no evil: for thou art with me. Thou shalt be gathered into the grave in peace. Amen!"

"Amen!" Joe heard himself croak.

After the burial ceremony, Buck conducted a council of war. "Little Ned's gone. We can't do anything about that. But we can track down his killers. If we don't, sure as shooting they'll be back with a war party."

Hawk Beak nodded. "Maybeso, a couple young bucks on a spree. I cain't understand why the mules didn't kick up a fuss. Wind must've been blowin' the wrong way. Usually they sniff out hostiles quicker'n we kin skunk."

"Well they didn't," Buck said, "probably because it happened too far from camp. Strange there weren't any tracks around the body. The only sign the killer left is this arrow." He inspected the shaft taken from Little Ned's back. "I make it out Crow." He handed it to Francois who confirmed the identity with a curt nod.

"Quit palaverin'," Deacon said impatiently. "Killers could be lookin' down our throats. Didja see anythin' whilst on guard?" he asked Joe.

Joe shook his head, then remembered the shadowy movement near the petroglyph cliff. "I did wonder if there was an animal or someone near the petroglyphs. When I looked nothing was there."

"Yuh should've turned out the camp," Hawk Beak accused. "We could've caught this killer afore he ambushed Little Ned."

Joe swallowed hard. The thought that his laxness might have caused his father's death left him numb.

"Hawk's right," Buck said. "Any unusual sign should be reported. Indians are cunning as coyotes. Trappers who forget that don't come home with their hair. Anyway, we had better take a looksee. Francois, you have the sharpest eye, let's reconnoiter."

Francois went directly to the tracks as if he knew exactly where to find them. The moccasin imprints were so faint Joe hardly could make them out. "Looks to be a party of four," Francois said.

Buck knelt down. "Must be young bucks new to warpath -- small feet and they made no attempt to cover their trail."

With Francois leading, they moved forward to follow the tracks. They had not gone far when Francois held up a warning hand. "He's got a whiff of somethin'," Deacon observed. "Look at him, like a beagle hound on the heels of a fox."

Buck waved Francois forward. "We'll let him scout a bit," he whispered to the others. "Spread out and be careful. We don't want to stumble into an ambush."

Although a cool breeze blew down the canyon, Joe was wet with perspiration. His heart thudded so loudly it made his ears ring. If he saw a savage, would he be able to shoot to kill? Without warning, the sharp report of a rifle shot echoed off the canyon walls. Joe's heart pounded in his mouth. For a moment the silence was deafening. Then a second shot echoed through the canyon. The trappers glanced uneasily at one another. Suddenly Buck held up his hand. He leveled his Hawken at a clutch of brush. Huddled there were two brown-skinned youths.

"Saplin's," Deacon exclaimed. "They's youn'uns still wet behind the ears."

Francois came up. In one hand he held two objects dripping with blood. Bile rose up in Joe's throat. The bloody scalps reminded him of Little Ned's denuded head. He turned aside to retch behind a bush. "What're you waiting for?" Francois demanded. "Put the varmints out of their misery." He advanced toward the youths. Tauntingly, he waved the scalps in their faces. A splash of blood struck the nearest, making him flinch.

"They're jest pups," Deacon said. "I hope we ain't stoopin' ta shootin' youngsters. Yuh know a bit of Crow, Buck. Speak ta 'em. Find out what they're doin' here."

In a quiet voice, Buck questioned the youths. They stared at him, hiding their fear with looks of defiance. The smaller of the two finally spoke.

"I say," Hawk Beak exclaimed. "The buggers're on a vision quest."

"Put finish to them," Francois snapped.

"Be reasonable," Buck admonished. "Little Ned wouldn't take revenge on boys. His first son is about the same age as these lads. What do you say, Joe? You and Little Ned were partners."

"Let them go," Joe quickly replied. All he wanted was to forget this terrible day. Nothing would bring back his father.

Francois eyed Joe with disgust. "Indians are like rattlesnakes. The young are just as poisonous as the full grown. Turn them loose and they'll rise up and stab you in the back." Francois turned and stalked toward the campsite swinging the scalps.

"Why's he so all-fired heated up?" Hawk Beak asked. "Acts like he's got a scorpion stabbin' him in the butt."

Buck put aside his Hawken and spoke to the two vision seekers who continued bravely attempting to hide their fear. From the signs Buck made, Joe guessed he told the youthful Indians they were free to leave. One sidled away, his eyes fixed on Buck. Soon the other youth followed. When they were some distance away, they started to run, bounding through the brush like frightened antelope.

"Good thing yuh happened on 'em, Buck, 'stead of Francois. They'd been dead meat," Deacon observed. "I don't understand him. He sees blood an' turns meaner'n a new sheared sheep."

"Yeah!" Hawk Beak agreed. "He's plumb scalp happy. I'll betcha he plugged two other kids jest fer their topknots. Maybeso we should hev a looksee. Ain't right leavin' 'em to the buzzards."

"No," Buck said. "Our handling the bodies would taint them. The vision seeker lads will do the burying. Let's get back to camp."

Deacon watched Buck leave and shook his head. "Thet's Buck fer yuh, knows the Injuns like he was an Injun hisself. But I've got afeelin' this ain't the end of this bloody business. If those kids didn't shoot an' scalp Little Ned, who the blazes did?"

#

The death of Little Ned and Francois' slaying and scalping of the Indian youths left the trapping camp subdued. For the first time since leaving St. Louis, Buck lost his composure. He sat in front of the trappers' lean-to nervously running his fingers through his thick corn-colored hair, his countenance lined with worry.

"It's best we don't test our luck any further," he said. "The vision quest boys will soon return to their homes and report the death of their companions. Any day a war party will ride hell bent into the canyon after our hides."

"When do we divvy Ned's catch?" Francois abruptly asked. "When a man falls it's customary to divide his takings among the rest."

Buck gave the French Canadian a sharp glance. "This is different. Little Ned and Young Joe were partners. The catch goes to the remaining partner."

"That'll give the kid more than twice as much as anyone else," Francois protested.

"If I remember right, yuh were the one who insisted on keepin' the ketch separate," Deacon said. "Ain't thet so?"

"That's right," Buck agreed. "Little Ned made it quite clear he and Joe were partners. There's no argument about that."

Francois picked up his rifle and stalked away on the trail to the petroglyph canyon.

"I hope those Injun kids had their visions an' vamoosed," Hawk Beak commented. "Thet Canuck's mad enough to chomp the barrel off his Hawken."

The remainder of the day the trappers spent preparing to break camp. They collected their traps, broke down the shelter and work place, and pressed the winter's catch of pelts into neatly bound carrying packs. When they finished pressing and packaging Little Ned's and Joe's pelts, Deacon sat back and scratched in his beard. I knew there was somethin' missin' -- Little Ned's white pelt. Where is it?"

"Maybeso, for safety sake he kept it separate, perhaps in his duffel bag," Hawk Beak suggested. A search of Little Ned's meager possessions revealed no white pelt.

"Yuh don't suppose the pesky redskin thet killed him sneaked in and took it?" Deacon asked. "The varmint could've done it whilst we was chasin' those vision seeker youngsters?"

The trappers searched every place they could think of, still the rare pelt did not appear. The loss greatly disturbed Hawk Beak and Deacon but Joe did not care much. Ever since Little Ned brought the pelt in the partners' luck had turned sour. Yet, it still gave Joe the shivers to think that someone had taken them unawares, sneaked in and stolen it, perhaps while he, himself, was on guard.

#

Two days after Little Ned's death, Buck Stone and his brigade set off for the rendezvous, held again this year on the Green River. Leaving the pleasant valley where they had spent the winter gave Joe a wrench. There would always be a special place for it in his heart. It was here that he had been introduced to the life of a mountain man. Here he almost came to know his father, and here his father had been killed and buried. At the top of the first ridge of hills he paused to look back. For all of its pleasantness, the rugged country mocked him. He had been tested and had been found wanting. His lack of experience and lack of diligence well could have been responsible for his father's death. What a terrible burden to bear for the rest of his life. Before he turned away he caught sight of the line of horsemen carved in the sandstone cliff. He was glad that they were there, standing guard over Little Ned's grave. Joe finally turned to follow the others. Mist covered his eyes until he barely could make out Buck and Francois who led the way.

For the first few days Buck hurried the column along. "If a war party is on our trail, it's best not to dilly-dally," he warned.

The fast pace did little to put to rest the turmoil that kept churning in Joe's brain. What would he do now? After the experiences of the past year, would he ever feel comfortable at home again? Then there was the most burning question of all, who for certain had killed Little Ned? Like Deacon and Hawk Beak, he couldn't believe it was the vision quest Indian boys. And what happened to the rare white beaver pelt? He glanced in the direction of Francois. He hated Little Ned and coveted the white pelt. Did he kill Little Ned and steal it? The thought made Joe feel sick to his stomach. How could he ever find out? "Agh!" He groaned so loudly the horse he rode broke into a trot.

As the miles rolled away, Joe's thoughts gradually lightened. There was no way he could wish Little Ned back to life. He was the man of the Jennings family now. He had to go forward and do what he thought best. He owned two horses, four mules and packs of pelts that in a good market could bring a couple of thousand dollars, Deacon said -- considerable wealth for a lad of eighteen. When he sold the pelts he would send the money home. That was not as good as bringing his father home but at least the money would make life easier for Tildy, Granny and Granddad.

At night the ritual of camp making followed the same routine. First, the trappers unloaded the mules. Then they placed the packs to form a triangular breastwork before they watered and led the animals out to graze. At nightfall each man brought in his stock to tether them within the breastwork where they were safe for the night. At this point losing one mule or horse would be disastrous.

At daylight precautions were again taken. Two men searched the area outside the camp to make certain hostiles were not present. When satisfied it was safe, the animals were once more put out to graze until everyone had breakfasted. The stock was then brought in and the business of packing for the day's journey commenced.

The trappers whiled away most evenings talking of the rendezvous. "Maybeso, I'll enter my chestnut in the hoss racin'," Hawk Beak announced one evening. "Old Blaze has fared the winter well an' is as full of beans as any two year old. Might as well bet a pelt or two an' add to my wealth."

"Yeah, there'll probably be some Injun riders who'll take yuh on. They'll make yuh earn yer money," Deacon warned. "Some of those critters look kinda scrawny but they kin sure skedaddle."

"My Blaze'll out run any Injun pony," Hawk Beak bragged. "They may be good for the short haul but in a race of any distance, they cain't stay the course."

"I know an Indian pony that'll pass your clod hopper like it was standing still," Francois said unexpectedly. "In fact, I 'd guarantee a good contest in Nez Perce country. Those riders cling to the back of a horse like ants sticking to a honey tree."

"Ah! Those people thet call theirselves Nimpau, are yuh expectin' some of 'em at the rendezvous?" Hawk Beak asked.

"Maybeso, maybe not. Those people come and go as they please."

THE LAST RENDEZVOUS

Joe, who was preparing to go on guard duty, would have liked to have stayed and heard more. Little Ned's Indian family was Nez Perce. Deacon said they lived at a place called Lapwai. Had that also been Francois' home? Now, with Little Ned dead, would the swarthy trapper return to Lapwai and take over Little Ned's family?

Joe carried the grim thought with him as he went to stand guard. The possibility of Francois moving in on Little Ned's family made him furious. They were his people, Little Ned's sons were his half brothers. He did not want to see them under Francois' cruel hand. Joe made a half circle of camp and stopped abruptly to listen. There was someone on the trail. His heart beat quickened. Indians! He hurriedly cocked the Henry. No, it couldn't be Indians. It was the grating sound of iron-tired wheels. Holding his rifle at the ready, Joe walked forward. The creak of harnesses, pulling and stretching with the weight of a heavy load, announced the approach of a wagon. From the noisy way it rolled over the rough track Joe guessed it a freighter.

"Hey, you in the wagon. Hold up!" Joe shouted. The men around the campfire picked up their weapons and quickly stepped into the shadows.

"Halloa! Halloa, the camp," came a return shout.

"Pull in and show yourself," Joe ordered.

A string of oxen, plodding slowly along, emerged out of the darkness. Alongside them walked a barrel-chested man covered with dust and spattered with mud.

"Name's Beamer," the teamster said. "This is my son, Clay." He motioned to a bareheaded young man with blonde, dust-covered hair. "Drivin' supplies to the rendezvous." Beamer took off his hat and mopped his forehead. "Had a mite of trouble. Broke a wagon tongue an' had to leave the regular supply train. We'd be obliged if yuh'd allow us to jine yuh fer protection. Some Injuns a piece back got mighty curious."

When the teamster stepped into the circle of light, Deacon uttered a profanity. "'Pon my soul it's ol' Dan Beamer. I thought I recognized thet cracklin' bull frog voice."

"Bless me, if'n it ain't the unfrocked deacon. Yuh still hitched to thet Bear Claw woman? If so, why ain't she here?"

"She'll be proud yuh remembered. I left ol' Bear Claw an' his people on the Sweetwater. Maybeso I'll go back an' see the folks soon."

The conversation left Joe speechless. He had trapped, rode the trail, camped with the old trapper for the better part of a year; only now did he learn that, like Little Ned, Deacon was married and had an Indian family.

Every night after the chores were done and evening meal was consumed, the garrulous teamster and Deacon entertained the camp with tales of past meetings and past rendezvous. Beamer's son, Clay, a slender youth with freckled face and bright blue eyes, sat in the background and barely uttered a word. Joe had the feeling the father's constant flow of speech condemned his son to everlasting silence. Only when they were away from camp did the young fellow speak.

One evening Buck enquired of Beamer what news he brought from the outside world. "What does the fur market look like in St. Louis?" he asked.

Beamer took a big chew and spit. "If yuh ask me, things'er goin' downhill. 'Twouldn't surprise me none if this was the last rendezvous. Some of the big boys hev quit trappin' an' gone to buffalo huntin'. I'm told Louie Vasquez and Andy Sublette had a whoppin' huntin' season. They floated bateaux down the Platte with seven hundred buffalo skins an' four hundred barrels of buffalo tongues."

Hawk Beak snorted in disgust. "What's the matter with those galoots? They built up a big fur trade an' go inta buffalo killin'. Don't seem right. Mountain men hev no business doin' somethin' like thet. 'Tain't honorable somehow."

Beamer shook his head. "The good ol' days're gone, I fear. Mountain men, like the Meeks an' Ewing Young're gone. They plan to settle in Oregon Territory's Willamette Valley an' take up farmin'."

"Wagh! Kin yuh see Joe Meek behind a plow. He'd otta shoot hisself afore stoopin' to somethin' like thet," Hawk Beak de-

THE LAST RENDEZVOUS

clared.

"If things're so bad, what kin we expect at this year's rendezvous?" Deacon asked.

"Should be right excitin'," Beamer enthused. "I hear One-Eye Link's comin' to settle a score — layin fer a couple of funsters who lifted his duds while he was performin' in Madame Melissa's back rooms. The poor naked brother was a week in the city jail before anyone could get clothes big enough to fit him. They say he was in temper that'd scorch the hinges of hell. From what I hear, he ain't cooled down since." Beamer slapped his leg and guffawed. Only Francois joined in.

THE LAST RENDEZVOUS

XIX

Believing as he did that the world was full of spirits, every Indian hoped that one would come to him and be his protector....
                                                            Edward Goodbird

News of Michael Two Feathers' miraculous vision quest swept through the tribal homeland like a prairie fire. For days it was the main topic around the Nimpau homeland. People came from as far away as Kamiah, Weippe Prairie and Asotin to see if the story was true and to view the feathers. Thunder Eyes, the *tewat*, sent a runner to invite Michael to his lodge. Weasel Face, who knew the history of Lone Wolf's son's tragic death, stopped by Raven Wing's cabin on the pretext of reporting on her sons' ponies. They had strayed from the pasture and into the mission grounds, he claimed. While at the cabin Weasel Face slyly inquired about the vision quest; was the rumor true, did the firstborn return with feathers of the uncle who had passed to the Great Beyond?

When shown the feathers Weasel Face was struck dumb. If they were not Many Horses' feathers they were exactly like them. At one time he had coveted them and often wondered where feathers of such white purity came from. It had to be from the far north where it was said animals and birds were white as fresh fallen snow all seasons of the year. He did not touch the feathers. He was half afraid of them. This was indeed powerful medicine. To keep the feathers in such perfection guardian spirits had held them in some sacred hiding place and watched over them through the years. Weasel Face first thought to report the phenomenon to Missionary Spalding, then discarded the idea. The bitter memory of how the missionary failed to baptize him into the church still rankled. He had worked like a slave for the missionary and received nothing in return. He had been the missionary's eyes and ears, reporting the villagers' every misstep. He would do it no more. From now on Missionary Spalding would have to find out for himself the sins the people committed.

Excited by the success of her eldest son, Raven Wing quickly prepared Second Son for his *Wyakin* search. Young Wolf bravely marched into the mountains, remained there for three days and three nights finally to stumble home, famished, exhausted and feverish with mosquito and other insect bites. Raven Wing listened impatiently to his stories of night flying owls chasing after fleeing mice, bears plodding through the woods and opossums snuffling around fallen logs. Lone Wolf, who expected more messages from the spirit world, was also disappointed. Why did the spirit of Many Horses grant gifts to Eldest Grandson and ignore Second Grandson? What did it mean?

Vision Seeker observed the goings-on with misgiving. The hypnotic drink, the removal of all evidence of their evening together, and placing the feathers under the sleeping robe, were meant to produce illusions that would convince the boy he had received his personal *Wyakin*. He had no idea his plan would work so well that even Thunder Eyes, the *tewat*, believed Michael had a visitation from the spirit world.

The matter bothered Vision Seeker greatly. Had he done harm or had he done good? One morning while the dew was still on the grass, he strode up the trail to Raven Wing's log cabin lodge. Near the doorstep stood the black and white pony Lone Wolf had given Buffalo Boy, the lad who now called himself Michael Two Feathers. The sight deepened Vision Seeker's distress. The youth was so taken with himself, like a warrior of importance, he kept his horse tethered close to his lodge. The boy believed he had one foot in the Spirit World and the other on Mother Earth. Vision Seeker rapped on the door and called out to announce himself. Raven Wing, her eyes still puffed with sleep, thrust her head out the door.

"Why do you disturb us?" she asked. "Is there trouble in the village? Are the folks ill?"

"Everyone in the home lodge is well. I cannot sleep. Worrisome thoughts trouble me. I come to see if everyone in your lodge is well."

"Do not worry over us. We have a young medicine man of great importance in our lodge. Some day he will be the medicine man of the tribe," Raven Wing's face glowed with pride. She shut the door, almost closing it in his face.

Vision Seeker knew he was defeated. He had never seen his sister looking so radiant. Michael had immersed himself in his new role so completely Raven Wing believed her son was destined to become the tribe's spiritual leader. Every day Michael went to Thunder Eyes' lodge to learn the secret ways of a medicine man. Raven Wing thought of herself as giving birth to a sacred person much as Mary, mother of the Christian God, Jesus, had done. If he told her what really happened to her son on the mountainside she would say he lied. He did not want to quarrel with his sister so he turned away and left more disturbed than when he arrived. Somehow he had to stop this nonsense. There was no telling what it might lead to. Should Missionary Spalding learn of it he would be infuriated. There was no need to get the missionary any more upset than he already was.

Later in the day Vision Seeker again passed by Raven Wing's cabin. This time he stopped and asked Michael to ride with him to inspect the herd. Their route took them by the mission grounds where Spalding's crew still labored on enlarging the millrace. Vision Seeker noted more hairy faces were at the work sites. More items of iron and machinery were standing ready to be installed. Vision Seeker urged his mount faster. The surroundings had changed so much he barely felt at home. The familiar smells, sounds and beauty were gone. From the blacksmith shop came the pounding of steel against steel. The smithies inside were making special tools to slice the skin of Mother Earth. The woods were filled with the ring of axes as trees were chopped down, trees that had provided the village with shade since the first villager chose Lapwai Valley as home. Without asking permission of man, animal, bird or fish, the missionaries changed the course of Lapwai Creek into channels that powered the clanking wheels which ground grain into powder. It was the sawmill that disturbed people most. It was like a voracious beast. Into its mouth disappeared tree trunks like frogs swallowed by snakes. The screeching sounds made horses skittish and hurt the ears of dogs so badly they howled and whined, keeping babies awake and villagers' nerves on edge.

Thoughts of what was happening to his homeland suddenly made Vision Seeker burn with anger. Why had his people allowed this to happen? They had a good life before the coming of the missionaries — now life was one upset on top of another. "Aiiee!" He kicked his mount into a gallop. Only when they came to a shady meadow did he stop. "Let's dismount and talk," he said when his nephew rode up.

Mystified, Michael slid off his pony and hunkered down in the shade. Respectfully, he waited for his uncle to speak. He owed Vision Seeker a lot. Without his counsel he would still be without *Wyakin*, a person without honor — a man of little importance.

Vision Seeker studied his nephew. Now that he had him by himself, he did not know what to say. Above all, he did not want to cause more harm than he had already done. He searched the cloudless sky for a sign. It gave him none. Two hawks circling the hills caught his eye. They flew higher and higher until they were mere specks, no larger than flies.

"Ah-hoh!" Vision Seeker finally exclaimed. The hawks — they were the sign. His thoughts went back to the blue-eyed trapper, Buck Stone, who once read him a story — the perfect answer to the message he wished to convey. He had enjoyed all the stories that came from Buck's black books but seldom did he have the opportunity to make use of the wisdom they contained.

Vision Seeker pointed to the hawks gliding south, hanging almost stationary, held in place by thermal currents that rose from the valley floor. "Have you ever wished you had wings and could sail away like those feathered creatures up there?"

Michael stared at his uncle. He wanted to be a medicine man, not a foolish bird that did nothing but float in the air all day. The last time they talked Vision Seeker spoke of the uncle who sailed out of the clouds on a great white horse, now it was hawks . . . !

"A man with eyes as blue as the sky above that hilltop and

hair the color of aspens in the Season of Falling Leaves read me a story once, a story so meaningful I want to tell it to you," Vision Seeker said, ignoring Michael's apparent lack of interest. "I don't remember it word for word but I am certain you will understand its message."

    Vision Seeker paused. Once again he was back in the trappers' sour smelling lean-to lodge. It had been the Season of Deep Snow. He had guided the hairy faces to the Bitterroot beaver grounds. He hadn't intended to stay but a heavy snow left him trapped with the three mountain men. What strange adventures he experienced that season. There was Buck Stone, who introduced him to talking paper and taught him to read. Deacon, who revealed the mysteries of the Bible, and Michael's father, Little Ned, who taught him the skills of trapping the beaver.

    At first Vision Seeker disliked the enforced stay with these bearded men. Their bigness made him feel small. They had an offensive smell. Their ways were strange. Besides, he did not like the taking of beaver. The little animals were too much like humans. Like people, they built lodges, lived in them together and protected each other from harm. The beaver fared well until the bearded ones came with their traps. The beaver had no protection against the merciless steel jaws that snapped their feet and legs and would not turn them loose.

    Vision Seeker noticed Michael's quizzical expression. "Aiiee!" His mind had wandered like a bird in search of an elusive worm. What was he about to say? Ah, the story Buck Stone read from a book called Mythologies. He glanced at his nephew to see if he paid attention. Satisfied he did, Vision Seeker began to repeat the tale yellow-haired Buck Stone had read to him nearly a dozen years before.

    "In ancient times on the far side of Mother Earth, a wise man and his son were seized and held prisoner. On all sides of the prison were deep wide waters filled with monsters. The only way prisoners could escape was to cross these dangerous waters. Since they had no canoes and the waters were too dangerous to swim, the wise man decided they had to fly. Secretly, he fashioned wings for himself and his son, fastening the feathers together with a special paste. When the wings were ready they tried them out. They worked. They were overjoyed. They could fly like giant birds. While their captors were sleeping they took their wings to a cliff overlooking the monster-filled water.

"'Now, son,' the father instructed. 'We must fly with care. We cannot fly too high or too low. If we fly too low the water will dampen our wings, make them heavy and drag us down. If we fly too high the heat of the sun will soften the paste. Like a molting grouse, the feathers will loosen and fall away. Without feathers the wings will not hold us in the air. We will drop into the water and be devoured by the monsters.'

"The wise man and his son put on the wings and soared away. The son was so proud of flying like an eagle he forgot his father's warnings. He soared high toward the sun. It was so wonderful to be so far above Mother Earth, he flew higher and higher. As his father warned, the heat of the sun softened the paste. One by one the feathers fell away. The son frantically struggled to stay in the air but without feathers the wings were worthless. His father found his lifeless body floating on the water."

For a long while Vision Seeker and his nephew sat silent. Finally, Michael spoke. "It is a good story. Is it a lesson? Do you tell me something I should know and do?"

"I speak these words to let you know of dangers that wait in ambush. Like the boy in the story, you fly too high. I do not want to see your wings come apart as they surely will. You must come down to Mother Earth and walk on two legs like everyone else. You are not a special person with one foot in the Spirit World. The two feathers you found came from your uncle but did not descend from the Spirit World. Do you not remember the first night in the mountains when we sat by the campfire and I gave the feathers to you?"

Michael looked crestfallen. "The happenings of that night gave me strange thoughts and frightful dreams. When I awoke I wanted to tell you about these terrible things. You were not there.

There was no sign of the fire. I thought, like the cunning coyote, you played a trick on me. You did these things so I would believe I had a vision. To make you feel good, I pretended; I acted the way I thought would please you."

Vision Seeker grimaced. "Ugh!" he snorted to himself. He had been caught in his own trap. This nephew of his had more sense than he thought. "It is time we stopped playing tricks on each other. What is done is done. These things will be our secret. Our people believe you are special, and you are. We won't say anything to disappoint them but you must start acting like a normal human being again."

Michael nodded. "Father said it is not good to live a lie. We must be ourselves."

"Your father spoke wisely."

"Perhaps Father will come home and be my *Wyakin* — teach me what I should do and what I should not do. I wish he would."

Vision Seeker again studied the horizon. The circling hawks had descended to glide low over the hills, their keen eyes alert to every move that was made on the expanse of Mother Earth below. One suddenly swooped down. It had spotted its prey. Vision Seeker looked back to his nephew to see the wistful expression that crossed his face. If he was ever going in search of the boy's Boston father, now was the time. Every Season of Tall Grass, trappers from every corner of the mountains met at a place called rendezvous, the summer fur fair. Where was it this summer? Perhaps he could find out from the Red Coats of Hudson's Bay.

THE LAST RENDEZVOUS

XX

*What counts most is not the size of the dog in the fight,
it's the size of the fight in the dog.*
Robert C. Savage

The rendezvous encampment reminded Joe of the Middlesex county fair. It was an outing Tildy and he looked forward to all year. Three-legged races, sack races, barrel races, egg and spoon races, long jumps, high jumps and greased poles to climb. However, the pleasant memories did little to ease the sinking feeling in his stomach. In spite of Buck's brilliant plan to deal with One-Eye Link, the looming encounter weighed heavy on his mind. Bleakly, he viewed the field of tents, lean-tos and makeshift shelters which housed the rendezvous crowd. At the edge of the trees a number of tipis were erected. Around them dark-eyed children scampered in play, camp dogs barking and nipping at their heels. The scene reminded Joe of Little Antlers' Cheyenne village and the slender, doe-eyed lass. How he wished he was there, anywhere but here about to encounter One-Eye Link. In his mind he went over Buck's plan that last night had sounded so good. Now it made no sense at all. He had been an idiot to think it would work. Buck got the idea from reading the legend of King Arthur. "Agh!" Joe felt like a fool.

Near the edge of the encampment Buck, who rode slightly ahead of Joe and Deacon, drew up to survey the scene. "Where's Hawk Beak?" he asked. "If he's let us down we're in a tight fix."

"'Pon my word, Buck, yuh shouldn't hev put so much faith in the rascal. If there's an open jug aroun' Hawk Beak cain't hep hisself. He's onta it like flies on a sugar spill."

"Perhaps he ran into trouble. You're kind of a neutral party, Deacon. Why don't you scout a bit. Joe and I'll hunker down and wait."

Deacon handed Joe the halter leads of his mules and spurred ahead to wend his way through the assortment of living quarters.

Buck dismounted to sit on a boulder. He also was worried. Would his plan work or would it not? It was so farfetched the mountain men present at the rendezvous would have good reason to scoff. He didn't care about that but he certainly did not want young Joe to get hurt. It was too late now, everything had been set in motion. Joe and he would have to suffer the consequences.

While Buck and Joe sat stewing over the plan to best Link, out of the conglomeration of makeshift shelters, lumbering like an enraged bull elephant, the one-eyed man appeared. Joe was completely taken unawares. He surprised himself by standing firm.

"Now, yuh young pilgrim prig," Link bellowed. "I've got yuh cornered. I'm goin' ta thresh yuh within an inch of yer life. I'll larn yuh ta disturb a man whilst he's doin' business with Madame Melissa's girls. Get off thet nag an' take yer medicine. I'm goin' ta hev at yuh if I hevta throw yuh, horse an' all."

Link looked larger, uglier and dirtier than Joe remembered. He glanced nervously at Buck who nodded and winked. "We have him going. Keep to the plan," the wink said. "Are you challenging me to a duel, sir?" Joe inquired, surprised his voice didn't squeak.

The politely worded question increased Link's fury. "Git off thet nag an' I'll show yuh — whup yuh from one end of this camp ta the other."

"One minute," Buck said, stepping forward. "My friend asked you a civil question. Will you be so good as to give him an answer?" Buck's right hand rested lightly on the hilt of Betsy, the finely honed knife.

Link glowered. "Buck, this ain't none of yer affair. This kid needs ta larn western manners, an' I aim ta larn him."

"Is thet the kid thet left yuh nakkid in Melissa's parlors?" a voice from the crowd asked. "By gum! Give him a good spankin', Link. He's too young ta be messin' around in a place like thet."

Hawk Beak stumbled up to stand alongside Link, waving a jug of liquor. "Throw yer gauntlet down, Link. Challenge the varmint to duel."

"Duel the tenderfoot. Show him who's king aroun' heya,"

an onlooker urged.

Link, his one eye flecked with blood, swayed forward to throw his hat on the ground. "Yer challenged ta duel, git off yer horse an' take yer medicine like a man."

"The challenge is accepted," Buck said quickly. "In a duel each man has a second. I'm this man's second and will answer for him. According to dueling rules the person challenged chooses the weapons."

Link's one eye blinked. "Yuh mean there's duelin' rules?"

Hawk Beak leaned heavily on Link. "Don't matter, yuh kin whup him standin' on yer head. Let 'em chose the weapons. Let's git on with it. We're missin' our drinkin', an' there's wagerin' to be did."

"Yippee!" a ragged trapper shouted. "Ten prime beaver pelts on Link."

"They ain't settled on weapons," his partner cautioned.

"A grudge match like this calls for a special fight," Buck announced, "an encounter historians will record in history books. Are we not all knights of the fur trade? Of course we are. We must establish a chivalry equal that of the knights of King Arthur's Round Table. The weapons we choose are jousting poles."

"Jousting poles!" the ragged trapper exclaimed. "Hell, these're modern times. Civilized people don't joust."

"By George! What sport, jousting like the knights of old. Why ain't we did it before," his partner enthused.

The idea of jousting appealed to the rough and tumble mountain men. They cut long slender pine poles, padded the shoulder held end with a beaver pelt, mounted up and started to charge back and forth across a pasture field near the rendezvous grounds. For a while bedlam reigned; spectators shouted and waved their arms to corral runaway horses; a gaggle of dogs and children ran barking and screaming from the Indian village. A drunk was run over and trampled and had to be carried away. Finally order was restored. Judges were appointed. Rules were established. Only two jousters could be on the field at once. Each pair of jousters was allowed three runs.

To win a match rivals had to unseat their adversaries two jousts out of three. The winner of a match was allowed to challenge the winner of the next until all jousters had a turn. Traders racked up barrels to serve drinks. Betting stations were established where wagers were made and winnings collected. The Indians loaned gladiators their ponies and helped shag down the runaways. There wasn't a person who was not involved in some small way.

"'Tis the best rendezvous ever," Deacon chortled.

The novelty of riding pell-mell at each other with long spear-like poles had enough danger and required sufficient skill to satisfy the mountain men's combative nature. They were so taken up with it they hardly allowed Joe and his one-eyed opponent to have a turn. Buck had to order the field cleared. He then declared the next bout the feature match: a greenhorn youth from the east against a mountain man who wrestled grizzlies -- a scrap between David and Goliath.

The Indian horse wranglers brought a big bay and a gray, both animals fighting the bit and jerking at the halter lines. "They're a bit wild," observed Francois, who seemed to have some authority among the Indians, "but that adds spice to the fun, don't you think?"

Joe's pony crow hopped around the field, trying its best to buck him off. Link's mount took a sudden jump, pitching the big man to the ground. Cursing, Link lumbered after it, spooking it even worse. Indian riders caught the pony and held it while Link got himself aboard. From the gallery of spectators, comments and advice came from every side. "Link, yuh don't need a horse. Jest take thet big toothpick, run along an' stab the man all by yerself," someone shouted.

When the horsemen were mounted and armed, the judge reminded them of the rules. "The object is to unhorse the opposing rider. Jousting poles are the only weapons allowed. If a jousting pole is lost or breaks, fists, elbows or feet can be used." The judge walked a safe distance away and shot a pistol in the air, the signal for the jousting to begin.

Link thumped his mount into a trot. Joe's feisty pony did a couple of hops, almost knocking him off. He took the reins in his teeth. With his free hand he rapped the horse on the rump. Then, with both hands clutching the jousting pole, he aimed it at the big mountain man's girth. The distance between the two ponies narrowed. Onlookers yelled encouragement. "Hold steady there, Link. Yer gonna pin him like a bug," someone shouted. But before the horsemen clashed, their mounts veered sharply away from the intended path. Joe's clinging legs kept him astride his mount. Link went flying to land in a cloud of dust.

Once again the Indian horsemen caught Link's horse and brought it back. They helped Link aboard. Again the judge fired the starting shot. This time Link grasped the jousting pole in two hands. Using it as a cudgel, he swung it in an arc above the pony's ears. The startled pony bowed its neck and skidded to a stop. Link sailed over the horse's head, the pole went skittering through the grass to end up in the crowd. Link staggered to his feet. "Ain't a fittin way ta fight," he bellowed. He picked up his fallen hat and plodded off the field, ignoring the entreaties of his backers to continue the match. The rest of the day he remained in his tent, growling at anyone who attempted to draw him out. In the morning One-Eye Link was gone.

The victory gave Joe no satisfaction. The jousting affair had settled nothing. If anything, it made matters worse. Link would brood over the humiliating affair until their paths crossed again.

#

On a rise overlooking the rendezvous site a lone Indian riding a colorfully marked Appaloosa, reined up. The special jousting match had begun. The horseman, Vision Seeker, swung down to watch. He had arrived at the right time. No one noticed him. He had no desire to draw attention to himself. He had never liked these gatherings called rendezvous. Something bad always seemed to happen. At Bear Lake, the first one he attended, his brother, Many Horses, had been mistaken for an enemy warrior and was shot and scalped. At Pierre's Hole the Gros Ventre attacked. Ten Nimpau men were slain in the battle that followed. Then there were the disappointing times when the Nimpau attended rendezvous to invite teachers of the Great Spirit Book to their homeland only to be cruelly rejected.

However, he never had seen anything at a rendezvous like this -- men with long spear-like poles on horseback, charging each other. They didn't appear skilled at wielding the weapons or riding horses. They kept losing their grip on the poles and were constantly falling off the horses. Then came a bout pitting a slim youth against a man as large as a full grown bear. It was quick to see the youth had more skill than the bear. He sat his horse well and handled the pole with ease. He was not surprised the bear was no match for the youth.

Vision Seeker moved nearer. The youthful jouster with his shock of black hair and eyes as blue as a clear autumn sky, reminded him of someone he had seen in the past. He studied him at length and searched his memory, singling out every hairy faced one he had ever known. All his efforts were in vain. His mind remained a blank. "Aiiee" he muttered in disgust. He was getting old before his time.

The jousting matches ended with shouts and the appearances of jugs. Vision Seeker hesitated. Trappers full of firewater were not good to be around but he could not leave until he accomplished his mission. He staked his mount out to graze and walked toward the encampment of shelters. He spoke to a trapper. He answered with a shake of the head. The second man he questioned made the sign of the cross. A third offered a jug of fire water. Vision Seeker walked on, then abruptly stopped and quickly retraced his steps. A rotund trapper set down his jug and stared. "By gum! If thet ain't . . ." He started to run after the slender departing figure but lost him in the maze of makeshift shelters. The rotund trapper returned to his companions and reached for his jug. "I'll be dadburned! I'd swear I jest saw Little Ned's Injun brother."

"Yuh've had too many pulls on the jug," Hawk Beak scoffed. "If it was Vision Seeker he'd of come said howdy."

Joe stared in the direction Deacon pointed. Vision Seeker! What a romatic sounding name. He suddenly wanted very much to meet Little Ned's Indian family. Francois snatched up his Hawken and backed into the shadows.

THE LAST RENDEZVOUS

XXI

If you find a path with no obstacles — it is probably a path that doesn't lead anywhere.

Robert C. Savage

In general the rendezvous of 1840 was a flop. The trapper/trader gathering saw its house of cards about to collapse. The price of beaver pelts was low. Most trappers had less than an average catch. The combination of low price and scarcity of pelts left purses flat. This had a sobering effect. No matter how much they tried, after the rousing jousting competitions, the activities and spirits of the mountain men deteriorated until even the most rampageous members were subdued.

There was the feeling in the air that this was the last rendezvous. No longer would they get together each year to frolic, trade and exchange views. Every day an individual or group broke camp, said sorrowful farewells and departed. Bill William, a respected old timer, thought California had promise. Black Moses and Doc Newell decided the Willamette Valley was the place to go.

Further depressing the encampment's spirits were new gaps in the ranks of the mountain men. Little Ned's tragic end at the hands of the Crow came as a shock. He was well liked and had been a fixture at a dozen or more rendezvous. Others also had gone to their reward. Joe Meek's former partner was slain in Blackfeet country. The Gros Ventre had claimed the lives of two old timers. Several new to the trade had fallen in Rogue and Umpqua country.

Like so many others, Joe Jennings could not decide what he should do. He had sold his pelts but they had not brought as much as he had hoped. Beamer offered to take the money to St. Louis and send Tildy a draft from there. She would be expecting news of their father, but what could he say? Sooner or later Tildy would have to know that their father was dead. Joe borrowed a quill pen and piece of paper from Buck. He stared down at the empty page. How did one couch such heartbreaking news?

Through all the gloom Buck Stone was optimistic. He could see as well as anyone the end of the mountain man era was at hand, but he had a special beaver grounds up his sleeve. "One more year," he said, "and I'm through."

"Not another spook hole like the last place," Deacon groaned, but he and his fellow trappers would not desert Buck. As they completed their preparations for leaving the rendezvous, Beamer and his son rode up. "This lad of mine is crazy ta ride with yer gang," the teamster said to Buck. "Can yuh see fit ta take him on?"

Buck shook his head. Although he was certain a beaver bonanza awaited, he had no idea if he could find it and if he did, it was no place to take a tenderfoot. The loss of Little Ned still weighed heavily on his mind. He did not want to have another death on his conscience. "Where we're going everyone has to know his trade."

"But-but," Beamer stuttered. He motioned toward Joe. "What about thet young un? I betcha he ain't a day older'n Clay."

"Yes, but I know his worth. He's proven himself."

Buck turned to see the crushed look on Clay's face. He glanced at the rest of the trappers who had suddenly busied themselves with their gear. The Beamers had done favors for them all. The teamster gave them discounts on their supplies and carried their money and messages back to St. Louis.

"All right, but I can't be held responsible if anything untoward happens," Buck said. "The place we're going isn't for greenhorns, and that's a fact. Joe, take the kid in hand and see he's properly outfitted."

"I'll never fergit this," the elder Beamer said gratefully.

"You sure won't if the kid gets himself killed," Buck brutally replied.

The teamster was too pleased to take offense or heed the warning. He quickly helped Clay prepare for his first trapping expedition. Beamer lavishly handed over trade goods, traps and edibles until Buck held up a hand in protest.

"After all, this isn't Marco Polo making an exploration of outer Mongolia. We may have to travel light and fast."

THE LAST RENDEZVOUS

When the band of trappers filed away from the encampment, Clay turned back to wave to his father. Beamer stood with one hand on the side of an ox, wigwagging his hat. Clay grinned at Joe. "I never thought the old man would let me go. He made up his mind when you bested Link. He said if a young whippersnapper from New England could turn into a mountain man, a Missouri-bred son of his could, too."

Joe rode along puffed up. Buck's acknowledgment of his worth and now Beamer's praise, lifted his spirits. "Ah!" If his father were only alive his cup would runneth over.

The trappers pressed on to the headwaters of the Snake. Joe and Clay were overwhelmed by the beauty of the region. The older trappers ignored the breathtaking splendor. They grumbled about the scarcity of game and lack of beaver sign. They came to the Three Tetons, the snowcapped, rock-sculptured mountains that towered high into a yellowish-colored sky. They continued on through the place of geysers the Indians called "Land of Many Smokes." They were now nearing the home of the Blackfeet. No one knew their destination but Buck. "It's a hidden pocket somewhere in these mountains," he explained. "I came upon it by chance. Didn't have time to get my bearings. Blackfeet were on my tail. I do remember the beaver were so tame they practically ate out of my hand."

"Quit funnin'," Hawk Beak exclaimed. "There ain't no place like thet. This country's been trapped out. Ol' Joe Meek an' his gang saw to thet."

Deacon, who had been with Buck the longest, also took a dim view of Buck's search for the elusive beaver grounds. "I think we best look ol' Mother Fate square in the face. She's done give up on beaver trappin'. The last rendezvous was proof enuff of thet. We had prime pelts, didn't git fiddlesticks fer 'em. What'll it be like next summer? With all those galoots goin' off ta Californy an' farmin', whose goin' ta come ta another rendezvous? Suppose we find these beaver grounds. We'll look mighty foolish showin' up with a bunch of skins an' no one ta buy 'em."

Buck was not deterred. Over every hill and mountain pass he

expected to drop into his enchanted valley. At the end of every ravine and draw he hoped this beaver wonderland would pop into view. Then one windy morning the mountains opened up. Buck led his brigade triumphantly through a narrow canyon and into a pleasant valley. The aspen leaves had fallen, but row after row of white barked slender tree trunks stood like white sentinels circling the valley floor. Everywhere else it was green. Thick grass rose waist high to the horses' bellies. On the far edge of the grassland grazed a herd of deer. When the horsemen appeared they glanced up and switched their short tails. They wandered a few steps and stopped, quizzically watching the horsemen approach.

"Heaven's sakes. Those critters're as tame as milk cows," Deacon uttered. "Now where're these beaver thet eat outta yer hand?"

The trappers rode a little farther to see a stream meandering from one side of the valley to the other. Over the years one beaver dam after another had backed the water up until the steam resembled a lengthy lake. As they approached, guardian beaver slapped their tails on the water. The busy beaver disappeared only to reappear swimming toward their lodges.

"I swan, Buck, I knew yuh was funnin' us. They ain't eatin' outta our hands at all," Hawk Beak complained.

"Maybeso yer not offerin' the right grub. These critters look like they dine on nuthin' but the best," Deacon said. "I ain't seen so many prime beavers at once in me born life. Why trappers' ain't been in here's a miracle. Tell us 'bout it, Buck, is the place also filled with haunts? It's gotta hev somethin' wrong with it."

Buck looked pleased but did not answer. He was busy counting beaver mounds.

It was an ideal place to spend the winter. High above the rim of the valley floor rose a palisade of towering mountains capped with snow. The cold wind that had blown into the riders' faces from the north was gone. It was almost like spring. Everywhere there was wood for fuel, and ample water and forage abounded. There were so many inviting places to set up camp the problem was deciding which to chose. They finally agreed upon an aspen enclosed vale near a

THE LAST RENDEZVOUS

sparkling spring. The setting was so perfect Deacon asked Buck again.

"What's the secret this time, Buck? This place is too perfect ta be real. Must be some powerful Injun ghost perteckin' it."

"Not exactly," Buck answered. "You see, the Blackfeet people believe they have a maker similar to our Christian God. This Old Man, they call him, knew and understood all of nature. The Old Man created it. He walked about the regions making rivers here, placing mountains there. He covered the plains with grasses and the mountainsides with trees. He decided which animals should live where, and what purpose they should serve. He put beaver in the streams to make dams to hold back the rain and snow runoff. He placed buffalo on the plains to keep the grass clipped. The coyote, wolf, magpie and buzzard were to keep the land neat and clean."

"I suppose the Old Man set aside this valley just for Buck Stone's trappers," Francois spoke for the first time.

"No, as the legend goes, after the exertion of creating all these good things, the Old Man lay down to rest. The broad plain we crossed was where the Old Man's body laid. The canyon that opens into the valley is where the Old Man's neck was and this valley cradled the Old Man's head."

"Thet don't tell why the animals're so tame an' there's no hostiles about," Hawk Beak said impatiently.

"I'm told the Blackfeet aren't certain the Old Man is gone for good. They believe someday the Old Man will return. They want everything to be like it was when the Old Man was first here."

"Sounds a bit spooky ta me," Deacon said. "What're these blinkin' Blackfeet going ta think of us campin' here?"

"I don't rightly know," Buck answered. "They might not take it kindly, so we'd better keep on our toes."

"One of these days Buck's gonna lead us right smack inta a hornet's nest," Deacon said as he walked with Hawk Beak and Joe to picket the livestock. "He hears an Injun legend an' believes every word. Jest goes ta show a man of larnin's dangerous. Look at him. He knows those mythology books back'ards an' for'ards... puts his faith in 'em like most folks do the Scriptures. It ain't quite Christian-like. One of these days . . ."

"Quit carryin' on like a locoed bedbug," Hawk Beak scolded. "Yuh won't leave the beaver trade until some Injun drives a stake in yer heart."

"Maybeso, the time's here. I'm feelin' mighty nervy. We been takin' chances the Devil wouldn't take, an' look at the price we've paid. Last year Little Ned bit the dust. Who'll it be this year?"

Joe silently listened to the two trappers quarrel. The thought of Little Ned left in the lonely grave brought back the sickening feeling of grief and guilt. The campsite in the Bighorns was nearly as lovely as this valley, yet it turned into a place of death; would the same happen here? The surrounding beauty with its wealth of beaver reminded him of the day he and Little Ned came upon the Bighorn beaver grounds. They had been like two boys stumbling onto a priceless treasure. Ah! If moments like that could last forever. Now he had to start a trap line all by himself. Joe glanced up at the palisade of snowcapped mountains and tried to think of something else.

As the rich catch of beaver started to roll in, Deacon's apprehensions and Joe's melancholy were forgotten. Clay and Joe teamed up. At first their catches were small, but gradually they began to swell. To improve their take, Joe searched through what remained of Little Ned's possessions for his magical formula but, like the white beaver pelt, it was missing. Joe wondered if one of the trappers had taken it, but it did not seem to matter. Everyone had good luck.

The season went surprisingly well. The mild winter provided a long trapping season. The horses and mules waxed fat and frisky on the abundant forage. Even idle time was spent pleasantly. Buck immersed himself in Greek mythology. Deacon read his Bible through. Francois kept to himself, went hunting with his bow and arrow, worked on pelts and sharpened his many knives. Hawk Beak ate and slept while Clay and Joe spent hours exploring the valley.

Joe found Clay an agreeable companion. He was interested in everything around him. He studied the tiny winter birds that remained through the winter. Why did they not fly south like other birds did, he wondered. He came upon a badger hole and waited half a day until the animal finally emerged. One day they discovered a cave. Clay wanted to crawl in and see if bear were inside sleeping the winter away. Only when Joe suggested it could be a rattlesnake den did he change his mind. However, there was a special place Clay enjoyed most. It was a rocky ledge from where one could see the length and breadth of the valley.

"If I should take up ranchin', this is the kind of place I'd want," Clay said one spring day at this special place that overlooked the valley. "I would build my house on this knoll. From here I could watch over my entire spread."

"What will you call your ranch?" Joe idly asked. "A place this special should have a name like Paradise Valley, something that expresses it's wondrous beauty."

For a moment Clay thoughtfully studied the valley. "I think I would call it something simple, like Beamer's Nest. Not very spectacular but I don't intend to do spectacular things. I just want to do normal things like raise livestock, farm a bit, rear a family . . . I'd keep this place like it is for my kids and their kids. What better inheritance could one hope to give?"

"Hmm," Joe grunted, surprised by Clay's domestic thoughts. "Now that you've decided to make this Beamer's Nest, tell me how you would lay out the ranch."

"I'd put the corrals over there." He pointed to the far side of the valley. "Right behind them I'd build a mammoth hay barn. I think I'd paint it red. Then I'd . . . Oh! God! There's a bunch of riders! Indians! They're after the stock!" Clay scrambled down the hill toward the pasture, slipping and sliding amongst the rocks.

Without hesitation, Joe fired his rifle, the signal that hostiles were sighted. The valley's restful scene was shattered. A flock of magpies flapped out of the brush to send up shrill chatter. Two startled rabbits dashed from under a bush to disappear in the tall grass. Joe quickly reloaded and ran for the campsite, shouting as loud as he could. Buck and the other trappers were already stationed behind the protective breastwork, shading their eyes against the afternoon sun.

"Hey! Get back! Take cover!" Buck shouted as Clay continued to run toward the grazing animals. Buck shouted again. He ran out from behind the breastwork, waving frantically for Clay to take cover. Uttering blood thirsty howls, the mounted Indians swept down on the herd. Clay threw up his rifle and fired at the nearest painted rider. The horse fell but, like a cat, the horseman landed on his feet. With a bound he was upon Clay. Buck went to one knee; he took aim and fired. The warrior dropped in the grass beside Clay. Buck reloaded and fired again. A horseman painted with stripes of black, white and red, bore down. The trappers gasped. Buck had fallen.

Howling and brandishing weapons, hideously painted warriors were suddenly everywhere. They overran Buck and Clay's inert forms to charge the campsite. The trappers dropped behind the breastwork and fired. Three riderless horses veered away. Two more horsemen rode full out, directly for the barricade. They came so near Joe could see the whites of the riders' eyes. He seized Buck's scatter-gun and fired both barrels. The recoil knocked him down. The nearest warrior pitched forward, the body skidding to a stop against the breastwork. The horse leaped over Joe and landed in the trappers' lean-to shelter, knocking it to the ground. Francois dispatched the second horseman with pistol shots.

The action had been so fast and furious Joe had barely had time to think. Now, with a pause in the fight, chills ran up his spine. He shivered and shook as if he had the ague. The staring, unblinking eyes of the dead warriors made him sick to his stomach. Just moments before these people had been breathing, living human beings like himself. A couple of pulls of the trigger and they were pieces of bloody meat.

Deacon punched Joe in the ribs. "This is no time ta go squeamish. Reload an' get thet hatchet ready. These varmints'll be back afore yuh kin say scat."

This time the warriors charged in two groups. One galloped straight at the left side of the breastwork, the other held back, waiting to circle around from the right.

"Ah! They're gittin' smart," Hawk Beak calmly observed, "plannin' to divide our fire. When we shoot to the left those on the right will come at us whilst we're reloadin'."

There was no time to plan their defense. The first line of riders lashed their mounts into a gallop, charging straight across the open space. Francois fired the Hawken and grabbed for his pistols. Hawk Beak fired and reloaded. Two horses went down, another galloped away riderless. Two warriors on foot emerged out of the grass swinging war clubs. Joe threw up his rifle.

"No! Behind yuh!" Hawk Beak shouted. While fighting on the left raged, the horsemen from the right had charged. Joe whirled around. A horse was on top of him. The flying hooves and the swish of a war club passed inches overhead. The horseman wheeled about. The galloping hooves were on him again. Joe threw himself prone and fired. The horse reared, the rider pitched off, falling almost on top of him. He clubbed the fallen rider with his Henry only to glance up in time to see the sun's rays glinting on a raised war club already spotted with blood. There was an explosion of flashing light, an excruciating pain, then all was darkness.

THE LAST RENDEZVOUS

XXII

I have heard talk and talk but nothing is done. Good words do not last long unless they amount to something.

Chief Joseph, Nez Perce

The summer of 1840 found the missionaries of Lapwai and Waiilatpu in as much disarray as that of the trappers at the Green River rendezvous. Indians and missionaries were at dagger points. Henry Spalding's trading policy was at the seat of the trouble. In attempting to wean his flock away from traipsing to Hudson's Bay at Fort Walla Walla, Spalding stocked an inventory of trade goods at the Lapwai mission. He did so against his better judgment. He did not like to have knives, guns, lead and powder around. He had little talent for merchandising and was somewhat greedy. He priced his goods higher than did Hudson's Bay and gave short measure. The trade experienced Indians saw through these petty shenanigans immediately.

Also, the locals were upset when outsiders, Joseph and Timothy, who Spalding had baptized into the church, were encouraged to remain in Lapwai, which they did, cultivating plots of land Lapwai villagers claimed were theirs. However, the greatest threat Henry Spalding faced came from within the mission family. Reverend Hall, who had been learning the Nimpau language under the tutelage of Hallalhotsoot in Kamiah, left his post in a huff. He did not like the direction the missions were taking. He was so critical of the way Spalding managed the Lapwai mission, Church Board members in the east turned down the reverend's request for additional help and supplies.

William Gray, once Spalding's stalwart supporter, became the missionary's implacable enemy. Gray had been the leader of a party who took Nimpau horses east to trade for cattle. Along the way the party was ambushed. Gray fled, leaving all the herders who accompanied him at the mercy of the enemy, a war party of Sioux.

In the encounter every Nimpau herder was slain and their horses seized. Lapwai villagers never forgot nor forgave Gray for his cowardly behavior. It was with some satisfaction that they watched the missionaries quarrel and fight among themselves.

Gray did his best to undermine Spalding. He wrote a twelve page letter to the Church Board attacking Spalding. Before the letter was barely on its way, Gray wrote a second castigating letter. Like Hall, he deplored the way the missions at both Lapwai and Waiilatpu expended their efforts. His principle complaint was that rather than save souls, the missionaries spent their time turning Indian people into sedentary settlers. The making of plows, hoes, scythes and other cultivating and harvesting equipment had priority over prayer meetings, Bible readings and sermons.

To add to Spalding's woes, Thunder Eyes, one of his stalwart supporters who he had named James, turned against him. Like Weasel Face, Thunder Eyes had received no reward for submitting his will and skills to Missionary Spalding. He brooded over the matter until it consumed him. "The missionaries take and never give," he told his mate.

Thunder Eyes did more than talk. He launched a campaign against the missionaries. He announced the valley belonged to the people of Lapwai. All outsiders must go. Life had to be made so miserable for them they would not stay. To urge outsiders on their way, Thunder Eyes embarked on a program of harassment. One of his first acts was to send youths to the schoolhouse to disrupt classes. Every day a group of rowdies came to shout and march around the schoolhouse, distressing Eliza Spalding to the point of tears.

The attacks on the missionaries and other outsiders, created ferment among the villagers. People took sides. Quarrels erupted. Neighbors who had lived side by side for a lifetime, stopped speaking to each other. In the long lodge blankets were hung from the rafters to keep wrangling occupants separated. Families were split. Children and parents were at loggerheads. Work in the fields and on the pasture lands limped to a crawl.

No one was more upset than Running Turtle. He had attended the mission school since the first day it opened. He applied himself with such diligence he rapidly graduated from one class to the next, finally to be named Eliza Spalding's assistant. When she was absent from the classroom, Running Turtle was left in charge. He also was assigned the task of tutoring students who had fallen behind.

Running Turtle enjoyed his role as teacher's assistant and tutor. At the mission school he was not looked upon as a bungling, overweight youth but as a learned man. Eliza Spalding held him in high regard. She claimed he was the brightest star in her crown. Missionary Spalding also had his eye on Running Turtle. Perhaps one day he would take him east and enter him in the seminary.

Running Turtle was keenly aware of his standing in the missionary establishment. Anything that threatened the mission, threatened him. When Thunder Eyes began his campaign of harassment, Running Turtle became furious. To see his beloved teacher in tears, turned him into a ferocious lion. He caught two troublemakers and clacked their heads together, another received a vicious clout with a ruler. He had learned this behavior by watching Reverend Spalding.

Shortly after these incidents, Running Turtle stomped up the porch steps and into Raven Wing's log cabin lodge. He plunked himself down with such vehemence Raven Wing thought her one and only chair would collapse. She gave her brother an angry glance. "What is it? You are as puffed as a bull frog."

"Ah! You are worse than a mole. You see nothing. You hear nothing," Running Turtle scolded. "The mission school is finished."

"Why come to me? I have nothing to do with the mission school."

"Foolish sister. Your son, who calls himself Michael Two Feathers, takes lessons from Thunder Eyes. It is said he will be a big man. Thunder Eyes is an enemy of the school. He tells people it is not good. Can you not see? If your son can be a big man by taking lessons from Thunder Eyes why should people send their sons to the mission school? Soon the classrooms will be empty. The school will close. There will be no place to learn."

Raven Wing gave her brother a glance of scorn. The temper that was always near the surface, erupted. "You are a thoughtless, foolish young man. You are like the grasshopper in the reading book. You waste the seasons away. What good is your learning? Has it added horses to the herd? Does it put food in the lodge? Are you a better hunter, horseman, warrior? No, the mission school does none of these things.

"Ah, yes. You read books. You tell stories. You put words on talking paper. What are you to do with them? Are you to live with the bearded ones where they use such things? What kind of life will you live — away from your people, away from the valleys, streams, and mountains of our tribal lands? When you are sick who will tend your needs? When you desire a mate, who will you take, a woman with hair the color of falling aspen leaves and skin as pale as flour? When you pass to the other side, where will your spirit go, to the Great Spirit World hairy faces call heaven? Brother, open your eyes. Quit school. Do the things Mother Earth put us here to do."

Running Turtle stared at his sister. Why was she taking on like this? Why did she dislike the missionary people so much? Ah, yes. It was the dark man, the second man she had taken as a mate. She could not get over the way Missionary Spalding's flock had chased him away. He glanced at his nephews who had sat silently through the tirade. They were unperturbed. They had heard this before. Running Turtle started for the door. Like his father, he hated defeat. If nothing else, he would have the last word.

"You are foolish. The missionary woman says learning is a treasure that is never lost. It is like *Wyakin*, it travels with us through life."

"Wagh!" was Raven Wing's answer.

#

Vision Seeker had ridden away from the rendezvous sick at heart. The man who taught him so much was no more. He had made the long trip in search of his Boston brother only to find he had passed to the other side. Not one, but three trappers had given him the tragic news. There was no reason for them to lie, but he had wanted to hear the words from his old friends, Buck, the man with hair the color of aspen trees in the Season of Falling Leaves and Deacon, the man with the hairless head. As he approached Buck Stone's lean-to he received an equally terrible shock. The first person he saw was Francois. Immediately, he knew this evil man was involved in sending Little Ned to the Great Beyond. Rage overtook him. Why should this man live and his Boston brother die? The urge to plunge a knife into Francois' heart was so strong he could not trust himself. He hurriedly turned back to avoid being recognized. Even so, Deacon, the man with no hair on his head, saw him and came running.

All the way home Vision Seeker had been tormented by the beauty that surrounded him. Why should evil Francois continue to enjoy these good things Mother Earth provided and Little Ned never see them again? He arrived in Lapwai to face another disagreeable situation. The village was in turmoil. He was appalled at the rancor that had reared its ugly head in his absence. His own family was caught up in the bickering between the followers of Missionary Spalding and those banded together under the leadership of Thunder Eyes. Running Turtle, who had blossomed into a promising responsible adult, was a rabid supporter of the missionaries. Raven Wing disliked everything about them. Lone Wolf and Quiet Woman were caught in between. They held their peace but Vision Seeker could tell they were troubled. Every harsh word exchanged between Raven Wing and Running Turtle was a dagger thrust to their hearts.

Vision Seeker attempted to bring peace and quiet to the family. His efforts were in vain. The only solution to the squabble was to keep Running Turtle and Raven Wing apart, but this was near impossible. The grandparents doted on their grandchildren. Now that the two older boys were not going to school, Lone Wolf insisted they come to the long lodge. Daily the boys appeared to listen to their grandfather's counsel and tales of the days before the missions when life in Lapwai Valley was peaceful, when the people could hunt, fish and travel anywhere they wished.

The most disagreeable task Vision Seeker had faced, however, was confronting his nephew, Michael Two Feathers. "Did you see Father? Will he come to Lapwai?" were his first words.

Vision Seeker put his hand out to grip the boy's shoulder. What was to become of the fatherless boy in this era of trouble and strife? No matter how much one hated to see them go, the old days Lone Wolf liked to recall were gone. The new ways were here. What did they hold for the young? For that matter, what did they hold for any of his people? For a moment blind rage gripped Vision Seeker. He hated the hairy faced intruders who had taken over their lives. Every one of them: Buck Stone, Hawk Beak, Deacon . . . yes, even his own Boston brother, Little Ned, had had a hand in changing the lives of the Nimpau. His people were like uprooted trees; never again would their feet be planted in the soil that gave them birth and nourished them to adulthood.

"I fear your father has passed to the other side," Vision Seeker finally said. "From what I could learn, he died pierced by an arrow."

Michael silently turned and walked away. Vision Seeker did not follow. This was one of those special moments in life when a person wanted to be alone with the Great Mysterious.

THE LAST RENDEZVOUS

XXIII

Fate has terrible power. You cannot escape it by wealth or war. No fort will keep it out, no ships will outrun it.
                                              Sophocles

The sound of voices came from far away, deadened as if heard through a dense fog. Joe listened, trying to understand what was said.

"It was the kid's fault. If it hadn't been fer him, Buck'd still be alive."

"Too late to worry about that. Buck's dead."

Joe opened his eyes and quickly closed them. Lying nearby were two buckskin clad figures, the heads topped with blonde hair. "Ah!" Joe groaned. It had been no nightmare.

"Quit playin' 'possum," Deacon scolded. "Yuh might think yer dead but yuh ain't. Wake up an' suffer like the rest of us. With only a bump on yer noggin yer probably good fer another hundred years."

Joe struggled to a sitting position. Gradually, the thickness in his head and ringing in his ears cleared. He averted his eyes from Buck's and Clay's bodies and glanced across the valley. The raiders who remained were busy collecting their dead and wounded. Around the pasture grounds riderless ponies trotted aimlessly, their heads high, spooked by the smell of blood and gun powder. One by one the Indians ran them down. The bodies of slain warriors were loaded onto the backs of the ponies and then led away. When the last rider disappeared into the far canyon, silence fell over the valley. Except for three dead warriors sprawled near the barricade and the two buckskin bundles that were Buck Stone and Clay Beamer, it was as pleasant and peaceful a scene as before the raid. Joe almost had to pinch himself to realize the horror that had occurred.

"We cain't jest sit here," Deacon scolded. "Believe me, these varmints ain't finished. They'll be back afore yuh kin say scat."

"Right you are," Francois agreed. "Let's get these bodies planted."

The trappers took turns digging a grave at the edge of an aspen grove below the point that overlooked the valley, the place where Clay Beamer said he would build his ranch home. When the grave was sufficiently deep, they lowered the blanket wrapped bodies to lay them side by side. Their faces, before Deacon tenderly covered them, looked as peaceful as though they had merely fallen asleep.

Deacon pulled himself out of the pit. He took off his cap and crumpled it in his hands. He looked up at a sky pierced with streaks of crimson and orange. The sun was hidden by a cloud. Shafts of escaping sunlight glittered on the mountain tops, making the snowy summits a luminous circle tinged with red. The trappers paused to stare at the incredible sight. It was almost as if a ring of blood encircled the valley. Joe noticed Francois furtively make the sign of the cross. "Quit wasting time, let's get on with it," the French Canadian's harsh voice rasped.

Deacon cleared his throat. Tears ran down his cheeks to disappear in his unkempt beard. "Oh, Lord," he called in a quavering voice. "Please take these brave souls an' lift 'em up ta heaven where they'll be safe from this bloody battleground . . . ."

Remembering the lone savaged form of his father, and now seeing the two blanket wrapped bodies of Buck and Clay laying in graves of bare dirt, a terrible thought struck Joe. Was this the way the lives of all mountain men ended, cut down in their prime and buried in the wilderness in unmarked graves? After their many courageous deeds they went unheralded into the great beyond. It did not seem fair.

Joe rubbed a sleeve across his wet eyes and started to push dirt onto the bodies. This prompted the others to join in. Afterward, they heaped a pile of rocks above the grave to blend it into the landscape. Blackfeet warriors were known to dig up their victims, take their scalps and other body parts as battlefield coups. Before they finished, a cold wind blew down from the north. It clouded up and began to rain.

"I've had it," Francois said abruptly. "As soon as we divvy the pelts, I'm off."

"Ain't it risky leavin' by yerself?" Hawk Beak asked.

"If you've a mind to, come along. I'm goin' south, probably Fort Hall."

"Maybeso, I'll jest do thet," Hawk Beak said. "I don't aim to stay an' lose my hair. Yuh galoots fixin' to go?" he asked Deacon and Joe.

Joe remained silent. It was wise to stick together in Indian territory but he did not fancy riding with Francois. Without Buck to keep him in check, he was a doubtful companion. Francois hated Little Ned and never liked Joe, especially after he fell heir to Little Ned's catch.

Deacon answered for them both. "We'll think on it."

"Why wait? You think Buck'll rise up from the grave and lead us out of here?" Francois asked, his voice heavy with sarcasm. "After all, he's not Jesus Christ."

"I know thet," Deacon replied testily. "I jest don't want ta be rushed inta doin' somethin' foolish. The Good Book says he thet's hasty of spirit exalteth folly."

"Are yuh tellin' us we're fools fer wantin' to shake the dust of this here killin' ground?" Hawk Beak demanded. "I don't care what yuh think. We're goin'. We're takin' half of Buck's an' Clay's catch, ain't thet so, Francois?"

Without waiting for a response, Hawk Beak and Francois seized the fallen men's stacks of furs and callously divided the spoils. Deacon glanced at Joe. Without Buck's steadying influence the two trappers had turned into a couple of snapping, snarling wolves, scrapping over the remains of a kill.

Hurriedly, Hawk Beak and Francois saddled, packed their mules and departed. The little pack train filed across the valley to disappear in the dusk. Not once did either Francois or Hawk Beak look back.

"Yuh'd think Satan, hisself, was on their tails," Deacon sourly observed.

"The loss of Buck hit them hard," Joe said. "I guess they can't put his death behind them fast enough."

"Cain't say I blame 'em. These blinkin' Blackfeet ain't goin' ta stand fer us decimatin' their troops like we did. Soon they'll be dancin' the war dance. When they git het up enuff, they'll be ridin' back ta finish us off. We gotta git outta here, but where do we go? We cain't wander around like a couple of homeless dogs."

Joe did not answer. All he wanted was to get away from this blood soaked valley. They brought the mules in and started to pack. Dusk turned into darkness. Then to the east a full moon came over the mountain range. It was so near and bright the valley was bathed in light.

"Well, at least we're blessed in one thing. We don't have ta feel our way around in the dark. Of course, it lights the way for the cursed Blackfeet, too."

Joe was tempted to ride away leaving everything but their pelts behind. He didn't want a thing to remind him of this terrible day. Besides their own gear, they had to do something about that of Buck Stone and Clay Beamer. Clay had possessed little except a few clothes, his riding equipment and a collection of special rocks he had picked up on tramps around the valley. Joe stuffed the small stuff into a bag. Teamster Beamer would be heartbroken. He should have at least a few mementos of his dead son.

Buck's belongings were harder to manage. Joe opened the pack of books. A journal fell out. It lay open, exposing Buck's beautifully crafted script. In the bright moonlight Joe could make out the words. "His name was Na'pi, Old Man, he created all creatures on Mother Earth. They all knew him and understood him. He told them to work together. They should not quarrel; they should not fight . . . ." Joe closed the cover and stuffed the journal into his own pack.

"Hell, we cain't cart all this stuff around. Buck's got more books than my ol' preachin' college," Deacon complained.

Joe leafed through one journal and book after another. He

had had sufficient schooling to recognize that several books were in Greek and Latin. Joe shook his head. What was an educated man who could read Greek and Latin for pleasure doing in the western wilderness? Joe came to the volume Buck always referred to in his discussions of myths and legends. On the fly, written in his father's firm hand was a dedication, "A gift to my good friend, Buck Stone, true scholar and true friend, Little Ned."

    Joe put the book in his own pack. This was something he could never leave behind. He glanced at another book Buck enjoyed. He couldn't leave it either. After sorting through all the books and papers, Joe decided he couldn't leave a single sheet of paper. There was Buck's horse and mule. Transport was not a problem.

    "Come on, come on," Deacon urged. "Yer wastin' time. What're yuh goin' ta do with it, anyway? Hardly a soul out here kin make head or tail outta brainy stuff like thet."

    "Little Ned once spoke of a mission school in Oregon Territory. It could probably use these books. Buck's books might give them a start on a library." The idea grew on Joe. He would look up Little Ned's family. He had half brothers . . . ! The thought of meeting them pleased him so he clapped Deacon on the back. "I know where to go, Nez Perce country. Isn't that where a trapper friend of yours went to live?"

    Deacon thoughtfully scratched in his beard. "Yep, ol' Red Craig hitched a Nez Perce woman. Far as I remember, he figured on settlin' with her people on the Clearwater. Believe he said his ol' woman's papa is a big medicine man. Has a name somethin' like Thunder Head — Thunder Eyes, somethin' like thet."

    Upon leaving, the two trappers rode by the aspen grove. The moonlight outlined the rock covered grave. The moon's rays, reflecting on the gray granite stones, created a fuzzy halo that seemed to glow. The rustling aspens and the babbling stream joined together to create a lonesome, haunting tune. Joe closed his eyes to keep back the tears. The haunting harmony reminded him of the muted music of a chapel organ.

    They traveled through the night; even the horses and mules

seemed to feel the urgent need to hurry. As dawn began to break, Deacon's horse, cantering in the lead, shied, nearly pitching him off. The trailing mules snorted and bolted into the brush. Deacon and Joe scrambled to keep the pack string from running away. Even after snubbing them up close, the mules continued to toss their heads and snort. The horses held back, their big eyes wide and wild.

"These critters act like they smell fresh blood," Deacon said. "Maybeso a mountain lion. Keep yer eyes peeled whilst I sneak ahead an' hev a look."

Deacon barely took a few steps before stumbling over a large mound in the trail. "It's the Canuck's broomtail! Tarnation! It's had its throat slashed."

They ducked into the deep shadows. The hair on the back of Joe's neck bristled. Hideously painted Blackfeet warriors flashed before his eyes. How many savage eyes watched? How many deadly arrows pointed their way? From off the trail came an unearthly moan. Joe's blood ran cold. The moan turned into a stifled cry.

"Thet ain't no mountain lion; thet's a human bein'. Maybeso an Injun trick. Stay with the critters. I'll scout a bit."

Deacon slid away to disappear in the early morning gloom. Before long Joe heard him utter a startled oath. Joe followed the sound to find Deacon on his knees. "It's ol' Hawk Beak!" Deacon said. "Looks in bad shape, cold as a dead fish."

They hoisted the body from the gully where Hawk Beak had fallen and laid him on a grassy spot. The unconscious man had a bullet wound in the shoulder. A wicked slash across his forehead was caked with blood.

"I swear, someone near scalped the poor cuss," Deacon exclaimed. "Those cussed Blackfeet'll do anythin' ta count a coup. He's comin' around! What've yuh been upta anyways, tryin' ta take on the whole Blackfeet nation?" Deacon asked testily as Hawk Beak opened his eyes.

Hawk Beak struggled to sit up, his thin lips drawn in pain. "A war party ambushed us. Francois's quick thinkin' saved our hides — jumps off his hoss an' cuts the poor critter's throat. We flop behind the carcass usin' it as a barricade."

Hawk Beak gritted his teeth as Deacon pulled back his shirt to inspect the shoulder wound. "Injuns was everywhere. Francois sent a couple to the hereafter an' I got one, dropped him on top of the dead horse." Hawk Beak groaned. "Don't suppose yuh got a spot of medicinal whiskey? Could sure use a jolt; I'm feelin' mighty low."

Deacon impatiently dug in one of his packs. "What'n tarnation happened next? Here yer shot an' near scalped whilst Francois is missin', so's all yer livestock an' pelts."

"Francois hollers, 'lookout!' The mules spooked. I was tryin' to hold 'em when this here bullet struck. There I was, half outta my head when a scalpin' knife starts to bite, guess must've passed out."

"I cain't understand why they didn't finish the scalpin'. It ain't like these Blackfeet ta slip up on a sure coup like thet."

"Yuh don't need to sound so disappointed," Hawk Beak croaked. He got unsteadily to his feet. In the early morning light his sharp features were so pale he appeared bloodless. His right arm hung limp. "I ain't perzactly fit but we'd better vamoose. Look fer my critters. I ain't about to leave 'em behind."

A search for Hawk Beak's horse and mules proved fruitless. "Maybeso, Francois thought yuh done fer an' skedaddled with the whole kit an' caboodle," Deacon said. "He's not one ta leave anythin' valuable layin' about."

Hawk Beak swore. "Jest like the miserable rascal, left me high an' dry without findin' whether I lived or died."

"Never mind," Deacon said. "Main thing is ta get outta here afore those Injuns take a mind ta call again. Now, hold still." Deacon hurriedly cleaned and bandaged Hawk Beak's wounds. He and Joe then helped the wounded man aboard Deacon's horse. Deacon swung up behind to steady Hawk Beak in the saddle.

"Where we goin'?" Hawk Beak asked. "I ain't feelin' too smart."

"We cain't stay here," Deacon answered. "Best go south, straight fer Fort Hall."

For two days they traveled. Hawk Beak could barely sit the

saddle. He developed a fever and hacking cough. He could hardly swallow the morning gruel Deacon prepared. On the third day, in crossing a rough patch, Hawk Beak collapsed. He pitched head first to the ground and lay still as death. Deacon got to him first. Hawk Beak's eyes were rolled back; his breath came in short gasps.

Deacon shook his head. "The ol' boy's in a bad way. We'd best stop fer a spell an' . . ." Deacon stopped, his eyes fixed on the trail ahead. "Oh-oh! We're in trouble."

Joe glanced up. On the crest of a hill a party of Indian horsemen were outlined against the skyline. As they approached Deacon reached for his rifle, then left it in the boot. "Look ta be Shoshones. Could be worse. Maybeso, we kin palaver our way outta this mess."

Deacon clasped his hands in front of his chest, the sign of peace. He took two steps forward. "How," he greeted. "Sick man. Need medicine bad!" He pointed to Hawk Beak. The lead horseman came close to inspect the prone body. A rapid conversation among the Indians followed. Two riders wheeled their mounts about and disappeared. In a short while a horse trailing a travois appeared. The Indian leader pointed at the sick man and then at the travois.

"A-hoh!" Deacon uttered. "Like Ma always said, never look a gift horse in the face." They hoisted Hawk Beak onto the primitive vehicle and dragged him along the trail to their benefactors' village. An elder waved a hand toward a brush covered shelter. He clucked sympathetically as the trappers carried the wounded man inside.

"Medicine man come," he said and then disappeard

"Where did these people learn English?" Joe asked.

"These folks git around . . . do a bit of tradin' an' travelin'. Probably picked it up at Fort Hall er some sech place."

The elder returned with a bent, wizened old man. "Medicine man. Big medicine man," the elder explained.

The medicine man hunkered down by Hawk Beak. He listened to his chest, lifted an eyelid and studied the bloodshot orb. He stood up and brushed off his hands. "Much sick," he said. He stared at the feverish, pale face and repeated himself. "Man much sick." Pushing the elder in front of him, the medicine man scuttled outside.

"He's afeered," Deacon said. "If the medicine man don't cure the patient, shoot the medicine man. Thet's what he's thinkin'. It's up ta us. We hev ta do somethin' quick. Poor fella's breathin' worse than a horse with the heaves."

While the two men debated, an ancient woman passed the shelter. She saw the two white faces and paused to display buckskin articles decorated with beads and quills. She wanted to trade. "G'wan, ol' woman. We ain't got time fer thet." In his concern for Hawk Beak, Deacon spoke gruffly.

From within the shelter came the sound of Hawk Beak's distressed breathing. Like a hunting dog alert to the rustle of game birds, the old woman cocked her head, listened intently, then went directly into the shelter. Her knees creaking, she lowered herself to examine the sick man. Deacon gave her a hopeful glance. "Kin yuh do somethin'?"

The old woman did not answer, but her eyes glinted with a knowing look. She struggled to her feet and left. In a short while she returned with a basket reeking with the smell of skunk. She rolled up Hawk Beak's shirt. She emptied the contents of the basket on the sick man's bared chest. The odoriferous ingredients were expertly fashioned into a poultice. Afterward, she took a flat stick to force Hawk Beak's mouth open. She depressed his tongue and clucked at the sight. "Much bad," she said.

Once again she went away. This time she returned with a handful of small sticky burrs. To each burr she fastened a stout thread. She covered the burrs with a sticky mixture. The trappers learned later it was made of honey and tallow. With a notched stick, she forced the burr down Hawk Beak's throat until he gagged. She then pulled the burr out, bringing with it a coating of pus and bloody sputum. A particularly deep probe made Hawk Beak cough and splutter. He opened his eyes and stared wildly about. "What the blinkin' blazes is this ol' woman doin', torturin' me to death?" he rasped. He sniffed the air. "Keerist! I stink worse than a friggin' polecat. What's all this skunk cabbage doin' here?"

The old woman grinned. "Him quick better," she said.

In less than a week Hawk Beak got up to stand briefly and take a few steps. Several days later he prowled around the Indian camp, scattering squealing children and barking dogs. The tall, cadaverous trapper, with his shabby buckskins, long face, hooked beak and bad arm hanging limp, had the appearance of a stalking vulture. Shortly after the wounded man's first walk around the village, Deacon traded a few pelts for an Indian pony and made Hawk Beak a makeshift saddle by strapping a sheepskin to the pony's back. "Thet'll at least keep yuh from rubbin' the skin off yer arse," Deacon said.

"Yeah! Yeah!" Hawk Beak said doubtfully. "Anyways, it's better'n walkin'. We're wastin' time. I wanta git to Fort Hall afore thet Canuck trades my pelts an' skedaddles."

"First we gotta do somethin' fer these people," Deacon said, pulling on his beard. "If'n it hadn't been fer 'em yuh'd be sleepin' under a blanket of dirt. Maybeso, we kin gift the elder Buck's hand ax an' his knife, Betsy. Buck wouldn't mind. He was always kind ta the Injun. Now, the ol' woman, she's the one who saved yer hide. Maybeso, a slab of bacon an' bag of beans'll make her happy."

The trail south took the trappers west of the three Tetons. They passed Pierre's Hole where the mountain men had gathered for rendezvous in 1829 and 1832. From there Deacon led the way through miles of pungent sagebrush lands leading to Fort Hall on the bank of the Snake River. Lulled by the monotonous miles of sand and sagebrush, the sight of the white fort gleaming in the sun above a verdant valley, made even the mules take notice. They quickened their pace as if they knew they neared the end of the trail.

At the fort gates, the saddle-sore trappers wearily slid off their mounts and tethered the pack string. "Maybeso, we should celebrate with a spot of libation," Deacon suggested.

They walked by the cannon that guarded the courtyard and into the trading room. In his impatience to get to the bar, Hawk Beak, in spite of his bad arm, did a little hop and skip. They pushed through the door and stopped stock still. Joe's feeling of well-being vanished. In one corner, conversing with Francois, was the one person he had hoped never to see again -- One-Eye Link.

THE LAST RENDEZVOUS

XXIV

We must seek unity within. The time for division is over.
We must reach out to each other, come together and unite.
Peter MacDonald, Navajo

The sky above Lapwai Valley was clear and azure blue. Father Sun bathed the hillsides with a warmth that turned the grass to a rich brown. Small whirlwinds gathered up dust only to let it settle back down. Flocks of magpies chattered in the trees. Blue jays boldly darted about village grounds. A mother bear and her cub were seen on the creek bank, sending dogs barking and children screaming. A flight of white birds were seen for the first time that year. A rider on a galloping horse thundered up the Kooskooskie Trail shouting. "Hiya! Hiya! The salmon have come!"

People spilled out of the lodges on the run. Differences that had split families and made enemies of neighbors, were forgotten. Every able person in the village from babes to elders gathered at the river side to watch the silver tide sweep up the Kooskooskie. The excited throng laughed and joked as the first wave of salmon appeared. So thick were they, the bodies carpeted the river surface with a shiny sheen. Nets that long had been prepared were brought to the water's edge and cast into the churning, struggling horde. Men pushed canoes into the river. With special made dippers they scooped up fish as though ladling stew from a kettle. Women and children waded into the shallows at the mouth of Lapwai Creek to make catches by hand. Upstream mother bear thrust out a paw to hook salmon on her claws. Everyone wanted to have a hand in harvesting these creatures that had made the trek from the Great Water called ocean.

Long racks of the harvest quickly appeared in village open spaces, the orange of the split salmon flesh making a brilliant splash of color among the drab earth-topped lodges. The black and white magpies, blue jays and white gulls that had followed the silver tide from the Great Water, added to the colorful scene as they swooped to feast on the offal. The harvest grew until the village had been transformed into a field of orange. The people walked up and down the rows of drying fish and smiled. Their ceremonies of thanksgiving had been taken away but Mother Earth had not been offended. Her rewards were as great as ever before.

Not all members of the valley were filled with thoughts of thanksgiving and good will. A chilling pall had fallen over Raven Wing's log cabin lodge. The family took little interest in the salmon harvest. The death of his father had taken the joy out of Michael Two Feathers' life. The fantasies he dreamed of would never be realized. In his mind's eye he and his father would meet in buffalo country or at the place the hairy faced trappers called rendezvous. Once, when Teacher Spalding spoke of the land beyond the River of Many Canoes, an entrancing thought had occurred to him -- he and his father would live in the city called St. Louis; he would attend school in classrooms where books covered the walls. What a foolish thought that had been. At the moment his mother would not even allow him to attend the local mission school.

Gradually, Raven Wing noticed the change in her firstborn and was deeply troubled. What was wrong? The boy should be in the highest of spirits. He had the most promise of any youth in the tribe. He would be the greatest medicine man Lapwai Valley ever knew. She redoubled her efforts to please him every way she could.

The attention only made the heaviness in Michael's heart worse. It became more and more difficult to act like a person who possessed a powerful guardian spirit that guided him in everything he did. He ceased to visit the *tewat*, Thunder Eyes. He found the medicine man's hostility toward Missionary Spalding distasteful. He could not bring himself to join the gang of youth who harrassed Eliza Spalding. More and more he kept to himself, taking long rides into the mountains, sometimes remaining there overnight.

The first time Michael remained away from home overnight Raven Wing gave it little thought. Powerful medicine men had to renew themselves by communing with the spirits. In the deep primeval forest all creatures and things of Mother Earth whisper messaages to those who seek their help and knowledge. But when her firstborn returned, instead of the tranquil appearance of one who received spiritual wisdom and blessings, he appeared distraught. That night she heard him weeping.

Raven Wing was shocked and a little frightened. What had happened to her boy? Wild thoughts raced through her mind. Vision Seeker . . . he was the trouble. It had something to do with his journey to the rendezvous. Upon his return she had seen them speaking quietly. Her brother had brought news that shattered her firstborn's spirit. What could it be? "Aiiee!" Something serious had happened to Little Ned. Had he been wounded in battle? Could he have gone to the other side? She felt faint. She went outside and sat down on the porch bench. The flower garden Little Ned had painstakingly planted and cared for, greeted her. He had said he wanted her to have the wondrous beauty of Mother Earth at her front door.

"Ah!" He had been so good to her. She remembered clearly the first day they met. It was on the grasslands of Sun River where Lone Wolf had taken his hunting party. The hunters and their families were waiting for the buffalo to arrive. Instead, three hairy faced mountain men appeared, their packs loaded with trade goods. At first the big man with black hair did not seem special. He wore a wide brimmed hat and his face was covered with a mat of hair. Only after the hairy faces laid out their trade goods did she notice him. From his pack of trade goods came an item that obsessed her, a beautiful dress decorated with elk teeth. He held it up to her. Their eyes met. He spoke in his low, soft voice. She did not understand his words but she never forgot the thrill that coursed through her veins. His eyes caressed her like the breath of a soft summer breeze.

The thought that she might never see her Boston man again left Raven Wing feeling numb. Ah! Greed had turned her into a silly fool. She had wanted that elk skin dress so badly she had no thought of this good man. How cruelly she had treated him. Would she now have to pay the price for her scheming ways? Would she have to live the remainder of her life without a mate? Could she alone bare the awesome responsibility of rearing three sons? Again she reproached herself. Why had she left Little Ned, run away like a spoiled child? Francois was not worth Little Ned's big toe. If she had remained home they would be together. The boys would not be fatherless and she would have a man in her lodge.

For days Raven Wing kept her tortured thoughts to herself. One morning Vision Seeker appeared to take the boys riding. While her sons went to the pasture for their ponies, Raven Wing accosted him. "You brought bad news from the rendezvous," she bluntly stated.

Vision Seeker hesitated. He should have told her. She had a right to know. "Yes, your Boston man has made the journey to the other side."

"Oh!" Raven Wing put a hand to her lips to keep from crying out. The emptiness in her heart turned to a block of ice. Even though she feared the truth, hearing the words from Vision Seeker made it real. She darted inside, away from her brother's keen eyes.

#

The mission in Lapwai was struggling through a painful period. The upheaval caused by William Gray's vitriolic letters and his abrupt departure, continued. Reverend Asa Hall, the second missionary posted at Kamiah to learn the language of the Nimpau, found himself ostracized. A group influenced by Thunder Eyes, insisted he pay for the land his cabin occupied. Smith packed up his family and departed. On his way through Lapwai he stopped overnight with the Spaldings. Disappointed in losing a fellow worker, Spalding attempted to change his mind. Asa Smith bluntly refused. "There is no hope for the Indian Race," he said. "These people are doomed to destruction. All of our efforts have been wasted. They will never be civilized, at least not in our lifetime. I see only troubled times ahead."

Spalding dismissed Smith's dire prediction with a careless wave of his hand. Later he would know he should have taken it seriously. Thunder Eyes was only beginning his campaign to drive outsiders from Lapwai Valley. Spalding's newly built millrace dam became a target of Thunder Eye's expanding force of villains. They demolished it, rendering the gristmill and sawmill useless. When the dam was rebuilt they ruined the ditches that channeled irrigation water to the fields. In other ways the roisterers also frustrated the missionary. Spalding caught them playing buffalo dice, violating his no gambling edict. When he remonstrated they set his house afire. Spalding's best cows mysteriously disappeared and later were found dead. The missionary suspected Thunder Eyes' supporters of poisoning them. He discovered yet another group stealing his corn. For this and other malicious acts, the beleaguered missionary ordered the miscreants to be publicly whipped. No Nimpau would carry out the order so the missionary had to do it himself.

During the height of the disorders Thunder Eyes received additional support. Two mountain men appeared to take up farming: William "Red" Craig, who had married one of Thunder Eye's daughters, and Lariston who also had taken a Nimpau wife. Spalding, hopeful the newcomers would support his missionary efforts, called upon the mountain men who were building Craig's cabin.

"On week nights we hold prayer meetings and Bible study," Spalding informed the mountain men. "On the Sabbath we have Scripture readings, singing of hymns and a sermon. We have need for folks with good voice, especially people like yourselves who have been accepted by the Indian community. Perhaps you would like to take part. I invite you to read Scripture from the pulpit."

Red Craig studied the black-coated figure with a face as white as paste. The man ought to do a little honest work, he thought. "I have nothing against the Christian faith," he began, "but in all good conscience I cannot attend your sessions of worship or take part. The way you treat these people is flat out un-Christian-like. You blundered in here like a blind pig, knocking down everything they hold dear. From what I hear, you took advantage of them in every possible way. You tyrannize them. You belittle their way of life. You force them to do mission work with no pay. Have you ever stopped to listen to their problems? Of course not, you've been too busy trying to make them into what you call civilized folk."

"We are called to do the work of God," Spalding retorted. "God and the Church Board want these people in the fold of Christ."

"Ah, yes, the churchmen who sent you told you exactly how

to deal with these people, isn't that it? I'll wager not a one of them has been west of the Allegheny. Their knowledge comes strictly from study of the Scriptures. You and your upstanding cohorts are like mules wearing blinders. You can't see anything but what's straight in front of you. You balk at anything that interferes with your narrow views. Let me tell you something your study of the Scriptures has failed to reveal. For centuries these people have made a go of living in this wilderness. Instead of pooh-poohing the way they live, you should praise it, borrow some of their wisdom. You would do yourself a lot of good and make them feel worthwhile. You can push these people just so far, then watch out. Frankly, unless you and your do-gooder churchmen don't change your ways I, for one, would be happy to see you leave."

Spalding was too shocked to respond. He had come dripping with good will and received the scolding of his life. He rode home in such a fit of fury he took the Lord's name in vain. He wrote in his journal, "I have seen enough of mountain men to last me a lifetime."

#

To please his mother, Michael had resumed his visits to receive medicine man lessons from Thunder Eyes. He soon met Red Craig. The redheaded mountain man had known Little Ned and took special care to be kind to his fallen friend's son. He approved of Michael's medicine man study. "The white man won't admit it, but native medicine men know many helpful things our medical men could and should learn. For centuries the natives have relied on medicine men and have remained healthy and strong. Medicine men know the healing qualities of roots, plants, barks and a tranquil mind. They care for the whole person, not just the injury or infection that occurs to one part of the body. Someday, the things medicine men practice will be recognized by our medical profession. That will be a good day for everyone's well-being."

The mountain man's words were balm to Michael's sore heart. Yet, Red Craig spoke of other things that were cause for alarm. Craig's and Thunder Eyes' stand against Spalding left Michael in a quandary. It was not right to destroy things and harass people who were trying to do good. The destruction of the millrace dam and the irrigation system disturbed him so much he sought out Vision Seeker.

"Why do these people quarrel like crows fighting over a kernel of corn?" he asked.

Vision Seeker studied his nephew. The boy was growing up. He was seeing the world through adult eyes. The truth of the matter was hard to explain. Two peoples of different backgrounds, with different religions and different ways of life had come together. When they lived apart these differences went unseen or were given little heed. Now that these people attempted to coexist, their differences popped up like gopher mounds in a pasture field. Unless these differences were recognized and accepted, their presence would keep the people restive and uncomfortable. "Aah!" he inwardly groaned. Would life ever return to the tranquillity his people enjoyed in the old days?

"We quarrel among ourselves," Michael continued. "The mission folk quarrel among themselves. We quarrel with the missionaries and the missionaries quarrel with Thunder Eyes and the mountain men. Where does it all end? What is to become of us if this goes on and on?"

Vision Seeker studied the distant horizon. Clouds hovered over the hills. The breeze carried the smell of rain. He did not know how to answer his nephew. He saw much darkness ahead. He feared many, many storms would come before light shone bright again on the land of the Nimpau.

THE LAST RENDEZVOUS

XXV

Trust the friends of today as if they will be enemies tomorrow.
Balthasar Gracian

The Fort Hall trading room crackled with tension. The scene was like a badly staged play. For a split second the actors were struck dumb, frozen in place only to recover and pick up their cues at the same time. Every eye was on Hawk Beak, who leveled his rifle and thumbed the hammer back to full cock. The deadly message set the actors in motion. Francois backed away, his swarthy face the color of chalk. The trading room clerks ducked behind the counter. Link alertly moved his bulk to one side. Forced against the wall, Francois held up one hand in a gesture of surrender. The other arm, swathed in bandages, was held across his chest by a sling fashioned from a strip of rawhide.

"Hawk! I thought you were done for!" The dark eyes shifted from trapper to trapper only to come back to the menacing rifle.

"Yuh sure didn't waste time to make certain, didja?" Holding the rifle level with his one good arm, Hawk Beak walked steadily toward his cornered victim.

"Hold on!" Francois barked. "You can't shoot a man down in cold blood! Don't you see, I was shot in that fracas, too." He gestured at his immobilized arm. "I just made it away by the skin of my teeth."

Hawk Beak stopped and brought the rifle muzzle level with Francois' midsection. "Quit squallin'. I ain't gut shot yuh yet. I'm after my outfit an' pelts yuh took."

"They're yours. I haven't mislaid a single pelt."

Somewhat mollified, Hawk Beak lowered the rifle barrel. "Yuh'd better not be lyin'. Every pelt'd better be jest as I packed 'em."

"A course, a course. Why don't you put that rifle away and have a snort?"

"Thet's what I like ta hear," Deacon said, easing the tension. "This ain't perzactly a rendezvous gatherin', but still a proper time an' place ta do a bit of hurrahin'."

Like strange dogs guardedly sniffing each other, the mountain men converged. Joe kept his thumb on the hammer of the Henry and stationed himself some distance from the bulk of One-Eye Link. The jug a fort clerk promptly handed over at Francois' urgent command, began to make the rounds. As the contents decreased, wariness turned to garrulousness.

"I swear, I'm sorrowful 'bout Buck Stone's passin'," Link said. "We wasn't partic'lar friends. It's jest thet another good trapper departed this earth. Buck knew the mountains better'n 'most anyone. When a fella like thet bites the dust, yuh git ta wonderin', whose next?"

Link looked as though he had experienced a hard year. His buckskins carried more than the usual amount of grease and dirt. The patch that covered the missing eye limply hung from his forehead, leaving much of the grievous scar exposed. His scraggly, uncombed beard had taken on streaks of white. For a moment Joe almost liked the rough old cob.

"The ol' rendezvous bunch's fadin' away like spring snow," Link continued. "I hear Ewin' Young took sick an' died. Joe Meek an' Doc Newell're workin' farmin' claims in the Willamette Valley. Big Neck Bridger's built hisself a tradin' post on Green River. Then there's Sublette an' Louie Vasquez killin' buffalo. Yep, the handwritin's on the wall. There ain't goin' ta be any more rendezvous. There's hardly a trapper left in the mountains."

Joe was so relieved not to be involved in another confrontation with Link, he leaned against the counter and let his thoughts wander. The one-eyed trapper's presence brought back poignant memories of Buck Stone. The first day he met Buck they went to tackle Link in Madam Melissa's back rooms. At the rendezvous Buck's jousting scheme saved him in another encounter with Link. Joe almost looked on the one-eyed man with fondness. Link and his rascality had done much to influence the course of his life. If it hadn't been for Link, Buck Stone would probably never have taken him trapping. Little Ned would have sent him packing back home.

Deacon, who had matched the others drink for drink, handed the jug to Hawk Beak and turned to Joe. "Maybeso, it's time ta leave. No one's guardin' the animals. Everythin' we own's out thar waitin' ta be stole."

Their departure was barely noticed. Hawk Beak was in the midst of an account of the Blackfeet raid. He had forgotten his animosity toward Francois and gave him credit for saving the day. The animals were where the trappers left them, tethered to a hitching rail. Deacon led the way to a cottonwood grove where they made camp. After unloading the pack mules and tending to the horses, Deacon flopped on the ground. With his head propped on a pack of pelts, he instantly fell asleep and began to snore. Joe built a fire and started to cook. When the food was ready he aroused Deacon. The rotund trapper awakened with a snort. Through bleary eyes, he wildly looked around.

"Ah!" he said at last. "I was back in the valley. The Blackfeet was comin'. Buck was runnin' . . ." Deacon shook his head. "I'll never fergit thet day as long as I live. Blast ol' Hawk Beak, why does he keep blabbin' about it? Where is the galoot? Didn't he show up? I hope he didn't get inta a fuss with the Canuck. If Francois didn't hev his arm in a sling I'd swear he tried ta do Hawk Beak in fer his pelts. Yuh saw how sheepish he looked."

Near dark, Hawk Beak, trailed by his horse, Blaze, and two loaded mules, meandered around the corner of the fort. "Got my outfit," he announced. "Don't think the Canuck had a chance to touch it. Factor Grant tells me he's been low with gunshot ever since he showed up."

To give Hawk Beak a chance to recover his strength, Deacon insisted they spend a full week at Fort Hall. "Now thet Hawk's got his outfit, there's no need ta hurry off. Might as well dicker with Factor Grant on the pelts. He'll be tightfisted, but it's better'n packin' 'em all over hell's half acre an' still git nothin' fer 'em."

Near the week's end two trappers rode in from the west. Sourdough Sam, noted for making uneatable biscuits, and one-legged, Peg Leg Smith, both acquaintances of Hawk Beak and Deacon, stopped by the camp.

"What've yuh two varmints been up ta, anyhow?" Deacon asked.

"We was Oregon way," Sourdough answered. "Didn't much like what we saw. People spillin' over the land like flood water after a thaw, wrong kind, if yuh ask me. Preachers're everywhere, sermonizin' agin' womin an' whiskey. Place's drier'n Peg Leg's wooden leg. Cain't git a drink nowhere. Missions're poppin' up like toadstools. Jason Lee's goin' up an' down the Willamette Valley spreadin' religion like barnyard manure; he's even got ol' timers like Joe Meek down on their knees.

"On the way up the Columbia there's Wascopum, a' outfit of Methodists. Bless me if those folks ain't tryin' ta tame the Wascos, Deschutes an' Chinooks. On the Walla Walla Doc Whitman ministers ta the Cayuse. We ran inta ol' Red Craig an' John Lariston. They've settled near a mission on the Clearwater. From what they said, things ain't goin' too good. Claim the Injuns're gittin' their belly full of a pulpit poundin' preacher named Spaldin'. Yep, Oregon Territory ain't what it was. More people than yuh kin hit with a stick. Say, ain't thet Francois, the Canuck?" The trappers turned to see Francois on a tall black horse loping along the trail to Fort Boise.

"Look's fit as a fiddle," Hawk Beak observed. "Maybeso, he wasn't as bad off as he put on. Where do yuh suppose he's goin'? Look at him! Ain't he the fancy dan? Thet saddle has enuff silver on it to start a mint."

"Probably up ta no good," Sourdough commented. "There's plenty of yarns of his scalawagness down Fort Vancouver way. Seems he got inta a fix at the Injun tradin' center in The Dalles. Loses his nags in a hoss race then goes mad an' proceeds ta cut the throat of a Chinook, takes his canoe an' all the poor fella's kit an' caboodle. Nasty business. Course no one did nothin' 'bout it, the dead man bein' Injun." Sourdough took a pull from a jug and handed it to

Hawk Beak, who had trouble handling it with his one good arm.

"What's the matter, ol' hoss?" Sourdough asked. "Yer a proper mess with a bad wing an' from those marks on yer forehead I'd say someun near lifted yer hair."

"Hmm," Peg Leg grunted when Hawk Beak related the story of his wounds. "Maybeso yuh should head west an' see Doc Whitman. He sure fixed up ol' hoss Bridger. 'Twas the '35 rendezvous, if I remember correctly. The doc cut this whoppin' big arra outta ol' Jim slicker'n yuh kin skin a cat."

"Yeah, I remember." Hawk Beak flexed his arm and shoulder. The pain made him wince. "I cain't go on like this. I couldn't catch a beaver if it hopped into my pocket."

The next morning Peg Leg and Sourdough continued on their journey east. The three former members of Buck Stone's brigade went in the opposite direction, following the Snake River west to Fort Boise on the route to Dr. Marcus Whitman's mission. From Fort Boise they forded the Snake to enter a rocky, desert region, then crossed a second river, the one Peter Skene Ogden named the Malheur.

As the miles passed, Joe's excitement grew. Every step brought them nearer the homeland of Little Ned's Indian family. He pictured himself greeting his half brothers. Should he make it known Little Ned was also his father? What would the family say? What would they do? Would they welcome him into their home? If they did how should he act? How would it be to have a dark-skinned stepmother? Would she speak English or would they have to resort to sign language? Should he introduce himself as Little Ned's son or should he keep the relationship to himself? They might not like to have a palefaced half brother and stepson. Thoughts such as these occupied Joe's mind as the miles passed.

The trappers entered the dry, rolling brown hills that hid Powder River. A day later they rode over the camas prairie at the foot of the Blue Mountains. Here lived the Bannock, led by warrior Hawlack. The Bannock leader was known to stop travelers and demand tribute, often stripping small parties of all they possessed. Aware of this, the trappers kept their eyes peeled and firearms ready. They passed through without incident. Only at a distance did they see signs of human habitation. Herders were rounding up livestock.

After two days travel through forested trails of the Blue Mountains, the trappers came to the western edge of the forest. Extending to the horizon was an expanse of rolling hills. They were now within a day's ride of Waiilatpu, the place where Peg Leg Smith said Doctor Whitman ministered to the Cayuse. In the distance an Indian camp sent up tendrils of smoke. Horses grazed everywhere. *Maumin*, the natives called them. Many of the animals stood fifteen or more hands high. Most were colorfully marked with white patches, black patches, others with zebra streaks down their withers; several were as speckled and spotted as turkey eggs.

Hawk Beak was impressed. "Francois said these people like nuthin' better'n a good hoss race. I'd sure like to put 'em to test against ol' Blaze. I betcha he could out run every durned one."

"Quit frettin' over thet hoss race yuh didn't get at the rendezvous," Deacon rasped. "The first thing yuh gotta do is git yerself fixed up. Trappin' season'll soon be here, an' look at yuh. Yuh got as much chance of trappin' beaver as a sick grasshopper escapin' from a hill of red ants."

That evening the trappers made camp on the Umatilla River. A group of inquisitive Cayuse horsemen rode up to inspect them. The leader held out the flat palm of his hand and greeted them in broken English.

"Friends. Welcome. You come trade?"

"No," Deacon replied. "We come to see Medicine Man Whitman."

"Ah! Mission man. Small day ride." He pointed to the northeast. "You want see trail?"

Deacon shook his head. "I'm sure we kin manage."

The leader held up his hand again. "Peace," he said. The horsemen reined away. They trotted a short distance and then, with a whoop, kicked their mounts into a gallop.

"Nice friendly people," Joe said, watching them ride away. Little did he know the Cayuse leader who greeted them was Stickus, who one day would become a good friend.

The next afternoon the trappers sighted the mission. In a pleasant open space, with cottonwoods in the background and a stream curving behind, sat several adobe buildings, the one in the foreground quite imposing. Except for the flat tablelands rising in the distance, the panorama was not unlike a New England farm scene. A corral encircled several horses and cows. Behind the main mission building a blacksmith forge gave off a faint trail of smoke. To the south was a cultivated plot of ground; neat rows of vegetable crops ran its length. The only unkempt ground was a steep brush covered hill on the far side of the mission grounds.

The domestic scene gave Joe a feeling of intense homesickness. So severe was the sensation, tears smarted beneath his eyelids. A woman in gingham with a sunbonnet shading her face came out of the large adobe building. She walked slowly along a path that led toward the hill. At the foot of the slope she stopped to kneel. Engrossed, the trappers pulled up to watch. The lady seemed to talk to herself. She placed something on the ground, got to her feet and retraced her steps. Later the trappers would learn Narcissa Whitman had been visiting the grave of her daughter, little Alice Clarissa, who drowned in the Walla Walla River the year before.

"Tildy now would look something like the lady in gingham," Joe thought. It was a year since he had written to tell her of their father's death. How had she managed? Were Granny and Granddad all right? He felt ashamed of himself. He should go home and help out. He was avoiding his responsibilities the same as Little Ned had done.

At the corral the trappers tethered their animals and attempted to beat away the trail dust. For a moment they debated what would make a suitable gift. The presence of the lady in gingham made them want to put their best foot forward.

"I bought a can of molasses at Fort Boise," Hawk Beak said. "It sure hits the spot with Injun women."

"Yuh crazy galoot, these people're civilized. Yuh cain't gift 'em stuff like thet," Deacon chided.

The trappers didn't need to worry about proper gifts. Narcissa Whitman, a gracious lady with sparkling gray eyes, made them feel at home. She invited the trappers into the adobe building to meet her husband. The soft spoken doctor rose from a rocking chair. He thoughtfully studied Deacon and Hawk Beak.

"Seems we've met before. Weren't you folks at Ham's Fork on Green River in '35?"

"Yep," Hawk Beak answered, happy to be remembered. "Yuh carved an arra outta ol' Jim Bridger slicker'n a whistle. Far as I know he's been right as rain ever since."

Doctor Whitman smiled. "Always good to put a person right. That's what doctoring is all about."

"Thet's 'zactly why we's here, to git put right. Yuh see . . ." Hawk Beak went into a graphic account of the encounter with the Blackfeet. Before he finished, the doctor had Hawk Beak's shirt off examining the wound.

"Yes, there's the lead. Shouldn't be difficult to remove. It's so near the surface you can see the color." The doctor pointed to a grayish lump close to the shoulder blade.

"Consarn it, if Hawk Beak wasn't sech a snivelin' baby, I could've cut thet out meself," Deacon said.

"Removing the bullet is simple. Healing the injured tissue afterward is the difficult part." As he spoke the doctor took a shiny instrument from a wooden case. Before the lanky trapper could resist, the doctor had him laid out on his stomach. Moments later a chunk of lead popped onto the floor.

Deacon picked up the bloodied object and wiped it clean on his buckskin shirt. "Tarnation! Thet didn't come from no Injun firearm," he exclaimed. "Only shootin' iron I know thet carries a load like this is Francois' Hawken."

THE LAST RENDEZVOUS

XXVI

*Humanness is not a thing which can be ordered by law.
It is an ideal to be lived.*

Luther Standing Bear, Lakota

In Lapwai, one hundred twenty miles east of Waiilatpu, the turmoil that plagued Reverend Spalding began to ease. Unexpectedly, two of his chief detractors, Red Craig and John Lariston, picked up and departed. Spalding watched them go with satisfaction. "If I never see another mountain man, it will be all right with me," he told his wife, Eliza.

However, there were niggling reminders the men were not gone for good. They had left behind their Nimpau wives. This was not unnatural for mountain men. They had the reputation for discarding old wives and picking up new ones. This ungodly behavior disgusted Spalding. It was another reason he wanted to see the end of mountain men in Lapwai. Their sinful ways were abhorrent examples for his flock. Spalding's joy was short-lived. News soon reached him Craig and Lariston had traveled to the Willamette Valley to induce more mountain men to make Lapwai their home.

Except for a few annoying forays by Thunder Eyes' destructive followers, the summer months in Lapwai Valley passed peacefully and productively. The people returned to work on the millrace and damaged dam. Farmers planted and cultivated their crops. Herdsmen delivered and cared for foals in the pasture lands. School reopened. Once again the discordant sounds of classroom recitations echoed across the mission compound.

On days when they could escape Raven Wing's watchful eyes, Michael and Young Wolf made it a practice to sit in the shade near the classroom windows and recite the lessons with the students inside. The desire to take part was stronger than the fear of punishment they would receive if caught by their mother. The brothers' actions did not go unnoticed. Running Turtle, who still had hopes of getting his nephews back into school, discovered them one day engrossed in the classroom recitation. The sight left him depressed and angry. The boys should not have to sit outside like this. What could he do? Pleading with Raven Wing only would make matters worse. He decided if they could not go to the classroom he would bring the classroom to them. He copied down the lessons. After school, he filched paper and books from supply cupboards and gave them to the boys.

Running Turtle was not as clever as he thought. Nothing missed the eyes of Eliza Spalding. She noticed Running Turtle's furtive manner and the bulge two books made under his hunting shirt. She planned to stop him in the schoolyard but when the time came she had a change of heart. She also had been aware of Raven Wing's sons sitting against the schoolhouse wall with mouths open like two fledglings expecting to be fed. "What a shame, having to steal to learn," she uttered to herself as Running Turtle hurried the brothers away to disappear behind a locust thicket. When Running Turtle reappeared his hunting shirt had regained its normal shape. The two younger boys skipped away from the locust patch, each clasping a book to his chest. Eliza Spalding shook her head in dismay. Books and paper were scarce. When Reverend Spalding made his weekly inventory he surely would notice the shortage. He would demand an accounting and she would have to tell him. She would receive a scolding and Running Turtle would lose the opportunity to attend the seminary. What should she do? She dropped on her knees to ask God for the answer.

From his hillside perch, Vision Seeker observed most everything that happened in the valley. He, too, saw the boys stealthily approach the schoolhouse to listen and repeat the lessons. Then for days they did not appear. Instead of going to the schoolhouse every morning, they rode their black and white ponies up the valley to disappear in the hillside brush where they remained for hours. Vision Seeker's first thought was that they plotted mischief. Perhaps to please Thunder Eyes, Michael, along with his younger brother, had joined forces with the medicine man's troublemakers. They were meeting at a secret hideaway in the hillside brush to plan their destructive campaign against Missionary Spalding. With this thought in mind, one morning Vision Seeker followed the boys. Slipping up silently, he caught them leaning against the side of a rocky draw. Each boy had a book in his hand, avidly reading aloud. Vision Seeker listened in amazement. The boys were surprisingly good readers, but where did they get the books? Ashamed of spying on them, Vision Seeker started to leave. In turning about, he dislodged a pebble that bounced down the slope. The startled boys snapped the books shut and thrust them inside their shirts.

"Who is there?" Michael called out.

Vision Seeker did not answer. He remained motionless until the boys decided the pebble had been dislodged by geckos or the ground squirrels that made their homes on the hillside. When they resumed reading, Vision Seeker slipped quietly away, irked with himself and with his sister. If the boys wanted to learn so badly, why should they not return to school? It was far better for them to study in the classroom than in a dry, rocky gully where snakes, scorpions and sand wasps abounded. He rode along so deep in thought he about collided with a rider coming down the trail from the south. It took him a second to recognize the man wearing a wide-brimmed sombrero. He sat tall on a handsome black horse with a white star on its forehead. The saddle twinkled with silver, as did a belt around the man's waist. Then Vision Seeker took in the face: dark eyes set too close together; skin the color of polished leather; a thin mustache over equally thin, unsmiling lips. The most recognizable feature of all was the left ear; nearly half of it was missing.

"Francois!" Vision Seeker uttered the name with such revulsion the rider wheeled to a stop. His right hand went to the bone handle of the knife at his belt.

"Stay away," Francois snarled. "Little Ned is dead. I now can safely take your sister for a wife. We will have a Christian marriage. No longer will the preacher say we live in sin. There is no reason for us to be enemies."

Vision Seeker stared into the cold hard eyes. He could not

stand the sight of the man, but what could he do? The half-breed trapper was right. Little Ned was no more on Mother Earth. Raven Wing was free to chose a new mate. He had no right to interfere. He wheeled his mount around. Michael and Young Wolf should be forewarned, particularly Michael, who was terrified of the cruel man.

Vision Seeker met the brothers as they left the draw with the books under their arms. They didn't have time to hide them from Vision Seeker's keen gaze. They looked at him foolishly, prepared for a scolding. Vision Seeker paid no attention to the books. Francois' sudden appearance and the effect it would have on the brothers, was uppermost in his thoughts. Young Wolf had little to fear. Francois had fathered him. It was Michael who would suffer.

"Ride ahead," Vision Seeker told Young Wolf. "Someone is waiting for you at the cabin. No, not you," he said as Michael reined away to follow his brother. As soon as Young Wolf left, Vision Seeker turned to Michael. He didn't have to say a word. Michael's face had gone pale. Somehow he sensed why he was held back.

"Is he here?" Michael asked, his voice hoarse.

"Yes, says he will stay with your mother," Vision Seeker said. "He can do so now without fear of Missionary Spalding. With Little Ned gone your mother and Francois are now free to marry if they desire."

The stricken look on Michael's face was terrible to see. "What can I do? Where can I go? I cannot stay in the same lodge with that man."

Vision Seeker attempted to think of consoling words but what could he say or do? The unexpected turn of events made his blood boil. From now on he would have to stand aside -- watch the arrogant Francois take over the care and guidance of Raven Wing's sons. When they married, Francois had the legitimate right to take Raven Wing and the boys anywhere he wanted and rule them anyway he pleased.

"Perhaps Francois has changed. He is willing to have a Christian wedding. That is a good sign. Who knows, he may become an important member of the village," Vision Seeker finally said.

"Wagh!" Michael uttered in disgust. His uncle was no help at all. He kicked his black and white mount into a gallop. He had to catch up with Young Wolf. If they approached him together perhaps Francois would not be mean.

"The book! Leave it with me!" Vision Seeker called out. "Taking it home will cause trouble."

The warning did not penetrate the torturous emotions that pressed against Michael's brain. The grim thought of a future with Francois as a member of the family crowded everything else from his mind. "Ah!" he groaned. There was no catching Young Wolf. He would have to face Francois alone. He tethered the black and white pony away from Francois' stomping black stallion. He trotted up the porch steps, took a deep breath and pushed through the cabin door.

Vision Seeker was right, the book should have been left behind. Although Michael had slipped it under his shirt, Francois' dark, searching eyes immediately spotted the bulge in the buckskin. "What are you hiding?" he demanded. The sight of the book infuriated Francois. He already had Young Wolf's in his hand. "You have both disobeyed your mother."

For a moment Michael thought Francois would throw the books into the fire. Instead, he waved them in front of Michael's face. "We are going to start by doing things right. We don't want these damned missionaries down on our necks again. The first thing we do is take the books back." He shoved them into Michael's hand and pointed him and Young Wolf toward the door.

Much to Michael's embarrassment, the three of them marched down the trail and through the village toward the mission grounds. Michael led the way, Young Wolf followed and Francois brought up the rear. It seemed to Michael everyone in Lapwai came out to stare. Spotted Badger shouted a taunt but quickly shut up under Francois' furious glare. At the mission house Francois rapped the front door with the butt end of his quirt. Reverend Spalding appeared. When he saw Francois' upraised quirt, his already pale face turned a shade whiter. He opened his mouth but no words came out.

"These boys are returning your two books. I don't know how they got them and don't care." Francois took the books from Michael and thrust them into Spalding's hands. Before the stunned preacher could say a word, Francois turned and motioned the two boys away. Back through the village they marched. Popping out of their lodges like prairie dogs, the villagers once again gathered to stare.

The following days were miserable ones for Michael. Francois kept him on the run. If he did not move quickly, Francois gave him a slap alongside the head. While he was moving the pallets and pieces of furniture around in the cabin to please Francois, the buckskin pouch which held Michael's two feathers fell on the floor. Before Francois could notice, Michael scooped the pouch up and thrust it inside his shirt. As quickly as he could get away, he ran to the field where Vision Seeker was preparing the herd for the trek to fresh pasture in the high country. Michael handed the pouch to his uncle.

"The sacred feathers," he said. "I fear for them. In your hands they will be safe."

"Yes, they will be safe with me." Vision Seeker studied the woebegone face. "Things are not good?"

"Awful! Mother is so happy to have a man in the lodge she lets him do anything he wants."

Vision Seeker stared at the far side of the valley. How could he help the boy? The brown hills, simmering in the late summer sun, did not provide an answer.

THE LAST RENDEZVOUS

XXVII

*Man is wholly the product of the environment
that nourishes and raises him . . . .*
Mikhail A. Bakanin

Life at Whitman's mission took the trappers by surprise. "Idle hands are tools of the Devil," was a slogan by which the missionaries lived. While dew was still on the grass, tillers began cultivating the row crops. Smoke from the blacksmith shop began to rise. A racket loud enough to awaken the dead resounded across the mission grounds. Horseshoes, plow shares, latches, clamps, hoes, shovels and other necessary tools and equipment were pressed, pounded and ground into shape by workers who had traveled across the continent to help "civilize the pagan Cayuse."

Occupants of the mission house were equally industrious. Narcissa Whitman had taken on the task of rearing two half blood children: Mary Ann Bridger, daughter of Big Neck Bridger, and Helen Mar Meek, daughter of Joe Meek. After breakfast things were put away, the girls, under Narcissa's direction, began a series of chores: scrubbed floors; aired bedding; fetched wood and water. Then came Scripture reading and classroom studies. There was always a great coming and going from the nearby Cayuse village. Men, women and children appeared at a moment's notice to borrow, bring a sick child to be doctored, or merely to watch the white man toil.

While the trappers waited for Hawk Beak's wounds to heal, Joe pitched in to help with mission chores. The farm atmosphere and the educated Whitmans made him feel at home. He helped with the harvest, plowed a field to be planted in winter wheat, fixed fence and did odd jobs in the same manner as if he were on Granddad Jennings' farm. His busyness annoyed Deacon.

"Fer tarnation's sake! Yuh take ta farmin' like a beaver takes ta gnawin' aspens. Tain't fitten fer a mountain man ta be doin' sech belittlin' work."

THE LAST RENDEZVOUS

Early in the fall a handful of immigrants meandered down the Blue Mountain slopes, across the rolling grasslands and into the mission compound. The travelers were on their way to the Willamette Valley and stopped at Waiilatpu to rest and replenish their supplies. The missionaries greeted the newcomers with great fervor.

"You are the advance guard of thousands who will follow," Doctor Whitman enthused. "You can be likened to Moses and his disciples who led their people across the Red Sea and into the Promised Land."

Joe and Deacon, watching the party of settlers ride into the mission grounds, were amused at the royal reception. The people and equipment were in the sorriest state possible. The horses and pack mules were as thin and bony as starvelings. The people shuffled along so worn and tired they could barely lift their feet above ruts in the road. Skinny dogs trailed the column, their tails drooping; their ribs resembled hairy washboards.

A body of Cayuse came to see the immigrants arrive. They were silent; their expressionless faces did not reveal a single clue as to their thoughts. After the last ragged plodder entered the mission grounds, they quietly filed back to their lodges.

"I'd say the natives ain't perzactly pleased ta see these folks," Deacon observed. "Cain't say I blame 'em. How'd yuh like ta see this riffraff on yer doorstep?"

The next day a delegation of elders from the Cayuse village strode purposefully up to the mission house and banged on the door. Doctor Whitman came out. The Indian men crowded around, everyone talking at once. The doctor raised a hand to quell the turmoil. The trappers could not hear what he said, but it did not satisfy the delegation. The leader brandished a hand ax. The missionary did not appear disturbed. He spoke again and held up his hand in the gesture of peace. The Cayuse delegation departed but a sullen mood hung over the mission grounds like a menacing cloud.

"They are afraid these people will settle here and more will join them," Whitman explained. "They're upset now, but they'll soon cool down."

THE LAST RENDEZVOUS 217

Dr. Whitman misjudged the temper of the Cayuse. That night a group of young men broke into the mission house. Shouting threats and banging on doors and walls, they turned the sleeping occupants out in their night clothes. Alarmed by the racket, the newly arrived immigrants seized weapons and ran to the rescue, but Missionary Whitman waved them away. He scolded the intruders and told them to go home. The disgruntled group departed peacefully, but hardly anyone on the mission grounds got any sleep that night.

"I ain't sure I like livin' amongst these Cayuses," Deacon complained the following morning as the trappers tended to the livestock. "I feel as weak an' worthless as yestiday's coffee grounds. Tarnation! Ain't thet ol' Red Craig an' John Lariston comin' up the road. Hey! Yuh varmints, are yuh lost?" he shouted a greeting.

The two horsemen entering the mission gate pulled up. "I'll be switched! What are you scalawags doing here, getting religion?" the lead rider, a man with a red beard, asked. The horsemen dismounted. The four veteran trappers exchanged slaps on the back and jovial slander. "You look as puny as a skinned muskrat," Red Craig said to Hawk Beak. "Come over to Lapwai and I'll fatten you up."

Before Hawk Beak could respond, Doctor Whitman came to welcome the arrivals. He invited them all into the house. "Since you just came from the valley you must tell us what's happening down there." The mountain men sat down at the kitchen table, their buckskin covered bigness filling the room. Over coffee and fresh baked bread, Red Craig and John Lariston reported the news. The talk turned from valley activities to troubles with the Cayuse. Joe sat quietly watching and listening. The picturesque language of the mountain men took him back to the gab sessions when Buck Stone, Gimpy, Little Ned, Deacon and Hawk Beak were planning the trip into the Bighorns. How long ago that seemed and how much had happened since then. He had to choke down a lump in his throat. Little Ned and Buck were gone and so was young Clay . . .

"I wish you would have a talk with these Cayuse," Doctor Whitman said to Red Craig. "I can't get across to them that these people who have crossed the plains are not out to take their land or their herds. Perhaps someone who speaks their language better than I can explain.

Red Craig pulled on his square beard. "I don't think it'll do much good." However, the following morning he visited the Cayuse camp and spoke with Tiloukaikt, the leader who had taken over from Umtippe, the man who played such an important role in the death and burial of little Alice Clarissa. Craig returned to the mission looking glum.

"From the looks of yuh, I guess things didn't go so good?" Deacon observed.

"I doubt if they believed a word I said. These people are not dumb. This handful of immigrants is only the beginning. Soon there'll be plenty more. So they are heading for the Willamette Valley, that doesn't mean they'll pass through without causing trouble. I don't envy the Whitmans. They're in for rough times ahead. Anyways, I'm off to Lapwai. Why don't you folks come along? The climate isn't much different there, but it's home."

Deacon and Joe readily accepted Red Craig's invitation. Hawk Beak would also have accepted, but Doctor Whitman advised against riding until his wound had properly healed. Joe barely could suppress his excitement. Within hours he would set eyes on his father's Indian home. The journey took the trappers across rolling plains with high bunch grass that swayed and rustled in the dry wind. They crossed the Snake and followed the Clearwater. The plain gave away to brown, barren hills. Everywhere rocky outcroppings jutted to the surface. They came to a rise that overlooked the valley where Lapwai Creek emptied into the Clearwater. Near the mouth of the creek lay the mission buildings, almost lost among a forest of tipi lodges.

"I hope these people're not fixin' ta go ta war," Deacon said apprehensively. "Cayuse country looked bad but this looks worse."

Craig and Lariston pulled up to study the mission grounds and Indian encampment. "Nothing to get nervous about," Red said. "Appears the reverend's having one of his revivals. Indians come from all over their homeland to hear Spalding preach his hell's fire, damnation sermons and to partake of the feast he gives afterward."

Joe's eyes could not take in everything fast enough. The settlement was far different than he had envisioned. Instead of an encampment like that of Little Antlers' Cheyenne village, Lapwai was a mixture of long earth covered lodges, log buildings and buffalo hide covered tipis. A heavy layer of smoke hung over the setting, rising from dozens of fires where pots boiled and spits of meat roasted. Youngsters and dogs dashed about, shouting and barking. In the flat land beyond camp, young men roosted on a corral railing watching a rider break a horse. On the far side of the valley horses grazed under the watchful eyes of two herders.

"Yep, the reverend is pacifying the natives," Craig caustically observed. "They were fussing when we left, and unless I miss my guess, they'll fuss again. The effects of sermonizing only lasts so long."

"Don't yuh approve of savin' souls?" Deacon asked.

"Not the way Spalding does it. He's ruining good people by turning their lives upside down."

"The fact yer hitched ta a medicine man's daughter don't influence yer opinion, does it?" Deacon asked slyly.

Craig laughed. "Not smart to go against the wishes of your father-in-law, is it?"

Red Craig quickly made his guests at home. They ate and then a jug appeared, which Red passed around. Joe declined. He was too engrossed in the surroundings. This was where his father had lived and reared his Indian family. He could almost feel his father's presence. He wanted to ask about Little Ned's family, but did not want to arouse the old trappers' curiosity. He had never confided in anyone that he was Little Ned's son.

The next morning, when Deacon and Red began to talk about old times, Joe excused himself. He would take a ride down to the mission, he said. Narcissa Whitman had given him a parcel to deliver to Eliza Spalding.

"Like as not you'll find her at the schoolhouse," Red advised.

"You can't miss it. You'll probably hear students reciting their lessons before you get there. However, with the revival going, school may be closed."

School was out but Joe found the schoolhouse without difficulty. Eliza Spalding was inside cleaning up. From Craig's caustic remarks on the missionaries' activities, Joe expected an unpleasant person. Instead, he found Eliza Spalding remarkably warm and intelligent. She graciously accepted Narcissa's parcel, thanking him profusely for delivering it. Proudly, she showed Joe around. She was particularly pleased the schoolhouse had been finished with boards from the mission sawmill.

Joe was impressed by her enthusiasm. If there was trouble in Lapwai, it did not appear to disturb Eliza Spalding. He would have been surprised to know her nerves were shattered. She had taken shelter in the classrooms to get away from her husband who stormed around the house, furious over the influx of mountain men. First there was the adulterer, Francois. Then four more rode in from Waiilatpu. He feared they would disrupt the revival meetings he had called to bind the wounds that had split the community.

"Many important tribal leaders come to take lessons," Eliza Spalding said in her pleasant way. "For the first time they are learning to read and write their own language." She handed Joe a pamphlet.

"Our people have translated the Gospel of Matthew into the native language. God willing, someday we will translate and print the entire New Testament."

They went outside to stroll under the trees of the mission grounds. Joe, trying to think of a subtle way to approach the subject of Little Ned's family, only half listened to the missionary lady's words.

"We have a long way to go," Eliza said wistfully. "Some of our brightest young people do not attend school. See that lad." She lifted a hand in greeting to a slender boy who walked by leading a strikingly marked black and white pony. "His mother has taken him and his brother out of school. I have pleaded with her but she is adamantly opposed to the mission school. It's terribly sad. Both boys enjoyed school so much and were doing so well."

The Indian boy turned to face them. He gave the teacher a hesitant smile and returned her greeting with a tentative wave. For a brief moment his eyes met Joe's. An uncanny sensation gripped Joe. It was as if someone from the past had looked deep into his soul. It suddenly dawned on him. This was his brother; this was Little Ned's son!

"What is his name?" Joe asked, trying not to reveal the excitement that gripped him. He was appalled he didn't even know his own brother's name.

"When he first came to class he was Buffalo Boy. Recently he changed his name to Michael Two Feathers."

"Two Feathers," Joe repeated. "I would very much like to speak to him."

"I am sure he will be pleased. Michael!" she called out. The boy stopped. He held the pony still, softly caressing the animal's sleek neck. He waited for his former teacher to speak. Instead, the young hairy faced one came toward him with his hand outstretched. Puzzled by the stranger's action, Michael took the hand and shook it in the manner of the hairy faces. Unsure of what the stranger wanted, he kept his eyes averted. The touch of the stranger's hand was warm, his look friendly. Who was this man? He knew from the expression on the missionary woman's face they had been discussing him. Why should the stranger be interested?

Joe, so overcome by emotion he could hardly speak, studied his brother's impassive face. He liked what he saw: hair black with a slight wave; complexion dark but eyes as startlingly blue as his own; body slender but strong; shoulders that would become as wide as Little Ned's.

"I knew your father very well," Joe finally said. "I was one of the last to see him alive."

"Ah!" Michael uttered. So that was why the unusual sensation. It was the work of the Great Mysterious. He had used this person as a messenger from his father. The thought made his heart leap. He glanced up. The young man even had the look of his father. "Ah!" he uttered again, this time to himself. The Great Mysterious worked in wondrous ways.

Joe waited for the boy to continue, but he said no more. While Joe pondered what to say, a curt command made Michael stiffen. He swung up on the pony and kicked it into a gallop. Joe knew without looking who had frightened him away. He turned around to face the dark sinister looking figure.

THE LAST RENDEZVOUS

XXVIII

Man is the most formidable of all beasts of prey, and indeed the only one that preys systematically on its own species.
William James

Michael Two Feathers rode furiously away from the mission grounds and up the valley. Eliza Spalding sadly watched him disappear. For almost the first time since coming to Lapwai she uttered a sigh of despair. The boy was so capable and so anxious to attend school it was cruel keep him away. She could not suppress her feeling of distaste for the man who treated the boy so callously. "Shame! Shame!" The censorious words were uttered before she could hold them back. But they had no effect. The man Francois had turned and walked away.

Far up the valley Michael pulled his pony to a walk. The pleasure he had enjoyed in meeting the young mountain man had been replaced with bitterness. He could not go on living in fear of Francois. He was like a horse that had been beaten around the head. Every time Francois appeared he cringed. It made him ashamed -- made him feel a coward. He thought of running away, but where? Even if he had a place to go Francois would track him down. It did no good to rebel. His mother only joined Francois in punishing him. Why did she put up with the man? She knew he was vicious -- unhumanly cruel, but when Francois was around she did not seem to have a mind of her own. She let him do anything he pleased.

"Aiiee!" Michael groaned. It was said they would marry. How could he ever bear it? Since returning to Lapwai, the dark faced man did everything possible to make himself obnoxious. Francois rode up and down the valley on his pure black stallion, the silver decorated bridle and saddle glittering in the bright sun. A line of curious youthful horsemen and cluster of dogs often trailed him, creating a spectacle few could ignore.

"Why do you do these things?" Raven Wing had asked.

"These people ran me out of the valley. I want to make certain they see I'm back and intend to stay," Francois retorted. "I'm just waiting for that missionary to preach against me again. I'll burn his damned mission down."

For Joe, the meeting with his brother, which he had looked forward to with such great anticipation, left him feeling ill. Just as he and Michael were about to get acquainted, Francois' appearance ruined everything. Not only did Francois treat Michael cruelly but his boorish attitude toward Eliza Spalding was appalling. The poor teacher who had sacrificed so much and was trying to do her best for her students, was treated like a stable hand. Joe had the irresistible urge to go after the man, haul him back by the scruff of the neck and make him apologize. But roughhousing on mission grounds was not done. Also, he was not at all certain he could pull it off. Taking on Francois was like tackling an irascible wild cat. Joe gave Eliza Spalding a rueful glance. "I'm afraid I know the man. His manners are disgraceful."

#

Joe returned to Red Craig's place to find Hawk Beak sitting with Craig and Deacon, taking turns at a whiskey jug. "I put up sech a fuss Doc Whitman said I could work the kinks out by meself," Hawk Beak explained. To demonstrate the arm's strength, he seized the jug with it, swung the crockery up and took a long pull. However, when he lowered the jug, he did so carefully with both hands.

The next day Craig took his guests to the revival. The sight of hundreds of Indian people sitting spellbound, listening to the preacher rant on the terrors of hell, astonished Joe. When Spalding brought the meeting to a close, many in the throng stepped forward to receive the reverend's blessing and "give their hearts to Jesus."

The revival spirit did not touch everyone. Near the back of the crowd a group of dissenters muttered throughout the ceremony. Among them were Red Craig's father-in-law, Thunder Eyes, and Looking Glass, so named because he wore a small mirror on a string for a neckpiece. Before the crowd dispersed, Thunder Eyes made a short, scathing statement that Red Craig translated.

"He says, 'Christians today, tipi Indians tomorrow.' To put it bluntly, he believes this religious fervor is short-lived."

The trappers rode up the valley in silence. The emotional revival meeting followed by Thunder Eyes' statement of obvious disapproval, left even garrulous Deacon without words. When they came in sight of Craig's lodge a black and white pony was in front with bridle reins at trail. Beside it stood Francois.

Hawk Beak kicked his mount into a gallop. He pulled the horse to a skidding stop almost on top of the swarthy trapper. He leaped down and rammed his rifle barrel into Francois' stomach. "I've a notion to blast yuh in two! Doc Whitman dug a bullet from thet Hawken of yers outta my back. What yuh gotta say 'bout thet?"

Francois' dark face grew a shade darker. He tried to shove the rifle barrel away but Hawk Beak pressed harder. The French Canadian's lips contorted into a savage grimace.

"I asked yuh, bushwhaker. Shoot me in the back, will yuh?" Hawk Beak gave the rifle barrel a painful twist.

"You're looney. Talk sense. If I'd shot you, you'd be dead! I came to challenge you to a horse race. You've bragged for two years how your horse can outlast any Indian pony. This pony'll make your Blaze eat dust. Since you're crippled, young Joe can ride in your place."

"All right, yuh stinkin piece of meat, we race. The stakes'll be my Blaze against thet painted Injun critter. An' let me tell you somethin', if yer thinkin' on pullin' monkey business, I'll blast yuh in two." He gave the rifle barrel another twist and thumbed back the hammer. "Don't think yer gettin' off easy. Yer hunk a lead in my hide ain't made me perzactly sociable."

Francois pushed the rifle barrel aside. "I'll see you at the race track mid-morning," he snarled. He swung upon the black and white Indian pony and urged it into a lope.

"Why thet broomtail cain't run," Hawk Beak declared, watching Francois ride away. "It hops up and down like a blinkin' jack-in-the-box."

Red Craig remained silent. It was obvious he did not agree.

Deacon finally spoke what was on everyone's mind. "What skullduggery's the Canuck up ta anyway? Why's he so hell bent on hevin' a hoss race?"

Craig pulled on his square beard. "I can only guess, but I'd say he's staging it for the home folks. He's about as popular around here as a coyote in a chicken roost. They drove him out of the village once. He's anxious not to have it happen again."

"How'n tarnation'll a hoss race help him?" Deacon asked.

"These people are so proud of these home grown nags they can't stand it. A win over Blaze will make them as happy as pigs in clover."

"Reckon it'll mess up Spaldin's revival?" Deacon inquired.

"Reckon so. Francois doesn't care. Probably figured on it. He hates Spalding. The parson announced from the pulpit Francois and his woman were living in adulterous sin, built an entire sermon around it. You can bet the Canuck hasn't forgotten that."

"Francois made one good point. He said let Young Joe ride," Hawk Beak observed. "Thet fer certain'll be to our advantage."

"It'll take more than Joe's riding to win," Craig said.

"Wagh! Thet nag hops up an' down like a huntin' dog in tall grass."

"Trouble is, that isn't the horse you'll be racing."

"What do yuh mean by thet? The wager was Blaze against thet black an' white patchwork quilt. Francois cain't get out of thet."

"That's exactly what you're supposed to think. Fact is, Francois has at his disposal two almost identical horses. The big difference is that one runs like a jack rabbit, the other one like an antelope. You can bet you'll be racing the antelope."

"Thet shyster kin pull all the tricks he wants. He still can't beat Blaze."

"That antelope sure can fly and the Canuck can't afford to lose. I'll bet he knows to a second what your horse can do. Has he ridden Blaze?"

"Yeah, blast him! Stole Blaze an' my mules. Had 'em a fortnight."

"You see, he knows exactly what he's doing. Right now I would have to place my money on the Canuck."

"Yer plumb serious, ain't yuh?" Hawk Beak said, perplexed. "What kin we do?"

"We'll just have to put the antelope out of action."

"Yuh mean, do away with the critter?" Deacon exclaimed.

"When it comes to horses these people know every trick in the trade. They have a simple way of temporarily laming a horse."

"Don't seem quite sportin'," Hawk Beak objected.

"Do you want to win or don't you?"

"Since yuh put it thet way, what kin I say? I sure don't want to lose Blaze."

After dark, Hawk Beak, Red Craig, Young Bull, a local horseman Red recruited, and Joe made their way to Little Ned's former cabin. Joe studied the place. A feeling of terrible sadness gripped him. This had been his father's home. He had raised the log walls and laid the shake roof with his own hands. How ironic to do all that work and have it fall to Francois, the man he hated.

They spotted the racing pony tethered near the lodge. As was the custom among the Nimpau, it had been left without food for the night. "It is believed the critters run better on empty stomachs," Red explained.

While the others stood guard, Young Bull crawled up to the horse. It was too dark for Joe to see what he did, but Craig helpfully explained that long hairs were plucked from the horse's tail and wrapped tightly around a foreleg. In the morning the horse would come up lame. Shortly after Young Bull returned and reported the job finished, the cabin door opened. Silhouetted in the escaping light was Michael's slender figure. He carried a sleeping robe. He had been sent to guard the pony.

All night Joe tossed and turned, unable to sleep. His half brother was certain to take the blame for the lame horse. He didn't like it at all but what could he do? Wearily, Joe picked at the food Red Craig's mate served the next morning. He wished he had never set foot in Lapwai. After eating, he made an inspection trip around the race course. He turned onto the final leg to see the hillside dotted with spectators. Joe grimaced. Craig was right. The Lapwai people took horse racing seriously. It was two hours until race time. Already a hundred or more spectators had gathered.

Joe arrived back at Craig's lodge to see Reverend Spalding and a group of his followers arguing with Craig and Hawk Beak. Before Joe could put his horse away, the missionary and his companions shouted a few final words and galloped off.

"The good reverend claims hoss racin' is a tool of the Devil," Deacon explained. "The Sabbath's holy. 'Stead of gamblin' an' cavortin' 'bout a race track we should be attendin' the revival. For all the fuss it's creatin' me thinks even winnin' the race'll serve no good."

Late in the morning Hawk Beak glanced at the sun and scowled. "If the Canuck don't come soon he should forfeit the race an' hand over thet patchwork quilt he calls a horse."

"He found the pony tampered with," Red Craig speculated. "He doesn't know which way to turn." He glanced at the hillside where the crowd had swollen. "Francois has no choice. He has to show. This bunch wants a horse race. If they don't get it, wouldn't surprise me none if they didn't run him out of the valley again."

Suddenly, the hillside spectators began to stir. Michael, dressed only in a breechcloth, appeared leading the painted pony. Francois strode alongside. Neither one glanced at the crowd. Francois' expression barely covered restrained fury. Michael had the abject look of a whipped dog. He kept close to the horse, his eyes intent on the race track. Francois carried two willow switches. As Michael vaulted upon the pony, Joe noticed the boy's back was a crisscross of welts. Furiously, he glared at the swarthy mountain man. It was all he could do to keep from attacking him -- whipping him with the same beastliness he had done poor Michael.

At the starting line Francois handed Michael the willow switches. In the same motion his hand smacked down on the backside of the pony. The startled animal gave a leap and took off down the track. "Get goin'," Hawk Beak shouted at Joe. "Let him have his lead. Blaze'll take him anyhow."

Belatedly, Joe swung astride Blaze and raced after the speeding pony. At the half-way point the Indian horse still led by several lengths. Gradually, the big bay closed the gap. When Blaze came abreast, Michael flailed the pony's sides with the willow switches. Steadily, Blaze drew ahead. The black and white jack rabbit pony could not keep up.

THE LAST RENDEZVOUS

XXIX

The wicked shall fall by their own wickedness.
Proverbs, 11:5

In the high country where Lapwai villagers had taken their horses for late fall pasture, Vision Seeker left Running Turtle in charge of the herd. He returned to the valley for supplies and additional clothes, for the nights were turning cold. He came through the gap that opened onto Lapwai Valley. The race crowd met his eye.

"What is this?" he asked a horseman who rode alongside.

"A hairy face stranger says he has a horse that can outrun any Nimpau pony. Your kinsman, Two Feathers, runs his patched horse against the stranger's bay."

Vision Seeker inwardly groaned. What business did his nephew have racing against some unknown newcomer? Did he still believe he was a special person with magical powers? Vision Seeker rode up on the hillside where he had a view of the race course. He surveyed the crowd on the opposite side of the valley. Everyone in the village appeared to be present. Clustered among Lapwai villagers were strangers, probably people attending Spalding's revival, Vision Seeker decided.

"Oh-hah!" Vision Seeker uttered in surprise as Michael led the black and white pony to the starting post, Francois following close behind. Now he understood. It was Francois' idea to race. He was not going to stop showing off until everyone in the valley knew he was back. But something was wrong. Francois was horse-wise. Why was he running Young Wolf's pony? It was far slower than Michael's Magpie.

Vision Seeker studied the group at the starting line. He was startled to see Little Ned's friends, the tall hawk-faced man so deadly with a buffalo gun and the man with no hair called Deacon. Michael was racing against the hawk-faced man's bay. "Ah!" Vision Seeker uttered. The pony was no match for the big horse. The bay's youthful rider looked very capable, too. The horses were off. Michael had the lead but Vision Seeker knew it would not last. The rider on the bay rode as well as Michael and he was on a stronger mount.

The race ended as Vision Seeker thought. He lingered awhile, watching the disappointed crowd disperse, but his mind was on the race. Why hadn't Michael ridden the swifter pony? Was it not well? And who was that familiar looking young man who rode the bay? Thoughtfully, Vision Seeker mounted and reined toward the village. There was something going on he did not understand. Why were Little Ned's old friends in Lapwai? They surely did not come to see Raven Wing. Vision Seeker had the uneasy feeling their presence did not bode well.

#

Almost sadly, Joe crossed the finish line. Blaze had won the race but it gave Joe no feeling of elation. All he could think about were the crisscross of switch marks on his half brother's back. The hillside gathering silently picked up their blankets and robes to walk slowly down the valley toward the mission grounds. His face aflame with fury, Francois also turned to leave. He took a few steps and whirled about. "Take your horse," he snapped at Hawk Beak. "Take it and be damned."

Michael dropped off the pony, leaving the reins at trail. With startling quickness, he darted away, losing himself in the crowd. He quickly out-distanced everyone to disappear into the locust trees that surrounded the Indian village.

"I wouldn't want to be in his moccasins," Red Craig said. "Knowing the little tyke'll catch hell kind of takes the joy out of winning."

"It does thet," Hawk Beak admitted. "But thet sneaky Francois deserves to lose. When he slapped thet critter off to an early start I should've crowned him with the barrel of my Hawken."

"That Canuck's as full of venom as a viper. You'd best watch your back," Craig warned.

"The best thing we kin do is ta hightail it outta here," Deacon said. "The reverend's mad, the Injuns're unhappy, an' the Canuck's edgy enough ta eat his scalpin' knife. What else kin we possibly do ta disrupt the peace?"

Joe silently agreed with Deacon. His insistence on coming to Lapwai had led to disaster. The trappers' presence had completely disrupted his half brother's life. The quicker they left, the better. He was glad he had not revealed that he and Michael were brothers. If Francois found out, his fury would have no limits. He would make Michael's life unbearable.

#

Michael's situation was far worse than Joe realized. He ran to the log cabin lodge and huddled in a corner, shivering as though he had the ague. Before long Young Wolf appeared. "You lost the race," he accused. "If I had ridden, I would have won."

Raven Wing, who came in later with baby Little Bird, was equally accusing. "You bring our lodge shame. You did not protect your pony? During the night someone came and made it lame." She dumped Little Bird down so roughly, he howled. Michael slunk out the door, leaped over the porch railing and ran. He had no desire to face the wrath of Francois.

#

The occupants of Red Craig's quarters were equally on edge. Craig snapped at Hawk Beak and growled at Deacon. It was clear he had had his fill of his trapper guests. Joe wondered if their presence had caused friction within Craig's family. They barely had seen Thunder Eyes and Craig's wife only appeared at meal times to serve food and clean up afterward. Still grumbling about the crook, Francois, Hawk Beak threw his things together and mounted up. "Maybeso, next time we come fer a visit thet Canuck'll be gone," Hawk Beak said hopefully.

"Ha!" Craig uttered. He rode with the trappers as far as the edge of the Indian camp. There he stopped and sat his horse until his guests were out of sight.

"Guess the ol' redhead's afeered we'll change our minds an' turn back," Deacon observed. "Can't say I blame him. It was all Hawk Beak's fault. We was doin' fine until he showed up. What the devil . . . !"

A crackle in the underbrush made Deacon's horse rear, nearly pitching him from the saddle. Joe's mount drew back with a snort. Blaze bolted down the trail before Hawk Beak could get him under control. When the animals were calmed, they rode back with rifles cocked. They expected to at least see a mountain lion or a bear. Instead, it was the Indian lad, Michael Two Feathers. Still clad only in the breechcloth, he ran up to meet the horsemen, his breath coming in gasps. "Take me with you," he pleaded.

The two older trappers glanced at each other in dismay. Taking an Indian boy from his tribe was a hostile act. Far better to steal a horse or someone's wife. The wife and horse could be replaced, but an Indian brave could not.

Naive in the ways of Indian people, Joe only saw a boy in trouble. Michael was his own flesh and blood, fleeing from a cruel stepfather. "Hop on the pony," he instructed.

"Yuh cain't take a lad from his people jest like thet," Deacon protested. "When they find he's gone, there'll be hell ta pay. Apt as not a war party'll hotfoot it after us. We've done enuff damage without startin' a war."

"No one knows I go," Michael protested.

"Thet Canuck'll figure it out. Yuh kin bet yer socks he'll be after yuh. He cain't let yuh go," Hawk Beak said. "He's already lost so much face he don't recognize hisself."

"Let the crooked, no-good Canuck come," Deacon said. "Sooner or later he'll force a showdown."

"Yeah, guess it don't matter," Hawk Beak agreed. "The fat's already in the fire."

It was late afternoon before there were signs of pursuit, the sound of hooves pounding up the trail. In a sheltered glade, the trappers dismounted and tethered the horses. The wait was short. Around a brush-lined curve in the trail came two riders, Francois and one of Thunder Eyes' ruffians. When they caught sight of the trappers, they pulled their mounts to a skidding halt.

"I want that boy," Francois shouted. He rode warily ahead

until only a dozen horse lengths separated him from the trappers.

"Hold it right there," Hawk Beak ordered, cocking his Hawken. "Maybeso, the boy don't want to stay. Cain't say I blame him. Yuh ain't my idea of a perfect stepfather, not by a long shot."

"You're meddling in something that's none of your business," Francois snarled.

"No, it ain't, but when a lad wants to better hisself, I aim to give a lift. Anyways, we'll leave it up to the boy. If he wants to go back, well an' good. He kin even take the patchwork pony."

There was more pounding down the trail. Another two Thunder Eyes' ruffians, young men armed with war lances, appeared. They pulled up alongside Francois. After a short palaver they rode into the thickets of brush, one on either side of the trail.

"Tryin' to surround us, are they?" Hawk Beak muttered.

"One way or another, I'm taking that boy," Francois said, "Just because you outsmarted me on the horse race doesn't mean you've a right to my kin. We weren't wagering for him."

The crackling made by the riders in the trail side brush became louder. For a brief moment, the trappers' attention was diverted by this new threat. The action suddenly became ferocious. A horseman from either side of the trail charged into the open. The trappers, who were on foot, scrambled to avoid them. Taking advantage of the distraction, Francois spurred the black stallion forward. The blade of his skinning knife glittered in his hand. The tethered horses reared, swerving into the path of the stallion. The trappers desperately waved their rifles. They couldn't fire for fear of shooting their own horses. The black stallion plowed ahead, knocking the trappers' mounts aside. Francois leaned over the saddle horn, the shiny blade poised ready to slit their throats. He made a murderous sweep and missed. He jerked the stallion around and made another attempt. Joe threw up his rifle barrel, blocking the deadly steel blade. Unable to control his reflexes, he pulled the trigger. The muzzle blast seared the stallion's face. The big animal reared. Francois frantically pulled on the reins and grabbed for the saddle horn. The pull on the reins was too much for the stallion. It toppled over backwards, pinning Francois underneath. Seeing their leader fall, Thunder Eye's three ruffians turned and fled. Francois' downed stallion struggled to its feet but the rider did not move.

For a short while, except for the heavy breathing of the excited animals, the tree surrounded glen fell silent. Then a flock of inquisitive magpies flew overhead and a chipmunk skittered down a tree trunk and scampered across an open space.

"I hope this ain't the calm afore a storm," Deacon said. "Now, why ain't this un movin'? Jest like him ta play 'possum." Keeping his rifle pointed at Francois' prone figure, Deacon walked up and gave the man a nudge with the toe of his boot. Francois remained still. Deacon seized the back of the downed man's hunting shirt and gave it a tug. Still there was no response. Deacon knelt down and turned Francois face up. The dark eyes were open, staring skyward. Joe heard Michael suck in his breath. The youngster was the first to understand the man was dead.

Deacon stepped back and mopped his face. "I swan! The bloody Canuck knifed hisself. Must've happened when thet big nag of his'ns pitched over back'ards . . . drove thet skinnin' knife inta his chest slick as a whistle. Now, ain't thet fittin'? Lived by the knife an' died by the knife, thet's what he did."

"Good riddance, if yuh ask me," Hawk Beak said callously. He seized the reins of Francois' black stallion. On its back was Francois' handsome, silver decorated saddle. "I always hankered fer a fancy saddle," Hawk Beak said, running a hand over the pieces of Mexican silver. "Yuh reckon the varmint kept valuables in these saddlebags?" Hawk Beak unbuckled the strap of the nearest one. He pulled out a bundle neatly wrapped in buckskin. He untied the thongs that held it tight. The buckskin wrapping fell away to reveal a mound of fur, white as fresh fallen snow.

"Why the dirty bustard," Deacon exclaimed. "He killed . . ." He glanced at Michael and clamped his mouth shut. The boy's stepfather had shot his real father in the back. How could the kid cope with a henious crime like that?

Hawk Beak handed the white beaver pelt to Joe. "Since yuh

an' Little Ned was partners, I guess by rights this's yers."

Joe gingerly took the pelt. The beautiful white fur appeared so pure and innocent. Yet, the only two people who had possessed it had met violent death. He glanced at Michael. It was their father's legacy. How could he share it without revealing they were both Little Ned's sons?

Hawk Beak growled they didn't have the time nor the tools to bury Francois' body, however, the trappers, with knives, hand axes and their hands, scraped out a shallow grave. They were still covering the grave with earth and rocks when the sound of galloping hoofbeats stopped them. They stepped into the trail side brush, cocked their rifles and waited for the rider to round the corner.

"It is Uncle Vision Seeker!" Michael cried out.

The trappers stepped into the open. Vision Seeker gave Deacon and Hawk Beak a slight bow of recognition. Many years ago he had trapped with them both. "You left without your *Wyakin*," he said to Michael, holding out the pouch that held the two feathers. Before Michael could grip the pouch, the flap opened. The white feather fell out. It fluttered tantalizingly out of reach, finally drifting toward Joe's feet. Before it touched Mother Earth Michael snatched it.

In amazement, Vision Seeker watched the antics of the feather. It was a sign! The feather acted like it did not want to go with Michael, instead it chose the young stranger. "Oh hah!" He recognized him. He was the one at the rendezvous — the jouster who reminded him of someone out of the past. He glanced from one youth to the other. They each had the same bearing and features . . . . Of course, why had he not thought of it before? The young Boston was also Little Ned's son! Like so many mountain men, Little Ned kept two families, one in the east and one in the west. Vision Seeker was stunned. "Ah!" It had to be the work of the Great Mysterious. His wonderous power had brought the brothers together.

Vision Seeker took the white feather from Michael and handed it to Joe. "You both are of the same blood. This is your *Wyakin*, the spirit that will guide you through life."

Atonishment crossed the brothers' faces. Joe was amazed this tall Indian man knew his secret; Michael was dumbfounded that Vision Seeker gave the young mountain man his white feather; and what did he mean, "You both are of the same blood?" Then the youthful mountain man smiled and held out the white feather.

"Keep both feathers," Joe said to Michael. "How can we call you Two Feathers if you only possess one?"

The trappers looked on aghast. Finally, Deacon understood. "'Pon my word, are yuh sayin' both of these boys're Little Ned's sons? Kin yuh beat thet? Little Ned, silent as a tomb, hevin' two families. Lordy! Won't tongues wag at the next rendezvous."

"There'll be no tongues waggin'," Hawk Beak scolded. "We've seen our last rendezvous."

The brothers were as stunned as the mountain men. It suddenly dawned on them that this was a momentous event, one that would change their lives forever.

THE LAST RENDEZVOUS

ABOUT THE AUTHORS

Bonnie Jo Hunt (*Wicahpi Win* - Star Woman) is Hunkpapa Lakota (Standing Rock Sioux) and the great-great granddaughter of Chief Francis Mad Bear who fought at the Battle of the Little Bighorn and Major James McLaughlin, Indian agent and Chief Inspector for the Bureau of Indian Affairs, who escorted the famous Chief Joseph back to his Wallowa, Oregon home after the Nez Perce Indian War. Early in life Bonnie Jo set her heart on helping others. In 1980 she founded Artists of Indian America, Inc. (AIA), a non-profit organization established to stimulate cultural and social improvement among American Indian youth. To record and preserve her native heritage, in 1997 Bonnie Jo launched Mad Bear Press that publishes American history dealing with life on the western frontier. These publications include the Lone Wolf Clan series: THE LONE WOLF CLAN, RAVEN WING, THE LAST RENDEZVOUS and the forthcoming CAYUSE COUNTRY.

#

Dr. Lawrence J. Hunt, a former university professor, works actively with Artists of Indian America, Inc. In addition to co-authoring THE LONE WOLF CLAN, RAVEN WING, THE LAST RENDEZVOUS and forthcoming CAYUSE COUNTRY, he has co-authored an international textbook (Harrap: London) and published four mystery novels (Funk and Wagnalls), one of which, SECRET OF THE HAUNTED CRAGS, received the Edgar Allan Poe Award from Mystery Writers of America.

No part of this publication may be reproduced, stored in a retrieval system, or transmitted in any form or by any means, electronic, mechanical, photocopying, recording, scanning, or otherwise, without the prior written permission of the publisher, except in the case of brief quotations within critical reviews and otherwise as permitted by copyright law.

NOTE: This is a work of fiction. Names, characters, places, and incidents are a product of the author's imagination. Any resemblance to real life is purely coincidental. All characters in this story are 18 or older.

Copyright © 2017, Willow Winters Publishing. All rights reserved.

Joseph
&
Lily

Willow Winters &
Lauren Landish
Wall street journal & usa today bestselling authors

From USA Today best selling authors, Willow Winters and Lauren Landish, comes a sexy and forbidden series of standalone romances.

She thought this was a game. She thought she could walk away. She thought wrong.

I've lived a cold, unforgiving life. I've seen things, I've done things, that would break a man if they didn't kill him first.

With my past behind me, I have nothing. No way to atone for my sins and nothing to lift me from the depths of despair. And no one to give me the control that I so desperately desire.

Until I saw Lilly and then something inside my cold heart flickered. There's a sweet innocence about her that steals the breath from my lungs. She brings my darkness to the surface, and what's more... she craves it just as much as I do.

The danger is what lured her to me. But she didn't realize how intense this would be when she signed that contract.

She thought it was all fantasy and make-believe.
I'm not a knight in shining armor. I'm not a hero from a romance novel. I'm the villain.

And now she wants to leave?
I won't allow it.

I own her. And I'm not letting her go.

Prologue

Joseph

I'm quiet as I walk into my bedroom, hoping to get a look at Lilly without her knowing. But those doe-eyed baby blues are shining back at me the second I enter.

Hating me. They pierce into me, giving me a look that could kill a lesser man.

I've been given more hateful glares. From deadly men who intended on killing me, who despise me and my very existence. I've never been affected.

But the look in her eyes guts me.

Because I know she's hiding pain behind the hate.

"Let me out," she says in a low voice as she wraps her fingers around the silver steel bars. Her voice lacks the strength and conviction she'd rather I hear. She adjusts slightly, and as she does she winces. My eyes follow her movements; the grates of the cage have left an imprint on her knees. It's only been a few hours since she's been given her punishment. And I'm already regretting it.

I have to remind myself that this is for her own good. She's being punished for a reason.

She *wanted* this.

She *asked* for this.

And now she wants to leave?

I won't allow it.

My hands ball into fists as I stalk forward, my bare feet sinking into the lush carpet with each heavy step. The cage is large, much taller than her own height, and she rises to meet me although she remains on her knees.

Here's a side to her I've never seen before. The fierce woman who was always there, hiding behind the facade of obedient eyes.

She liked to *play* the submissive. She thought this was a game.

She thought wrong.

Lilly looks back at me with daggers in her eyes as I crouch lower, leveling my gaze with hers. Even with the anger swirling in her blue eyes piercing into me, she gives off an air of purity, of innocence. She's so delicate, so sweet. *My flower*.

Her rage only makes me want her more.

"Are you ready to *obey*?" I ask her, tilting my head

slightly. My words piss her off. And I fucking love it. The comprehension of her predicament makes her eyes narrow for a moment. I watch as her hands attempt to ball into fists, but she corrects herself, warring between what she craves to do and what she feels she's expected to do.

She clenches her teeth, but her eyes water. Tears form in her eyes as her lush lips part, but then quickly close without a sound being uttered.

I question everything in that small moment.

"Fuck you," she finally responds with a sneer, but then instantly lowers her gaze. She's strong, courageous even, but she's a true Submissive. I have yet to earn that side of her. But I will.

"You want to," I answer with a sharp smirk that curves my lips up, and that brings her glare back. We're at an impasse. If she'd give in, so would I, but she's fighting it.

She didn't realize how intense this would be when she signed that contract giving her freedom over to me. Neither did I.

She doesn't respond, but I see her thighs clench ever so slightly. The small action makes my dick instantly harden with desire. She loves what I do to her. She still wants me, even when she hates me.

"All you need to do is obey, my flower." I regain my strict composure, waiting for her answer.

My nickname for her makes her lips part just the tiniest bit with lust. It makes me lean into her that much closer.

Wanting more. My fingers wrap around the bars just above hers, barely touching her, but feeling the heated tingle I always do when I'm with her.

She knew I wasn't a good man.

That's part of what drew her to me. I know it is.

"Fine," she says in a mere whisper. I cock a brow at her answer, daring her to continue with that disrespectful attitude.

Our days are numbered, and if I let her, she may leave me the moment she can and never look back.

But she craved this arrangement for a reason. The same darkness that drives my desires is also in her. Stirring low in the pit of her stomach, fueling her hatred for me, but making her want me so much more.

"You know that's not the way I'd like you to address me."

"Yes, sir," she says obediently, her voice the proper tone as she squares her shoulders. She's still eye level with me, and there's still a fierceness to her, but she's willing to play. *That's just how I want her.*

I'll show her how good this can be.

But first, she needs to be truly punished. The cage door opens slightly with a gentle creak. I need to leave a lasting impression.

She may be angry with me, but she's still mine.

I *own* her. And I'm not letting her go.

Chapter 1

Lily

"What in the effin' hell?" I slam *Playback*, the romance paperback I'd been reading closed with an angry growl. My blood is boiling like an evil witch's cauldron.

"How could it end... like *that*?" I grit my teeth, shaking my head at the gall of whoever's written this. I fell in love with this storyline, and totally felt the heartache and brutal pain the hero and heroine went through. I was rooting for Liam and Tilda. Their story gripped my heart from the very first page, and I was quickly drawn into their struggles to overcome the heartbreaking obstacles keeping them apart.

I'd read each page breathlessly, flipping through the book like a hungry wolf in search of his next meal, practically dying to find out how it all ended, and then... I gulp as my throat constricts into a ball of tight anger, unable to understand how someone could be so cruel. I'd invested so much of myself into the story, hoping to be rewarded with a satisfying conclusion to such a tragic relationship.

Then it ended abruptly. Just like that, with no happily ever after, no resolution. Only a tragic heartbreak that left me feeling raw. I can't believe how completely engrossed I was in the book, feeling like I was part of the characters' lives, only to be shafted at the very end.

Burning up with anger, I turn the book over and peer at the binding, determined to commit the author's name to memory so I can make sure to stay clear of reading any more of their future work. *Lauren Winters.* "More like Slutty Winters," I mutter angrily, feeling thoroughly cheated.

I know it's fiction and it's not real, but I hate when I get emotionally invested in characters and then something like this happens. It makes me feel absolutely cheated.

I groan my frustration, tossing the book on the end table. My eyes are drawn to the roaring flames of the marble fireplace in front of me. The heat of the fire pricks my already heated cheeks, and I relax slightly as I'm enveloped by cozy warmth. Despite my sour moment, I *love* this.

It's one of my favorite pastimes during the cold winter months, sitting in front of a roaring fire with a hot mug of coffee and burying my nose into an engrossing romance novel. I just like it better when it's a book that doesn't leave me feeling like my heart's been ripped out of my chest and stomped on in front of me.

"I need something more mindless and smutty after that," I mutter, picking up my cup of coffee and taking a sip. I'm calm now, but I still have a slight urge to toss the book into the flames. I must admit the author did a good job with everything else. I just didn't like her ending.

I just wish I hadn't stepped on my Kindle. I had like fifty awesome books piled up on my to-be-read list.

Sighing, I get up from my cushioned recliner with the book in my hands and stretch out my limbs, several of my bones popping as I stand. But it feels so good, I hold the position, letting my limbs come back to life.

My eyes take in my living room, and my mood lifts again slightly. It feels so homey in my new townhouse, especially with how cold it is outside. I've decorated it with warm earth tones that make me feel right at home. The walls are lined with decorative shelves that are filled with books. I've read every single one of these books. A few of them are even autographed.

I love my new bookends, too. They're pale blue mice carved from stone stone to look like they're holding the books up. Just seeing them makes me smile.

This room is completely mine, and finally feels like a home. I still have the rest of the rented townhouse to put my stamp on, but this one room is just perfect. I walk to the large window across the room to open the curtains and let the evening light in. I can feel the cold from the winter air coming through.

Outside, I can still see confetti lining the streets from the New Year's Parade as I place my hand against the window. It's a few days past the first of January, and a few pieces are still blowing along the edges of the building.

I grin as I take it all in, the ending of the book quickly forgotten. I could write a romance that would leave me with feelings that would brighten my day. It's okay to make my heart hurt a little, but I don't want it broken. That's not why I read romance novels.

I've actually had a very good year, albeit a long one. I just finished my next-to-last semester at North University and I've passed all my classes with a B or better. I even managed to get a B+ in Advanced Calculus, something that's always been a struggle for me, all while working hard as a guidance counselor with troubled students at a local high school. I will never understand why psychology students have to know calculus. At this point, I just want to graduate and start giving back by helping make a brighter future for others as a teaching counselor in the local youth detention center. It's their last chance before their delinquency sends them beyond public schools and straight to jail. It's not a job I take lightly.

I can't handle the high school kids though. That's for damn sure. For this past paid counseling internship, the program threw me in a classroom with twenty students. I'm only twenty-four and petite, so even on my best days, I hardly look over twenty-one. To say the students didn't take me seriously doesn't even begin to cover it. I cannot handle working with older teenagers. At all. Sure as hell not twenty of them at once.

Some of those kids got under my skin so bad that I thought I was about to have a stroke. It takes a lot to get me worked up and thinking negatively. But I found it difficult to stay positive as the semester progressed. I still managed to persevere though; a few students showed so much improvement, and I know I made a positive difference in their lives. In the end, that's all that matters.

That internship is over, thank God. Next year, I'll be in a middle school and that's where I really want to work. I feel like I could do the most help there.

And now I have the entire winter break to catch up on all the romance books I've neglected as reward for my hard work.

I glare balefully at the book in my hand, thinking, *I just need to make sure I don't read any more disasters like this one.*

Huffing out another small sigh, I walk over to my bookshelf and pause before I slip the book back into its spot. I really should toss the damn thing into the fire. I'll probably never read it again. In fact, I know I won't. But I can't bring myself to do it. Books are my biggest obsession; even ones I don't love. They keep me sane and positive. They give me hope.

It's time to get dressed and move on. I love my book boyfriends and getting lost in romances, but I have other plans tonight.

My body crackling with excitement, I put the book back on the shelf and make my way to my bedroom. I'm going to Club X tonight, a place that literally embodies the BDSM fantasy elements I love reading about. It's a fantasy come to life, and I freaking love it. It's been my secret pleasure for a while now, and I'm having a blast just showing up and observing the BDSM lifestyle. From the rich, powerful men, to the beautiful and willing sex slaves, and the hot and heavy playrooms with wild, untamed sex—it's all so incredible. I suck in a breath as heat burns my cheeks, and my nipples pebble at the thought. The experience has been so much more liberating and intoxicating than I thought it would be. Even if I haven't actually participated yet.

It's exactly the place I need to be to research the themes I'm putting in my romance novel that I've been writing on my downtime while at school. The book isn't anything I'm taking too seriously, and I don't expect for it to ever be published or seen by anyone else's eyes but mine. I just love writing the stories that come to me. It's a stress-relieving outlet I enjoy indulging in, especially when I've had a particularly bad day.

I walk into my bedroom, tingling with excitement, and dig out a beautiful red nightgown out of my closet. I bought it just for tonight. There's a PJ theme tonight at Club X, and I don't want to be sent home for breaking club protocols. I set it down onto the bed, running my fingers along the soft silk fabric, thrilling at how luxurious it feels.

My skin pricks as I stare at it. I hope I'll look beautiful in this tonight. Just thinking about the looks I'll get from those powerful, handsome masked men causes my breath to quicken, and my pussy to clench. A fiery blush comes to my cheeks, a little bit ashamed at how turned on I am. I don't engage with them though. I stick to the safety of the trainers. I'm not ready for this to truly be real.

I can't imagine how people at school would react if they knew I was attending a place like Club X. A twinge of worry pricks my chest at the thought. I don't want anyone finding out, and I'm filled with anxiety every time I show up at school after a night at Club X. I worry that someone will recognize me and out me. But with how strict the rules are at the club, and the non-disclosure agreements that have to be signed just to get through the doors, I let the worry slip by.

I'm still slightly shocked about how I found out about it. Or rather, *who* told me about it. One of the teachers at the high school I work at, Mrs. Nicole Flite, mentioned the place to me after she saw me with my nose stuck in an erotic romance novel over lunch break. She was cautious at first, probably scared that I would look down on her or rat her out to the principal when she told me about the darker elements of the club. But when she saw how intrigued I was by the whole thing, she let loose, filling me in on all the exotic details.

I couldn't believe that a teacher who looked as sweet and unassuming as her could even be part of such a dark, sexual world like that. But then again... so am I. And now I'm hooked. This place embodies what I've been dreaming about after reading my romance novels.

It took a lot of work to build up the courage for me just to go. But I finally did, and I don't regret it at all.

I still haven't seen Nicole there yet in the weeks I've been going. And I'm not sure I will. From what I know, she's married with kids and she doesn't get the chance to go often anymore.

I haven't been able to go that much either, occupied with school and work. Only on the weekends during this past semester.

But now that I have all this free time over the winter break, I'm going to make the most of it.

I slip the red nightgown into my bag, feeling the adrenaline rush through my blood, and walk out of my bedroom, intent on spending a night lost in fantasy.

Chapter 2

Joseph

I bring the whiskey to my lips, taking a swig and then wiping my mouth with the back of my hand.

The amber liquid warms my chest with a vicious burn on the way down. I revel in the feeling. I need it just to feel at this point. My life is devoid of anything meaningful to me. I have wealth, I gave up power, and now I'm alone.

I made the right decision though. I left the *familia*, taking the fall to get the heat off their backs. But now I have nothing, and no one. I'm bored, and that's what's pissing me off the most.

It's better than taking over the familia though. Even if that does make me an outcast.

I clench and unclench my hands into fists. My knuckles are sore from boxing earlier today. I spend most of my time in the gym in my basement. It's all I do at this point, workout and survive each day. Just like the prisoner I am. Caged within a prison of my own making.

I don't fit in anywhere. Like the fucking Beast in his castle. I huff a humorless laugh, swirling the whiskey in the glass before taking another swig. I can feel the warmth flowing through every bit of me, coursing through my blood and finally giving me the buzz I was after.

I want to drown in this feeling. I need it just to sleep. The visions of what they've done and the blood still on my hands burn into me when I close my eyes.

I killed them. I helped eliminate those thieving, lying murderous bastards. Not for revenge, not for a righteous vindication. Killing the Romanos was a message. One that the community and our business partners heard loud and clear.

But someone had to take the fall for it, and I was eager to leave. I don't want to be a monster. I don't want a life of corruption and pain. It's a ruthless lifestyle. But it's the one I was born into.

I stare down at the worn leather journal in my lap. I'm writing every memory down as they come to me. Partly for documenting it, partly to relive it. It's fucked up that I'm trapped by the memory of a world I was so eager to leave, but the sins of my past refuse to let me move on. And I don't know why yet.

I close the journal and run my finger along the stamped name on the front. Passerotto. *Little sparrow.*

But that's not my name. It's what my mother called me. And this journal is all I have left from her, save a few dark memories.

Joe Levi. Murderer. Villain.

That's the only name I go by now.

I'm sure this wasn't what my mother imagined this journal would be used for, but she's buried six feet under in the cold hard dirt. I down the whiskey at the thought.

I was raised to be ruthless and cold, brought up in an environment that breeds sick fucks, like my own father.

They think I'm corrupt or maybe even a snitch 'cause the charges got dropped. The ones I was meant to take the fall for, but they don't know how or why they got dropped. Some think I have more power than I do, which is helpful at times. I'm still feared, which is better than having a target on my back, but it leaves me lonely.

The fire crackles in the large den. I stare at the logs, the fire spilling from the splits between the wood. The back of the brick firebox is black with soot.

I enjoy their fear. I need it to continue to survive. What's worse is that it breathes life into me.

I didn't have a choice.

Lies! The voices in my head sneer at me. They hiss that I could have done more.

They all should have died. My father, my brother.

I shouldn't have stopped at just the Romanos.

I set the empty glass down and lean forward, my head in

my hands and my elbows on my knees.

I've done horrible things. I didn't have to. I chose to, so I could survive. So I didn't have to run my entire life with the threat of death hanging over my head. But I still didn't have to do it. And now the memories haunt me.

My phone pings on the end table, drawing my attention and breaking the repetitive thoughts that I can never escape.

I slowly reach for it. There are only three people it could be. I dread the ones from my *familia*. They can all go fuck off. But they don't seem to get the message. I read the name on the lit screen, and relief and something else flow through me. Comfort.

Kiersten. Or Madam Lynn, as she likes to be called nowadays.

She reminds me of the one good thing I ever did. The whiskey pales in comparison to the warmth that memory brings to my chest.

They left her for dead. But I helped him save her.

It wasn't enough for all my sins to be forgiven, for all my wrongs to be righted, but I'm proud that she's still here, even if he isn't.

She's a close friend and nothing more. It's only recently that I've begun to leave this house, and it's all because of her. She's always talking about how she owes me; she has no idea how wrong she is. There's no doubt in my mind that I'm the one who owes her.

She wants to help me, but she can't. I'm beyond repair, and there's nothing I want from her. It's a sweet gesture that she tries to fill my dark days with *something*.

I rub the sleep from my eyes. It feels late in the dimly lit room with the thick drapes closed, but the darkness is just setting in beyond the walls of this house. This prison I keep myself in willingly.

Are you coming tonight?

I read her text message and debate on my answer.

I have sinful fantasies, some a product of the way I was raised, but others I've grown to desire of my own accord. I've yet to give in to the impulse driving me to keep going to Club X. It's alluring and intoxicating in its nature. The atmosphere is a heady mix of sex and power; so intense, it alone is a drug.

Just last week I bid on a Slave at her auction in Club X. I'm not a fan of the term, I prefer pet, but neither really matters.

I've never paid for sex before. It's not about the money at the auctions, it's about the contract. About getting exactly what I want, and ensuring the lines are clearly drawn and everything is written in black and white. Everything consensual. ...even if its nature is not.

That bid wasn't a bid for pleasure. Although she made me curious, I didn't want her. Her Master called her Katia, his kitten.

I thought Isaac was humiliating her, making her go onto a stage knowing no one else would bid on her. Making her feel undesired. I know the man, and I know what he's capable of.

I was pissed. How could he treat her like that? She was trembling on the stage, her apprehension and fear apparent. I wanted to make him pay for what he was doing. And steal his kitten, set her free even.

But I was wrong.

I don't understand them, the members of the club and the elite circles who have grown comfortable there. This lifestyle is new to me.

But control isn't. Sex isn't.

Power is in my blood.

My phone pings again. I don't want to read it. She always convinces me to go. Maybe it's because I feel for her and what she's going through, but I'm not interested in playing games and trying to fit in where I don't belong.

I toss the journal and pen onto the end table and rise from my seat, feeling my muscles groan with a pain I find pleasurable. I take a peek at my phone in my hand when the reminder ding goes off.

Kiersten's text reads:

She's going to be there.

I stare at it, thinking about the one thing that's interested me in the last three years of living in this void. I ran into her when I left the last auction. Literally. I ran straight into her small, delicate frame and nearly knocked her over. I wasn't paying attention. It was my fault entirely.

But she took the blame.

Kneeling, improperly, and apologizing in a hushed voice.

She was perfectly imperfect. In need of a Master. But not yet accepting of one. She's still learning. Kiersten caught on to my interest when I started coming to the club more often.

I've been watching her. I needed to observe her.

She has desires I'm not sure I can fill. The way she craves pain is something that feeds a monster lurking inside of me. A depraved beast I've tried to keep chained.

I should stay far away from her. But she piques my curiosity, and she's made me truly desire her. Or at least I crave hearing those soft moans and forcing them from her lips myself.

I've watched her closely this past month. I'm not sure she's noticed. No one pays her much attention since she's still finding her limits. She's not eager for a partner either. She sticks with the trainers and stays in the shadows and corners, keeping out of sight.

I can't deny that she tempts me to possess her, to teach her proper techniques. I tap my fingers on the wooden end table rhythmically as I consider going tonight.

I picture the curve of her ass as she practices her poses, the way her lips part with lust when she touches herself discreetly. She may think no one's noticed her, but I have. And I want her.

I text Kiersten back, *I'll be there.*

Chapter 3

Lily

I walk up to the doors of Club X, the huge mansion-like structure looming in the background, its red ambient lighting illuminating the front of the building and casting a glow on its esteemed guests that are waiting to be admitted. A cool breeze blows through the area. My skin pricks as the air softly caresses my flesh, crackling with electricity, and the dark-suited bodyguard at the door recognizes me.

His eyes trail the skimpy outfit I'm wearing, the red silk short nightgown I changed into before getting out of my Honda. I feel almost naked under his gaze, but at the same time incredibly sexy; he makes me feel wanted. Although the attraction is firmly one-sided.

I should be used to this now, but I still get nervous with

anticipation. I know that in a few moments, men far more powerful than him will be looking at me, and it makes me feel anxious. Unconsciously, I trail my finger along my bracelet. It's rubber without any metal rings, meaning I'm still just learning. I haven't yet chosen a membership bracelet that will indicate what I want in a partner, Dominant or Master, or someone who enjoys the more painful side of BDSM. I'm afraid to admit that I'm still a virgin, although there's a bracelet for that. I would rather have a Submissive or Slave bracelet, although I'm not sure which one yet. The lines are blurred for me still. And I'm not sure how much control I'm really willing to give up. The fantasy of being completely at someone else's mercy makes me weak with desire. But the reality has an entirely different effect. I think the aspects of pleasure and pain are what intrigue me most. I haven't felt the sting of a whip yet. But I really want to. I crave it like a sweet-toothed freak fiending for their next Twinkie. I just haven't asked for it. It's as easy as letting a trainer know that I'm ready. But I haven't taken the plunge yet.

Deep down, I know that actually committing to it is going to take a lot. So right now, I'm just observing. It's all just research for my book. Or so I tell myself.

I'm admitted through the doors by the dark-gazed bodyguard, and as I step into the club I have to suck in a breath. I've been here a lot, at least half a dozen times, but I'm still floored every single time I walk in. Club X is beyond beautiful with thick lush carpet, extravagant furniture, gorgeous ambient lighting and soft, tantalizing music that makes my blood heat.

But the thing that gets me the most is the very air that surrounds the people.

The men who walk the floors of the club radiate power and wealth beyond imagine, and the women who follow them are too beautiful for words. I watch as a masked man pulls his timid partner along by a gleaming silver chain, his eyes filled with determination and swirling with lust. I keep my gaze safely away, knowing it's not my place to look a Master or Dominant directly in his eyes unless I want to draw his ire. I'm supposed to be Submissive, and acting anything otherwise will get me in trouble. Even if I'm only here to watch. I can't ruin the fantasy that Club X provides so perfectly.

I shiver as the atmosphere of the club seems to wrap around my body, my nipples pebbling. I love this place. It's even better than reading my books, and that says a lot.

My lungs fill with a deep, steadying breath, as I try to get control over my emotions. It's almost as if I've taken a hit of a powerful drug and I'm getting high. That's what this place does to you. It gets you high on lust, power... sex.

I lean against the bar just past the foyer and breathe in deeply, cooling my heated blood.

I know I want to go to the dungeon, but first, I think I need a drink. It's dark down there, and I'm not sure I can handle it without at first numbing a part of myself. I need to free my inhibitions.

As I wait for the bartender, I glance across the large hall. The stage on the back wall is dark tonight, with the curtains closed, and I don't know if that's a good thing. I look forward to the shows, since not only are they exhilarating, they're a great learning experience. I order a shot of tequila, making sure to keep my gaze in a safe place. Within seconds, the shot glass is placed in front of me by a beautiful bar vixen with long dark hair, wearing the same professional uniform the other employees have on. There's no mixing up who's working here, and who's here for play.

The liquid burns as it goes down my throat, but it's a comfortable feeling. I know it will help me deal with the experience of the dungeon. Even though I'm hungry for it, the alcohol aids me in handling the intense sexual emotions that run through my body. The alcohol is nothing in comparison to how intoxicating the sights in the dungeon can be. I bite into the lime and let it wash the taste of the liquor out of my mouth, the sourness making my eyes close tightly.

When I'm done with my drink, the fiery liquid warming my belly, I leave the bar and make my way through the halls, blending in and trying to disappear amongst the crowd.

A few men approach me as I pass the playrooms. I swallow thickly, my heartbeat racing as I pause in my steps. I don't look at them, but I make sure that my bracelet is in view.

Once they see it, they move on. No one seems interested in someone who still doesn't know what they want.

With the rubber bracelet on my wrist, the only people who talk to me are Submissives waiting for their partners, or the trainers. I like it that way. It makes me want to keep the bracelet forever. It makes me feel safe. But the days are limited. The membership here is expensive. Too fucking expensive. The first month with this bracelet was on the house. Madam Lynn, the owner I think, said that I could stay to see if it suited me. But next month I have to pay up if I'm not paired up. And I'm not sure I'm ready for that. Or if I ever will be. But the month is almost up.

It's hard not to stop and stare at the sexual acts taking place in the playrooms as I pass them. The men and women going at each other with untamed depravity. Their moans and cries and grunts and groans assault my ears, the smacks of their flesh pounding against each other filling my already heated blood with sexual desire.

I ignore it as best I can, although my breathing is coming in faster, and continue on into the darkened corridors, my pulse racing with excitement.

There's nothing in this world like the place I'm about to enter. The playrooms are an intense experience, but down here it's far more... primal, possessive. Raw in every sense of the word. I make my way down a dim hallway to where two men dressed in dark suits wait on either side of a large iron cast door. They're employees, guards who make sure that everything runs smoothly. And that no laws are broken. They give me a cursory glance before opening the door, the sound of its creaking making my heart jump in my chest.

I take in a ragged breath before I walk into a dark stairwell, the only lighting being small, glowing red sconces on the wall, giving the area an almost evil feel. A few masked men pass me on my way down and their way up, their dark gazes holding secrets that chill my blood. One man even stops to look at me as if thinking that I am looking to be taken, but when he sees my bracelet, he keeps moving like the men back at the playrooms.

They respect that I'm not ready, and not a single person has tried to push me. There are rules to the club, and they're strictly followed. It makes me feel safe. It's odd to think that way, given the nature of this place. But I do feel safe.

I shudder to even think about what goes on through the heads of the Masters and Dominants when they look at me. It arouses me in a thrilling and exciting way. A way that hardens my nipples, and sends a pulsing need to my clit. I'm almost ashamed at how turned on I am by their questioning glances and piercing stares, and the sinful thoughts I know are lurking behind their eyes.

It's just like how I imagine things in my books. I only hope I can write about this in a way that does this place justice. A way that captures the sensual seductive side along with the other emotions coursing through my blood.

As I get closer to my destination, a shrill scream that's a mix of pleasure and pain rips through the stairwell. It's followed by whimpers and moans. I pause, gripping onto the banister for support, my breath stalling in my lungs. I've been here many times, but I still can't prepare myself for some of the darker things that happen in the dungeon. It's so sexually intense that I become dizzy with desire and emotion. Thank God I've taken that hit of tequila. After I calm myself, I continue on until I make it to the bottom floor. The sounds of groans and seductive pleading fill my ears. It's a place that resembles a seventeenth century English dungeon, with cages and racks on either side of the room, and lit torches along the walls. The ambiance is everything that makes this room... it's all so tempting and forbidden, mixed with danger and fright.

It's more private here, especially this early, but I've seen many things here I never imagined I would. Things that have turned me on. Scenes I've watched play out, and then later been ashamed to have gotten aroused by. I've seen a woman beaten with a whip until tears were falling down her cheeks, her ass bright red from the lashes. But she leaned into it. She begged for more. Her Master gave her what he felt she needed, and the way he took her after made me desire the same ruthless touch.

I want to feel what she felt. I want to experience it to understand why she desired it as much as she did.

I watch, stalking along the edges of the room, as a naked,

dark-haired woman is bound to a bench. The rough rope is coarse and would chafe her skin, but her masked Master places a thin piece of silk under it. Her lips part in a soft mix of moan and whimper as he binds her so tightly she can barely move. I can see his huge hard cock pressing against his silk slacks. It forces an intense wave of arousal through every part of me.

The Master, or Dominant, I'm not sure, is wearing the membership bracelet. His rubber bracelet is joined by two interlocking metal bands of silver, and in the center, a red band. I shiver at what the bracelet signifies. This dude is into some dark shit. Sadism and Masochism.

I've seen this couple before, though I don't know their names. I don't know anyone's real name, actually, other than Nicole. It's funny--I've been coming here for a while, and I don't know anything about anyone. But it doesn't bother me. I'm here for the experience. And names are rarely used inside Club X.

Another couple is seated on a bench, and I've seen them before, too. The man gives me chills like no other. And not in a good way. His eyes are beady, and pure black. His hand is gripping his pet's shoulder, squeezing. He's always touching her, or pulling her collar. I've never seen them interact in any way other than what they're currently doing. She's on her knees on the ground, looking straight ahead and he's behind her, whispering into her ear.

Her hair is wispy and unkempt, which also makes them stand out. None of the others look like her. They're taken care of in ways she's not. Most of the women here are given looks of jealousy from me; I can't help it. But not her. I can't help the sympathy I feel for her.

Of all the people here, he's the only one that doesn't seem to belong. And it's all because of the way he treats her. The way she doesn't beg him for more. The way his touch seems to wilt her spirit, rather than enhance it.

I rip my eyes away from them, hating that they're here. I have to ignore them whenever they come down to the dungeon. Instead I focus on the couple in the center of the room, the reason most everyone is in this room. The ideal couple. The one that exemplifies what I consider to be the fantasy of this lifestyle. I watch as he kisses her softly on the lips and places a blindfold over her eyes. There's a guard to the right of them, watching vigilantly. There's another one stationed at the end of the room, also watching the couple and the onlookers like me. These men observe every detail. They see everything. The men in the suits are here to enforce order in case things go too far. They know the safe words ahead of time. Although everything is done discreetly. And some couples don't use safe words at all.

I was shocked the first time I saw one of these men disrupt a session. I could understand why though, because the woman was screaming for her partner to stop. The very fact that the guard felt the need to step in made me fear for the Submissive. The guard merely stepped forward and requested that the

Submissive give her safe word. The Dominant stepped back immediately, lowering the paddle he was using on her, and the Submissive gave it, out of breath and still writhing in the binds that held her down. She whispered the word green and then looked to her Dominant, waiting for more. I got the feeling it wasn't the first time a guard had interrupted them.

The man in the suit stepped back, and the scene continued. The Submissive kept screaming as her Dominant fucked her ruthlessly, using her body mercilessly, fucking her with vicious need and smacking the paddle against her skin as he took her almost like a caveman from prehistoric times.

It was a rape fantasy reenacted before my very eyes. It was very difficult to watch, and my eyes kept going over to the guard that was standing nearby. But he didn't move again. As long as the Submissive didn't say the safe word, the Dominant had complete control over her. They were free to act out whatever fantasies they shared in complete safety.

For couples without safe words, they merely nod at the guards when asked if they're alright. Or so I've been told. I've only seen a guard interrupt once. I'm surprised how many couples don't have safe words. Some simply use 'stop'. I suppose it's different for every partnership.

Most of the clients in here seem paired up, like these two. It makes me envy them. Especially when they're collared. Collars are like wedding bands. My eyes fall to the floor, and my heart thuds. Maybe that's more of my romance novels slipping in. I don't know for sure that the people here regard collars so highly.

It's hard not to confuse reality and fantasy. But that's easy to do here. This place is like a fantasy come to life.

A movement out of the corner of my eye causes me to look around. The breath stills in my throat, and my heart skips a beat. There *he* is. Looking at him, I can hardly stand, my knees are so weak. He's like a dark prince, dressed all in black with his matching half mask, the edges of it looking torn. It only serves to enhance his chiseled features. My breath quickens as his eyes bore into me with an intensity that makes my skin prick. The room seems to bow to him. Everything urges me to bend to his will. *And I want to.*

My heart pounds rapidly in my chest as I stare at the floor. A chill travels down my shoulder and through my spine. He has a power over me more intense than anyone else. A pull to him so strong I nearly give in and fall to my knees as I feel his gaze on me.

I've seen this man before. In fact, I ran into him when I was new to the club. My cheeks burn at the memory, remembering his dark regard of me, the flush of my skin as I sank to my knees and apologized for being so clumsy. He watches me sometimes when I come into the club, and I'm always almost overwhelmed. At first I thought it was all in my head that he was checking me out, and then I thought I was just getting carried away by my fantasies. But he followed me down here.

He must want something from me. The thought makes my body come alive with desire.

Or maybe it really is all in my head, I think to myself. No one knows me here. I've tried my best to make myself as invisible as possible.

But as I move away and walk over to the Saint Andrew's Cross that sits next to a rack of whips and rope, I can feel him following me, stalking my every move.

My breathing quickens as I do something new. I slowly fall into a kneel, trying to remember every detail one of the trainers showed me about proper posture. I can't believe I'm about to do this. But my body feels compelled by a mysterious force.

I show him submission.

I invite him to have power over me.

Chapter 4

Joseph

I can't take my eyes off of her. It happens every time she comes in here. *Lilly.* I follow her, staying a safe distance away, her gorgeous curves stringing me along. I'll never admit to her how much power she has over me; I can't help but follow her through the club, watching her and gauging her reaction to the variety of kinks. I know she's seen me this time.

She's not put off by it. She doesn't seem frightened, although I obviously affect her. It's as if she's waiting for me. She's never done this before. She's never invited anyone into her personal space. Let alone kneel as though she's been waiting for me, offering me a chance at her submission.

Seeing her kneeling there, looking vulnerable and sexy as fuck in that red nightie makes my cock harden, my heart beat faster. I take a quick glance around the room, a possessive side of me rising from deep within my veins, but no one moves to go to her. A few eyes are on me, narrowing with questioning looks, but they fall when I look their way.

I ignore them all. I always do.

They don't know shit about me. And I give zero fucks about what they *think* they know.

These masks are good for hiding the identities of the men from the Submissives. But it's no secret who we are to one another. The tight social circles that run this city, both from the highest highs of skyscrapers and penthouses, to the dirtiest lows of the pulses that run the streets—are all infamous in their own way. We all know each other. We know who has business with who, and what side each of us is on. Right now, I belong to neither, but I'm well-known to both.

I can tell from the way they look at me out of the corner of their eyes without moving an inch, without even breathing. By the way they stay away and avoid me at all costs. I know for a fact that they *know* who I am. And I sure as fuck know who they are.

We're all powerful men here, and with too much to lose to engage in this kind of activity around people we don't know. Even with contracts and NDAs, we're bred not to trust. With so far to fall and so much to lose, most of these men stay in the private rooms once they've found someone to pursue and indulge in.

But me? I have nothing to lose. And I know exactly what I want. Or rather *whom* I want.

I approach her slowly, almost cautiously, as if moving too quickly will frighten her away. The very notion that she's offering this gift to me, thrills me.

She's been coming to the dungeon more often as if she's looking for something, as if she needs some kind of depravity that she can only find here. But she's yet to engage with anyone. That's what I've been waiting for. For that moment when she's ready to test how her pleasure reacts to pain, and how much freedom she'd get by giving over control.

It piqued my interest to see desire flash in her eyes when she watched the tails of the whip hit against the soft skin of a Submissive. She wasn't frightened by it. She was intrigued. She was *aroused*. She hasn't experienced the pain yet. I have no idea if she'll actually enjoy it.

But I'm excited to find out. The anticipation clouds my judgment, and makes me focus solely on her.

The guards in the room are watching over the other couple. David and Nadine. They're well-known in the club. They've been together for over a year, but they don't have any safe words. They take their sessions to the extremes. It's intoxicating to watch, just as my Lilly is drawn to them, like a moth to a flame.

I stand next to Lilly for a moment, shifting my Barker Black shoes slightly across the cement floor. Her eyes dart toward them, and her head tilts slightly. A sharp breath is pulled through my clenched teeth at the thought of my flogger smacking along her back. She should be still. Her back is curved. She has so much to learn. I pivot and face her, but I don't address her; I'm merely letting her feel my presence.

From the way her breathing picks up, I know she's filled with anticipation as well. She's practically trembling beneath me.

I already know her name, since I've heard her tell it to a few others in the club. But I feel compelled to ask anyway, as if it's the polite thing to do. I crouch down next to her, my hand resting gently on her head. Her soft blonde hair is like silk beneath the rough pads of my fingers. The strands slide easily through my fingers and whether it's unconscious or not, Lilly leans slightly into my touch. Her eyes close, and her plump lips part. She is a woman in need of approval. And desperately in need of touch.

I clear my throat as I take my hand away, testing her obedience and knowledge. She remains in place, her eyes locked on the floor, although her tongue darts out quickly, wetting the seam of her lips. I wait a moment, rising to stand, but she still doesn't move. Good girl. It's not until I give her permission to look, that her pale blue eyes lift to reach mine. As soon as her baby blues meet my gaze with a look of pure desire, tiny golden flecks swirling in the mist of blue and sparkling with lust, I feel a spark between us that sets my heart afire.

This is the closest we've ever been; the first time I've ever touched her. I almost have to reach out to brace myself, surprised by the electricity flowing through me. It's the intensity in her eyes, the vulnerability that shocks me. I hadn't anticipated how emotional she would be so quickly, how trusting. Maybe it's in her nature. I don't like to think that way though. I want it to be just for me, and only me. The sight of her eyes in this moment will stay with me once we've parted, I know that.

"What name do you go by?" I ask her easily, ignoring the attraction screaming at me to claim her right here, right now.

"Lilly," she replies, and her voice is low and gentle. *Lilly*. It suits her. I call her by her name for the first time, letting the soft sounds of her name fall from my lips.

"And you?" she asks, chancing a look up at me, her doe eyes calling to me in a way where I almost feel a need to look in another direction. To break the intense contact, but I don't. I accept the challenge. "You can call me Sir," I tell her. She licks her bottom lip, her eyes darting away as her breath leaves her, and then quickly looks back to meet my gaze. I smirk down at her and ask, "Does that turn you on?"

I already know it does, but hearing the "yes" fall from her plump lips gives me undeniable satisfaction.

Nadine moans from across the room and then hisses in a sharp breath that echoes off the walls. It distracts us both. David has a lit candle above her, a match in his hand while keeping the fire on the wick. The wax slowly drips down onto her naked body, leaving splashes of red covering her milky white skin. She's bound to the bench on her back, unable to move very much, but each time the wax hits her she wiggles slightly to get away.

I faintly hear David admonishing her. "You need to be still, my love." Immediately, she stops writhing on the bench, her head falling back, and her mouth opening in a silent scream as the next drop of wax falls between her breasts. Her hands ball into fists and her feet move outward slightly, but the rest of her body remains perfectly still as she obeys her Master.

"Do you want to watch them?" I ask Lilly softly, gently lifting her chin and drawing her attention back to me.

She starts to look up at me. But she stops herself. "I would like to. If you would allow it." She barely whispers the second sentence. My dick hardens instantly, loving the vulnerability in her voice, loving the way she gives me power. And reveling in the fact that she's uncertain about her behavior. It's the uncertainty that makes me crave her as a Submissive. She's breakable. And I fucking love that about her.

"Are you playing with me, my flower?" I ask her in a deep rough voice.

Her eyes look up into mine, widening as my words register. She stutters to answer, her breath coming in quicker. Fear flashes in her eyes, not understanding what I'm asking her. I give her a soft smile to put her at ease and say softly, yet in a stern voice, "Meaning that you want me to play the role of your Master?"

I can practically see the relief flooding through her veins. The tension leaves her body as she looks up and answers me confidently, "I would like to play." The strength in her voice diminishes as she adds, "I'm not sure if I need a Dominant or a Master."

Submissives have more power than they realize. They truly control the relationship. They set the boundaries, they start and stop all acts with what they allow the Dominant to get away with. The Dominant has an illusion of control. I'm not interested in an illusion. I want absolute power. I want to be her Master.

"I'm not looking for a Submissive, my flower," I state clearly. I don't want her to get the wrong impression. I'll determine her boundaries, then I'll push her much faster than she's pushing herself.

Her eyes quickly look beyond me, staring at the row of cages that line the left wall as she considers what I'm saying. "I'm willing to play with you, for now." My body heats, and adrenaline pumps through my veins with an anxiety I'm uncomfortable with, something I've not yet experienced. I don't want her denying me.

She nods her head slowly.

"So would you like to play with me then?" I ask her.

"As a Slave?" she asks me, clarifying what I've just said.

I tower over her small body. "In this setting it doesn't matter. We'll only play for a moment."

Her forehead pinches slightly as she considers what I'm saying. "You'll do as I say while we're down here. And if you don't like it, you can simply leave."

She seems dumbstruck by my words at first, and the connection between us wanes as something else settles in between us. Insecurity. She's confused and uncertain not about what she should do, but about what I can give her.

I'm quick to put her at ease as I say, "You can always leave. Regardless of whether I'm your Master or Dominant. You can always leave without fear." Her expression softens as she comprehends what I'm telling her. In a sense, I'm twisting words to put her at ease so I can keep her. But I don't give a damn. I'll do what I must to get what I want.

Her voice comes in breathy as she responds, "I think I'd like to play."

"Good girl." My lips curve into a noticeable smile, and when she responds with a faint huff of a breath, it's slow and easy. And sexual. Everything about her right now from her posture and dilated pupils, to the way she's breathing and clenching her thighs depicts how turned on she is by my approval.

I walk over to the bench while she remains kneeling. I'm highly aware of the other men in the room, but there's no way they'd approach her. They'd be dead men if they dared to try.

I want her in my lap while we watch, grinding on my hard cock. She gets up on all fours before I tell her to, eager to come over to me. I wonder if she wants to crawl, if she wants to be degraded. I've yet to learn her limits. I'm confident that *she* doesn't even know her limits. But I'm going to find them by pushing them.

I need to see what her true fantasy is, and how much she can take. It may frighten her, but she'll thank me in the end.

"Come to me." I give her the command and wait for her reaction. She immediately crawls to me. Watching her move catlike across the floor, her bare knees against the cold, hard ground and her nightie riding up high on the back of her thighs while she obeys my command so swiftly, turns me the fuck on. It makes me harder than I've ever been before. As soon as she gets to me, I reach down and lift her up by her hips, settling her in my lap. She lets out a gasp at my powerful grip, which only makes my cock throb harder for her.

That sound. I want to hear it again and again and again.

I grip her by the nape of her neck. A powerful hold, yet I'm still gentle, barely holding her still in my grasp. Her body is so much lighter than I had anticipated. It's easy to move her, to grip her hips and direct her body which way I want it to go. Feeling the weight of her ass in my lap I can only imagine how easily I can take her. Her petite, pear-shaped body was meant to take a punishing fuck.

"You came down here for a reason, my flower." My hot breath tickles her cheek, causing her to shiver slightly.

"Yes, Sir," she says staring straight ahead, but she turns to me, looking me in the eyes as she adds, "I'm curious."

The focus of the dungeon is pain. The name is fitting, and we're gathered down here because the things that happen in the confines of these walls may be disturbing to others. I've watched Nadine and David before. I enjoy their play. I've also seen much, much worse. But what they do is nothing short of erotic to me.

"Put your hands behind your back." Lilly looks at me hesitantly, but even as she does, she obeys me, putting both of her hands behind her back and balancing herself by shifting slightly in my lap. I want to get rid of that hesitation. The more she plays with me, the more she'll learn to trust.

My dick throbs against her soft ass, and I know she has to feel it. I shift in my seat, making sure it presses deep into her flesh, allowing her to feel the pulsating thickness. I want her to know how much I want her.

There are rope ties, leather belts and all sorts of instruments of bondage in a storage bench next to me. More different varieties hang on the wall on hooks to my right. I'm quick to choose a hobble for its versatility and ease of use. It's a wide piece of leather with holes in it for a buckle, complete with D rings and O rings so that the band can be used as restraint, like handcuffs or, without the rings, a simple collar. I wrap the leather around her wrist and secure it and then do the same to the other wrist before fastening the two ends together with the buckle.

I make sure that both are tightened and fastened all the

way so that her wrists are completely restrained behind her.

"I want a safe word," Lilly speaks quickly, her words laced with fear, as I tuck the leather strap into the loop. I can practically hear her heart beating faster and faster, mixing in with the sounds of Nadine's pleasure.

A scowl forms on my face and knots my forehead. I fucking hate safe words. I'll know her limits before she does. I'm good at reading people, and I know the difference between pleasure and pain all too well.

I can feel the eyes of the guards on me, no longer watching the scene unfold in the center of the room. Instead they're focused on the two of us, and my reaction to her wanting a safe word. My body heats with anger. But I need to get the fuck over it, she's only just now let me hold her. She's never done this before. She'll learn.

"And what would you like that word to be?" I ask her. I don't miss the look of surprise on some bastard's face across the room when I give in so easily. I don't know his name, and I don't give a fuck; he's seated across the room and enjoying the show. And not the one starring David and Nadine.

"Lollipop," Lilly answers quickly.

I almost huff out a laugh at her answer. *Lollipop?* Does she think this shit is funny? That it's some sort of a joke? I furrow my brow for a moment and then I nod my head, shoving the anger down. It doesn't matter if she thinks this is a game, she won't be thinking that once I'm done with her.

"Lollipop it is then." I lean forward, placing my lips just barely against the shell of her ear and whisper, "Now that I've given it to you, you need to make sure that you use it wisely." Her thighs clench in my lap as she nods her head. I quickly spread her thighs apart, gripping both her knees in my hands and placing her legs outside of my own. The shocked gasp that spills from her lips at how quickly I've made her available to me makes my lips curve up.

My hand slips between her thighs, my fingers barely caressing her skin. I make sure that my movements are slow, not so that she can see them coming, but just so I can send a chill of goosebumps down her body as I slide my fingertips along her soft skin. I want her to *feel* everything. I want her soaking wet by the time I slide my fingers inside her tight cunt.

I run my finger down the center of her lace panties. And again I whisper, "Next time you'll take these off before you come here." A soft moan escapes her lips as I brush my fingernail against her clit, back and forth. "Do you understand?"

"Yes, Sir," she breathes her answer. Her nipples are hardened and poking through the thin fabric of her nightgown. I want to take it off and suck her nipples into my mouth, swirling my tongue around them and heightening her pleasure. But not here. Not with everyone watching. I need to take her home. But I have to be patient. She needs to learn, and I need to find her limits.

Fuck, she makes me so fucking hard. I want to take her

right now, thrusting my dick into that wet, tight pussy of hers.

My back hits the concrete wall as I spread my knees wider, which in turn spreads hers. She bites down on her bottom lip, but she has no protests. I push the thin lace fabric away and run my fingers over her soaking wet lips and groan in the crook of her neck. "You're so ready for me." Her eyes close as a shiver runs down her body.

I'll focus on her clit as she watches the scene. She's so fucking responsive. I'm in awe of how beautiful the subtle changes of her pleasure are expressed on her face. "You are going to watch what a Master does to his Slave," I lean a little closer, gently kissing the lobe of her ear and then adding in a softer voice, "and you're going to get off to it, but only when I say."

She nods her head and immediately answers, "Yes, Sir."

I grip the nape of her neck, not hard, just enough that she knows I have control of her positioning. With her wrists bound, her legs spread, one of my hands between her thighs and the other on the nape of her neck, I have complete control over her.

A silver gleam shines across the room as David produces a knife. He scrapes the wax from Nadine's body, the knife tickling her skin as he does it.

Nadine whimpers as he gets close to her hardened nipple, scraping her sensitive skin but careful not to cut her. She moans as the sensation becomes overwhelming. Every little touch gives her pleasure. Even those that are dangerous.

"It's a good thing that she learned to be still," I whisper

in Lilly's ear, careful not to disturb the scene. A few other members of the club have gathered and are watching. Scenes like this are rare in the club. It takes a lot to trust someone so wholeheartedly. Most have their eyes on the couple in the center of the room. These two always manage to draw a crowd.

But some of the men are focused on us.

I run my fingers down her lips all the way to her entrance, teasing her and then trace back up to her clit. I'm toying with her and testing her sensitivity. "She must have so much trust in him." I kiss her neck, breathing in her scent. So sweet. She's truly a flower.

I open my eyes and see that David has traveled down Nadine's body, flicking off the wax as he goes along with the knife. The skin on her belly is red from the pressure of the blade. The sensitive stroking of the sharp edge against her skin brings the endorphins to the surface. That's the entire point. It makes every feeling that much more intense. I watch as he travels down farther, crouching between her legs. A few drops of red wax have pooled and hardened around her pubic hair. And he scrapes them off, cutting the short hair as he goes.

I slip my middle finger down the center of Lilly's hot pussy, and then back up to her hard, throbbing clit, putting more and more pressure on her as I rub in hard circles. I pinch the hardened nub slightly as David leans in between Nadine's legs and begins licking her pussy.

I wasn't anticipating her to react so strongly, so quickly, but

Lilly's body trembles and her thighs tense, immediately trying to close in my lap. Her head falls back, hitting my left shoulder and she moans loudly as she cums in my lap. My dick pulses with need at the knowledge that I brought her to her edge so quickly.

I make my strokes harder, rougher, making sure to get every bit of her orgasm out of her trembling body. She shakes in my grasp, my left hand moving from the nape of her neck to wrap around her waist, steadying her as her orgasm reverberates through her.

I stare at her in wonder, amazed by how fucking beautiful she is. It only makes me want to get her off even more.

Her body wavers in my grasp, completely unsteady, unhinged from the intensity of her orgasm. I've seen her touching herself before, but it was nothing like this. I should admonish her for cumming without permission. A wicked grin slips into place on my lips. My sweet girl needs to be punished. She's really going to enjoy this.

Before I can move her back to my chest and spread her wider so I can feel the arousal dripping down her pussy and onto my lap, she calls out to me, "Lollipop."

Her eyes are wide open, seemingly just as shocked as I am. I hesitate, but only for a moment. Only because I'm pissed. I don't want a safe word; I know she doesn't need it. I feel ripped off in some ways. My grip on her tightens for a moment, hating whatever I've done to make her safe word me. I imagine it was the intensity of the situation. I can only begin to guess that's why. Unless she knew her punishment was looming...

I'm quick to unbind the hobble around her wrists. Not because I want to, and certainly not because she can't handle this. Only because I agreed to it.

"I'm sorry," she breathes the apology, her breath coming in faster. "I just didn't-"

She doesn't finish, looking up at me with wide eyes shining with fear and shock. I press my finger to her lips. "This is new to you. You're going to be surprised by what I can do to your body, by what arouses you. Don't let it scare you."

She swallows thickly and starts to apologize again, but I won't allow it. She seems genuinely upset. But I don't want her to remember this moment with a single negative thought.

Still hard and pissed that I wasn't able to bind her to the Saint Andrew's Cross and give her a lashing, I steady her on her feet and stand behind her. "Don't apologize, my flower. You did very well." She could have done better. If only she'd given me more control. But that requires trust. And I'm willing to wait to earn it.

As I lead her out of the dungeon, I pass a few men. All of them wear masks, but their eyes follow us as I walk by them, a look flashing in their eyes that lets me know what they think of me. None of them trust me. But I don't give a fuck. I don't trust them either.

Even here in this dungeon beneath a house of sin, I can't escape my past.

Chapter 5

Lily

A rush of endorphins flows through my limbs, filling me with excitement as the previous day's events run through my mind. I'm trying to remember everything as I prepare to write, sitting at my Ikea desk in the corner of my living room.

I've never felt anything like this before. I've never had someone own me so utterly and completely. So quickly taking possession of me. The feel of that masked man's hard body pressed up against mine, the way he took control of me, his hard cock pressing against me, throbbing and pulsating, making me want to beg for it...

I have no idea what came over me, submitting to him like that. But I don't regret one moment of the experience. It was so intoxicating that even now my body refuses to relax, little jolts of electricity shocking my nerves throughout the morning. I can already see myself mirroring a scene in my book, making it even hotter and heavier than what went down in that dungeon room. What I wish had taken place afterward if my fear hadn't made me safe word.

Fuck. I'm already getting wet, and the day hasn't even started yet.

Shaking my head to clear it, I open up my laptop and bring up the desktop. I need to write to get my mind off my sinful thoughts. Before I can open my Word document and begin writing the scene that won't leave me alone, I see an email notification pop up on my screen followed by the telltale *ding*.

From: Zach White
To: Ms. Lilly Wade
Subject: I need ur help.

Hey, I know ur probably busy with ur family over vacation and all, and I really hate to bother u, but can u do me a favor? I got myself into some major shit and now I have to do community service if I don't want to end up in juvey. I'm not going into details about what happened because I don't want u to be pissed off at me. I remember the talk we had before the semester ended and I'm really ashamed that I didn't listen.

I'm lucky as fuck tho. The judge said he might let me choose where I put in my hours if I show him that I'm really sorry, but it has to be something that he will approve of. Right now, they have me signed up for public bathroom cleaning. I can't do it. Public bathrooms make my skin crawl. Like seriously, I'm a total germaphobe after the shit mom put me thru with her dirty fucking needles and pipes all over the place and those cockroaches she had crawling everywhere. I know it's shitty to ask, but can you please help? Could you get me assigned somewhere else or something?

I can fucking hardly stand it when I have to use one at school and there is no goddamn way I'm doing that shit unless I have to.

Zach

I sit back in my chair as I read his words. My first reaction is to respond and tell him to just grow up and deal with it. Cleaning a public bathroom, while pretty gross, is a small price to pay in exchange for not winding up in a more serious place. I'm pissed off, too. We had so many talks, and I poured my heart and soul into every single one of them, about him getting his act together and putting more effort into his schooling. And figuring out where he wanted to be in a few years. He could do great things. We set up a plan together, and he promised that he'd do better.

But then I remember all the things he's gone through, and my anger subsides.

Zach was dealt some rough cards coming into this world. He had an abusive father who beat him regularly before he abandoned him, leaving him with a mother who was strung out on drugs and let her son live in absolute squalor, resulting in his germaphobia. He's just a kid in so many ways. I could see the pain in his eyes every day that he came into my office, the hurt that haunted him. Seeing that tore at my heart. No child should have to go through what he went through. I let out a soft sigh as I position my fingers over the keyboard. I can't be angry with him, that's not going to help him. Without someone in his life that shows that they care about him, he might as well give up. I can't let that happen. No matter what bad thing he's done, I have to offer what help I'm able. I refuse to give up on him, and I refuse to let him give up on himself.

But I can't enable him either.

Blowing my bangs out of my eyes, my fingers fly across the keys as I type my response.

From: Ms. Wade
To: Zach White

Zach,

I'm so very sorry to hear that you've gotten yourself into some trouble, but I did warn you that if you kept on your current path, that something like this might happen. I'm not going to lie and say I'm not disappointed. I'm pissed, actually. I put a lot of time and effort into trying to help you, and it doesn't look like it stuck with you. I hope that you're able to prove me wrong. I understand why you don't want to have to clean public bathrooms, given your past with your mother.

And I will try my best to figure out the options that are available to you... but only if you tell me what you did, and why. I want to help you, but I'm not going to let you walk all over me. I can't help you if I don't know what exactly you've been caught doing. I'm available to talk and work on the plan we've set for you. This is yet another obstacle that I know you'll overcome. I look forward to hearing from you.

Sincerely,
Ms. Wade

I sigh again as I press send. My heart hurts, hating the fact I can't give him an easy out. I can't just pluck him from where he is now and move him somewhere better, where he's surrounded by encouragement and more opportunities. This very situation is going to close even more doors for him, and I hate that simple truth. He's just made things harder on himself.

I hate that the kid is in this predicament and I feel really bad for being tough with him, but I can't let him off easy. He can't come asking for my help and then try to gloss over the crime he committed. I hope he does the right thing and comes clean. I really like him and want to see him do something with his life, not end up a deadbeat father, or a druggie like his mom, living a life of crime.

Helping troubled students like Zach gives my life meaning, and it means a lot to me. There are times where I wish I could just wave my hand and change all of their lives for the better. Ha, if only such magic existed. The world would be a much better place. But sometimes... I just have to admit...

You can't help them all. They need to want to change. And I don't know if Zach really does or not.

Ugh. Just thinking about how helpless I feel in the moment, makes me depressed. I need to try to write, get my mind off this.

After making a mental note to check my email for his response later, I go back to my Word document. For the next five minutes I sit there looking at the blinking cursor trying to think of what to write. Nothing comes to me. It's frustrating. I have so much material from the previous day, yet I can't write a single word. Seriously, my fingers should be flying across the keys like a roadrunner, filling the screen with steamy paragraphs that would have even the most chaste woman wanting to go on a date with Mr. Rabbit.

I let out a frustrated sigh.

I guess I'm just not in the mood to write anymore.

Sighing again, I get up from my desk and go over to my bookshelves and begin rummaging through my erotic romance sections. There's nothing like a good book to pull me out of a slump. I grab one with a shirtless hot guy with six pack abs on the cover, entitled *Deep Inside*. I already know what I'm getting with such a title, and I'm hoping it's just what I need to forget about my depressing work. Some days are hard. But it makes the good days that much better.

I settle down in my favorite recliner and begin reading. After a couple of paragraphs, I decide that I need something hotter. I skip straight to the first sex scene, but after several paragraphs of that, I find my mind wandering. The words are filled with passion, but I don't feel any of it. They seem dry. Empty. It doesn't even begin to compare to...

My mind wanders back to my masked Sir that I submitted to the day before, and the sadness I feel falls away. Images of how he handled my body and how he got me off flash before my eyes. A soft moan escapes my lips.

God, it was so hot, so incredibly intense. Just thinking about it now, leaves me breathless. The intensity of my orgasm and how he controlled me made me call out the safe word without even realizing it.

Lollipop.

I huff out a little giggle at the word. I don't know what I was thinking when I told him that I wanted it to be that. Maybe I thought it was cute. He didn't look like he thought it was, but in the end, he didn't care. He was more concerned with my body and pushing me to my limits.

I think I pissed him off by saying it. But I couldn't help myself. I was overwhelmed.

One thing that keeps bothering me though, is that he didn't show any commitment to me. He didn't ask for my number, or show any interest in following me from the club. He let me leave without mentioning anything, other than not wearing underwear next time. It's not like that's a normal occurrence. I'm sure there are rules against men following a woman from the club, but it still would have made me feel special if he'd asked me for more. I sure as fuck want more.

I'm curious to see where this goes. I've read all about BDSM, and I've researched Master and Slave relationships. I figure that I can at least try this if he pursues me, knowing the only way I'll really understand a M/s relationship is if I experience it for myself. My knowledge from reading about it makes me feel confident that I can handle it. It's a win-win relationship for me. I get to explore this dark sexual world, and further my research for my book at the same time.

Still, the forbidden and dark aspects keep me from committing fully. Thank fuck for Club X. A knock on the door pulls me out of my reverie. Clearing my throat, I get up to see what it is. The postal truck is driving off when I open the door, and down at my feet there's a large parcel sitting on my front steps, a beautiful white box with a white bow tied around it. Furrowing my brow with curiosity, I pick it up. It's rather light for its size, and I take it inside, setting it down on the kitchen table.

As I unwrap the item from the tissue paper, I can't stop

the gasp that escapes from my lips, my heart skipping a beat. It's a rather revealing white lace dress that is see-through in seductive places. My cheeks flame with a blush at the thought of wearing it. As I hold it up to the light, my heart races.

It's so beautiful. Luxurious and obviously expensive. And exactly my size. As I press it up against my chest, the significance isn't lost on me. Tonight, Club X's theme is all white. I can hardly wait. I set the dress on the table, but something brushes against my arm. I look down.

There's a note attached to the dress. I pick it up, and my heart only speeds up even faster as I read the simple words.

I'll see you tonight, my flower.

Your Sir.

Chapter 6

Joseph

As I wait at the long mahogany bar at the front entrance of Club X just outside of the foyer, I take another look at the text from my brother. I don't know why I do this to myself. I have no intention of texting him back. There's no reason for me to be involved at all with my family anymore. They have nothing to offer me, and I have nothing to offer them, despite what my brother seems to think.

Roberto may be a few years younger, but he'll be the one taking over the *familia*. I don't need to listen to a damn thing that he says right now though. I sure as fuck don't have to listen to my father either.

I'm not getting sucked back into that life. I have no intention of going back to them. I'm not going to be a puppet for them. I'm not going to take over like I was supposed to. I played my part and took the fall; I'm done with them.

I don't ever expect to live a normal life. I know that's not meant for a man like me.

I wasn't brought up to be normal. There are things I've done that are unforgivable. The sins of my past will always stay with me, and they made me into the man I am. Whether I like that or not, it's true. My own mother was a whore. My father, Angelo, and the Don of the Levi *familia*, wanted sons, so he knocked several women up, one after the other, until he was given two boys. I grew up surrounded by prostitutes and drug cartels. I've sat through dinners that were ended with gunshots or stabbings. It was normal, and there was never a moment where safety was a possibility. There was a promise of loyalty, but in actuality any and everyone was waiting to stab one another in the back.

That's the kind of life I'd be living. It's the shit that I lived through. Even when I left the *familia*, my past followed me. My name still follows me.

Not responding to my brother, half-brother really, sends a strong message. I don't give a fuck though. I have no intention of sending one back. There's no reason for us to meet up. We have nothing in common. I have a conscience. It may have taken me a long time to find a way out, but I have a desire to lead a different life, even if I'm already condemned to hell. My brother doesn't share that desire. All he cares about is money, greed and selfishness. I wouldn't be surprised if he kills our father one day. Not that I'll shed any tears over it. They're both despicable for what they've done.

I have enough money I never need to work a day in my life again, one of the unforeseen bonuses of having the Romanos' funds sent to my account. It was meant to be evidence used against me, but never came to fruition. I need a new life; I need something to look forward to. Something to give me purpose.

I think back to Lilly, and my hand gently starts swirling the whiskey in the tumbler. She more than interests me. I click the button on the side of the phone before slipping it back into my pocket and take a swig. The burn does nothing to soothe the sickness stirring in the pit of my stomach at the thought of Lilly not coming back.

I know I need to be gentle with her. I can't be the ruthless man that I used to be. I need to hide the darkness that's inside me as best as I can until I have her fully and completely trusting me. I need to get the fuck out of here, too.

The couples walk around me, the Submissives completely unknowing, nor do they care who I am. Most of their eyes are focused on the ground. Some of the men walk by me without taking a second look, but most of them hold contempt for me. The newspapers crucified me, as they should have. My name is practically a slur. I look up at the one man that dares to give me a hard look. The moment my eyes meet his, he breaks his gaze, pretending to stare past me. Fucking coward.

I look to my right, signaling the bartender for one more. There's a two-drink limit in Club X for obvious reasons, but my tolerance is high enough now that the drinks hardly have an effect on me. As the bartender catches my eye, I notice a man to my right staring at me once again.

It's Zander. Zander Payne. I'm well aware of who he is and what he's capable of. Even if most of the men in here have no idea. I snort at the thought. He's someone the men here should truly be afraid of.

There's an odd look on Zander's face. A look like he has something to say.

I hold his gaze as the bartender sets my glass of whiskey down on the counter in front of me. I wrap my fingers around the glass and bring it to my lips, not moving my eyes off Zander. He doesn't drop his gaze either.

I've never said a single word to the man. I've never said a word to any of the men here except for Isaac, the head of security, but that was brief and inconsequential. I have no fucking reason to talk to them.

I only came as a favor to Kiersten. She was worried about me. She's always worried about everything and everyone.

As the whiskey burns down my throat and fills my chest with the heat I've come to rely on for comfort, Zander finally walks toward me with purposeful steps. He has to walk around a few of the couples. One girl notices Zander walking by and obviously pushes her breasts up and out. She's sitting on a stool leaning forward, her white lingerie wrapped around her body and tied around her neck. Her head lowers until she looks up at him through her thick lashes, attempting to be submissive, although she's doing a poor job of it. But he ignores her.

Just as he ignores all the women here. No one else may see it, but I know the only reason Zander's here is for business. He likes to keep an eye on his assets. He likes to have an eye over everyone around him. That's just the man he is. And I truly admire it, although it's hard to admit that. I do the opposite, I try to stay away from anything and everything that reminds me of what I used to be. The only problem is I have no idea what that leaves me with.

"Mr. J? Is that what you go by here?" Zander asks me, standing a few feet from me as he rests his hand against the bar, in a seemingly casual stance.

"I prefer Sir." I set the whiskey down and leave it there, squaring my shoulders and waiting for him to say whatever it is that's on his mind.

"Ah," he says easily. This is the way he approaches all things in his life. With a casual air that makes him seem harmless. Charming, even. But I know what he's capable of. I've seen it firsthand. Everyone owes him but me. And I won't be making any business deals with a cunning shark like him.

"Sir?" He lets out a small laugh while shoving his hands into his pockets and looking past me. "I was wondering when you were going to begin indulging."

I don't respond to him. I'm not sure if he's referring to Lilly, or my bid on the auction last month. Either way, I don't give a fuck. What I do in here and outside of the club is none of his business. The less this man knows about me, the better. I look past him, toward the front entrance, waiting for Lilly. I know that she received my package. I'm only curious whether or not she's decided to obey me, to wear the dress I've given her and to come without any undergarments on. The latter is what I'm truly curious about. Not only did I give her the order yesterday, but from what I know about her, it's out of her element to be so brazen.

Zander shrugs as he says, "Not that it's any of my concern." He signals the bartender and orders a draft beer.

"Is there something you wanted to ask me, Zander?" I say to get to the point and end this charade.

His pretty boy face flashes a smirk, although he still staring at the back wall where the shelves of liquor bottles are lined up. "I may have heard something I thought you would be interested in knowing."

A man walks quickly in our direction. I've seen him before a time or two, although his name doesn't come to memory. He's a businessman, not someone that I would ever be involved with in the past. Although he does seem to know who I am, judging by the way he avoids my gaze at all cost. The last time I saw him was while I was in the dungeon with Lilly. I search around him for his pet, Adela, but she's absent today. My blood simmers, thinking he's hurt her again. Kiersten told me about him, about an *incident*. I glare at the man, hating that I have to share the same air he breathes. He clears his throat as he pats Zander's right shoulder, taking his attention away from me.

"Master Z," he says, and the man's voice is rougher and lower than I would've anticipated. My eyes hone in on a bruise at his throat, like fingers still wrapped around his windpipe. I look back at Zander and put two and two together. I back away slightly, turning and giving them privacy. Before I can turn from them completely, I notice Zander's annoyance with the man. He looks at the man's hand pointedly before responding in a low voice laced with a threat, "Yes?"

The man seems fidgety, leaning forward and whispering not so softly, "If you have a minute, I'd like to talk."

Zander nods at the man and then turns back to me, grabbing the beer off the bar.

"If you want to talk," Zander says to me, only looking me in the eyes for a moment as he stands. The permanent smile on his face is nowhere to be seen, "I heard something you may be interested in knowing." Without anything else he leaves, walking from the bar of Club X down the hallway with the man following him and away from the onlookers.

I have no idea what he could have heard, or why it would concern me. I'm not willing to make a deal with him, but I won't deny that I'm the least bit curious. My eyes follow the two men as they disappear from view.

I down what's left in my glass, setting it on the bar behind me as I swallow the amber liquid.

As soon as the glass tumbler hits the wooden bar, the doors open for Lilly. The bouncer gives her a small nod and she continues forward with confidence, both hands gripping her wristlet. She's in a long trench coat that goes down to her knees, although her calves are bare. Her high heels are nude with rose gold tips and matching rose gold heels.

She walks to the desk to check her coat, just as most of the other guests do. Some walk past her and make their way past me and off to the right down the hall to the private rooms. Many guests here don't even bother with the public. They just like the privacy and protection that the club offers. The black and white tweed trench coat slips off her shoulders down to her elbows, exposing her bare back from the white lace halter dress that I've given her.

She's a vision dressed all in white. The shimmering silk only makes her tanned skin look that much more kissable. As she takes off the coat, it brushes against the hem of the dress, pulling it up slightly and unbeknownst to her, showing more of her upper thigh. Several men around her take in the sight of her gorgeous curves. She doesn't notice them. She doesn't realize how tempting she is. I could wait for her to come to me. She's obedient. And the fact that she wore the dress I sent her, signifies that she wants me still.

After seeing the two of us interact in the dungeon, she'll be getting more attention than she ever did before. So long as I don't put a collar around her neck.

But I'm not going to give any of these men a chance to come between us.

I push off of the bar, walking straight toward her as she hands her coat to the man behind the counter.

I'm going to make sure they all stay away and that they know she's mine.

Chapter 7

Lily

I step into Club X, my limbs trembling with excitement, my eyes taking in the themed decorations. There's white everywhere, the usual red sconces on the wall giving off a soft, pure glow, the tables decorated with silk ivory tablecloths, and even the walls have been draped with temporary white lace curtains, giving the ballroom an almost heavenly feel.

The air inside the club seems to crackle, only adding to the anxiety twisting in my stomach. Keeping in with the theme, everyone is dressed in white finery. I inhale in a sharp breath as my eyes flit about the room, in awe of the other women. They all look gorgeous, angelic even. The men still wear masks, but they're all white.

If I didn't know any better, I would think the attendees

were dressed to gain entry to the gates of heaven, or a slutty version anyway, I imagine. I huff out a small laugh at the thought. It's comical when I think about it. I'm pretty sure with all the debauchery and fornication that goes on under this roof, everyone here is going straight to hell. Worry mingles in with my excitement as I peer down at my white lace dress that Sir gifted me. I think I look alright in comparison to the other Submissives and Slaves, but it's hard not to feel a sense of inadequacy. I thought I looked good in it back at home, but I'm slightly nervous that I may disappoint him. *My Sir.*

Slowly, I remove the overcoat from around my shoulders, the cool air of the club hitting my flesh and causing goosebumps to travel over every inch of my body. I shiver at the sensation, my nipples almost pebbling against the soft white fabric as it shifts against my skin. That's when I see *him* over at the bar, his intense, dark eyes boring into mine. My heart skips a beat as I gaze back into his handsome visage. He looks heavenly, dressed in an all-white suit, and I love how his white winged mask frames his chiseled features. His hard jawline and piercing eyes remind me somewhat of Thor, but I know this hero would rather wield a whip than a hammer.

My breathing quickens as I stare at him, my mind filled with the image of him wielding a whip. My skin pricks from the desire that flows up from my stomach.

His eyes seem to call to me with hypnotic power, and before I know it, I'm moving toward him without even thinking about it. My coat falls into the hands of the coat check attendee, quickly forgotten. By the time he reaches me, I feel as though I'm completely under his control. He could tell me to jump, and I wouldn't even ask how high. I'd just do it.

Up close, he's even more handsome than he was from across the room, putting my memory of him to shame. His white suit is crisp and spotless, his winged mask glinting in the soft lighting. His eyes, which are a deep brown, continue to hold my gaze, enchanting me with their intensity. My legs tremble, and it's hard not to show the anxiety coursing through my limbs as I resist the urge to reach out and run my fingertips along his chiseled jawline, wanting to feel him to make sure he's real.

I can't believe this is the same man that took control of my body the other night. The man who wanted me. The man I safe worded and walked away from.

I swallow as I take in all of him in his majestic glory, barely remembering to breathe. He's almost too sexy to be real. He radiates a kind of cold power that makes me shiver, his eyes filled with dark secrets I know should horrify me, but only serve to turn me on even more. It's an odd contrast, the darkness in his eyes, and the pure white he's wearing, but I fucking love it.

For a moment, I consider kneeling before him. I've seen other women do it, but I'm not sure if I should. I'm not even sure what we are, or what this is yet. He's not my Master, and yet...

He chuckles as he appraises me, his deep rich baritone sending electric shocks through my clit. "Do you like it?" he asks, his dark eyes sparkling with amusement. He must be able to sense my anxiety and uncertainty, and it pleases him immensely. "Like what?" I ask breathlessly, trying in vain to seem confident.

He smiles at me broadly. "Your dress."

I know he thinks I must be a fucking idiot. How could I be so clueless? What else could he have been talking about? The snow in Antarctica?

It's because he's so damn hot that I can't think around him, I tell myself. I blush furiously, my cheeks flaming. "I do, thank you," I reply.

"You mean 'thank you, Sir'," he corrects me firmly, an eyebrow arched sternly.

My skin pricks at my mistake, the heat of shame making it feel as if my cheeks might burn off. "Sorry, Sir. I thank you so much for the dress, Sir. It's beautiful." My words almost trip over themselves to get out. My heart seems to trip in my chest as well.

His eyes roll over my curves, and my skin tingles everywhere they seem to go. "Beautiful," he agrees huskily. I can only stand his hungry gaze for a moment before I'm forced to look away. All I can hear is the thumping of my heart in my chest. He isn't having it. He cups my chin, forcing me to look back at him, and pulls me in close, his hot touch burning my flesh. As he gazes into my eyes I can almost feel the possessiveness radiating from him. It should make me want to run away, but it only draws me to him like a moth to a flame. I didn't think it possible, but I desire him even more than the night before.

"Come, my flower." His words are not a request, but an order. I *must* obey. *Flower*.

He leads me through the club, walking with a confidence that's undeniable. As we walk through the hall, several men look our way, but each time they do, my Sir looks at them as if daring them to challenge him, and they look away. I thrill at the power he radiates, impressed by how some of these men, who are powerful in their own right, don't want to fuck with him.

It makes me feel secure. *Safe*.

Still, I feel eyes on me as we walk past the playrooms. This is different now. Before I was hidden in plain sight, but now that I'm with *him*, they're all watching. I pick at the hem on the dress, realizing how self-conscious I feel as we walk down the darkened hallway, past the double bodyguards, and to the stairwell of the dungeon.

There are a few more people here than the night before. I wish it were empty; I want privacy, but that's not going to happen. All eyes turn on us as we enter the room. Even the couple who obviously had the attention of the crowd before, stops to stare at us. Anxiety twists my stomach, and I look away.

"Look at me," my Sir commands.

I bring my gaze up to his eyes, trying not to shiver. In the background, the couples go back to their sessions and I hear the sing of whips flying through the air and smacking against flesh, followed by pained, but pleasured cries.

"What are you most interested in?" he asks, his deep voice punctuated by another *smack*. I want to look at the couple, the woman writhing in her rope binds as the man alternates the vibrator and the whip.

I shake my head, trying to keep my gaze focused on him as another lusty cry echoes off the walls. "I'm not sure. There's so much..." my voice trails off as I try to find the words. My heart won't stop racing in this room, especially standing here with him. I don't want to tell him that I'm partly here for research, and that I want to live out the fantasies I've read about in my favorite erotic romance novels. He might not like that. It'll only give him more evidence of my inexperience.

His eyes search my face. "Why do you keep coming down here?" he asks.

Smack. Smack. Smack. Another cry assaults my ears. "The pain," I whisper almost as if in response to the cracking of the whip and the cries that follow. "I'm curious." I swallow thickly and add, "I want to know why they beg for more."

He arches an inquisitive brow, the trace of a smile on his lips. The thought that I've pleased him with that knowledge makes my pussy heat for him. "Have you been whipped before?"

I shake my head vigorously, my breath quickening, my nipples pebbling. "No."

A grin plays across his firm lips as if my reply delights him in a way that I can't imagine. "Would you like to?" he asks, his deep voice dipping lower than I thought possible.

My heart races as I gaze into his eager expression, my pussy clenching with need. "Yes," I whisper. I've read about the pleasure it can bring. Every scene I've read turned me on with a passion that surprised me, and now I get to experience this sensation firsthand. I'm excited to see what it's like, but also apprehensive. To be completely honest, I'm terrified.

"Come." Taking my hand, he leads me over to the Saint Andrew's Cross. I watch as he loosens the leather straps on the cross, my legs slightly trembling, my pulse racing. His grip on my wrist is firm as he binds it to the cross. And then the other.

A guard I hadn't noticed before steps forward, a serious expression on his face.

"Lollipop is her safe word," Sir says before the guard can say anything, his voice laced with irritation. He doesn't even turn to face the guard as he straps my ankles to the cross, spreading my legs. The cool air flows up my white dress, and my heart stalls as the guard looks at me, searching my face for any objection. I clear my throat and nod, trying to swallow my heart as it tries to climb out of my throat, then he steps back into the shadows. Sir moves on to binding my other ankle, as if nothing had happened. As he tightens the leather strap, a realization washes over me.

This is *real*.

My heart skips a beat and I swallow thickly. This is not a fantasy I've read about in my books. If he whips me, I'm really going to feel it. I gulp again, my chest rising and falling sporadically. Based on everything I've read; I should like it. Love it, even. At least... I hope.

But it's a fucking whip.

Trembling with anxiety, I watch as Sir grabs a cat o' nine tails off the wall, and the ends of the braided tails look frayed. He holds it up for me to see before letting the tails tickle down my body, over the pure white silk and down my belly. To my surprise, they're soft to the touch, but at the same time thick and unforgiving.

My throat constricts as anxiety threatens to overwhelm me, and I find myself struggling a little against my binds as sweat beads my brow. I need to chill. I can endure this. I've read about it in my books. The pain mixes in with pleasure, and you don't feel it after a while. Or so they say.

I need to just keep telling myself that, and I'll be fine.

He runs the whip along my flesh again, and I almost laugh at the sensation. It tickles. But I know it won't for long. I suck in a breath at the pain I know is coming.

Sir gentles his hand on my waist, his touch soft and comforting. "Relax, don't tense your body." His command is soft at the shell of my ear. His low voice is seductive and washes a sense of ease over me. My breathing still comes in deep, but this time it relaxes me. He relaxes me. I loosen my hands and try to ease my muscles. *Relax.* I must obey him. *Don't tense.*

"I could use this to make you feel… so many different things," Sir says, his breathing heavy and husky, and his eyes are darker than I've ever seen them. I know he's turned on by what he's about to do, but that still doesn't make me feel at ease.

Without another word, Sir pulls back his arm and then brings it forward with an almost animalistic grunt, the whip singing through the air.

Smack!

I gasp as the air is ripped from my lungs and the thick leather lashes my flesh, my raw cry ripping through the chamber. Fuck! It hurts, the sting bringing tears to my eyes. But at the same time, my nipples harden and my pussy clenches repeatedly around nothing, my breath coming in short, panting gasps as I try to recover.

I pull at the binds as Sir runs his fingers gently over the slight marks. From the pain, I expect the marks to be a bright red, maybe even breaking my skin, but they're merely a soft pink. All on my upper thighs. The throbbing pain dims instantly.

His touch is so soft, but it feels like electricity, directly connected to my clit. That's the best way I can explain it.

It's an odd sensation, feeling pain and pleasure at the same time, but I like it. The adrenaline that's rushing through my body is downright intoxicating.

Sir gazes at me, watching my reaction intently, his eyes blazing with intensity. "Did you like that, my flower?" His deep voice is low and husky, his breathing ragged. I can tell he enjoyed the lash as much as I did, his crotch sporting a huge bulge pressing against his dark pants. My mouth waters just looking at it.

"Yes," I whisper weakly, my limbs trembling uncontrollably, my palms moist and clammy as I clench my fists and teeth at the residual stinging pain.

He cocks a brow at me as he says, "Yes?"

I realize my mistake, but it's too late.

"Sir, my flower," he says as he twirls the whip a bit, watching the tails sing in the air. "You keep forgetting."

"I'm sorry, Sir."

I close my eyes, tensing my body.

"You should be punished," he says in a husky voice while he grips the tails of the whip in his left hand. "A little more pain this time."

The sing of the whip whistles in my ears followed by a powerful lash against my thighs that forces another raw cry from my lips.

The pain is more intense this time, making my skin prick all over my body, my flesh red and heated in the areas where the leather tails have struck me. It's crazy what it does to me.

It hurts like fuck, but it feels so good. I'm wrapped in almost dizzying euphoria, the room feeling as if it's spinning around me.

After a moment, I force my eyes open to see Sir gazing at me, an amused grin curling the corner of his lips.

"You will call me Sir," he says firmly with authority, his chest heaving from exertion. He put a lot of strength behind that last blow, and I can feel it, my flesh feeling like it's caught fire. The flames sending a hot sensation to my pussy.

"Yes, Sir," I gasp, barely able to fill my lungs with breath, my body teeming with pain and arousal.

The words haven't even finished leaving my lips before his fingers are tracing the marks and then his lips, and then his tongue. I hardly pay attention to it. Pain and pleasure become my existence as the room whirls around me, and my vision blurs almost to the point of darkness.

He pulls away from me while my eyes are closed. I instantly miss his soothing touch over the stinging heated marks.

Pain and pleasure, wrapped in leather. The sensation is addicting.

I want him to whip me again, harder, taking me to the next level, but a part of me knows I won't be able to take it. If he does it again, it will push me beyond the brink. I don't want to say it, but the word *lollipop* starts to form on my lips as I sense him preparing for another blow.

As if sensing what I'm about to say, Sir suddenly drops the whip to the floor, the loud clack on the floor making it obvious even with my eyes closed. He steps right in front of me, his shoes thudding against the stone floor, his breathing heavy and ragged from his exertion. Close up, I can see the sweat on his brow and the slight perspiration making his dress shirt cling to his chest. The smell of his masculinity fills my lungs and I breathe it in deeply, almost as if I'm inhaling a powerful drug.

"You've had enough, flower?" he asks me although we both know it's a statement, his deep, sexy voice low and filled with lust.

I'm unable to speak, my skin burning like it's on fire, but I manage to shake my head no. I can't be left like this. After that, I need a release. *Now.*

He grins at me, as if expecting my inability to answer, and runs his powerful fingers along my heated flesh, my skin stinging wherever he touches. A sibilant hiss of pain escapes my lips as I tremble with need at his touch, watching him trail his fingers down further until he reaches where I'm soaking wet.

He pulls his fingers away, and I instantly pull against the leather straps to bring his touch back to me. "Yes, Sir," I answer with the last bit of breath I have.

I watch him close his eyes, a satisfied groan leaving his lips at being able to touch my pussy as he feels my wet, dripping folds. I shiver at his seductive touch, moaning with pleasure.

"You're soaking wet for me, flower," he growls, slowly rubbing my clit in a circular motion, causing me to throw my head back and my eyelids to flutter. Fuck, his touch feels so good, heightened by the pain he's given me. I've read about this, but nothing could prepare me for it.

I want more of this, more of *him*. But before I can say anything, he suddenly curves his fingers into my pussy, stroking me hard and fast against my front wall. I cry out, fighting against my binds, my eyes rolling into the back of my head. I quickly forget the harsh pain stinging my skin, it feels so fucking good. Wet noises mix in with the pleasured cries of the other Submissives surrounding me as my thighs tremble around his arm, his fingers massaging the walls of my pussy. I let out several cries as I struggle against my binds, wanting to arch my back, but unable to. The intensity of the sensation is driving me wild, and I know I'm not going to be able to take it for much longer.

A thought makes my breath come to a halt, interrupting my pleasure for just a moment, although I'm not sure if he can tell. I've yet to be touched by a man. Not in any way. My anxiety courses through me, but the pleasure is too much.

Sir stares up at me as he pushes his fingers deeper inside of me, his eyes burning into my face, almost bidding me to cum for him. But all I can think is, *can he tell? Does he know my secret?* My head thrashes, and I close my eyes. I don't want to think about it. Right now, I'm someone else. It's only a fantasy.

I writhe against my binds, whipping my head this way and that way, crying out for release, a fiery crescendo building inside the pit of my stomach. *Fuck.* I can't take it. I'm about to cum.

Just as I'm about to find my release, Sir stops, leaving me gasping for breath, my forehead covered in a cold sweat. Anger surges through my breasts as I stare down at him in disbelief, my pussy clenching in fury as the orgasm it was chasing flees.

Sir rises to his feet and leans in, giving me an intensely hungry look as I breathe raggedly in his face. "You've been a good girl and you can cum, but I want to fuck you and make you cum on my dick," he explains as my lips part in protest.

His words should fill me with overwhelming excitement, but they don't.

My desire ebbs somewhat as I stare into his hungry eyes, a feeling of wariness washing over my limbs. I wasn't expecting it to go this far. Him getting me off with his fingers was fine, but I'm a virgin. And though he's sexy as sin, and turns me on like nothing I've ever felt before, I'm not going to give myself to him. Not like this. I don't even know his name.

A part of me wants it badly, though. As my breath comes in frantic pants, I can already imagine him plunging deep inside me with his thick cock, fucking me with a ferocity that would have me screaming with pleasure within seconds.

But I know it'll be a mistake.

Looking at the absolute hunger in his eyes, I feel the heavy weight of fear pressing down upon my chest, constricting my breathing.

I have to break this off before I cave to the desire he makes so hard to resist.

Lollipop, a voice urges in my head as Sir moves in closer, softly brushing his hard bulge against my leg and causing my skin to prick and my pussy to throb with insatiable need. *Say it now before it's too late!*

My skin flushing a deep scarlet shade, I suck in a deep breath, parting my lips to say the word that will bring me to safety.

Before the first syllable escapes my mouth, he surprises me by suddenly releasing me from my binds.

Immediately, I slump to the cold stone floor covered in sweat, my limbs sore, stinging and red, feeling drained and exhausted, his arm wrapped around my waist and holding me up.

"Are your ankles alright?" he asks me, bending over to massage my wrists, his voice coming out clear.

A feeling of confusion washes over me at the tone of his voice. His demeanor, which was hot and heavy moments before, is replaced by a coolness that makes my skin burn.

He knows you're hiding something, the voice at the back of my head says as my heart pounds wildly within my chest. *And that you were going to safe word him.*

I hate not being able to tell him the truth. But I'm not ready. Not ready to tell him, not ready to lose my V-card, I'm not even ready for a real M/s relationship... or whatever this is.

"Yes," I barely manage with a strained whisper as he helps

me to my feet.

My skin stings as he examines me in the places where I was bound, making sure that I have good blood flow to those regions.

My lips part to tell him I'm sorry, that I'm a virgin and not sure if I'm ready, but then I close them. I'm not sure he'll even care to hear my pathetic excuse for denying him. He just seems ready to leave.

And there's no sense in making things worse.

Our session for tonight is over.

CHAPTER 8

JOSEPH

Lilly's gone for the night. And yet again, I feel as though I've scared her off.

It's my own damn fault, but I'm still in shock.

I knew there was an innocence about her; I assumed it was because this lifestyle was new to her. But when my fingers slipped into her tight cunt even deeper, I felt her hymen. I couldn't believe it. How could she keep something like that from me? The look in her eyes told me everything I needed to know.

I stare at the lush carpet as a couple passes me in the halls of Club X, remembering that look on her face. Scared and vulnerable... and raw. She was completely at my mercy in every way.

No wonder she's taking this so slow.

This should ward me off of her. I should stay away for her own good. No matter how much she wants this, the mere fact that she's a virgin is going to make what would be an erotic exploration into something *emotional*. I'm not an idiot. I won't be fooled by the notion that she knows better. If I take this from her, there will be an attachment that can't be undone.

It makes me even more of an asshole that this knowledge only fuels my desire to take her. I fucking wanted her right then and there. The moment I realized... I'm damn proud of my restraint, but my reaction made her run away... again. She'll come back. I won't let her slip through my fingers. Not that easily, anyway.

"Kiersten," I call out to her as she walks through the main hall of Club X.

Her heels are muted on the carpet, and her eyes whip up to me as she purses her lips and searches the empty hall.

"Quiet!" she snaps in a hushed voice, scowling at me and gripping my arm to pull me aside to a darkened corner. It's comical that the sweet little woman thinks she can pull me around, but I let her. After all, she's been a close friend of mine for a lifetime, and at this point, she's the only person I trust.

"That's not my name here." Her voice is low and her eyes dart down the hall again, but it's empty. The theme night has nearly everyone in the dining hall.

A chill goes through my blood. I forget sometimes. "I'm sorry... Madam Lynn." I give her a small smile and she purses her lips, but I know she's not angry with me. She's too forgiving.

"What is it that you want?" she asks, crossing her arms and cocking a brow. I resist the urge to smirk at her. Here she's in control, the Madam of the house. But I know her too well to look at her the way the other members do.

"I wanted to make a Submissive an offer," I clear my throat and tear my eyes away from hers for a moment. When I look back, confusion is etched on her face, so I continue, "Outside of the auction."

"Oh!" Her posture relaxes slightly, although she remains skeptical. "And what offer is that?"

"A monthly contract outside of the club. I'm willing to split the fees of course. I'm simply not interested in the charade of the auction." I try to make my stance and voice casual, but the reality is that I don't want my flower coming back here. Not until we both know she belongs to me, and every person in this club knows to stay far away from her.

Kiersten raises her brow and I add, "No offense." I don't at all mind giving the Submissive whatever amount she desires, and the club the same. The money goes toward women's shelters. It's a good cause I already donate to, for the same reason Kiersten's chosen it.

It's not about the money. It's about ensuring I'll get exactly what I want.

I've been wanting to take her away from here. I don't have an interest in engaging in activities here, but I want her. I want to break her. That sweetness about her, I crave it. But I covet her tears of desire more. I see the way her back arched as the braided tails of the whip smacked against her skin. The way she touched the marks with a reverence after being lashed. I could show her so much more. I could give her indescribable sensations; things she's never dreamed of. And I want to.

All in time, but not here. She's taking things slowly and going under the radar. I need to take her away now.

"May I ask who?" Kiersten asks with a teasing smile on her lips. She knows exactly who. She's going to take credit for this, I know she will.

"Lilly." My flower.

"I'm sorry Joseph, but the rules are in place for a reason, and Lilly is still finding her limits." Kiersten looks as though she's ready to leave, and if it were anyone else, I'm sure she would. But it's me. So she rocks on her heels, waiting for my response.

I know Lilly is still learning, but she can handle everything I want to give her. She's perfect.

I clench my fists, hating that I'm living by these sets of rules.

Since when did my life revolve around the commands of others?

I've lived my life making demands and seeing that they're

met. I've murdered, committed crime after crime and lived a life without consequence. I have more power than any man in this room. More wealth.

I do whatever the fuck I want, when I want it.

But in the last few years, I've simply been biding my time in this empty world I'm living in. I don't feel at all like the man I used to be.

It's time for a distraction. And Lilly is the perfect candidate.

"Don't give me that look," I hear Kiersten's soft voice, laced with sympathy. "I know you're hurting, Joseph," she says just beneath her breath.

I scoff at her. "This has nothing to do with that."

"If you want Lilly, you can approach her and ask to be her Master, although I'm not sure she's ready. If she goes up for auction, you may claim her that way as well. But there will be no deals outside of that." Her voice is strong, although her face is an expression of compassion. I hate it. I hate that she knows me better than I know myself.

A couple's footsteps echo in the hall as she speaks. I concentrate on the patter of the Submissive's bare feet and clacking of her partner's shoes. I'm sick of being here. Surrounded by other people I don't give a fuck about. I want Lilly where she belongs. In my home, in my bed, *in her cage when she forgets to call me "Sir"*.

"Joseph?"

My eyes snap to Kiersten's, her soft voice bringing me

back to the moment.

"Are you sure you should be taking a Slave? Outside of the club, that is?"

My heart sputters in my chest, and my blood runs cold. I know why she's asking. But I'm tired of waiting and living in this limbo. I'm done living by *their* rules. I've never known anything other than the environment I've grown up in, but that doesn't mean I can't care for Lilly. I know I can.

"I'm certain." My words don't convince her, and I know Kiersten's unhappy, but I don't care.

I want Lilly.

And I'm going to take her.

I'm going to *own* her.

Chapter 9

Lily

I blow my bangs out of my eyes with a sad sigh as I go through my emails and work documents. I'm trying to make sure that my lesson plans are ready for my new students. My heart breaks when I think about them. They're just middle schoolers, but they've already been through so much. I've read over each and every one of their files, and I can't believe what they've lived through at such a young age. Some of the kids already have a record, some of them coming from families so abusive that it makes me wish that I could take these kids away from their shitty parents.

My pen taps on the desk as I go through each study plan, making sure that they all draw from everything I've learned in these classes. I try to make them as perfect as possible for the kids, hoping that they'll take something from it that helps them. If it can change even one student's life, it will make me happy. I want each and every child to have a chance at a good life, no matter how hard their upbringing, no matter how terrible their circumstances. Just like I did.

A knock at the door pulls me out of my thoughts. I twist in my seat, looking at the door and wondering who it could be. I'm new in this city and I don't really have any friends other than classmates, but all of them are busy right now, most of them home for the winter break. I know it can't be one of them at my door. No one here even knows where I live. *It's probably a package or a neighbor*, I think as I scoot the chair back from the desk.

It makes me wish I was home with my family. But I only have my father, and now that he's remarried, we've lost touch. I know he still loves me, and I still love him, but I don't want to intrude on his new relationship and family. My birthday's coming up soon, and I know he'll be thinking about me. I smile at the thought. He always manages to send me something nice and sweet. Something from the heart.

I at least need to call him, to let him know I'm doing fine.

I make a mental note to give him a ring as I open the front door. There's a white box with an elegant bow on top sitting on the ground outside.

Sir? My heart does a backflip, and the small smile grows on my face. It can only be from him.

Arching a brow and sinking my teeth into my bottom lip to keep the smile from growing, I pick it up and bring it inside to the kitchen table.

I can't wait to open it. He's been all I can think about, although my thoughts have been a confusing mix with me being a bundle of nerves and insecurities. I suck in a breath when I open it and see what's inside.

Several white roses, and a smartphone with a platinum cover on it. My heart pounds in my chest as I pick it up out of the box, examining the high quality finish. A phone? *He could have just asked for my number!* I shake my head at the thought, but my heart won't stop beating erratically and my head won't stop shaking.

I place my fingers against my throat as I stare at the sparkling phone. I'm not sure why he would get me a phone. It's gorgeous, and more than what I could ever hope for or afford, but I already have one. It seems like such an awful waste of money, even for someone rich.

I'm shocked that Sir got me this and sent me flowers, especially after the way we left things yesterday, with me turning him down. I wasn't sure he'd want to see me again. I thought I'd ruined it all.

Maybe there's something really there. God, my heart. I stare down at the roses, gently petting the petals and inhaling their floral scent.

I'm about to close the box, when I notice a note at the

bottom with a phone number and several words scribbled on it in a smooth font, a strong masculine one. It's definitely his handwriting.

If you need me, you can reach me here.
Sir.

My breath quickens as I stare at the words, my pulse racing inside of my chest and my knees going a little weak. I know that I should just box this and put it away, that this may have gone a little bit too far. But I want more... of whatever this is. I hate it. It feels like I'm getting ahead of myself, like I'm running straight into trouble. I've never had a relationship that lasted more than a few weeks. I'm always the one to send them away, not wanting them to get too close to me.

But this isn't like that, is it? I want him to get close. I'm practically haunted by the thought of him almost taking me against the cross. He could have. I was bound and there for him. The very thought sends shivers down my back.

Whatever this is between me and Sir, doesn't have to be anything more than what I want it to be. It can just be the fantasy I've always wanted to explore. It doesn't have to go any further than that. It doesn't have to be *real.* ...although I'm starting to think I want more than a fantasy.

The air fills with the ringtone on my real cell, going off across the room and pulling me out of my thoughts.

I set the note down and walk back to my desk, trying to calm the mix of emotions as I answer the phone absentmindedly.

"Hello?"

"Miss Wade?" a woman asks on the other end.

"Yes?" I furrow my brow, wondering what this could be about.

"This is Sarah Parker with Parks and Recreation."

My heart drops in my chest as I realize this is about Zach. That's the only explanation. I pulled every string I could to get his public service moved. I lean slightly against the chair, my hand resting on the back as I lower myself down into the seat. "Yes?" I ask again cautiously.

"I'm calling because Zach White didn't show up for his service today. And he had you listed as his contact." I nod my head, my throat closing and my eyes shut tight.

"Oh," I finally manage to say, disappointment lacing my reply.

There's a slight pause before the woman continues. "I just wanted to let you know that I'm going to have to give a call to his parole officer."

Anger rips my chest as I force out my words. "Okay, thank you for letting me know. I'll try to get a hold of him." I'm so pissed at him. I'm upset, but more than anything, I'm angry. Why couldn't he just do this? Why?

"I'm sorry. You have a nice day."

"You, too," I say as the line goes dead.

Feeling the hurt spread through my chest, I turn in my seat and face the laptop. I need to email Zach and try to talk some sense into this boy's head. It really pisses me off that he wasn't there today. I thought he was really going to try. He told me he would. He told me he was grateful. Some gratitude.

Muttering angrily under my breath, I open my inbox, but before I can start drafting an email, I see a message pop up.

To: Ms. Wade
From: Zach White

Hey don't be mad at me

I know ur gonna be pissed at me and think I'm lying but i wasnt able 2 show up to my community service because I cut my hand really bad and ended up in the hospital. Then I went home and caught a fever. If you can call my parole officer and tell him what's up? My cell doesn't work and the land line is dead.

Thank u

Zach

"Oh Zach, how I want to murder you," I practically growl as I finish reading his message. I'm not sure that I even believe him. I grit my teeth, trying to decide what the right move to make is. I remember the way he was in class. The way he tried. He was honest with me then. I nod my head, remembering the days where he really put forth effort. He is a good kid. I know he is. I'm going to call his parole officer and try to smooth things over.

I pick up my cell and dial the officer's number. No one answers, but I leave a message on the voicemail, stating that Zach is going through some things right now and if the officer can please bear with him and not come down too hard on him. He'll be there next time. I let out a frustrated sigh when I hang up the phone, wondering what I should do. After a moment I mutter, "fuck it," grab my coat, and walk out the door. I need to check on Zach. I slam the door shut behind me. I shouldn't go there; this is a job for his parole officer. But I need to really talk some sense into him. And I need to see if he's lying to me and playing me for a fool.

Anxiety grips my stomach as I roll through the seedy neighborhood, the dilapidated houses making my skin crawl. I don't ever like coming to the south side of town. It's known for its gangs, drugs, violence and prostitutes. I only come this way if I have to. Or if I care so much about a person that I'm willing to risk my personal safety, like now.

Damn it, Zach, I growl inwardly, trying to calm my frayed

nerves.

After passing several rundown townhouses, I turn a corner onto the street Zach lives on, my palms clammy as hell as I grip the steering wheel, my eyes darting around like a cat, looking for any sign of danger. I relax a little after I pass several residences that have decent lawns. The houses look a little better on this street, but I still wouldn't want to be caught walking here after dark.

I drive past several more slightly beat up houses until I see a crowd of kids standing just outside a gated two-story stucco house. I spot Zach almost immediately, his tall figure and platinum blond hair standing out like a sore thumb. They're all out there laughing, some of them smoking weed, while others twist around on skateboards on the cracked concrete. Anger washes over me as I watch Zach laugh at a joke one of the kids cracks as he huffs out a large cloud of smoke from his lips. Both hands are visible. He cut his hand so fucking bad that he had to go to the hospital, but doesn't need a bandage? Yeah, okay. Tears prick my eyes, but I hold onto the anger.

I grip the steering wheel tightly, gritting my teeth as it hits me. He *lied* to me. I knew he probably wasn't telling the truth, but seeing it confirmed before my eyes makes my blood boil.

A part of me wants to jump out of the car and drag him to community service. But he has his own car, and I know he can take himself. He obviously just didn't want to.

I roll up alongside the crowd and several heads turn my

way, including Zach's. I give him a look as he spots me, letting him know how much he's pissed me off. He stares back at me for a moment, but makes no move to come toward me. I tap my fingers against the steering wheel, waiting, hoping he will. I'm giving him a chance to come over, apologize and explain himself. To make things right.

But to my absolute surprise, he turns his back to me, pretending as if I'm not even there.

"Zach!" I call out to him and he pauses in his step for a moment, but keeps going.

Shocked, I watch as he walks off with the group of kids, one of them even pointing at me and making some sort of joke that causes Zach to burst out into laughter.

Anger and hurt twist my chest as I watch them walk away, being rowdy and unruly. I know he may not want to seem uncool in front of his friends, but I can't believe Zach would do this. This isn't the kid I know.

I don't know what to do. I want to help this boy, but you can't help someone that doesn't want to be helped. That's what's so hard about this job. It's not easy to turn someone's life around. You can give them the best advice in the world, but if they don't listen or take the initiative, there's nothing you can do.

It's definitely not how I thought it would be when I signed up for this. I thought I would be able to tell children my story, give them a sense of hope, let them know that I was here for them, and everything would be alright.

It's a job that's much harder than I ever thought it would be.

Maybe it will get better with the middle school kids, I tell myself. But deep down, I feel like I'm lying to myself. I shake my head as I sit at the stop sign in my car. I refuse to let Zach give up on himself. I won't stop trying. Even if he doesn't listen. I won't give up on him.

I reach the highway and get on it, flying down the road like a bat out of hell. Shaking my head and biting back tears, I turn the radio on full blast, mindlessly singing along to a pop tune. I don't even slow down when I pass the highway exit that will take me to my townhouse. Instead, I turn onto a highway that will take me to the upscale part of town.

I need a distraction.

And I know exactly where to get it.

Chapter 10

Joseph

It's private in the dungeon today. Without the crowds of people, the air is chilled. It's perfect for Lilly's training. "Curve your back more." I swish the flogger in the air, and Lilly's eyes are drawn to it as she curves her back, raising her ass beautifully on all fours, and showing me her glistening pussy.

She loves it when I use the flogger. I think it's her favorite.

We've only had three sessions here since I've found out her secret, but each one makes me more and more anxious. I want her out of here, but she doesn't take me up on my offer to play outside of the club. She's always anxious at the end of training. She expects me to want more in return, she expects me to push her for sex. But I haven't, and I won't. Not yet, and not here.

This week, I've been showing up every night, because she

has been, too.

I keep forgetting to tell her that she needs to call me before she comes, and ask for permission. Not that she needs to, with the tracker and the phone I gave her. But she needs to start using it. Or else the phone will be useless to her and forgotten. I can't have that, not until we've made different arrangements.

The tails of the flogger gently brush along her back as she crawls on all fours in large circles around me. I can just imagine training her in the study at my house. Her knees would be on lush carpet, rather than this concrete floor. I've already started gathering things for her arrival. She's yet to consent to it though. Every night she comes here, and she obeys every command that I give her. The commands are simple; the tasks at hand are her choice.

I've given her so much control, although she doesn't realize it. I never thought I'd want to give up control, to win her over, but it's becoming addictive. Like a game.

I know she wants a collar more than anything, and I've been hanging it over her head. I see the way her eyes linger on the couples whose Submissives have collars and leashes. She's jealous. I can give that to her, and I want to. I want her to be mine in every way. I have no reason to give it to her here though. No man here would come between us. No one has even tried. They're all aware that she's mine--with, or without a strip of leather around her throat.

And the only bargaining chip I have to get her out of this

club is that collar.

"Stop," I tell Lilly, my firm voice echoing off the walls of the empty room, although the command was spoken softly.

Lilly's breathing comes in quicker, and I watch as her pussy clenches. She loves being told what to do. She holds her position easily. She's learned well. Every small mistake that's corrected with the whip or paddle, she's quick to memorize. Not because she doesn't like the sting that travels through her body and the heated pleasure left behind. No, it's not that. It's because she wants to please me. Lilly desires approval.

I can give her that. I want to.

I let the tails of the flogger scratch along the concrete floor so she can hear it. I enjoy it when I tease her like this. Making her wonder what I'll do next. Heightening her anticipation.

"Are you enjoying this, Lilly?" I'm tempted to purchase us a private room upstairs. I could have it fitted with any equipment I need. But it's not the same as being home. And I'm not interested in only having this arrangement within the walls and confines of Club X. I'm holding back so much. For nearly two weeks I've been holding onto this desire for her.

I unbuckle my belt and unbutton my pants as she answers, "I am, Sir." I circle her a few times, lifting the flogger in the air before gently slapping it against her ass. She hardly feels it, although each time her body gently pushes forward; she's expecting more. It's a natural instinct.

I'm conditioning her to be still, to stop expecting my

reaction during play. She'll get what I give her. Part of me doesn't want to though. I love this side of her. I love that she's not broken in. I love that I can train her to be exactly what I want her to be. She's a virgin in every way.

I bring the flogger up higher in the air behind her, whirling it to make a perfect circle and landing it directly on her right ass cheek.

Smack! She didn't see it coming. She takes the hit well even though she tenses her body, which I'd rather she didn't do. It creates more pain that's unnecessary, and the point of this isn't to hurt her. It's to elicit a higher threshold of her sense of touch that will intensify her pleasure beyond what I could give her otherwise. She knows this, and she knows better than to tense her body.

"Curve your back!" I give her the command, and she's quick to obey. I slowly crouch in front of her as she catches her breath, recovering from the sting on her backside. My hand wraps around her throat as I talk, my lips just inches from hers. "Don't you dare move." I watch her thighs tremble as she stays in position. With a flick of my wrist, the flogger rips through the air and strikes her along her upper right thigh. It's not a hard blow. I still don't know how much to push her, but more than that, from this angle it's difficult for me to see whether or not the tails of the flogger are only hitting her thigh or whether they're also hitting her pussy. And I sure as fuck don't want to hurt her there.

She gasps and nearly straightens her back, but after her instinctual reaction, she curves her back a little bit more. The tempting curve of her body is gorgeous. I kiss her shoulder as she moans into the air, swaying her hips slightly. "I told you not to move, flower," I say teasingly against her lips.

Quickly moving away from her, I release her throat and bring the flogger behind me, hiding it from her sight. I circle her again, loving the heavy pants spilling from her lips. Her panting is the only sound in the room other than the smacking of my boots against the floor. I take a look at her ass, and her right side is beautifully flushed. Tails of the flogger have left red lines in their place. They've blurred together as the adrenaline and blush of her skin spreads. I smack her again on her left cheek. *Smack!* And again on her right.

Each time she gives me a beautiful cry of pleasure, breathing raggedly between the blows. She doesn't move anymore though. She acts like the good girl I know she is. I continue cracking the whip through the air and landing it on her tender lush ass. Her left side, then her right side, hitting only her cheeks and upper thighs. With her focused on her back, her body is less tense. And the lashings are affecting her as they should.

The natural reaction to move away from the flogger greeting her flesh with a hot sting soon turns to her pushing her ass higher in the air, greeting it eagerly upon impact. Wanting more. And that's when I know she's there.

I place my hand along her heated flesh, massaging her ass and thighs before bending lower to lick the center of her pussy. I suck on her clit, but I don't get her off. She tries to stay still, I know she does, but she shifts her balance and arches her back. I've yet to take pleasure from her while she's learning. But I'm ready to change that.

Her curiosity and being my pet have evolved to a genuine desire and craving of my touch. Last night was the first time she asked me if she could please me. I knew what she meant, but I answered her with a simple fact, "You already are." She didn't press the issue, although she kept her gaze on my hardened cock.

I lick the taste of her from my lips as I stand. She groans slightly in protest, but she's quick to be quiet. She's learned that she'll get hers; I'm good to her, she knows that.

I unzip my pants, pulling out my throbbing cock and stroking it once, and again as I stand in front of her. Her chest rises and falls with heavy quick breaths. She looks up at me through her thick lashes, her baby blues begging me for my cock. She nearly crawls forward, my dick so close to her lips, and her so eager to please me.

"I'd like to be your Master," I tell her with her eyes on my dick, watching me stroke myself.

"You are, Sir," she answers me with a breathy voice full of desperation. Her hips sway again, and her thighs clench. She's so close to getting off. We both know I'm not really her

Master though. I want more.

"You've been so good, my flower," I tell her sweetly. "What would you like most right now?"

Her eyes dart to my dick, focusing on it, and then quickly move back up to meet my gaze as she says, "I'd like to suck you off, Sir." She hesitates before saying "suck." She's so innocent. Fuck, it's hard to keep my eyes open and hold back the groan threatening to climb up my throat.

A blush rises to her cheeks, and she shifts slightly in her position. Out of all the things we've done, simply telling me what she wants seems to be the most difficult. She's not very good at voicing her desires. But she'll learn.

A rough chuckle rises from my chest. "Don't worry, my flower, you'll be doing that soon. Is there anything else?" I ask her.

"I want to know your name." She tells me immediately, with no hesitation, no shame, and she holds my eye contact the entire time.

"I'll tell you if you come home with me," I'm quick to answer. Her eyes widen slightly, comprehending what I'm telling her.

She's quiet for a moment, truly giving my request consideration. It's the most she's given me so far. I asked her to come home with me three days ago, and she made it clear that she wasn't ready. I'm tired of waiting. "Would I see your face?" she asks me.

"Yes." Although I've given her the answers I know she

wants, she's still hesitant. My heart races, waiting for her answer. *Don't deny me.* I know she wants me, but I also know she's very aware of the fact that she's a virgin. That she's scared to commit so much.

She looks at the ground for a moment before telling me, "I'm scared."

"You should be." I hold her gaze as I tell her, "I want full control, and that's a hard thing to give someone." Her eyes close slowly as she sucks in a breath. The idea turns her on; I've known that from the start. She's smart to be so resistant though. I can't be angry about that. Maybe I shouldn't be so forward, to tell her I want so much. But at least I'm being honest.

"Open your mouth," I tell her after a moment. She keeps her eyes on me as she does what I tell her. "Wider." My own breathing quickens as my body heats at the sight of her curving her back, her wide mouth opens eagerly, waiting to please me. I place the head of my dick just inside her mouth. Only the head. "Suck."

Her mouth closes around the head of my cock, her tongue massaging the underside of the tip. Her hands move along the cement floor as I pull back slightly, desperate to touch me and stroke my length and do everything she can to get me off.

The sight of her so desperate for me makes me crave even more.

I want this whenever the fuck I desire her. I don't want to have to come here. I'm getting sick of it.

She moans around my dick, but I pull away. Leaving her wanting, and falling forward slightly. Worry makes her beautiful eyes seem that much wider. She's concerned she did something wrong. She didn't, but I'm not ready to give her what she wants. I need more from her.

"I want you to come home with me tonight. I don't want to have to come here to see you." I'm completely honest with her.

Her wide eyes stare up at me, flashing with genuine concern. "I'm just not sure if I'm ready," she answers softly with disappointment in her voice.

I need to sweeten the deal. I need to be able to provide her with something that she won't get from coming here.

"I can pay you... two hundred and fifty grand... if you come with me." My thoughts are on the monthly auction the club hosts when I make her the offer. I know it's a bit lower than what she'd get from the auction, but it was the first number that came to mind. Even if Kiersten disagrees, I don't give a fuck anymore.

But the second the words come from my lips, I regret them. She moves from her position, still sitting in a respectful kneel, but she knows that moving from how I requested her is displeasing.

"I'm not a whore." She doesn't look me in the eyes as she answers me, barely above a murmur. Her chest seems to stutter on her inhale. Fuck.

"It's just an incentive," I say quickly. "It wasn't meant to offend you. I'm fully aware that you are not a whore. And I would never see you as that." I'm quick with my words as my heart races, and my body heats. Fuck!

I crouch in front of her, meeting her eyes and taking her hands in mine, rubbing soothing circles on her wrists. I ignore the fact that she's completely disobeyed me.

I'm that desperate, and I should have known better than to say it the way that I did. "I apologize, my flower." I lean in and kiss her. Her lips are hard at first as she holds onto the anger I've caused her, but then they soften, molding to mine. The tension ebbs from my body. Good girl. *Forgive me.*

"I know leaving here is going to be hard for you," I whisper against her lips, cupping the sides of her face and trying to explain myself. "You deserve to be compensated. Especially with what I want from you."

"It doesn't feel right," she answers calmly; at least she's looking me in the eyes now. The moment is lost between us. I nod my head, my chest feeling tight, disappointment lacing my blood.

I stand, tucking my dick back in and buttoning my pants, feeling like a fucking fool. I reach my hand out for her as I lightly say, "Let's go see the show." I haven't gotten her off yet, but I will. I always do. Especially during the shows. I offer her a tight smile, but what we had was ruined.

Her brow furrows, with concern etched on her face. Her eyes focus on my crotch as she stands and frowns. "I'm sorry," she says and her voice cracks as she realizes that I'm once again not allowing her to please me sexually. Not that she'd want to now anyway.

"You haven't done anything wrong," I answer her honestly. I lead her to the exit as the door to the stairwell opens, taking her away from here, and having no commitment from her to leave yet again.

Chapter 11

Lily

It will definitely make me a whore, I tell myself over and over again.

I've never read a book where a woman accepted money in exchange for sex and I didn't think she was a whore. So if I'm going to judge myself by that same logic, then that makes me one, too.

If I accept Sir's offer. The key word being "if".

No matter which way I look at it, no matter how it's said, I can't see the offer in a positive light.

Sir called it an incentive, but the wording doesn't matter. You can put lipstick on a pig all you want, but it's still a pig. What he wanted was a contract with me.

And isn't that what prostitution is? A contract between two consenting adults involving sex and money?

Anger burns my throat.

I feel insulted that he would offer to pay me. It cheapened the experience that I had with him. I don't even know why he felt the need to offer me money. Did he think I was that cheap and could be bought after I rebuffed his advances to take me out of the club?

I bite my thumbnail, remembering the look of want in his eyes. I fucking want him, too.

I'm tempted. The kind of money he was offering could make such a huge difference in my life. I could pay off my student loans, my car payment and stash the remainder of the money away for future investments. There's no shortage of things I could do with that money. And it means I'd get him. I'd get to live out a forbidden desire that keeps me awake late at night.

Do whatever you want with it. It will still mean you're a whore, that annoying voice at the back of my head whispers.

I grit my teeth, angry that I'm even considering his offer. But at the same time, I'm breathless just thinking about it. The very idea of being *paid for* makes my body tingle with excitement and exhilaration. It's something forbidden. And that in and of itself is tempting.

"But I am not a whore," I mutter, closing the textbook on my desk. It's not like I could focus on it anyway.

Every time I'm with him, I feel safe. Even though there's something behind his eyes that scares me, something that warns me away, it's what draws me to him. I know I love the way he turns me on and how he gets me off. I've never experienced anything this sexually intense with anyone. And I think... I bite down on my thumbnail again, staring aimlessly straight ahead, I think I want to give myself to him.

I need to shake this off. I want to just pretend like he never offered, but I know the topic of me going beyond the safety of club acts is going to come up again. Not only that, but he's going to keep withholding himself from me. At first I didn't get what he was doing, but now I know exactly what he's been up to. I should be happy, I get all the rewards of being an obedient pet to him, and I don't have to pleasure him in the least. But I want to. I feel like I *need* to. Even worse, the pit of my stomach sinks as I think I'm failing him. He gives me so much, and I give him nothing. I groan, arching my neck back and staring at the ceiling. Why is this so fucking complicated? Why can't I just be normal?

I flip open my laptop to my document for my book, brushing the hair out of my face and ready to focus on something else, *anything* else. My fingers itch to tap away at the keys and get out all of my frustration by getting lost in the world of romance. I stare at the cursor blinking on the screen of the blank Word document for several moments as I run through the images of me with Sir in my head for inspiration. My breath comes in shallow pants, and my thighs clench. After a moment I close my eyes, place my hands over the keys and begin writing the scene that plays before my eyes.

It's a quarter past eight and I can't get him out of my head. His chiseled, handsome smile, his rock hard abs, and his thick, ten-inch cock. Fuck. He's so sexy. I can't stop thinking about his slicked-back dark hair, or the way he looks at me. His incredible eyes bore into me with an intensity that makes my skin burn with desire. I've never met a man that's looked at me in this way, who's made me feel this way. His hands caress my body, running along every curve, making me feel like a possession. Like he owns me. A soft groan escapes my lips as I feel myself clenching below. I need his hands on me now, caressing me, feeling me. I want to be fucked hard, and...

My eyes pop back open and I suck in a deep breath, pulling my hands off the keys. I was getting carried away with the last passage. I swallow the tightness in my throat, and shift in my seat. I shouldn't be ashamed, it's what some books are about. I place a hand on my chest as my breathing picks up. But I don't want my heroine to come off as an oversexed horn dog the entire book. At least not hornier than the male lead.

I want this story to be...

I purse my lips, wondering how I can make something that's just about sex... something *more*. The darkness in Sir's eyes immediately come to me. They stare back at me, luring me to write about them. About what happened in his past that made him into the dominating man he is today. I place my elbow on the desk, my pointer tapping on my bottom lip as I wonder if he'll tell me. I imagine my heroine, knowing she'd have the courage to ask. If she met a man like Sir...

What would she do? Chewing my bottom lip, I sit there for a moment and try to come up with something. But all I can think about is how the heroine in my book has the courage and strength that I don't.

After a moment I get up from my seat, deciding to pull inspiration from one of my many romances. The second my ass leaves the seat; I hear a telltale ping. I sag back into the seat, clicking on the email notification that pops up on my screen.

I crinkle my nose at the sender. It's from the director of the counseling department. I wonder what it could be about. My heart jumps as I read the subject line. What the fuck?

From: James Cricket
To: Lilly Wade

Subject: Notice of Severance

Dear Lilly Wade,

You are receiving this email because you are part of a counseling internship program that has been defunded by state lawmakers.

Over the last year, the Children in Need Foundation has fought tooth and nail to keep the funding for our program. We realize how important it is that children who are disadvantaged get the help they need so they can get a fair shot at life.

Unfortunately, the city council doesn't agree, and has voted to take away the funds that keep the Children in Need Foundation running.

What this means is that all members working under this program are being terminated forthwith, and you will no longer be employed by the Department of Education. It saddened us deeply to have to send out this message to all our hardworking employees, knowing how much so many of you care about these children, and how you all want to make a difference in their lives.

The world needs more people like you, and the entire Children in Need family wishes you all the best of luck in future employment. Don't hesitate to use us as a reference for any future employers. You will all receive our highest and most glowing recommendations.

In the meantime, we will be doing everything in our power to get funded in the future.

Yours truly,

James Cricket
President & CEO of Children in Need Foundation

My body is like ice as I sit there staring at the screen, numb with shock. I can't believe what I just read. My eyes stop at every word, not wanting to comprehend what's written on the screen. I'm hoping that this is some sort of cruel joke. But when I check the sender address, I know it's real. A pulsing pain hits me out of nowhere in my temples. I wince and seethe in a breath, rubbing my suddenly throbbing temples. Great. Now I have a fucking headache.

I continue to massage my temples, hoping it will all just go away. I just can't get over how sudden this is. I really wasn't expecting it. My heart squeezes in my chest as it really hits me. I just lost my job. I lost my fucking job. And the kids... fuck. The pounding in my head intensifies as I focus on just breathing.

For a while now, I believed that I could depend on this job, that I would remain employed until I was done with school.

Boy, was I dead wrong. Now my entire living situation is in jeopardy if I don't find another job in a reasonable timeframe. I only *just* moved into this place. I lean back in my chair, trying to calm my breathing and get rid of this headache. Tears threaten to form in my eyes, but I won't let them. I won't cry over something like this. I rock back and forth in my chair, taking in soothing breaths like I learned in a yoga class. I will fix this. I will find a way. There's always a way.

I don't know what to do, but I *will* figure out something.

My cell goes off just as I feel like I'm starting to calm down, the shrill beeping making my head throb even more. For a moment I debate on not answering it, but then I think it might be my job calling with some miraculous news, and I jump to answer it.

"Hello?" I answer breathlessly, hope soaring in my chest. It has to be one of the counseling administrators. Please God, let it be.

"Miss Wade?" a deep, authoritative voice that sounds somewhat familiar asks. I narrow my eyes trying to place the voice, but nothing is coming to mind.

I hold in a groan of despair. My left hand rubs the throbbing pain from my head as I keep the phone to my ear, closing my eyes and wishing I would wake up from this nightmare. This isn't my job calling to deliver a fairytale. This is more bad fucking news. I just know it.

"Yes?" I try to keep my voice steady, though I'm inches away from breaking down.

"This is Officer Johnathan Johnson with the Department of Corrections. You left a message on my voicemail the other day for Zach White."

My mouth goes dry, and I'm unable to even put forth the effort for an answer.

"I'm calling to inform you that Zachery White is in jail for committing a third offense." If my laptop wasn't right in front of me, I'd slam my head against the desk. Today is nothing but a cruel joke.

"What was the crime?" I ask, my voice barely above a whisper. My heart sinks in my chest, and my throat closes.

The state has a three strikes law. My hand runs down my face as my elbows fall to the desk, my left one hitting the keyboard. I want to shove the whole thing off my desk right now I'm so upset and angry. I'm so emotional and feeling overwhelmed.

"Vandalism. He and several other kids went onto an elderly woman's property and spray painted the side of her house." Officer Johnson snorts a derisive grunt. "They almost gave the woman a heart attack.

I close my eyes, my temples pulsing even harder as I remember the crowd of kids Zach was hanging with. Why couldn't that boy have just gotten in the car and gone with me? It would have gone a long way in helping him, and none of this would've ever happened. I shake my head as my eyes close, and I wish I could go back in time and just grab him. But you can't force people to change. I can't force him to make the right decision. No one can.

Now things are fucked.

A sharp pain lances through my skull. *God.* I definitely don't need any more shit right now.

Officer Johnson obviously hears me sigh and must sense the anger and sadness behind it, because he quickly speaks up. "Don't worry Miss Wade, I'm recommending that he be sent to The Boy's Academy, one of the best juvenile corrections program in the United States. If anything will turn your boy around, this place will. It has an impeccable record."

Officer Johnson sounds very hopeful and upbeat. I suspect

it's mainly for my benefit, but I don't share his optimism. I just can't right now. The Academy is a few counties over. Strings will have to be pulled to get him there. It makes me happy though, because it really does have a good reputation. I suck in a breath and try not to cry. I couldn't help him, but maybe they can. I feel like I failed Zach.

"Okay," I say, trying to sound strong, but my voice cracks. "Thank you for calling to tell me, Officer Johnson. I'm going to try to reach out to Zach as soon as I'm able. You have a wonderful day."

"Zach's going to be all right once he's in that program, Miss Wade," Johnathan tries to assure me one last time. "Don't you worry. You'll see."

The line goes dead and my headache seems to increase tenfold, my head pounding like it's stuck in a vice.

Just when I thought things couldn't get any worse, more shit hits the fan. Now I lost my job and probably Zach, all in one day. It makes me sick to my stomach.

I open my eyes to see the email still up on the screen. The one telling me I've been dismissed, and the program doesn't even exist anymore.

I need to find a job. *Fast.* I need to find a way to raise funding for the program. My to-do list just got a lot longer. I need money for my rent, and the bills aren't going to stop coming just because I unfortunately lost my job.

My heart skips a beat as I suddenly remember Sir's offer.

No, I tell myself, shaking my head. *No fucking way. I can't- I won't stoop that low.*

Surely I can find another way to support myself. But every option I can think about requires immense time and work. Time that I may not have.

The offer from Sir is immediate. *Easy.* And more money than I could ever dream of having all at once.

I don't have to be Einstein to know which path I should take.

It doesn't make me feel any better about it though.

Fuck it. It's not like I don't enjoy being with him. Like I haven't been fantasizing about exactly what he offered me.

Sucking in a deep breath, I walk over and grab the phone that Sir gave me. My head pulses even harder, almost as if warning me away as I bring up his number and the text screen.

My heart beats along with my pounding headache as I stare at it. Everything in my mind screams at me to drop the phone, but my hands move of their own accord.

I close my eyes briefly before I tap out the message.

Sir,

How soon can we talk about your offer?

Chapter 12

Joseph

Kiersten is so pissed. I didn't have to tell her that I was doing exactly what she told me not to. But I did.

I don't know why I bothered, but now I'm looking at all these text messages and avoiding her phone calls. I don't have to explain myself to anyone. The only thing she can do is kick me out of her club. I'm sorry that I've hurt her and that I've broken her rules, but I'm not going to allow her to get in my way of getting what I want.

And I fucking want Lilly.

I rise from my seat at the dining room table at the back of the restaurant as I see the maître d' walk through the aisle with Lilly. I button my jacket as I walk toward them.

She's already checked her coat, at least I assume she has,

because the thin lace dress she's wearing would have her freezing outside in the chilly January air. The black fabric clings to her curves and ends just about mid-thigh. What's most striking are her exposed shoulders, the lace straps hanging loosely off her shoulders. She's so tempting. She calls to me like no one else ever has.

She's absolutely breathtaking. Her lips are made up a darker shade of red than I've ever seen them before. Any other makeup she's wearing only emphasizes her natural beauty. Her long blonde hair is pulled into a loose bun, looking slightly messy with her bangs swept to one side.

Lilly sucks in a breath the moment she sees me, and takes a small step back. She's obviously nervous. I nod at the maître d', letting him know he can fuck off as I take Lilly's hand in mine, wrapping my arm around her back. She walks with me, her strides even, but she stares straight ahead. My throat tightens at her distress. I lead her to her seat across from me, pulling out her chair and helping her sit down. She desperately needs the help, she's practically shaking.

I take my seat, eyeing her curiously. The sound of my heart thudding in my chest is getting louder. This isn't starting as I imagined it would.

"Thank you," she says nervously, finally looking me in the eyes.

Her small hands grab the white cloth napkin off the table and she places it in her lap, smoothing it over and she seems to calm slightly. But then her eyes hone in on the stack of papers on the table. Instead of looking eager and excited, she looks uncertain and scared.

This isn't what I anticipated. I didn't know why she finally agreed, but I wasn't expecting her to be so... terrified.

"What's bothering you?" I ask her.

She twists the napkin in her lap nervously and takes a deep breath. Her mouth opens with her eyes still closed, but then she shakes her head, placing an elbow on the table and putting her head in her hand.

She's obviously not all right. I'm not sure what's gotten to her but whatever it is, I don't like it. I've never seen her like this.

I place my hand palm up on the table in front of her. Her eyes open at my words. "I'd like you to tell me now, my flower."

She holds my gaze with her beautiful doe eyes. "I lost my job," she says, and her voice is hoarse.

So it's about money. Maybe it's not a bad thing that I offered to pay after all.

She adds, "The entire department lost funding." Clearing her throat with her eyes on the glass of water in front of her, I watch her break down in front of me. My heart hurts for her.

She shakes her head and swallows thickly, looking past me and at the wall blankly. "So there aren't any more of-" she clears her throat again and takes a sip of water quickly before continuing. "So there aren't any more programs at the schools, and I don't know how to change that or help."

"Funding?" I ask. I can fund whatever the fuck I want. My heart pounds in my chest as my fingers slide down the cold glass of water in front of me. Maybe I can take some of the burden off of her, whatever it is.

"I work with underprivileged kids that have gotten into a little bit of trouble." She takes an unsteady breath, but it seems to calm her. "It's only an internship for now until I finish the last semester of school." She takes a deep breath before adding, "It was both my job and coursework for this past semester until the last two classes are available next semester." Her blue eyes meet mine as she answers the question on the tip of my tongue, "I'll be done in December." She readjusts in her seat and finally places her hand in mine. "I'm sorry. I know that-"

She starts to apologize, but I cut her off. "Don't be sorry," I say and rub the pad of my thumb on the back of her knuckles, giving her hand a comforting squeeze. "So that's what you do?"

She nods her head, a small confirmation coming from her lips. "Yes."

She's nothing like me. She's good and pure, so sweet and innocent. For a moment I consider backing out of this. I could give her the money and move on, continuing what we have at the club, or not.

But I fucking *want* her. And I haven't wanted anyone or anything in a long fucking time. Maybe it makes me an asshole for taking advantage of her and the situation. But

I don't give a fuck. It's not like I only offered it now when I know she's in need. I never claimed to be a knight in shining armor. Everyone knows I'm the fucking villain. I push the papers in front of her, letting go of her hand and getting back to the contract. She came here for a reason. I need to strike while she's willing and vulnerable.

"Have a look and see if this is to your liking." As I say the words and look up over Lilly's right shoulder, I catch sight of the waiter holding a decanter of red wine as he returns to pour me a glass. I chose cabernet just before my flower arrived.

Just as Lilly's eyes settle on the papers, his presence startles her; she pulls the papers close to her chest, hiding them from his sight. But it also draws attention to her and to the papers. I hide my smirk behind the goblet of red wine, swirling it gently and inhaling the sweet scent before taking a sip.

I nod at the waiter, letting him know it's to my liking and setting the glass back down. I can't take my eyes off of Lilly as the waiter refills mine first and then fills hers. I can practically hear her heart beating out of her chest. This isn't her simply agreeing to something she's familiar with. She's yet to tell me she's a virgin. I'm not taking this lightly.

Although this isn't an auction at Club X, I'm still taking the same precautions. As the waiter leaves, another comes behind him, setting down a tray of hors d'oeuvres. Arranged neatly on the silver pebbled tray are two of each: mini caviar parfaits, pancetta crisps with goat cheese on thin pear slices, marinated mozzarella with chili and thyme, as well as a variety of olives, soft cheeses, and shaved meats.

I'm not sure what my flower really enjoys eating yet, but I'll be finding out shortly. Lilly's eyes glance to the tray and then back to the waiter, as he turns his back to us, leaving us alone and to our private dinner as I requested. Her eyes don't linger on any of the items on the tray. Instead she sets the contract back down on the table, focusing on each line.

"Would you like to eat first?" I ask her, popping an olive into my mouth.

She gently shakes her head and returns to reading the contract before her eyes widen, realizing what she's done. She looks up at me with slight fear in her eyes as she says, "No thank you, Sir."

I nod my head once, keeping my eyes on hers. She waits with her body stiff before I reply, "I know it's different here, in a new environment." I quickly lick the salt from my fingertips before wiping them on the cloth napkin in my lap, her eyes drawn to my mouth. "It'll be like this when you come home with me. But you'll get used to me being your Master at *all* times, and in *all* settings."

She sucks in a breath, and her eyes cloud with lust as she answers, "Yes, Sir." She maintains my gaze, waiting for me to give her permission to continue reading. Such a good girl. I nod down at the papers in her hands, and say, "Go on."

I have the contract nearly memorized.

Contract to be signed on this day, January 13, 2017, by the following participants.

Master: Joseph Levi.
Slave: Lilly Wade.

Definition of Master and Slave needs.

The Master requests the Slave to be available to him at all times for any needs he deems suitable.
The Slave requires safety at all times, as well as free periods when her Master deems appropriate. There will be no punishments during these free periods, however, the Slave must continue to respect her position and address her Master appropriately.

Definition of Master and Slave responsibilities.

Lilly Wade agrees to obey Master in all respects with her mind as well as her body. She is also responsible for the use of her safe word, lollipop, when necessary and trusts that her Master will respect the use of that safe word.
She will keep her body available for whatever use her Master deems appropriate at all times.
Joseph Levi may use her body in any manner within the parameters of her safety.

Lilly is responsible for answering any questions from her Master honestly and directly, and will volunteer any information he should know about her physical and emotional condition.

She is not to interpret that as permission to whine and complain. She must always address her Master in a respectful manner.

It is the Master's responsibility to make it clear when a punishment is being given, and why it has occurred.

In public, the Slave will conduct herself in a manner that doesn't call attention to the relationship.

No part of this agreement will interfere with Lilly's career, her physical or emotional wellbeing.

Of her own free will, Lilly Wade offers herself in slavery to Master Joseph Levi for the period beginning on January 14, 2017 at noon, and ending on February 14, 2017 at noon.

Both parties must also note and acknowledge that this contract is not legally enforceable. It is a tool to help guide the relationship, and monetary gains will be provided to Lilly as compensation in the form of two hundred and fifty thousand dollars. Lilly Wade, Slave, may at any time leave without fear of losing Joseph Levi as her Master for the duration of the contract. Although in doing so, may be met with punishment if she is to return.

With my signature below, I agree to accept and obey what is detailed and outlined for the contract noted above.

Slave, Lilly Wade _____
Date_____

Lilly looks up at me hesitantly. "Joseph?" She says my name softly, so sweet coming from her lips. I've always hated my name, but hearing it from her, with that look in her eyes, makes me proud of it.

I clasp my hands on the table and nod once, holding her baby blues firm with my gaze.

She smiles shyly before returning to the contract.

"The terms are negotiable," I say easily, waiting to see if she's comfortable with the amount I blurted out in the dungeon. It's the minimum of what she'd get if she were to go up for auction. I should offer more, but I'd rather keep the opportunity open for me to extend the contract into the next month if I'd like to.

"This contract ends on Valentine's Day." Although it's a statement, Lilly looks at me as though it's a question.

"Yes," I nod again and say, "It's exactly one month."

I stare deep into her pale blue eyes, willing her to tell me that she's a virgin. It's been days since my fingers have been pressed inside of her tight cunt, but I can still feel her hymen on the tips of my fingers. I know she's untouched, and I expect her to tell me before signing.

She looks like she's going to tell me something, but she doesn't. Instead she returns to the paperwork, but she's not reading it. Her eyes are focused on the line she's supposed to sign.

"If you're not comfortable with this..." I hate myself for even giving her an out. But in this moment, I fall victim to the vulnerability in her eyes.

"I want to fuck you," Lilly blurts out, covering her mouth with both hands. Her cheeks brighten with a beautiful blush of embarrassment.

Although her little outburst is adorable, I need to make sure she's ready for this. "But are you ready to be my Slave? To give yourself to me in all things for a month?"

Lilly takes a deep breath and then another, all while staring into my eyes. She nods her head and without speaking a word, she picks up the pen on the table, and signs her name on the line.

Chapter 13

Lily

I blow a strand of hair out of my eyes as I pack away another tank top, one thought running through my mind.

It's only one month.

It's something I've been telling myself all morning to make myself feel better about accepting the money. That, along with, *after thirty days, I'll be free.* The words are helping some, but not totally alleviating my anxiety about the contract. I went over every single line of it several times. It was nothing like the contracts Madam Lynn showed me at the club when I first came. There weren't any specific boxes for things I was interested in or uninterested in. There weren't any hard limits or soft limits that were indicated on the last line.

I was agreeing to be his Slave. Period.

My heart skips a beat at the thought, my breath quickening.

The whole contract is very much in Joseph's hands. It scares the *shit* out of me, yet at the same time, it turns me on. It's a paradox.

There's something about giving this man total control over me that drives me absolutely wild.

I should be ashamed, but I'm not. I want it.

I want *him*.

It isn't lost on me that I'll be giving him my virginity. My *V-card*. It's not that it's something sacred to me, something that I've been holding on to as long as I can remember. I've just never... been with anyone who's made me want to give it to them. I wasn't waiting until marriage. Just waiting until I found someone who turned me on and wanted me just as much. Joseph is definitely that man.

I hardly know the man, and here I am, knowingly about to give myself away. I shouldn't be doing this. I should know better. At the same time, I can't help but think there's something more between us, something I've never had with anyone else. I toss another tank top into the small pile on my bed.

Or maybe I'm just trying to justify it.

He's so much like one of the heroes in one of my romance novels; handsome, dark, brooding, mysterious and most likely hiding a damaged past that'll pull at your heartstrings. That's part of what draws me to him, how much of a living, breathing fantasy he seems to be.

But I need to remind myself this isn't a fantasy. It's real

life. And I've gotten myself into some serious shit. Except it hasn't really sunken in yet. I'm not sure when it will. I'm infatuated with the romanticized version of Joseph.

Even now, my heart flutters at how concerned he seemed with making me feel comfortable with the contract.

I stare at the pile on my bed, remembering how he told me to bring only the things that make me happy. I glance down at my half-stuffed bag, looking to see what I have so far. My most favorite books and a new Kindle I bought that has loads of titles on my to-be read list already downloaded, but I'm still missing a few things.

I glance at my list, and go down the line of things I still need to grab, then go about gathering them.

I grab a small blue pillow that's on my bed that I use to prop up my knees when I'm sleeping and toss it in the duffel bag. Walking into the bathroom, I grab my aromatherapy oils and some cherry bath bombs and stuff them in my small toiletry bag. While I'm in there, I grab some nail polish and my three favorite lace nightgowns that are hanging on the rack. I rub my fingers over the lace; they're not nearly as beautiful as what Sir gifted me, but maybe he'll like them.

My body heats, imagining what he'll say. I close my eyes and stop that train of thought. I walk out of the bathroom with my personal items and I go down my list again, getting anything else I might have left out. Comfortable socks and flannel pajama pants that I wear when I'm really happy are next.

In the kitchen, I grab a box of my favorite homemade tea that I absolutely love and get from the farmers market. I start packing it away, but then pause, wondering if he'll even let me use this. I have to remember. He owns me. I have to do what he says, whether I like it or not. So if he doesn't want me to drink my favorite tea, I can't drink it.

Anxiety twists my stomach as I begin to doubt my decision to sign the contract. I'm not sure if I can make it through thirty days of being told what to do. I like to think that I can, but it might be harder than I imagine.

Even though it's a contract, you can always walk away, that voice in the back of my head whispers.

I shiver at the thought of breaking the terms of our agreement. But if I find that I can't handle the situation, I'll have to.

Pushing away the troublesome thoughts, I finish packing and go through the house, making sure I have everything that makes me happy or feel good. My laptop is the last item on my list. I'm about to pack it away when I decide that I want to check my email one more time before I leave. I've been hoping to hear some good news back from the counseling administration and from a lady that I sent the first two chapters of my novel to.

As soon as I open my inbox, two email notifications pop up. My heart jumps in my chest at the first email.

From: Jenna Ramey
To: Lilly Wade

Lilly,

I just got done reading the chapters you sent me. And I have to say... I absolutely love them! I love how sensual you made the heroine seem, and how dark and dangerous you made the hero. I think you're definitely on the right path with the story, and you should really explore the hero's dark side. Trust me when I say that you have great potential as a writer. And I look forward to reading your next chapters. If they're good as the first two, you might have a bestseller on your hands!

Love,
Jenna

A feeling of warmth flows through my chest as I read Jenna's words. It feels good to get feedback on my work. I've always thought of myself as a crappy writer, and have had horrible confidence in my ability. To actually hear someone say that I have potential fills me with joy and almost brings me to tears. Even if she is just a friend who edits for a publishing company. Still, it means so much to me.

I read Jenna's words over and over, each time feeling a little bit better, until my eyes fall to the next email and my joy dampens slightly.

> From: Zachery White
> To: Lilly Wade
>
> Lilly.
>
> *I'm sorry.*
>
> Zach

I stare at his words, trying not to feel anger after getting such a lifting message about my writing. He's sorry? That's all he can say after everything I've tried to do for him? I take a moment, sucking in a deep calming breath, trying to look at the entire situation, rather than being consumed by my immediate feelings.

Zach is going somewhere where he'll be able to turn his life around. What he did before is in the past now. Getting mad over it won't help either of us. My eyes flicker across the one line on the screen again. I should just be relieved he's being given the opportunity at a second chance.

Rising from my seat, I shake off the uneasy feelings and close the laptop, putting it into my travel bag.

I leave the bag on the desk chair, as I go through the house and make sure that I haven't missed anything else.

A whole month away. Of giving myself to someone else. *All of me.*

Is it really worth doing this?

I heard about the auction. It would've paid me more than the amount Joseph offered. I'm fully aware of that. Maybe even three times the amount. Possibly more. I overheard a few of the girls talking about how much the virgins go for. But when I think about how anyone other than Joseph could have put in a higher bid, essentially taking me for their Slave, I don't regret it.

It has to be him. I want it to be Joseph who I give myself to.

Shame burns my cheeks as I think about what I've done. I've sold myself to another human being. For money. I would have been with him in time, without this though. My heart clenches, and the nasty voice in the back of my head whispers, *does that make it any better though?*

I pick up the strap of the bag after zipping it closed, and hoist the heavy thing over my shoulder. The strap immediately digs in. I may have packed too much.

I'll never tell a soul what I've done. I'm ashamed, but this is about more than just me. This money is going to be used for a good cause.

I'm sorry.

I think of Zach's words in his email. I'm sorry, too.

I'll never tell anyone, but as I turn out the lights to my living room, I know I want Joseph. And nothing's going to stop me now.

CHAPTER 14

JOSEPH

I know that I fucked up the moment that Lilly walks through my front door. Her shoulders are hunched inward as I carry her duffel bags into the foyer, leaving them in the corner of the room.

Her vulnerability is intoxicating. I know it's taking a lot for her to do this, so I'll make today easy. The first few days I'll be gentle with her, and ease her into this lifestyle. I only have her for a month though, and I intend to take full advantage of our time together.

Although it's freezing outside, she wore a beautiful dress that ends above her knees. The hem brushes against her thighs as she walks in, taking off her tweed winter coat and hanging it over the crook of her arm. She shivers slightly as she walks in, holding onto the coat as if it's her anchor.

The chill from outside has made her cheeks a bright red, as well as the tip of her nose. The house is warm and inviting though, the sound of her heels echoing as she walks closer to the hall.

I close the door, my back to her as I imagine all the things I'm going to do to her. She's mine now.

I could bend her over the foyer table right now, I could take her with a bruising force from behind and fuck her like I've been dreaming of doing. I can practically hear her hips banging against the wooden edge of the table. I can see how the trinkets I've gathered from all the places I've traveled would rattle as I pounded her tight cunt, taking her virginity in a swift thrust.

I own her; I can do whatever the fuck I want with her.

I know it would turn her on. I know in the moment she would enjoy it. I would make sure of that. Strumming her clit while I positioned my hips against her ass, shoving my dick deep inside of her over and over again until she screamed out her orgasm.

I clear my throat and the thoughts from my head as I lock the door. The gentle click fills the room and makes her turn on her heels to face me. I ignore all the ways I could claim her as I walk to her, embracing her and planting a small kiss on her cheek.

"It's all right, my flower." I lower my lips to hers, pressing them against her mouth gently.

She pulls away for a moment, pushing her small hand against my chest and breaking away. I don't like it. I don't like her pushing me away at all. That's not what she's here for. My heart races in my chest, and my body stiffens slightly. I'll allow it for the moment. But only until she's comfortable. Only until she fully realizes what this is between us.

"It's different here," she says, her voice small.

I stare at her for a moment, registering what she's said. Different? Looking to my left, I take in the open layout of my home. It's modern and dark. From where we're standing in the foyer, she's easily able to see the kitchen and den.

She focuses on the white marble fireplace on the back wall to the right. It's lined with large rectangles of black slate. Although the stone holds a cold feel to it, the warm coloring of the worn leather loveseat and chair, combined with the lush carpet balance out the room.

I watch her face as her eyes skim across the room, taking in the details. Her curiosity makes the corners of my lips kick up into a smile. She obviously approves.

My home is littered with two things: fireplaces, because I love the atmosphere created by the crackling of wood in the warm glow of a natural fire, and artifacts from the places I've traveled in the last two years. As soon as I could leave my family, I did. And I went as far as away as I could get.

Cigars are my favorite keepsake. There are several boxes, some antiques, holding cigars throughout my home. There are a plethora of maps as well. Mostly hand-drawn ones I've collected from the places I've traveled, mountains I've climbed, taverns I've explored. The other trinket I've collected a mass number of are weapons. A set of bow and arrows are showcased in the den. It's from ancient Greece, and one of my favorites. I never used it for fear of breaking it. Lilly's eyes widen when she catches sight of it. She blinks several times, as if doing so will make it disappear. My fingers itch to take the bow off the wall and let her hold it.

She noticeably swallows. I can practically hear her gulp. I know she's just now registering that she doesn't really *know* me. That she signed a contract handing her freedom over to me. And only now is she even beginning to learn who I really am. I don't like seeing her fear. Especially since she's only just gotten here.

"I think you'll feel better once we discuss things a little more in detail." I let my finger trail down her collarbone, down to her shoulder, pushing the fabric out of my way as I go. I only use my middle finger, my blunt nail scraping along her skin gently. Her eyes close, and her body relaxes under my touch. I've conditioned her to do that.

"For now, I'll allow you to be clothed." I talk softly, my words gentle and caressing. Calming her. "It'll be your first privilege that I'll take away. Do you understand?"

"Yes, Sir," she responds immediately. She's falling into character, so to speak. Remembering how we were inside of the dungeon of Club X. That's most likely what it was to her, *an act*, a character she was playing. But now it's real life. When she's done playing but realizes she can escape, that's when I'll see the real her. The piece that she's kept hidden from me while we played.

"If you disobey me again, then you'll be whipped." Her head falls back slightly at my words, her chest rising with a quickening breath. Again this turns her on; she's used to me giving her pleasure with the whippings. But there's no pleasure and punishment here. She has yet to go through a true punishment.

"Yes, Sir." I take her coat from the crook of her arm and set it on the foyer table behind me before returning back to her. She stands obediently, hands clasped in front of her, waiting for me to give her a command. This is the way she should have been from the start. Waiting and ready for me. That's how she'll always be in this house. I just need to train her. I step closer to her, standing in front of her but not touching. Her fingers twitch, but she stays still. "The third punishment is orgasm denial." I smirk at her as her eyes widen in surprise. "That's something you've yet to experience, isn't it?"

"Yes, Sir... May I ask a question?" She's hesitant and I can understand why, but I need her to know that she can always talk to me. There may be consequences if she speaks to me disrespectfully. But I always want to know what she has to say.

"While you're here you can speak freely. So long as you address me properly."

"How long?" I smile broadly at her question, holding back my laughter. My greedy little flower. My reaction makes her smile, her shoulders relaxing slightly.

"Are you already planning on getting into trouble?" I tease her, my middle finger now running up and down her throat.

"No, Sir." There's still the trace of a smile on her lips.

"Are you so certain that you're going to displease me?" I ask her, my finger pausing on her soft skin.

She takes a moment to swallow before answering again, "No, Sir."

"Your punishment will fit the crime. So the length of your denial depends on what you do."

I have to tell her about the cage. These punishments are for minimal offenses, if she does something out of character. But if she does something to intentionally upset me or disrespect me, then that's where she'll stay. I've seen the way she looks at the cages in the dungeon. The one I have for her is larger. There's curiosity behind her eyes, but it truly is a punishment. Both for her and for me. My hope is that I'll never have to use it, although I imagine with her curiosity she may ask me if she can go in, just to see what it's like. Just to tease me with her being unavailable.

"We have a lot to discuss." I splay my hand on her back, leading her away from the front door and farther into my house, her new home for the next month. "Come. Let me show you your room."

Chapter 15

Lily

L*uxury.*

It's the only way I can describe my bedroom when I step inside with Joseph at my side, his eyes on my face, watching for my reaction.

I don't disappoint him. My jaw nearly drops to the floor as I survey the room, my breath catching in my throat.

An amused grin curls the corners of Joseph's lips up as he eyes my stunned look. He knows I'm floored by his impressive wealth, and he's enjoying every second of it. *Pure, unadulterated luxury.*

Seriously, I can hardly believe this will be my bedroom. The rest of the house is amazing and I can't wait to explore it all, but this... I shake my head. This is absolutely gorgeous.

I press a hand to my chest. This room is the stuff dreams are made of. It's large and spacious, contemporary, urban and chic, all in one. The walls are lined with an intricate high-gloss gray paisley wallpaper that literally takes my breath away, and soft lush white carpet that looks and feels like a mink fur coat. I kick my heels off as I let it all sink in.

As I move across the floor, my feet are enveloped by the soft carpet, and a soft sigh escapes my lips at the caress of it against my skin. It feels so good to walk on it. I've never felt anything like it. A large king-size bed with a canopy lies at the back wall, the soft white gossamer curtains billowing out from the gentle air circulating around the room. Above it is a tray ceiling painted a pale blue with a diamond chandelier in the very center.

Directly across from the bed lies an exquisitely shaped white hearth over a grey marble fireplace, with a large white recliner sitting in front of it, adorned with pale blue throw pillows.

I spin around, taking in everything from the crown molding, to the expensive finish of every piece of architecture in the room. With all the white, it really looks like a place of purity. Sweet innocence.

Like my virginity.

I try to push the unwanted thought away, not wanting to think about what the cost of the contract entails.

Then I see them. *The toys.* I shake my head. I must be imagining things.

I close my eyes, and then pop them open. *Nope*. Still there. I don't know how I didn't see them before, but now that I have, I can't *unsee* them.

They're all the color of the room, white and grey, so I guess they blended into the background. But not now. Now, they're all I see.

There are white whips hanging off the end of the bed frame, white riding crops on the wall along with large foreign objects that make me shudder at the thought of what they're used for. I start to walk to them, my hand at my throat, and as I do, I hear and feel Joseph walking behind me. I can hardly breathe. I stop in my tracks, lowering my head and just trying to breathe. This is why I'm here.

I lift my eyes and nearly laugh.

There's even a white cage in the corner of the room and a white bench with white leather straps.

I stare in disbelief, wondering how my eyes could have deceived me so. Here I am, enraptured in the upscale beauty of the room, when it's a goddamn torture chamber! A very nice, plush comfortable-looking one, but a torture chamber nonetheless.

Anxiety twists my stomach as I stare at these objects, knowing what they'll be used for. *How the hell did I get myself into this?*

I look over at Joseph and see his eyes on me. He hasn't said a word since we've walked into the room, content on watching my every move and expression as if trying to read my mind.

I part my lips to ask something, but then close them, my legs feeling weak. I don't trust myself to speak yet.

To hide my anxiety, I walk over to the closet and open it. It's pitch dark inside, and I have to search around for the light switch.

Once again, I have to keep my jaw off the floor.

Fuck. The closet is huge. It has its own island, and tons and tons of space. It's the kind of closet that every girl dreams about. With a ton of rack space to dump the latest trendy pumps on. But I'm surprised to see it mostly stuffed with feminine clothing; corsets, silk and lace lingerie. It looks like they're all my size, too.

After a moment, I turn off the light and leave the closet, walking back into the bedroom, feeling stunned.

Joseph is standing there where I left him, his eyes on me. My heart skips a beat at the hunger I see in them. A growing sense of dread rises from the pit of my stomach. I know what that look means. And I know what I haven't told him.

"This is beautiful," I say quietly, trying to keep my voice steady, not wanting to betray the anxiety twisting my stomach.

An amused twinkle glints in his eyes. "I thought you might like it," he murmurs, his voice husky and confident.

"I don't think I've ever stayed in such a nice room before," I say, and then jokingly add, "Minus the whips, chains and cage of course."

Joseph huffs out an amused chuckle. "Those will have no effect on how well you sleep in that bed. You will find it quite soft, actually." For the first time, he takes his eyes off my face, casting a quick glance over to the corner of the room where the white cage is. "But if you disobey me…" his voice trails off, but I know what he means. It's almost like he's itching to see me in the cage.

I slightly shudder, my nipples pebbling. A part of me thinks I would like the cage. I'm turned on by it. But I think I would only enjoy it for a little while--an hour, maybe two, but definitely not for anything longer than that. The thought of being in it for more than several hours absolutely terrifies me. I clasp my hands in front of my dress, swinging my shoulders back and forth, trying to shake the nervousness that keeps running through my limbs.

Joseph steps forward, sensing my emotions, stopping a few feet from me. He reaches out and places a hand on my shoulder, halting my rocking. I almost groan at his touch, feeling small shocks where his skin touches mine.

Fuck, what this man does to me.

Up close, I'm enveloped by his masculine scent and it calms me, if only slightly. *Jesus*, I love how he smells.

"What's wrong, flower?" he asks me with concern.

I look into his eyes, and my heart flips. The hunger is still there, and it's enough to make my skin prick, my cheeks burning red. I know that it won't be long before that hunger will demand to be sated. I just need to... I swallow thickly. I need to tell him. I know it's going to happen soon.

"Can tonight be different?" I blurt out, my heart skipping a beat and then starting to race.

Joseph's eyes never leave my face. "Can what be different?" he asks, and his voice sounds so deep and low.

My forehead crinkles as I frown. Is he toying with me? He has to know what I mean with the way he's been looking at me since I've got here and that giant bulge in his pants that he's done little to hide.

My cheeks still burning, I gesture at the king-size luxurious bed. "Uh, you know."

A grin plays across his chiseled jawline. "No, in fact I don't."

Okay. Now I know he's toying with me.

I shake my head. "I just always thought... it's silly... but I've always been..." I search for a way to say what I want without giving myself away. "I'd like this to be outside our contract? I just... can we just pretend I'm not your Slave for the first time?"

Joseph shakes his head firmly, and my heart falls into my stomach. "I don't pretend, Lilly."

I search his face for some sign of softening, but his jaw is firm. I don't think I'll convince him. My heart races in my chest. All the ways I've imagined him fucking me have been ruthless. But right now, I don't want that.

"Can you be gentle at first?" I ask hopefully. "Just for tonight."

I see amusement flash in his eyes, but his expression remains flat. "That's not in my nature."

It's hard to keep my face steady and my knees from shaking as I look at him. I don't know what I should do.

I've never had sex before, but now I'm supposed to be able to endure a man his size, who's going to fuck me like a wild animal?

Holy fuck.

I'm just as scared as I am turned on.

More than that, I'm uncertain. I'm about to give away my virginity to a man I've hardly known for more than a few days. The realization nearly makes my head spin.

What the fuck is wrong with me?

My next words come out small and tiny sounding. "Is it going to hurt?"

God, I sound so fucking naive, but I can't help myself. I'm terrified.

Joseph reaches out, gently cupping my cheek. "The only pain I give you will be followed by pleasure."

Oh God. Yes.

I close my eyes, shuddering, hoping to find the strength to endure what's to come. I hear him as he takes a step closer, pushing me with him until the back of my knees hit the bed.

You could always end this, says that annoying voice. *You could just walk away right now.*

I don't get to answer it.

I feel Joseph move closer, invading my private space and pressing his hard body up against me. I want him. I've never known anything else to be as true as that single fact.

Fuck. I feel his hard cock pressing up against my hip.

And *damn*. It feels *SO* big. I take an unsteady breath. It's happening.

His hot lips suddenly press against mine, sending electricity shooting through every one of my nerve endings. I tilt my head back, my lips parting in a sigh, my nipples hardening and my pussy heating with need. The sensation is like nothing I've ever felt, and I feel like I'm being turned into pure liquid honey, ready to melt into him.

"You want me, Lilly?" Joseph stops kissing me to murmur, his hot breath scorching my neck.

I groan, wanting his lips back on me, not wanting the sensation to end. "Yes, Sir," I moan. "Please, Sir."

Even though his lips are at my neck, I can feel his grin, along with his throbbing cock pressing insistently against my pussy.

"Good girl," he whispers. I swallow thickly as he unzips the back of my dress slowly. I can hardly breathe as his hot breath sends chills down my body, his fingers brushing against my shoulders as he pushes my dress down my waist and over my ass. It falls into a pool at my feet.

His fingers tickle around my hips. I knew better than to wear undergarments. I only packed a few for the entire month, although I'm not sure he'll ever let me wear them.

He leaves an open-mouth kiss on the front of my throat, humming with satisfaction as his fingers move to my pussy. I stand still, waiting for any direction he's willing to give me. I can hear the words at the tip of my tongue, begging for me to say them. *Please be gentle with me. I've never done this before.* But instead I say nothing as he grabs my hips and lifts me onto the bed.

A startled gasp is ripped from my throat as my back hits the mattress. My heart races in my chest, beating uncontrollably. I glance up to see him unbuttoning his top button and pulling his dress shirt over his head. His muscles ripple in the soft light.

Holy fuck.

I can't take my eyes off of him as his deft fingers unbuckle his belt, and then the button of his pants. He slowly unzips the slacks, pushing them to the floor and stepping out of them along with his boxers. The only thing I can hear is my hammering heart. I lie as still as I can on top of the bedding. I need to tell him I'm a virgin. But I can't, the words refuse to come out.

He crawls onto the bed and hovers over me. His bulky shoulders make him look even more intimidating than usual. The look in his eyes freezes my body. Possession. Power radiates from his very being. He owns me. It's never been more clear to me that in this very moment. He. Owns. Me.

"Spread your legs for me." His voice is soft as he commands me, and then he gently kisses the edge of my jaw, trailing kisses toward my ear and down my neck. I do as he says, spreading my legs as far as I can. He moves between my thighs, his fingers cupping my pussy once again.

I'm soaking wet, shamelessly soaked for him.

He lays his body so close to mine. Only centimeters away. His forearm to the right of my head braces him as he strokes his cock, and gently pushes the head through my folds.

Tell him! I scream inside my head.

My body heats, and begs me to move. I don't. I lie perfectly still, waiting for him to take from me one thing I can never get back. I've committed to it. Fuck, I hope he can't tell.

"Are you ready for me, Lilly?" he asks with a different tone in his voice. Something I don't recognize. I nod my head quickly, swallowing the lump in my throat. "Are you ready to give me your virginity?" Shock paralyzes me for a moment. My mouth opens and closes, nothing coming out. He nuzzles his nose into the crook of my neck, giving me a moment to realize what he's said. I still can't respond when he kisses me sweetly on the lips. My eyes refuse to close.

"Tell me," he says, then kisses me again before moving away from me slightly to rest his thumb on my bottom lip. "You're ready for me?" he asks me, his eyes moving from my lips to mine. I can't deny the want reflected back at me. The pure desire. I nod my head once and with that simple response, the powerful man towering above me closes his eyes and groans as though I'm torturing him.

"Answer me," he says simply, his eyes still closed as his dick presses into my entrance.

"Yes, Sir." At my answer, he slams into me with a forceful thrust that makes my back bow and my neck arch, pushing my head into the mattress. I instinctively reach for him, my nails digging into his back. A silent scream falls from my lips. It feels like a pinch. A hard fucking pinch, followed by stinging pain.

He stays buried deep inside of me, my tight walls refusing to adjust to his thick girth. It hurts! The stinging pain refuses to dim as he stretches me. My eyes close tight, and my forehead pinches, willing the pain away.

He shushes me in the crook of my neck. His hand gently strokes the curve of my waist as he stays deep inside of me. I want to writhe under him and move away, but he holds me still, planting soft kisses down my neck to my collarbone and then back up my throat. Tears prick my eyes; I didn't think it would hurt like this. My heart isn't even moving. My body is so still, so paralyzed with the shocking pain. Joseph puts his hand between us and rubs my clit as he kisses me.

The sensation quickly morphs into something else. My body relaxes slowly and then tightens as my pussy heats, and tingling stirs in the pit of my stomach. I finally swallow, feeling my muscles ease and the pleasure increasing as the pressure builds.

"Does that feel good, my flower?" Joseph asks me in a low voice. I can only moan an answer at first. His hand moves from my clit as he pulls out of me slightly before pushing all the way back in. Fuck! My legs wrap around his waist, ankles crossing and digging into his ass. When he moves, oh God, when he moves, my sensitive nipples rub against his chest. I need more.

"Yes," I answer in a mere whisper as he pumps his hips again. And then again. Each time he brushes against my clit. The sensation becomes nearly overwhelming. Oh fuck yes. This is what I thought it'd be like. My body heats with a cold sweat breaking out along my skin. It's too much. I can't... I can't.

His fingers wrap around my hip, holding me down as his pace quickens. My nipples harden as goosebumps form over my entire body as a cold sweat breaks out, traveling along every inch of my skin. My nerve endings are on high alert. My forehead pinches as I realize I'm about to cum. My body slams into the bed, Joseph's hard thrusts pushing me higher and higher. I'm so close. I force the words from my lips, "May I-" He cuts me off before I'm able to finish. "Cum freely," Sir says in a voice I've never heard, one laced with desperation, his speed increasing as he races for his own release.

The realization of what I do to him is my undoing. I make him lose control. I throw my head back, the intense sensation running through my body in waves. The first is slow, starting from my stomach and working its way out to each of my limbs, tingling the tips of my fingers.

Before the first is even finished, the next comes crashing through my body and as I feel him cum deep inside of me, the final wave forces me to call out his name, "Joseph!"

My body shakes and trembles. My heart is pounding so loudly I swear he can hear it.

As I try to catch my breath, Joseph slips out of me slowly, hushing me when I wince. I open my eyes to see his shining back at me.

He knew. My breathing comes in slower as he plants a kiss on my lips. I can't close my eyes though.

He knew.

CHAPTER 16

JOSEPH

It's been a long time since I felt the warmth of a woman in my bed. It's been years. A soft sigh gently spills from Lilly's lips as she nestles into my arm. Her left leg is propped up on top of mine, and every little movement is making my dick even harder.

I own her. I could take her again right now if I wanted. But the sight of her sleeping so soundly is something I never thought I'd want to see as much as I do.

Her hair is a tangled, messy halo of golden locks. Her face is partially buried in the comforter that she has up around her neck. The warmth gives her skin a slight blush. I've seen her naked so many times. Last night I felt her raw, not only in the way I took her, but also in her emotions when she gave me something she can never have back. After I cleaned us up, I held her as a lover should, and I was happy to give her that. She fell asleep in my arms, and that's where she's stayed.

She's at peace and relaxed. It's an odd thing to me, the feelings washing over me as I look at her, something I didn't expect.

"Lilly," I say her name in an even cadence, and her breathing comes to a halt as she readjusts in her sleep, still not waking. I move my arm out from under her, the air feeling cool without her warmth.

Her head falls to the mattress without my support. She gasps, opening her sleepy eyes and bracing herself with both hands on the mattress. I give her a minute to wake and to recognize where she is. The moment she sees me, her pupils dilate with both recognition and desire.

I sit up on my knees, shoving my silk pajama pants down along with my boxers so my cock springs free. My little flower is such a naughty girl. She licks her lips staring at my cock, but she's as still as can be on the mattress as she waits obediently for my command. Such a good girl.

"What are you?" I ask her as I stroke myself from end to end, spreading the moisture over the head of my dick.

She breathes her answer, "Yours." Fuck, hearing her lust-filled voice admitting my claim to her with such pride makes me want her that much more. I reach down, grabbing her by the hair at her nape, fisting it and bringing her lips to my dick.

"Damn right you are," I tell her as her lips slide down my

cock and my head brushes against the back of her throat. Fuck! She feels too good. It takes everything in me not to groan out loud and shove deeper down her throat. Although I have a firm grip on her, controlling her if I need to, I let her move at her own pace. She nearly gags on my cock, her wide eyes looking apologetic. I don't give a fuck. Her mouth feels like fucking heaven.

I buck my hips once, feeling her throat stretch around my cock. She takes it, her hands almost reaching up to grip me, but she quickly puts them back down, gripping her thighs. Her eyes water as I pump my hips, forcing her to take more, and holding myself at the back of her throat. Only for a moment, right before pulling out and giving her a moment to catch her breath.

She breathes in deep, keeping her mouth open and ready for more. Fuck, she's too good to be true.

She moans around my dick, loving how I'm using her. She gets on all fours, hollowing her cheeks as she sucks my length, eager to take more. Her tongue massages the underside of my dick and her throat closes around my head as she goes as far as she can, her nose almost reaching the coarse pubic hair. Again she moans and her lips push down, stroking my length as she blows me. She moves her lips all the way to the ridge of the head of my cock. It sends tingles down my spine, my toes curl and I nearly cum just from that sensation.

The tip of her tongue dips into the slit, licking up the

small bit of precum that leaked out. She moves her hand up to stroke my dick, and that's what I've been waiting for.

Thank fuck she did it before I came. I'm quick to grab her wrists before she can touch me. I pull out of her mouth, pushing her backward and pinning her down on the mattress. Her eyes flash with fear as I hold her down, staring at her with narrowed eyes.

"Did I tell you that you could touch me?" I ask her, my head tilted. A spark of knowing darts across her blue eyes as she realizes what she's done.

"I'm sorry, Sir," she says as her hips tilt and her upper thighs clench. "I had no right." She gives in so easily, accepting what she's done. My fingers dig into her hip before loosening my hold on her and letting go of her wrist.

"Mistakes will be made," I tell her. "I'll allow you one warning for now." She stares at me, her breath barely coming in as she waits for her punishment.

I back away from her and her lips part to protest me leaving her, her eyes flashing with worry.

I've kept myself from her for so long, refusing to let her please me. And although it wasn't a punishment then, I'm sure she saw it as just that. But I have no intention of not taking from her every fucking day that she's here. She'll learn that soon enough.

"Get on your hands and knees," I tell her as I sit on my knees, ready to feel her tight cunt wrapped around me again.

She's quick to get into position, turning her body so her ass is the closest thing to me. I grip her hips nearly violently in a bruising hold and pull her quickly toward me, reveling in the sweet gasp that comes from her lips. She curves her back like a good girl. She's trying, I know she is. She's desperate to please me. I take her hair in both of my hands before wrapping it around my wrist, gripping and pulling her hair back slightly.

My fingers play at her wet pussy lips as I look over her body in complete submission to me. "You fucking love this, don't you?"

With her neck arched, her voice comes out in a higher pitch, "Yes, Sir." I nearly slammed myself into her tight cunt to the hilt without waiting for her response, but I stop before doing so after hearing those sweet words. But I already know that I can't.

She's swollen from last night. I spread her lips and see she's red. I'd love to ride her hard and fast, to give her the brutal fuck she truly desires. But instead I ease in slowly.

She feels so good, and I knew she'd feel just like this. Somehow I knew.

I slowly slip deep inside of her, letting her hair relax around my wrist and losing my grip on her. Taking her hips in both of my hands, I bend forward and kiss her neck. Her eyes are closed tight, and her mouth is pressed into a small frown. I know she hurts. My hand slips between her legs to rub her clit. I pull back on her clit slightly, exposing the raw sensitive side and press my middle finger down, rubbing merciless circles against her. Her eyes pop open as her mouth forms a perfect "O".

I stay buried to the hilt until her face softens to show more pleasure than pain. Her pussy strangles my cock as I move deep, sliding in and out of her. My fingers are wrapped around her hips and my stomach presses against her back as I bite down, nipping on her earlobe and making her gasp before I pull nearly all the way back and then slam into her. Her hands slip on the mattress, and she falls forward.

With her small body under mine, I buck my hips over and over. I brace my heavy body with one forearm, my other hand holding her hip and keeping her angled just how I want as she fights under me to control herself. I piston my hips, loving how her pussy spasms around my cock and the sounds of her wet cunt being so brutally fucked filling my ears.

Her cheek presses against the mattress with each blow I give her. Her eyes shut tight, and her teeth sink into her bottom lip. She's holding back her screams of pleasure, her hands fisting the sheet beneath us.

"Let me hear you," I tell her in a strong voice I don't recognize in this moment. I'm so lost in her touch. My heart beats fitfully, and my body heats then freezes with an intense pleasure that radiates outward. I'm so close to losing it. But I want her with me every step of the way.

Her mouth opens instantly, obeying me as I continue my ruthless pace. She screams out my name over and over, not addressing me as Sir but instead calling me Joseph. I wasn't expecting it, just like I wasn't last night, but my name on her lips sends me over the edge. I desperately rub at her clit as thick streams of cum fill her tight pussy.

Her small body shakes under me as her own release finds her. Thank fuck!

My mouth parts as I take in a sharp breath, loving the way her tight cunt strangles my dick.

I brace myself with my forearm, wiping the sweat off my forehead and gently stroking her side, until her body stops trembling and her breathing finally steadies.

My own breathing is coming in heavy as I sit up on my knees. Her small body is lying limp on the bed, her shoulders rising and falling with heavy breaths. Her eyes are wide open, darting from me, back to the bed as she stays still. Her body shivers uncontrollably, but I'm not sure if it's from a chill or from the intense pleasure of her orgasm. As I climb off the bed I grab the edge of the comforter and bring it up to her shoulders.

"Don't go back to sleep now, my flower." I kiss her forehead, loving how she closes her eyes and trembles beneath my comforting touch just as much as she did from the ruthless way I fucked her. I whisper against the shell of her ear, "We're just getting started."

CHAPTER 17

LILY

I lie back against the mattress, my chest heaving, my pulse racing as I look up into his eyes. God, he's so handsome. I could look at his face all day. He leans in close, his hard body pressing up against my soft skin. Down below, I can feel his hardness pressing up against my stomach. I can feel it throbbing, pulsating along with my heartbeat as he brings his lips against my neck.

A soft sigh escapes my lips as I arch my back against the bed, pressing my body into him.

I want him.

I need him.

I'm just not sure if I'm ready.

He pulls back as if sensing my anxiety, his deep brown eyes searching my face.

"Do you trust me?" he asks softly, his breathing heavy.

I stare back into his concerned gaze, not sure what to say. Do I trust him? I've only known him for a few weeks, and while I am infatuated with him, I'm not sure if I trust him.

At the same time, he's treated me better than anyone else has ever treated me. He's shown more concern about my well-being than anyone ever has. Most of all, I'm sure he's willing to wait until I'm ready.

But I'm not going to make him wait.

Not today.

"Yes," I breathe, my heart in my voice. "I trust you."

His handsome face splits into a grin, his eyes sparkling with happiness. "Good."

As he comes in closer, bringing his lips close to mine, I relax my body and prepare to surrender myself wholly to him...

Smack!

The memory of being spanked jolts me out of the book I'm working on and I pull my fingers back from the keys of my laptop, my breathing ragged. I can still feel the sting of the paddle against my ass. Joseph disciplined me for talking back to him this morning.

At the time, I thought I was being myself and it was all just harmless banter. He even smiled as I was doing it. He played along. My heart warms at the memory.

But I was still *punished*.

Harshly.

My eyes fall down to my naked legs and I see the goosebumps covering them, the faint red marks my disobedience has earned me. I squeeze my thighs together, feeling my clit pulse, turned on by the sight.

I've lost my clothing privileges, all because I sat incorrectly at the table. Joseph wants me seated with my legs spread if I'm in a chair. His rules are simple and easy, but unnatural. I purse my lips. These punishments aren't really fair. But at the same time, I welcome them. Being bad has never felt so good.

They're erotic, sensual even, and they bring back memories of being whipped in the dungeon.

My nipples pebble, and my pussy clenches around cool air as I think about these *punishments*.

It's been a crazy last few days, and I still can't believe I gave myself to him. Or that he *knew* about my virginity. My fingers tap on the keyboard and I look over my shoulder and out to the hall, shifting on my bed with my laptop balanced on my thighs.

I was concerned I'd regret giving myself to him. But with everything I'm feeling, regret isn't even on the radar. Even when I unknowingly disobey him.

He's taught me so many things in such a short amount of time, gave me pleasure that I'd never dreamt possible. The way he makes me feel, taking my body, ravaging it, devouring it. *Owning it.*

I shake my head, at a loss for words.

I love it.

I love both sides of Joseph. The nice and caring side, and the dominant side. Although, he's been showing the dominant side more these past few days. It seems like he's controlling everything I do or say now. Just this morning he had clothes laid out for me that he wanted me to wear, along with the oils that he wants me to put in my hair. I love the smell of them actually.

And strangely enough, I want more of this. More of his control.

More of him.

Thinking about him makes me wonder what he's doing.

Crawling off the bed, I leave my laptop and go search through the house for him.

I look through several of the rooms, including his bedroom before I find him in his study. He's sitting at his desk, his head down as he writes in a notebook. It looks worn and I tilt my head, narrowing my eyes as I notice the binding is leather. His brow is furrowed; he's clearly focused on whatever he's writing.

I bite my lower lip as I look at him, my heart racing as my hand stills on the doorframe. He looks so gorgeous sitting there in slacks and a white dress shirt opened at the chest. I don't know if I should disturb him. He did tell me that I have permission to come to him at all times, but he looks busy and I don't even remember why I came to find him. I almost turn and leave, twisting on my back heel, but he looks up, freezing me in place.

I step fully into the doorway, clasping my hands out in front of me like he taught me to do, and then I wait patiently.

I don't have to wait long.

"Yes?" he asks in a low voice, slowly setting the pen down. My heart thump, thump, thumps.

Opening a drawer off to the side, he places the notebook into the drawer and then closes it, his eyes on me the entire time.

A feeling of suspicion washes over me at his actions. What was he writing?

Joseph clears his throat and says, "Lilly?"

I stare at him for a moment, noticing for the first time that he looks stressed; something's bothering him.

He's sitting in his chair, tense as can be, worry lines etched in his forehead. I've never seen him like this.

I lick my lips, hesitating to respond. I don't want to say anything now. I'm not here for anything important anyway. I was just coming to play around and do something to get punished, but it all seems so trivial now.

Joseph's going through something.

It's insensitive of me to expect him to stop what he's doing to indulge me. My fingers twist around one another. A strange sense of loneliness washes through me.

I think back to the hero that I'm writing about, with his dark hair and dark eyes, and how much he reminds me of Joseph.

"Flower," he growls warningly, his deep voice pricking my skin.

Shit. I have to say something now.

"I was hoping I could please you, Sir," I say softly. The

moment the words leave my lips, I regret them. Looking at him, I know that he's not in the mood for playing.

His pause hurts almost as much as his next words. "Not right now."

I was expecting it, but it still hurts, a heavy weight settling on my chest. I try to turn away quickly before my face crumples into a frown, intent on running back to my room and closing the door behind me. I don't make it two steps before he calls me back to him.

"Come here," he commands me. "Now."

I bite my lower lip, holding back tears, and turn on my heel and make my way over to his desk to stand beside him. I don't know why I'm so emotional. But something about this moment is off.

He looks up at me, a sadness in his eyes that tugs at my heartstrings. "Kneel," he commands.

I obey his command immediately, sinking to my knees beside him. Swallowing, I look up at him, not sure if he's going to punish me, scold me, or both.

I startle when he reaches out and pets my hair softly. "You've been a good girl," he tells me. "You can put your clothes back on if you'd like."

My heart drops in my chest. I don't want to put my clothes back on. I want him to take me. *Punish me.* Anything.

"Okay," I say, rising to my feet, my throat closing. I try to hide my displeasure, but I can't keep the frown off of my face.

I wish I could just disappear.

Anger sparks in Joseph's eyes. "I didn't tell you to get up," he growls, his deep voice low and dangerous.

My heart skips a beat and then starts racing, excitement coursing through my limbs. Maybe he will punish me after all.

I cross my arms over my breasts and try to think of something smart to say. But before I can say a word, he jumps up to his feet and grabs me by the wrist.

"I can see exactly what you're doing," he says in a calm, controlled voice. "I don't want you to deliberately disappoint me, do you understand?"

I stare into his eyes, my heart pounding. There's anger there, but a different kind. One that isn't attached to sexual emotion. I hate it. I hate that he's making me feel this way, like I've done something so horrible to turn him off.

"I wasn't trying to do anything-" I begin.

"Don't lie to me, Lilly," he growls, cutting me off. My heart clenches. I don't like this. I want to go back in time five minutes and never have stepped in here.

I square my shoulders, and rather than tell him how I'm feeling, how I'm craving his punishment in the pleasure that he gives me, and how I hate that he's in whatever mood he's in right now, I snap, "I don't know what you're talking about."

His grip tightens on my wrist, his eyes narrowing. I can tell he's pissed off that I won't tell him the truth. But fuck him. I don't have to give in to him when he doesn't give in to me.

His next words are cold and harsh. "Stop denying it."

Anger tightens my chest at his threat. All I wanted was to have a little playful fun, get each other off. It's not my fault that I'm begging for sex. He did this to me. He made me want it. He made me need it.

Need him.

Even now, I'm breathless with desire as he stares at me angrily, his lower jaw bulging out from being clenched tightly. But he doesn't want me right now. And that pisses me the fuck off.

Too angry to speak, I raise my chin in defiance, letting him know that I'm not going to do what he wants. He can fucking punish me.

That's when something inside of him seems to snap and he pulls me into him with great force, causing me to cry out in shock.

Next thing I know, his powerful fingers are wrapped around my chin, forcing me to look into his eyes. My blood turns to ice as I look into them, and for the first time that I've been with him, I feel very real fear.

There's darkness there. A cold emptiness that makes a chill shoot down my spine.

I don't know this man. Or what he's truly capable of.

And that terrifies me.

The next thing he says frightens me even more, his voice low and very dangerous sounding.

"Go to your cage."

Chapter 18

Joseph

She thinks she knows everything, and I've been pushing her to find her boundaries. To find that breaking point where she'll realize she isn't getting what she wants. So far, she's wanted to obey me. And every command she's met head-on. The perfect slave.

I knew at some point she'd break. I knew I'd ask too much of her. I imagined it would be something much more than simply not telling me that she's deliberately disobeying me. She's always had a problem expressing herself though, so I shouldn't be as shocked as I am.

I can read her so easily. I know she was disappointed. But this relationship isn't me being available to her. It's her being available to me. I'm restless in the leather armchair in the living room, her laptop on my knees as I read through the scene she's been writing. I've given her permission to write every day. When she feels the inspiration, she can do so. I huff a humorless laugh. I've given her permission to do whatever the fuck she'd like when my dick isn't in her. Maybe that was my first mistake. It's my fault she's in the cage.

I take a small sip of the whiskey before sitting the glass back down on the end table.

I scroll through her scene, reading about the collar the hero has given the heroine. She's romanticized everything. Her perception of what this lifestyle is, is missing an important aspect. The one where I have control.

This is why I didn't want a Submissive. My fingers tap on the short glass in my hand before bringing it to my lips again. I didn't anticipate that the boundary that would send her to the cage would be refusing to tell me the truth.

I thought better of her than that. Of everything I've asked her to do, that seems to be the least difficult. But maybe she doesn't want to believe it herself.

My eyes read over the next scene she's written, the hero of her book taking the virginity of the heroine. It's not difficult to see that it was inspired by how I took her. This hero kisses her sweetly, talks to her gently. He *makes love* to her.

This man is nothing like me. The stark contrast reminds me of where I came from.

I remember the first time I saw my father kiss my mother. She was always quiet. Always in the background and never allowed to be around us. I didn't quite understand it. She wasn't allowed to interfere, that's what my father told us.

She approached him, her eyes wide with worry as she talked in quiet whispers, pleading with him for something. Her eyes kept darting toward us as we sat on the floor of the living room, cleaning the guns.

My father was rough with her. I watched as he grabbed the back of her hair so tightly he ripped some out. He kissed her hard on the lips, smearing her lipstick across her face before throwing her down on the ground. I remember how I jumped up, how my heart raced in my chest. I knew how hard my father hit, all too well. She landed hard, wincing with pain as she braced herself. But the look on her face changed when she saw me watching, slowly walking toward them. She shook her head, her eyes warning me to stay away.

That was what we had as an example. It sickened me. I loved my mother, and I couldn't watch as my father hit her. Day in and day out, she became an outlet for his anger. As my mother whimpered on the floor, I looked back to my brother. Wanting to make sure he was all right. We were only children. But the look in his eyes sickened me. It still does. The smile on his face showed what kind of a man he would be. If you can even call that a man.

That's the day I realized that my father was a sick fuck, and the cold dark look was echoed in my brother's eyes.

I down the whiskey and close the laptop at the unpleasant

memory, setting it on the ottoman and rising from my seat. I ignore the fact that I feel like an asshole. I'm fully aware that she's under a different impression of what this is. She shouldn't be. It's my fault, and I need to fix this.

I look at the clock and see it's been an hour. The time has passed by slowly; tick-tock, tick-tock. I wanted to go to her every minute that she's been in there, but she needs to learn she can't top from the bottom. I'm the one with control, and she won't force my hand to get what she wants.

All the punishment she's received up to this moment has been for conditioning. The punishment was to help her learn how to please me. Although there's pain, it's always been accompanied by far more pleasure. She takes a simple punishment, and then she's rewarded for accepting it.

Not this time.

Hopefully this will be the last time. But I doubt it will be. There is a ferocity in her. A strength that she doesn't recognize. She may not know how courageous she is, but when most people see me, they cower. She was drawn to my power. That in and of itself shows courage.

My blood rushes in my ears, and my body heats as I move to her room. I open the door slowly, peeking in to see her curled in a ball on the floor of the cage. The cage itself is large enough for her to stand. I imagined her in the corner with her knees tucked under her chin, her arms wrapped around her legs.

And that's just how she is.

She peeks up over her knees as I close the door.

Her eyes are red-rimmed. She's been crying. Seeing her like this hurts me.

"Are you ready to behave?" I ask her, slowly walking toward the corner of the room. The cage door is slightly ajar; I didn't lock it, but I know she didn't leave it. It's not in her nature.

She can leave if she wants. At any time, she could go and break the contract. But she doesn't truly want to leave. She wants to fight me; she wants me to earn her submission.

And I fucking love the challenge.

This part of it though, I'm not sure I want to do again. I'd rather fuck her into submission.

I crouch in front of the cage, opening the door all the way. She watches me with wide eyes. When the door creaks open, her body stiffens as she says, "I didn't unlock it." I stare back at her as she continues, her voice soft. "I think you forgot to lock it, Sir."

"Did you leave?" I ask as I sit on the floor with my legs crossed. I already know she didn't. She shakes her head and whispers, "No."

"I didn't forget anything, my flower." I pat my lap, waiting for her to crawl out to me. "I'll never lock you in here. It's in our contract."

She seems hesitant for a moment, her movements stuttering.

"You did read what you signed, didn't you?" My voice comes out playful. I know she read every word more than once. I know she takes it seriously. Her lips show the trace of a smile, but it quickly disappears as she wipes away the tears under her eyes.

"Yes, Sir," she answers beneath her breath as she crawls out. She doesn't hesitate to come to me, nestling herself in my lap and resting her cheek against my chest. I comfort her, rubbing her back with firm strokes.

"You know I had to punish you, don't you?" I ask her.

She nods her head against my chest as her fingers intertwine nervously. "I do." She clears her throat and says, "I'm sorry, Sir, I shouldn't have lied to you. I shouldn't have tried to push you."

I kiss her hair, petting her as she apologizes. I hate this. It's something I knew that was going to happen, but I didn't expect my reaction. Or hers.

"I-" I clear my throat and shuffle her in my lap. I don't mind that she came to me. I'm dealing with my fuckface of a brother. He wants the money back. The money they planted on me to set me up. He's trying to get me back under the *familia's* thumb. It's not going to happen. "I will attend to you when I can. But sometimes you have to wait."

Lilly nods her head diligently.

I hook my finger under her chin, and look her in the eyes as I tell her, "Trust me, I would have much rather been spending time with you."

I kiss her, the taste of her tears touching the tip of my

tongue as she gives into me, parting her lips. Her eyes are still glassed over with unshed tears. I brush my thumb along her cheek, and kiss her again. I say the only words I know that will make her smile again.

I brush my nose against hers and say, "I think you need to be punished, my flower."

I knot the rope at her wrists, tying them tighter. Her lips part, gifting me that beautiful sound.

Testing the give of the rope, I pull slightly, her small body falling forward. She's on her ass on the floor. Naked and waiting for me to command her.

I'm running out of these stupid rules. It's not about training her anymore, it's about pushing her limits and simply enjoying each other's touch.

I pull her closer to me, her arms bending as my lips brush against hers. My heart seems to slow when I open my eyes and find her pale blue gaze shining back at me. There's a look there I should fear. Something that tells me I should end this. But I don't want to. I refuse to.

Chapter 19

Lily

I let out a groan, rubbing soothing circles on my right ass cheek as I stop in the hallway outside of Joseph's room.

I'm sore all over. From being used. Deliciously used. But I need more of whatever it is he rubs on my ass after he's done spanking me.

Over the past several days, Joseph's given me nothing but sessions of rough, pleasurable sex. At this point, I can't tell if I'm aching from one of his spankings or his thick cock. I smile at the memory of this morning. No doubt the spanking when it comes to my ass.

It's a good problem to have. And I could definitely learn to love it. I just wish I didn't feel it right now. It's getting in the way of my snooping. A mischievous grin slips into place. I know I'm being a bit bad, but technically there's no rule against it.

For the past hour, I've been looking around the house, trying to figure out what Joseph's hiding. I *know* he's hiding something. A part of me is scared to find out. And the other part of me is hoping that I'm just being paranoid. I bite down on the inside of my cheek. He won't tell me about his past. Or whatever the hell makes him hide away in his study. I'm sure as fuck not gonna sit around waiting.

The wooden floor creaks in the hallway under my weight the second I slip out of my room. Dammit. I'm not the best at being quiet. My heart stills and I stand frozen in the hallway, glaring at the wooden floorboards. After a moment, I straighten and continue on into his room. I practically tiptoe, my tongue stuck between my teeth as I sneak into his room. I love it in here. It's so... him.

Furtively I look around, wondering where I should start first, my heart pounding in my chest. I don't have much time. I don't know when Joseph will come out of his study, so I need to move quickly. I should hear him, I keep telling myself. I will definitely hear him when he comes up the stairs.

I purse my lips as I walk over to his dresser and start digging through it. I go through five drawers, but don't find anything but neatly folded clothes. Where else do people hide shit? I figured the dresser would be a gold mine. That's where I hide all my shit. I shut the last drawer gently, feeling a little let down. I look up and spot his bed, a smile curling on my lips. *The mattress.* I search underneath the bed and then push my hand below the mattress, between the box spring and the frame. I'm weak as shit, and holding it up actually makes me winded. *Nothing.*

"Come on," I mutter, looking around the room frantically, "Everyone hides something under the mattress."

I get down on my hands and knees and look under the bed again. He's gotta have something somewhere.

I search the nightstands. Nothing again.

Frustrated, I stop and place my hands on my hips, biting my lower lip and thinking.

If I had a big house like this, would I hide anything in my bedroom? I mean, how stupid would that be? Maybe I'm in the wrong room. I sure as fuck can't search his study though. Not while he's in there at least.

I'm about to give up and leave the room when my eyes fall on the closet. The door is slightly ajar, and the light is on inside. My pulse picks up speed as I stare at it. I don't know how I didn't notice it already. I used to hide in the closets. The thought makes my heart hurt.

It's where I found my mother. I think she wanted me to find her before my father did.

He used to tell me how much I looked like her, until she killed herself. Then I would see that pained look in his eyes, and I knew it was what he was thinking, but he never said it again.

I know that's why he doesn't see me much; I remind him

of her. I know it hurts him. I understand it. He still loves me, and I love him. Even if our family is scarred from what my mother did.

I bite my lower lip, shoving the sad memory back where it belongs, in the past, debating on whether I should go digging around more. I've already been looking for the past half hour, and Joseph doesn't spend very long on his own.

I should leave, I tell myself. *I'm not going to find anything in there anyway.*

I start to walk out of the room, but when I reach the doorway, I can't bring myself to leave without at least checking the closet. Though I know I probably won't find anything, who knows when I'll have another chance like this?

I spin around on my heel and walk quickly to the closet, swinging the door wide as I walk inside. It bangs against the wall, and I wince at the sound. I don't think he'll hear it though. Damn my eager ass.

Not wasting a second, I quickly go about inspecting the large closet, but I have to pause to suck in a sharp breath at the sight before me. *Jesus Christ.* He has *so* many suits. And they all look so fucking expensive. Who owns suits like these? I want to run my hands down all of the fine clothing, but I'm not here to look at his wardrobe. Focus, Lilly!

I go through several of the suits, checking in all the pockets, looking for something, anything that will tell me something about the past I feel Joseph is hiding. I come up empty. I look around, looking for a safe, some sort of bag, anything where something can be hidden. But I don't see a damn thing.

I'm about to leave the room when my eyes fall on a shoe box that's sitting inconspicuously next to a row of shoes. Looking at it, I know it's probably just shoes in there, but I can't help myself. I rush forward, nearly tripping to get to the box, and grab it. My heart stutters in my chest at the bit of racket I'm making. I only need one more minute.

Yes! Finally! There's a leather-bound book inside with a worn gold latch. I take it out, marveling at the high quality feel.

I open it, quickly glancing over my shoulder as I sit on the floor of his closet, to see pages filled with neat handwriting. One name keeps popping up off the page; *Passerotto.* I say it over and over again, whispering under my breath. I don't know what it means. I have no idea, but it definitely sounds Italian. I try to read some of the entries, and it's hard to keep up, but there's a lot mentioning of the *familia*. What the hell? Joseph is part of the Mafia? My heart beats faster, and my anxiety starts to grow.

I read a little bit further and find out that he's left *the family*, but it doesn't give me any relief. I scan an entry, my heart breaking in my chest. He watched his mother being beaten. He didn't do anything. I can tell by the way he's written it, he blames himself.

I get several more paragraphs in, so absorbed in the

moment that I forget the time and where I am. I can feel my heart breaking as tears cloud my eyes. *Joseph*. I can't believe what he's been through.

A loud sound of footsteps coming up the stairs pulls my gaze from the pages of the book and a curse spills from my lips, "Oh shit!" I throw the book back into the shoe box and quickly set it back in its original place.

I'm about to run from the room when I knock over several suits on the clothing rack. My clumsy ass. Dammit. I'm the worst at this. Crap. I bend over to pick them up, but a metal glint catches my eye.

Holy fuck.

My heart jumps in my chest at the sight before me. A gun rack, hidden behind the fallen suits. It's filled with all sorts of guns.

"Tsk tsk," says a deep voice from the closet doorway.

I spin around, my heart pounding in my chest to see Joseph leaning against the doorjamb, gazing at me with amusement. I swear my heart wants to run away, and it chooses to try by climbing up my throat.

"Bad girl, my flower," he says playfully, a twinkle in his eye.

My heart is beating so fast it feels like it's about to burst out of my chest. I know I will be punished for this. And I know it will be the cage. I try desperately to come up with an excuse. Something. Anything. But I'm in his closet.

"Please sir," I plead, holding my hands out imploringly, "I

was just looking around –" My throat is so dry as I speak. My body is tingling with fear.

"It's all right, flower," he says easily, surprising me. My heart doesn't believe him though, and it's still fighting to leave my body, ruled by fear. "There's nothing wrong with you having a little look. I want you to feel comfortable here."

"I'm sorry sir," I say softly, relief slowly coursing through my blood.

Joseph motions at me. "Come here."

I look down at his suits that are on the floor, swallowing and bend to pick them up, but Joseph stops me with a terse, "Now."

That tone he uses makes me walk to him immediately, cringing as I step around his expensive suits left on the floor. He leads me back into the bedroom, pulling me by the hand and sitting me down on the bed. Gazing into my eyes, he gently strokes the side of my cheek, making my skin prickle all up and down my arms. I can still hardly breathe. I'm waiting for the other foot to drop, waiting for a punishment or admonishment. I knew what I was doing was bad. ...I also know I'm not really sorry. I'm only sorry I got caught. And I bet he knows that, too.

"There's nothing to be sorry about, flower," he tells me softly as if reading my mind. He pauses, and then gives me a playful nudge with his nose. "Unless you want to be sorry that you weren't waiting on my bed for me, naked with your legs spread wide."

A smile spreads across my face, and I let out a girlish giggle at his playful words. I really love these moments, when his playful side shines through. It's so different from the dark, dominating Master side. And I want more of it. I cup his face in my hand, looking deep into his eyes and rubbing my thumb across his stubble.

"I like you like this," I say softly, still not quite sure if he's really not mad at me. Maybe he knew I'd be looking. He always seems to know what I'm up to.

"Like what?" Joseph asks.

"I don't know, just when you're kind and playful."

He scoffs, shaking his head as he responds, "Those words aren't used to describe me very often."

"I really like this side of you," I say, placing my hand on his. A moment of silence falls over us, and I feel compelled to ask, "*Passerotto?*" I'm not sure if I pronounced it correctly. Or if me prodding is going to tip him to the point of being pissed off. But I want to talk. It's in my nature.

Joseph hesitates for a moment, and I fear he might close himself off. But instead he grabs onto my waist and pulls me onto his lap. I gasp and hold onto him, not expecting it. He seems to pull me into his lap whenever we "talk." I like it. Yet another thing to add to my Things-I-Like-About-Joseph-Levi-list. I nestle into his lap and wait patiently.

"Yes. It means little sparrow."

"Who did that journal belong to?" I ask, although I'm

certain it's his.

"My mother gave it to me when I was little..." Joseph's eyes are distant as his voice trails off. I place my cheek on his hot chest, listening to his heart and playing with the smattering of chest hair peeking through his unbuttoned shirt. I can sense that this is something he doesn't want to talk about, but I don't want to lose the opportunity to get him to open up.

"Go on... Please," I say very softly, stroking his hand and pulling away from him enough to look him in the eyes.

Joseph swallows audibly. But I'm pleased when he continues speaking. "I don't like talking about my past, but you seem to make me talk, my flower. I've had a fucked up life. There were a lot of times where I thought I wouldn't make it after the shit I had been through, after the shit I seen." He runs a hand down his face and looks past me.

The pain in his words pulls at my heartstrings.

"What did you see?" I ask, my voice barely above a whisper. I just want him to open up to me.

There's a long pause, and I can actually feel Joseph's heart pounding against my hand still at his chest. "A lot of death. A lot of murder."

I bring a hand to my lips in horror. "I'm sorry," I say in a choked voice, feeling tears well up in my eyes.

"It's okay," he replies thickly. But I know it's not. He's fucking hurting, and it tears me up. "I'd just rather not talk about it." My eyes flicker down to my lap, then back to his. I want him to talk. I want him to open up to me.

I know how he feels, not wanting to talk about things. But it helped me, so much that I know for sure I wouldn't be the person I am without having someone to confide in. Even if it was just a counselor at school. It's good to talk it out.

"Please?" I plead with him.

He shakes his head, and the look in his eyes tells me not to push him. I nod, trying not to feel like he's pushing me away. My eyes focus on the closet, where the journal is. Maybe that's his way.

I glance over at the closet. "Can I read it?"

"The journal?" he asks, and I immediately nod my head. "You can read it any time you wish."

We sit together in silence, and I swear I can hear Joseph's heart beating in tandem with mine. After a moment I turn in his lap, looking him in the eyes. I see the pain in his dark gaze, and I hate that I've partly caused it by bringing up the subject. I just want to help make it go away.

"I'm sorry," I tell him, rubbing his arm.

He doesn't respond. Instead, he leans down and kisses me on the lips very gently. Emotions swell up from my stomach and I find myself wrapping my arms around his neck and pulling him into me, smashing my lips into his with fiery passion.

I feel him hesitate for a moment, but it only lasts for an instant. He wraps his arms around my waist and pulls me back into the bed.

I've never felt more connected to anyone in my life. The more I learn about Joseph, the more I want him.

The more I fall for him.

And that could be a very dangerous thing.

Joseph

Although her hips are steadied by the bench in front of her, the rope tying her wrists behind her back and hanging from the ceiling is what's keeping her upright. Her ankles are bound to the bench and spread for me. Her hips are tied down as well. She's dangling naked, completely at my mercy. With the blindfold on, she doesn't know where I am. Each time my feet smack on the floor, her fingers twitch slightly. Her shoulders are going to be hurting her soon. This has to come to an end soon enough. I pull back on the blow as I smack the riding crop against her ass one last time. She yelps as her upper body is swaying, although her lower body is tied so tightly she doesn't move from the waist down.

Her ass is a beautiful shade of red. Some spots are a bit darker than the others. I trail the leather up the middle of her back; her body shivers, and her rose petal-colored nipples harden that much more. As I get to her arms and move forward, gently flicking the riding crop against her hard nipples, she moans.

It's only been thirty minutes, but she's so wet that her arousal is dripping down her thighs. I move the head of the riding crop up her neck and to her chin as I pull the blindfold off of her. The bright light startles her, and she sways away from me for just a moment as she closes her eyes. I allow it. Once she looks back at me, I bring my face closer to hers and plant a gentle kiss against her lips.

This is all because she got up from the table without asking for permission. Realistically, this isn't a punishment. I know she loved every minute of it. But that's what we're calling it.

"You do realize I own you," I tell her, my lips just an inch from hers. "You belong to me. Your freedom belongs to me." She holds my gaze as I speak to her. Her lips part in that beautiful way I've become addicted to.

She says her answer so sweetly, "Yes, Sir."

I walk around her, dropping the riding crop as I go and stroking my hard cock. I grip her hip in one hand although I don't need to, since she's not going anywhere.

I don't hold back when I fuck her.

And she takes it.

Chapter 20

Joseph

You can't keep telling me no.

I stare at the text message, nearly breaking the phone in my hand as I squeeze it, my anger rising and rising. I need to calm down. Every time this fuckface pisses me off, I fight with my flower. I'm not letting him come between us, and I don't give a damn what he wants.

I kept up my part of the bargain. I'm out.

They want the money back? They can come fucking get it.

I'm not dealing with their shit anymore. I pace the study, wanting to go back to the home I grew up in and beat the fucking piss out of him. But he never played fair. He'd pull a gun in a sword fight if he could. And he'd be damn proud of it. Going back there wouldn't be good.

The sound of Lilly turning off the water to the shower upstairs reminds me why I'm even letting him get to me. I finally have something worth giving a fuck about. This isn't the first or second or even the dozenth time I've had to put up with these assholes since I've left.

But lately I've been giving a fuck. I hear her pad across the bathroom upstairs. She's not a quiet little thing. Not in the least. The thought makes me smile until I hear the ping from my phone.

I scowl, looking down as my blood heats.

You don't have a choice.

Pissed. If I had less restraint, I'd hurl the fucking phone into the wall and scream out. Instead I calmly set it on the desk, staring at the phone and thinking of all the ways I'd love to kill him. I could have strangled him in his sleep. So many times I wanted to. I should have. Leaving that sick fuck alive was a mistake.

My desktop computer is still alive with light. With the sun setting and the thick curtains nearly closed shut, the study is dark. The faint glow of the computer draws me to it, back to the email Zander sent me.

If you'd like to chat, you can reach me here.
-Z

It's the third time he's reached out to me.

He's yet to be straight with me, and I don't fucking trust him. I don't trust anyone.

My eyes dart to the ceiling as a thump followed by another thump tells me Lilly is up to something. I'm not sure what she's getting into, but I'm sure she'll be enjoying herself.

I have no one, I never have, but right now I need someone on my side. I need to protect Lilly. My fingers pick at my bottom lip. They itch for a glass of whiskey, to drown out the problems pestering me. The men behind the scenes of crime each reach out to me, each wanting me for something. But not with her here. I can't do that to her.

My phone pings again, and I don't even have to get up or even touch the phone to see the message.

Answer me!

I feel the grin grow on my face. He never did enjoy being ignored. Fucking prick can go fuck himself.

We had a deal, I take the fall and I get the fuck out of the *familia*. What happened to loyalty? I clench my teeth and bite back my anger, finally doing the sane thing and silencing the cell phone.

I toss my cell phone back onto the desk, rising from my seat and ignoring my past.

Zander, my *familia*… I can deal with them later. I leave

the study, slamming the door shut behind me.

"Lilly!" I call out for my flower. For my beautiful distraction.

As I make it up the stairway, I see her scrambling out of her room. I've never called for her like this before. When she catches sight of my anger, she falls to the floor and into a perfect bow. A beautiful display of submission.

Her wet hair is sticking to her face and lying on the wooden floor of the hallway.

I climb up the last few steps and walk slowly to her, watching as her chest rises and falls. She thinks she's in trouble. My lips kick up into a smirk as she trembles slightly on the ground.

"What were you doing?" I ask her with a bit of humor in my voice.

She answers clearly and quickly, "I was trying to rearrange something." My brow furrows as I lower myself to the floor and cup her chin in my hand.

As I bring her lips up to mine, her body stays still, just as she should.

I plant a small kiss on her lips before searching her eyes. "Rearrange what?"

She swallows thickly. "I wanted to move the bed." I wait for more. At my silence, she adds, "So it would be across from the mirror." Her answer and the bright blush in her cheeks make me smile.

My flower. Ever the perfect distraction.

I rise, leaving her where she is and slowly taking off my worn leather belt. I let it slip through each loop on my pants slowly. "Did you ask permission?" I ask her. My voice is low and threatening. The punishment voice.

Her pupils dilate with lust as she shakes her head. "No, Sir."

I hold the belt in one hand, feeling my cock harden as I command her, "Get on all fours, now."

The belt cracks against her skin again. "Ten!" Lilly cries out. Her hands are braced on the floor, her ass in the air. She's hanging over the edge of the bed, half on, half off. I run my hands down her trembling thighs and back up to her hot pussy. She's soaking wet for me.

"You asked for this," I tell her, dropping the belt on her bed.

Lilly moans before answering, "Yes, sir." I've learned she needs this; she doesn't have many punishments anymore. What used to be a method of conditioning, a tool for her training, has now become the reward. And I'm more than happy to give it to her. I need it, too.

I brush my fingers along her folds, ready to pleasure her. But I stop when I see how red and swollen she is. I've been using her often, and my touch is rough. It's not surprising that she's sore.

As I run my fingers from her entrance to her clit, I wait for her to tell me, but she doesn't. Her forehead pinches, and she bites into her bottom lip. I do it again and she closes her eyes tight, but still she doesn't tell me I'm hurting her. It makes me angry. All this time, and she still doesn't talk to me. She wants me to open up to her, but she can't even tell me when I'm hurting her? I close my eyes and let out a frustrated sigh. She'll learn, I know she will. She's almost as stubborn as me, but I'll teach her.

"Get on all fours," I tell her as I unbutton my pants. I'm still waiting as I get behind her. Putting trust in the fact that she knows to tell me, and if nothing else she has a safe word. But she never utters it.

"You asked for a safe word, Lilly," I admonish her, placing my hand on her lower back. "But you're not even using it." She stills and looks back over her shoulder at me with frightened eyes. She realizes she's disappointed me. I leave her to grab the oil, and she gets up from her position, ready to protest, her soft voice apologizing.

She's breathing frantically until she sees the ointment in my hand.

This'll make her feel better.

"Did I tell you to move?" I asked her.

Lilly's quick to get back into position. "No, Sir," she breathes. The oil is cool on my fingers, so I warm it for a moment, massaging it between my hands before pressing my hand against her pussy. She winces for a moment, sucking a breath between her teeth.

I tell her as I massage her hot cunt, "I don't want to hurt you. If you desire pain, I'll give it to you in a way that's acceptable. But never like this." Her eyes close as I speak. She should know better. I don't want to injure her. I can give her what she craves in other ways.

"I'm sorry, Sir," she whispers her apology. "I just want to please you."

"You already do."

I move my fingers and spread the oil to her puckered hole, gently pressing my finger into her tight ring. My other hand is placed on her lower back as her mouth gapes from the sudden intrusion, and she nearly pushes away from me.

"Push back, my flower." Her back curves as she obeys me, my finger sliding farther in.

There's not an inch of her that I won't claim. But only when she's ready.

Chapter 21

Lily

I lie in my plush bed, staring up at the ceiling, my breasts gently rising and then falling with each breath. I can't stop thinking about Joseph. All the things he's gone through. The terrible life he's had.

I feel for him.

I wish I could be there for him. But he won't let me. I grab my blue pillow I brought from home and hug it against my chest.

I know why. He wants to appear strong, doesn't want me to think he's weak.

He needn't bother. I know he's strong, surviving what he's been through. I close my eyes and shake my head. He just needs to let me in.

I know he drinks when I lie down at night, trying to suppress those unwanted memories, smother those dark feelings. I saw him last night, drinking while writing in his journal. My heart hurt for him, seeing him sitting there vulnerable, and in pain. I stare at the journal, now laying on my bed.

I hate to see him when he's like that. Alone with his thoughts. Consumed by his past. He becomes a different man and puts me aside. I *loathe* it.

He needs someone to help him get over his past. And I want to be that person.

Isn't that what I'm supposed to do? Be there for him, like he's trying to be here for me?

I just want to get to know him. I don't like how he shuts me out, or when he goes to his study late at night. I'm grateful he lets me read what he's written. In a lot of ways that's his way of talking it through. Talking to me.

He needs that. I know firsthand how powerful it can be to just talk things out. Even if it's just your school guidance counselor. Maybe if I open up to him, he might then finally open up to me.

Gathering my courage, I sit up in bed and roll over onto the edge, my feet dangling off the side. I'm about to slip into a pair of plush white slippers, when I hear an angry shout downstairs. My heart racing, I slip off the bed and rush from the room.

As I'm rushing up the hallway to Joseph's study, the voices get louder. He's arguing about something with another man.

Their voices are muffled, so I can't understand exactly what they're saying, but it doesn't take a genius to know whatever it is, it's not good.

Stay out of it, the voice in the back of my head warns. I know I shouldn't go there. My blood is freezing, and my heart refuses to beat because yells are coming from both Joseph and someone else. It's more than a heated argument. But my feet are moving before I can stop them. I have to see. I have to make sure he's okay.

But I can't go unarmed. The thought chills my spine, paralyzing my movements before sending me quickly on a different path.

I make it down the hall into Joseph's room, the voices rumbling like thunder throughout the house, making my blood freeze. I hear Joseph yell something that sounds like an awful threat. I've never heard him sound so angry. Fuck, I'm scared.

I rush into Joseph's closet, shaking and trembling, my heart skipping every other beat. The room spins around me as I steady my clammy palms on my thighs. I can hardly breathe. What the fuck did I get myself into?

He was in the mafia.

He was a bad man.

I take in an unsteady breath, staring at the suits that block the gun rack. I didn't for one second think he had anything to hide other than his dark past.

My fingers are trembling as I push his suits aside and

swallow thickly at the sight of the guns. I stand there for a moment, my heart thump thump thumping as the noises downstairs gets louder. Staring at all the cold hard steel, my heart bounces around like a fighter in a cage.

I've used a gun before, but only for target practice. I don't know which to choose.

But I don't have time to sit here debating with myself. Joseph might need me. My throat closes as I quickly grab one of the Glocks and check if it's loaded. It is. The click of the gun makes my heart pound faster, but I rush out of the closet and out of his bedroom, and down the hall to his study, holding the gun down carefully at my side and trying to be quiet for once in my life.

I stop to the side of the door of his study, my heart racing, and dare to peek inside. My heart pounds. Thump. Thump. Thump. The cold steel seems to heat as my palm sweats, making my grip on it weak.

Joseph's sitting at his desk, his face a mask of rage and there's a man in a black suit standing in the center of the room with his arms crossed across his chest.

They're arguing with each other, the man in black waving his hands sporadically before running his hand over his shiny bald head. Neither of them can see me from this angle, so I slip into the study, hiding behind the table, eavesdropping on their conversation. I can hardly keep my hands from trembling and the grip on the gun slips a little as I listen.

"The *familia* wants you back," the man is saying, his voice incredibly harsh. "Did you think they just forgot about you when you left?" He has a thick accent, but it sure as fuck isn't Italian. I'm trying to be quiet, but I feel like they're going to hear me just from my breathing.

"I don't give a fuck what they think," Joseph growls.

"Oh really? Do you really want to play this game?"

"I don't want to play anything. I'm done with that life. I'm a different man." The confidence in Joseph's voice makes me proud of him. I find myself nodding my head, although my heart is still begging me to get the fuck out of here.

The man in black lets out a harsh laugh. "You're not done until the *familia* says you're done." His quiet answer makes me want to peek around the table. My fingers grip the edge, but I can't do it. I'm frozen in place. "You can lie to yourself all you want, but it doesn't change the fact that you've killed in the name of the *familia*. That'll never go away, no matter how hard you try to forget, or no matter how many lies you try to tell yourself."

My heart stutters. *Joseph's killed people.* Goosebumps run over every inch of my skin.

There's a moment of silence, and I swear the only thing I can hear is the pounding of my heart. I'm afraid even Joseph and the man in black can hear it. Maybe that's why they're quiet; they know I'm in the room.

"You have ten seconds to get the fuck outta here," Joseph

growls suddenly, his voice dark and deadly. My blood chills at the note in his voice. I don't think I've ever heard him so angry, so ruthless. It lets me know that whoever this man is, he's really gotten under Joseph's skin.

There's another pause, almost a hesitation, as if the man is wondering if he should press his luck and call Joseph's bluff. *Please don't.* My pointer finger steadies on the gun in my hand, although I'm too afraid to even open my eyes. I can barely hear the man respond, "The *familia* will be waiting for you."

He turns to leave, and when he does, I dare a peek from behind my hiding place. I catch a glimpse of dark hair, dark cold eyes and handsome features that remind me of Joseph's, except his are marred by the absolute ruthlessness stamped on his face.

For an instant, his cold eyes meet mine.

Fuck.

I sink down almost immediately, but I think he saw me. *I know he did.*

I can hear Joseph rise and follow the man out, the sounds of their shoes smacking against the ground so much softer than the sound of my wild heart. *He saw me. Fuck!!*

Before I can even move, Joseph returns and closes the door.

I sit there, clinging to the gun, my heart pounding, wondering what I should do. I'm fucking scared. I don't know what kind of shit Joseph is in, but I want no part in it. The man claimed Joseph killed before. He *killed* people.

After a moment, I decide to remain hidden until Joseph leaves the room, however long that takes.

But I don't get the chance.

"You can stop hiding now, flower," Joseph says, the sudden sound of his voice making my heart jump.

I close my eyes, swallowing thickly, and then slowly rise to my feet as a feeling of dread and two words run through my mind.

Oh fuck.

Chapter 22

Joseph

I can't stand the look in Lilly's eyes, accusing me. All this time she's been reading my journal, looking at me as though I'm a wounded animal. I don't want her sympathy. But her kindness and the sweet side she's given me have been addictive. I've grown to crave them.

Now she sees me for who I really am. What I represent, and where I came from. As if she didn't know. How did she think I got this fucked up?

You can't have one without the other.

"Hand me the gun," I command as I hold out my hand, and she's quick to look down at her hands as if only now realizing what she's holding. She rises slowly, her shoulders hunching in slightly and takes a step forward, handing it to me and quickly backs away. She looks around the room, still processing everything.

I gently set the gun on the table before turning back to her.

"What did you hear?" I ask her. More for her own safety than anything else. My brother isn't going to let up. I need to know what she heard.

She doesn't answer me. She stares at me wide-eyed with a mix of fear and something else.

I raise my voice and give her the command again, "What did you hear?" My heart hammers in my chest. I hate the look in her eyes. The way she's looking at me. I want my Lilly back. *My flower.*

"Nothing," she barely answers. Her voice is only just above a murmur. I narrow my eyes at her, hating that she's lying to me. I open my mouth to admonish her, but she cuts me off.

"I didn't sign up for this!" Lilly's voice wavers as she raises it. Her eyes are glazed with tears as her body trembles. Leaning forward, I can feel the anger radiating off of her in waves. As though I betrayed her.

"Who did you think I was Lilly?" I ask her, my head tilting and my voice low, filled with my own anger. She's a smart woman, she knew what she was signing up for. She had to know.

She stares at me with a look of contempt, but tears cloud her eyes. She shakes her head, unable to speak. She keeps looking at the door and then back at me. I can practically hear what she's thinking. She doesn't want me anymore. She doesn't want *this* anymore. I'm not the man in the books she reads. I'm not the poor boy whose memories of abuse are coming to front.

She thinks I'm *one of them*. One of the villains.

She swallows thickly and takes a step forward.

"Kneel," I give her the command, but she doesn't obey. She stares back at me, her eyes wide and disbelieving. My heart freezes. Don't deny me, Lilly. Don't do this. What we have is so good. It's so right.

"No," she says and shakes her head. "I want to leave!" she screams at me. My chest clenches with pain at the conviction in her voice. "The contract says that I can leave at any time." Her voice shakes as she speaks, mirroring the trembling of her body.

I can't let her go. I won't.

They've seen her. I saw the look in Ricky's eyes when he left.

They'd use her as a tool to get me. I take two steps closer to her, and she takes two away from me until her back hits the wall. She's staring back at me with her fists clenched, and her breathing is coming in sporadically. Her eyes flash with challenge, but they also contain fear. She's scared of me. It fucking kills me to see that look in her eyes.

I brace my palm on the wall beside her head, leaning forward and whispering into her ear, "You aren't going anywhere."

The only sound I can hear is her breathing. As though it contains her hate for me in this moment. She swallows thickly before answering, "You lied to me." The hurt in her voice is surprising. As if that's my biggest offense. Telling her she can go, and then taking it away.

I kiss her neck gently, but she's stiff and I wouldn't attempt to kiss on her lips at this moment. I pull away from her and rest my hand against her neck, my fingers wrapping around her throat in a possessive hold. "I've never lied to you Lilly," I speak softly, staring at her plump lips rather than the daggers in her eyes. "The game has changed though. You shouldn't have let him see you." I chance a look at her face, and her expression is one of sadness, her eyes staring at the hardwood floors.

Again she swallows, quiet and no longer fighting me. But that's only because she doesn't know how to fight back yet. She will, I know she will. She has too much fight in her to give up so easily.

"You directly disobeyed me," I say quietly; that draws her attention to me, and the sadness is once again replaced by anger. I prefer that. Because at least with anger, there's passion. I crave her passion.

"You need to go to your cage now." I deliver the blow.

Her lips part, and I can practically hear the words on her tongue, *"Yes, Sir."* But instead she snaps her lips shut, looking me straight in the eyes and refusing to obey yet again. It makes me want to smile. Her defiance, her new game move. I'll take it; I'll take anything she's willing to give me.

We're both quiet as I lead her to her room. I silently open

the cage, and she gets in without a fight. That's not to say she doesn't have one. I can feel her disobedience rolling off of her in waves. I shut the door just as I did before, not locking it. I never have, and I never will.

She stares at me through the bars of the cage, with a look of pure hate shining back.

But she doesn't use her safe word, and I cling to that knowledge.

Chapter 23

Lily

I lie in my bed, naked, the cool air from the ventilation system caressing my bare skin. I'm counting the days until this is all over. Just thinking that hurts my heart, my hand moving to it and tears pricking my eyes.

It hurts to think Joseph maybe isn't the man I thought he was. I knew he was hiding dark secrets, but this is just too dark for me. He won't let me leave. But as soon as he deals with this mess, as he says, then I'm gone. Money or no money, contract or not. I don't care.

It'll all be over. I roll over onto my side, clinging to the small blue pillow I brought with me from home and ignoring the pain in my chest.

At the same time, I don't want it to end. It's crazy. I both hate it and love it. Hate *him* and love *him*.

I blow out a frustrated breath as I think about my predicament, think about the position I'm in.

It makes me want to fight him, knowing he's keeping me here. And I'm getting addicted to it.

But even with the urge to be belligerent, I still obey him. Only to a degree. Pushing my limits, testing him. He knows it too, and that only makes me push harder. Because I want him to push me harder. The knowledge makes me lower my eyes to the beautiful white comforter.

And I still have feelings for him, even with my doubts. I can't deny how strong they are. How could I not?

A part of me hates myself for feeling that way. But I can't help it. I can't snap my fingers and erase what I feel just because Joseph may have done some horrible things. We have a connection, something that I've never had with anyone, though it feels very strained right now. Because of me. Because his past won't leave him alone.

I stretch out my leg, and lay it over the outfit he has laid out for me. My eyes are drawn to the beautiful short dress. Don't know why he laid it out. It's not like I'll be wearing it.

He wants to tempt me to wear it, that voice at the back of my head says. *So he can have a reason to punish me when I don't.*

As if he needs a reason. He can do whatever he wants to me. *He owns me.*

I can't even lock my bedroom door.

I never have a moment of privacy.

That's the part my romance novels left out. The cold, harsh reality of never having a moment to yourself, never being able to do anything without approval. It was fun and games before, when I wasn't angry at him. When I wanted it as much as he did. But it changed.

I hate that I even have to ask to work on my novel. But it's not like he denies me that privilege. He always gives permission when I ask. Somehow, that makes it more infuriating.

I wish I could be more pleased with him. Instead, I feel like I'm a spoiled pet throwing a tantrum.

I'm so confused.

My thoughts are swept away as I hear the soft creak of the bedroom door.

I hear him walk into the room, but I only move my head just enough to peek at him. My breath catches at the sight. He looks handsome as usual, dressed in black dress pants and a white dress shirt opened at the chest. I don't get off the bed to kneel or greet him. That's why I know I won't be wearing those clothes. I'm done playing. He can just throw me in the damn cage until he lets me go.

His eyes find my naked body and I blush fiercely, though I don't know why. It's nothing he hasn't seen before. Looking at him, I'm feeling so many emotions that I have to turn away, my chest heaving.

Anger. Hurt. Betrayal. Lust.

They're all there.

I startle slightly as I feel his arms encircle my waist. His hot lips find my neck and I find myself leaning back into him, my lips parting in a soft sigh, my nipples pebbling. I've missed his touch. My eyes close; he feels so good. My arm wraps around his, betraying me, but I don't care. I just want to feel him for a moment. Just a moment.

"I know you're still angry with me, Lilly," he says softly in my hair, his breath hot on my neck. I can feel his big, hard cock pressing against my ass, and I desperately want him inside of me. *Make love to me. Make me forget. Please, make me forget.*

I wish he couldn't read me so well. And I don't want to really respond. But I know he's expecting an answer.

"Yes, Sir," I say softly, my words sounding a bit stiff. I've come to hate them. But I love saying them at the same time. I'm just one big walking contradiction.

He runs his hand down my stomach, and circles it around my pubic hair. "When you shower, make sure you shave."

Anger swells up my throat, and I swallow. I'm glad he can't see me roll my eyes. He knows I'll shave; I just haven't gotten a chance to take a shower yet. I think he just knows that I'm pissed and wants to make me even angrier. He wants to rule over me. Fuck him!

"You're an asshole!" The words spew from my lips before I can stop them.

His arms leave my waist. I'm relieved and miss his touch all at the same time. I fucking hate how he makes me feel. "Why are you angry with me?" he asks, his voice even and low. Deadly.

I turn to face him, no longer able to hide the anger I feel. "You lied to me."

Joseph clenches his jaw. "I already told you that I didn't."

"And I'm supposed to believe that? That man said you killed people. How do you explain that?"

"Lilly, I'm going to ask you not to talk about that. It has nothing to do with us."

My jaw nearly drops as I stare at him with wide eyes. "Nothing to do?" I ask breathlessly, stabbing my finger into the mattress. "I'm a fucking Slave to a murderer! That's what I am! How do you think that makes me feel?"

Anger flashes in his eyes. I've really pissed him off by calling him a murderer.

He stares at me for a long moment, his chest heaving, the veins standing out on his neck. For a second, I think he'll even strike me. Maybe I just want him to, so I can have a real reason to hate him or at least a reason not to love him. But his next words make my blood run cold.

"Go to your cage."

I open my mouth to protest, but I snap it shut. It's useless. This is what I wanted anyway.

Tears well up in my eyes, but I fight them back. I don't know why I said anything. I should've known what would happen. All I needed to do was to shut the fuck up and keep counting the days until this was over.

I turn around, drop to my knees, and crawl inside my cage, hating him every second of the way.

He shuts the cage door before I'm even in the back of it. But he doesn't lock it. He never does. I wish he would. My heart breaks as I hold back the sob.

I glare at him balefully from in between the bars. He looks down at me with both pity and anger in his eyes. For some reason, it pisses me the fuck off, yet again.

"I'll spend every fucking day here in this cage if it means I can get away from you," I snarl with venom. I don't know why I say the words. I know I don't even mean it. But I can't help myself.

I regret it the moment I say it though.

I wait for him to say something nasty in response, but he doesn't. His face is an impassive mask, but his eyes are a storm of emotion. I've hurt him with my words, I can feel it. It hurts me to know that. I really shouldn't have done that. God, I'm such a bitch. Looking at the swirl of emotion in his dark eyes makes me hate myself.

He was opening up to me, and now he'll be closed off.

Fuck, I'm sorry. *I'm so fucking sorry.*

But I can't bring myself to say anything. My throat's closed off, and the tears roll down my cheeks.

I don't know why.

After a moment, his eyes heavy, Joseph turns and walks from the room, leaving me alone in my cage.

A feeling of guilt washes over me as soon as he's gone, along with a wave of loneliness and I can't stop the tears that are suddenly falling freely down my face.

I really should be careful what I wish for.

JOSEPH

Her nails dig into my forearms, scratching down my arms and leaving marks as I fuck her ruthlessly, claiming her once again. "Keep fighting me, my flower," I tell her as my hips buck into her and the bed shakes beneath us.

It's been three days since I've been able to feel the warmth of her cunt wrapped around my dick. Not that she hasn't wanted me, since her anger seems to only intensify her desire. I stare into her eyes, and she stares back at me with the same fierceness. In this moment I don't know who owns who.

She so close, I can see it on her face, but she's yet to ask permission.

"Are you trying to cum before I allow you to?" I pull away from her, pulling out of her warmth and leaving her on the edge of her release. I would have gladly given it to her, had only she asked. She breathes heavily, her blue eyes swirling with defiance.

The room fills with the sounds of our heavy breathing.

Hate fuck. Makeup sex. I'm not sure what this is, but I'm hopeful that once it's over, she'll forgive me. I want her to look at me the way she used to.

I crawl up her body, my hard dick wet with her arousal, pressing into her hip. Her expression softens as I gentle my hands at her hip. She doesn't know what to think as I kiss up between her breasts along her collarbone and up her neck.

"You only need to ask me," I say and stare at her lips, wishing I could kiss her like I used to. My eyes dart to hers, and I feel this familiarity of what used to be between us. I take a chance, pressing my lips to hers.

She kisses me back before breaking the kiss and asking, "Please, Sir." There's hesitation in her voice before she adds, "I miss you."

There's no trace of anger on her face. Only sadness. I'm not sure if this will last. But at least I have my flower for a moment.

CHAPTER 24

JOSEPH

The marks in the journal are smooth as the pen glides against the paper. The pages are worn and old at this point, and nearly come to the end. It's fitting, seeing as how I've come to the final scene between myself and my father.

The Romanos were easy to gun down. They didn't even see it coming. My father took the entire crew. Eighteen men. The first four littered the front of the restaurant with bullets. I remember how the glass broke, shattering onto the ground in splintered pieces. I stood in the background, my father to my right, my brother to my left. The screams and gunshots rang out clearly. Blood flooded the streets that night on both sides, although heavy in the Romanos. Their wives were with them. Their children were with them. Their deaths were quick. With a gun in each hand I walked up with my father, the glass crunching beneath my boots.

I shot a bullet in each of their heads from my guns. Evidence. I continued shooting until they were both empty. Part of me hoped that my father was going to put a bullet in the back of my head. Every bullet that went off, I expected it. I was meant to take the fall. And I didn't think that required me being alive at the end of this.

My father gave me a look with a hint of fear when he told me not to mention a single name. I already knew not to. What's more memorable than seeing fear for the first time in my father's eyes, was the cold look of my brother's face. I saw jealousy there. My father was willing to trust me with this task. A son who he knew never loved him. And my brother hated me for it.

Even if I was going to go away for life. He didn't like that I got any approval from our father, or any respect from the men of the familia. *But I didn't agree to do it for either of those reasons.*

I never uttered a word. I was ready to take the blame and get the death penalty or go to prison for life; I didn't care which. I deserved to be punished for my sins. All of them. But the cops let me go. They followed me, they waited. They were pissed I wouldn't talk, and they anticipated that letting me out would send up red flags to everyone on the streets.

They thought my *familia* would come for me. They thought the target they put on my back would have me running back to talk and give them the information they wanted in exchange for protection.

Their error was thinking that I gave a damn. I was ready

to die. I didn't care how. It didn't matter to me who pulled the bullet.

My father didn't make a move. If anything, he knew I was honest, and he gave me the only thing I truly wanted. Freedom from his rule. But now that my brother is gearing up to take over, my past is coming back to haunt me.

I'm not going back. I don't care how many men my brother sends here. I'll kill them all before I go back. I just hope it doesn't come to that. I haven't pulled a trigger in a long fucking time. But I sure as fuck haven't forgotten how to do it.

The pen stills on the paper as I hear the faint padding of Lilly's bare feet against the floors behind me. Her anger has waned tremendously. She's not trying to fight me like she was before.

Maybe she's forgiven me. Maybe she's realized that she wasn't as angry as she thought she was. She was hurt because she thought she knew me.

In many ways she does though, more than anyone else ever has.

Or maybe it's because I stopped fighting her.

I've been going easy on her. I don't want to give her a reason to go back to that cage. I don't want to give her a reason to fight me any more than she already has. I don't see a way out of this, other than meeting with my brother. But to do that, I have to leave Lilly, and not something I can't risk. I *won't* risk her.

"Joseph?" she asks me.

Although she's used my real name, she still kneels beside the chair. I never know which side of her I'm going to get until she approaches me. It's a funny thing. I thought I didn't want a Submissive. I didn't want someone else to control what we do, and when and what our rules are. But Lilly's gotten under my skin. I'm bending for my flower. I'd rather do that than see her wilt.

"Yes?" I turn to her, petting her hair and waiting for her to look up at me.

She visibly swallows and clasps her hands in her lap. She seems nervous, which in turn makes me nervous, but of course I don't show her that. I'm her Master at all times, and I must be strong for her.

"What are you doing?" she asks, her eyes on the journal.

I pat my lap and say, "Come sit with me." She stands slowly and obeys me, but there's still hesitation in her actions. I've yet to earn her trust back. Even if she gives me these small moments, I know what we once had is broken.

I place my journal on her lap. My heart races in my chest, every bit of vulnerability I've ever had is documented within. I don't know why I write it all down. Maybe the dark scenes that haunt me late at night will leave me if only I write them down.

"I like to write things I remember." Her pale blue eyes focus on mine through her thick lashes. And then look back down to the journal. I can see those wheels turning in her head; she wants to ask more. I don't wait. I pull her closer to me, my fingers tickling the curve of her waist as I sit back in the chair. "I used to do very bad things, Lilly." My heart pounds in my chest as I confess to her, "I've written down some more for you." I swallow thickly. "These ones are just for you." My body chills at the thought of her hating me when she reads them. It's all the truth of what I've done. I can't forgive myself, but maybe she will. She's kinder than me. She met me when I'd tried to move on.

Her breathing comes in a little louder. She licks her lips slightly and then asks, "Why did you do them?" The hurt in her voice kills me.

"You didn't want me to turn out to be a bad man, did you?" She wants there to be good in all people. I can tell that about her. It's one of the qualities I find endearing about her. I think that's one of the reasons she's so angry with me. I disappointed her. But I swear I tried.

Her voice cracks as she answers, "You aren't a bad man." She can't even look me in the eyes as she says it. She knows she's lying, and it breaks my heart.

"I didn't have much of a choice." I know I had one, but it was kill or be killed. For the first time in a long time, she lays gently against my chest. Her small hand rubs circles over my heart. I miss her comforting touch.

"Would you like to read it?" The offer spills from my lips in an attempt to tell her what I had been through and explain without having to actually tell her. I don't want to recount it all over again. I put it into this journal so I can forget. But maybe if she knows everything, the explanation of how I left and why, she can forgive me.

She doesn't hesitate to nod, the word slipping between her lips, "Yes." The eagerness in her response makes me smile.

"This is different from what I thought it would be," she says softly. The way she speaks makes it seem as though what she's telling me is a secret.

"It is for me, too." I have to agree; this isn't at all what I had in mind when I first laid eyes on Lilly.

I wasn't lying when I said the game's changed.

"How is it different for you?" she asks, playing at the hem of her dress. I suppose I'll have to go first before she'll tell me what she was thinking.

"That the Master/slave relationship is only for short spurts. I'm not stupid, Lilly. I don't control you. But I don't want to, either." I want something different from her now. More than just acceptance as her Master. More than forgiveness. Although I'm not sure what, exactly.

She looks a little bit upset and hesitant. I wish she'd just forgive me. I want to put her at ease. That's all I've been trying to do for the past week.

"I'm sorry, I've been..." Lilly's voice trails off. "I knew you... I knew you had..." She looks away, unable to finish.

"It's in my past. I promise you." I just need her to believe it. I know she doesn't want to fight me anymore. "I'm not the man I once was." She must know it's true. She knows me better than anyone ever has.

Her nod is small, but accepting. I can see it in her eyes that she believes me.

"Where does that leave us? Both of us thinking this was something it's not... and you... figuring," she waves her hand in the air, shifting in my lap.

I cup her small chin in my hand, tilting those soft lips closer to mine as I say, "It just means that sometimes we'll play, and sometimes we'll just be us."

She looks up at me and asks, "And what is that?"

I don't know how to answer her, so I'm quiet.

"Even if we aren't playing, you still need to treat me as though I'm your Master." Although it's a statement, it feels as though I'm asking her a question. I feel wrong for telling her that since all this time we've nearly been playing scenes. But I know what she's about to read. And I don't want her to think any differently of me. I am her Master, and it should stay that way. Regardless of what she reads. Regardless of how well she gets to know me.

"Yes, Sir."

"Hold still, my flower," I tell Lilly as her back rests against the wall. "Hands at your side," I say as I push her palms against her thighs. She's naked before me, finally obeying me again. It feels as though we're playing house. Like this is all pretend. We're ignoring what lies beyond these walls. My familia, the fact that she can't leave. Pretending to be blind to what's meant to keep us apart.

I get on my hands and knees, putting my face between her thighs and inhaling her sweet scent. Judging by her gasp, she didn't expect it. I smile against her heat before taking a languid lick and pulling back to look her in the eyes.

"Ride my face, Lilly," I tell her, noting how her eyes widen as she comprehends my words. "Take your pleasure from me. Cum freely."

I place my hands on the inside of her knees, allowing her legs to bend slightly. She rocks helplessly into my face, hesitant at first. But as I groan with approval, her hips grind harder and soft moans spill from her lips.

So long as she obeys me, I'll give her everything she wants. Every pleasure, every need. I just need her to obey me. I need her to stay with me.

Chapter 25

Lily

I take a deep breath, my fingers trailing over the high quality leather of Joseph's journal. I'm partway through reading it. I don't know if I'm ready today for more of the bad things that I know I'll find out while reading it, but I'm going to go through with it anyway. I want to see what happened in his life. It makes me feel that much more connected to him.

A ray of sunshine hits the golden latch of the journal, reflecting a flash into my eyes.

I'm curled up in Joseph's sunroom, reclined in a white, plush fabric recliner, soaking in the warmth of the sun. The view from here is gorgeous. The sky is a clear azure blue, and the ground is covered with a thick layer of white snow that reflects the sunlight, filling the room with brightness.

It's lifting my mood. I'm already feeling better from these past few days with the new rules Joseph has set for us. I like the idea he had about playing scenes. And I love that he's opening up to me bit by bit. He's adding details and writing notes to benefit my understanding of what happened. He won't talk to me about it though; the journal is all I get. He won't even be in the same room when I read it. Even now, he's in the kitchen because he knows I'm reading it.

I open the journal to the last passage I stopped on and pick up where I left off. It doesn't take long before I'm deeply engrossed in his story. Now that I know how the story ends, everything he's written is so clear. But when I reach a passage that's so heartbreaking, about his mother, I can't keep the tears from falling from my eyes.

"This is hard," I say thickly, wiping the tears from my cheek with the back of my hand.

I have to close the book. I can't read any more right now. I just can't believe all the things that Joseph has gone through. I feel absolutely awful for him.

I haven't forgotten that he's keeping me here. That I'm a prisoner. But I wouldn't leave if he told me to. If he commanded me. I'd refuse.

As soon as I see him, I'm going to crawl in his lap and kiss him and try to give him all the comfort that I'm capable of giving. I know he doesn't like to be held and he doesn't like sympathy, but I need it as much as he does.

But for now, I'll keep playing our game and pretend like I don't know that he's avoiding me because I'm reading the journal. He'll pretend he doesn't know that it kills me to see what he's been through. I don't mind playing this game, because it only makes me closer to him.

I push the journal onto the ottoman and grab my laptop, wiping under my eyes and my nose as I move.

I need to relieve some serious stress. I sniffle again, opening up the laptop as I sag in the seat. Right fucking now. And there's nothing that helps me to relieve it more than writing. It's always been my therapy for when my emotions are heightened, or I'm feeling down. It's the perfect way to release my emotions. Joseph needs something like that. I told him that.

And he told me that's what I am to him. My heart hurts, remembering his words.

I open on my laptop screen, my mind overflowing with ideas to use for the story. It should be easy. I have so much material to work with. So many emotions to play off of.

I'm about to turn over to the Word document screen, when an email notification pops up on my screen.

From: Aida White
To: Lilly Wade

Subject: MY BABY IS GONE

Lilly

My hands are shaking as I type these words. I don't know who to talk to, but I need to talk to someone. I haven't stopped crying since this morning. My baby is gone. I can't believe it. How I wish I would have turned my life around sooner. If only he would've waited just a little while longer and mommy would have been there for him. I feel like such a worthless piece of shit. I bet that's what you think of me. And you're not wrong.

The police called me this morning to tell me that Zach got into a fight. He was stabbed to death. He died this morning.

I know you were someone that was important to him, they gave me your email. You have to be someone special because he would talk about you when he called me. I just want to thank you for being there for my baby when I couldn't.

Sincerely,
Zach's mom, Aida

I stare at the screen in disbelief, my stomach twisting in agony. I don't believe it. It can't be true. This has to be some sick cruel joke. I shake my head. This didn't happen. This woman is a liar. She's a liar!

I shake my head, pushing the laptop away, refusing to

believe Zach is dead.

It might be one of his friends playing a joke on me. I can't accept this. It has to be! Tears roll down my cheeks as I rise out of the chair. Not Zach.

I refuse to believe it.

He was going to get his life together. Even the parole officer said it. Things were going to be better for him.

"It's not true," I say over and over in denial. "This is a bunch of bullshit!"

I have to believe it's not true, but a growing fear grips my heart. I have to find out.

I jump up from my seat and rush through the house in search of a landline phone. I find one in Joseph's study. My hands fumble over the ancient thing while I nearly rip the phone out of the wall in my haste to pick up the receiver.

I quickly dial the parole officer's number. I know it by heart. Pick up. Pick up! My fingers twist around the cord as I pace the small area.

It rings three times before someone answers.

"Hello?" a woman's husky voice answers.

My lips are suddenly dry, and my words stick in my throat. *It's okay,* I tell myself. *You'll see. It was all a lie. He's okay*

I suck in a deep breath and then blurt, "It's Lilly Wade... I'm calling to... find out about... Zach White?" That's all I can manage.

I don't know if it's protocol to just say a name when

calling to ask for information, but I can't say anything else. My throat feels so tight, I almost can't breathe.

The woman on the other end of the line gets it though, because I hear the tapping of keys.

Her next words nearly knock me off my feet.

"I'm sorry, Ms. Wade. He passed away this morning."

The phone slips from my fingertips and swings up against Joseph's desk with a bang. But I no longer care. The room is spinning around me. My heart is racing. I can't fucking think. Not him. I couldn't help him. But they were going to. They were going to save him. He told me they would. He told me he'd be fine!

Somewhere in the background, I hear the woman's voice coming out of the receiver, "Ma'am, are you there?"

I sink to my knees beside the desk, wrapping my arms around my chest, and begin rocking back and forth. Trying to calm myself. Trying to remember the moves I learned in yoga class to help me relax. But instead my rocking is fast. Too fast.

I'm not okay. It's not okay.

"No, no, no, no!" I repeat over and over, the tears rolling from my eyes, so hot my eyes are burning. I can't believe it. I failed him. I should have done more to help him. I should have snatched his ass and forced him in the car that day I saw him walk away from me.

It's all my fucking fault.

"Ma'am, are you all right?"

She tries again to get my attention several more times before hanging up, the sound of the dial tone mixing in with my quiet cries.

I don't even hear the sound of footsteps, but I'm suddenly pulled up into a hard chest by strong arms.

"What happened?" Joseph asks, pushing my hair out of my face as I try to calm down.

I can't answer him right away, the tears and sobs coming in even harder, seemingly brought on by his caring touch. But he waits patiently for me to get a hold of myself, his normally dark eyes filled with concern.

"Zach died," I sob when I can finally say the words. "He was murdered." Speaking haltingly, I tell him all about my relationship with the troubled kids in school and how I devoted a lot of myself to helping them and how special Zach was to me.

"I thought he was going to be okay." It's all I can say toward the end. His strong hand rubs my back in large, soothing circles.

Joseph frowns, squeezing me gently. "I'm so sorry. But this wasn't your fault, do you understand? You couldn't have changed what happened to Zach. No one could." I shake my head in denial before burying my face into his hard chest.

I want to scream at him, 'That doesn't make it right!', but when I pull away from him and look at the softness in his eyes, I know that he's only trying to make me see the truth. I couldn't save him, just like I couldn't save my mother. Just like my father couldn't save her. "Lilly, you can't save people from themselves. I know that. So much better than most people. But you try. And you never stop. You're a good person. Even if he's gone." I let out a small sob and try to pull away, but Joseph holds my chin firmly in his grasp and continues, "Even if he's gone, you can still help others. I'm sure you have. Even if you don't know it." He grips my chin and forces me to look into his eyes. The intensity that he gazes at me with actually stops my sobs and dries my tears. "I know you have."

I feel like shit. My heart is hurting. But I can't deny the power he has over me. I shake my head, not fully believing him.

His next words steal the air from my lungs. "You've helped me." He loosens his grip on me to brush the hair from my face as he says softly, "More than you'll ever know.

I stare up into his eyes, and I see something I've never seen before, something so powerful it makes me weak in the knees. Something I'm not sure that I'm seeing because it's truly there, or because I want it to be there.

That must be it. I'm only imagining the love I see reflected in his eyes.

Chapter 26

Joseph

I thought it was her that was playing a game when we started this. But it's more clear to me now that I was the one playing. The bottle of whiskey is empty. I keep bringing it to my lips, forgetting that it's gone, having nothing to take this pain away.

There's life beyond the hollow shell I've been living in. There's a reason to fight, there's a reason to *feel*. Lilly's shown me that. My heart hurts for her. I wish I could give her something to take the pain away. But nothing can soothe grief. I know that all too well.

Over the last few days, she hasn't been herself. I told her she's blaming herself for something she couldn't control. It's something no one could have controlled. But she doesn't want to believe that.

I'll show her with time. I'll help her however I can. I just want her to be happy again.

Knock. Knock. Two soft knocks from the front entry distract me from my thoughts.

I've ordered her a new laptop. I put the bottle down on the end table and quickly make my way to the door. I'm eager to get her something that will make her smile. She's been burying herself in her writing. I'm hoping this will make her happy. Even if it's only for a moment.

When I open the door without checking, my heart stops. I hate myself this very second. I should have known better. Fool! I'm a fucking fool for letting my guard down.

I stare down the barrel of two guns, held by men I don't recognize, but I know who sent them. I stand there numb on the surface, but internally I'm screaming. How could I be so fucking stupid? I don't have a gun. I have nothing! And Lilly's upstairs. Vulnerable. It's my fault.

"What do you want?" I ask without giving in to the fear and reflecting it in my voice. My hand grips the door keeping me upright, as though without it, I'd fall.

Lilly. She's all I can think about. I start to walk outside, my hand closing the door behind me, but they step forward, crowding my space. I need to get them away from here. As far away from Lilly as I can.

"We can discuss this somewhere else," I say easily, as they ignore me and continue walking forward, pushing me back into my foyer. One closes the front door and locks it. I start thinking about where every gun I have in this house is located. I have them stashed away in every room. My eyes dart to the corner of the foyer; the one here is behind these two assholes, so I won't be able to get to the gun in the closet. There are two in the living room though. I only need to get these assholes to follow me in there. But that's closer to Lilly. Fuck! I try not to clench my jaw and ball my hands into fists at the thought.

I'm not sure if these men know she's here. I can't risk them finding out. I wish I could tell her to run. To hide. I wish I could go back in time and never speak to her, never corrupt her with the sins of my past.

If only I could. I'd give it all up to keep her safe.

"You know how this ends, Joe," the one man says to my left. He's nearly bald and short, and his leather jacket is slightly too big for him. The man on his right is much taller, his military cut giving him an edge over the other fuckface. Both of them are holding their guns loosely. They're both arrogant. They think they've won. I take in a deep breath, quickly coming up with a plan. Something. Anything to keep her from them.

The bald man continues to point his gun at me as the other man asks, "We just need the code for your safe." I huff a grunt. Of course. Money. It's always about the money.

"And why would I tell you that?" I ask with a grin that

doesn't reflect a single thing I'm feeling.

"Because if you do, we won't make you watch what we're gonna do to your girl." He smiles a crooked grin, showing his yellowed teeth. "We'll put you out of your misery first." The bald man's answer chills my blood. My heart pounds in my chest.

As I swallow thickly, registering what they're saying and trying not to give into the urge to beat the piss out of him, I see movement over the tall man's right shoulder.

Lilly.

I swear my heart stops. What the fuck is she doing?

"You need to go back where you came from," I tell the man standing in front of me, but I'm not speaking to him. I wish I could look at her as I talk, but I can't. I'm afraid they'll follow my line of sight, turn around and see her.

I'm fucking pissed as I say the same words louder. Both men seem thrown off by the command in my voice, but I don't care. I can't even think about them. She needs to listen. She needs to get out of here.

I dare to take a step forward when the floor creaks with Lilly's steps, it distracts them enough that they don't hear her; both men point their guns at my head. "You should go hide," I tell them, a sick grin on my face with false confidence in my voice. *Run, Lilly!*

Lilly must know that I'm speaking to her, but she doesn't listen. Of all the times I need her to just listen to me, now is the time. But she doesn't, she just continues forward, entering the foyer and holding a gun in her hands high, pointing at the tall man to my right.

"You have two minutes, Joe," the bald man says. "Or else Nicky here..." he sticks his thumb out pointing to the other man and turns his head slightly to look at him. My heart jumps up my throat when he does, because as he turns to look at his partner, he catches sight of Lilly. I see it all happen in slow motion.

Fuck!

He shouts and raises his gun at her, whipping around on his heels and I react instantaneously, pushing forward with all of my weight, shoving him down to the ground. All the sounds and screams turn to white noise, my lungs freezing, my heart beating frantically. A rush of heat takes over my body, nearly numbing me. I've never felt so much fear in my life.

"Run!" I yell at Lilly as several gunshots go off at once. Bang! Bang! Bang!

Lilly, not Lilly. My throat hurts from my screams as I fight for the gun. Trying to keep him from shooting it, but trying to look at Lilly. Run! Just run!

I hear her shrill scream as another bullet echoes off the wall. A stray piece of drywall falls into pieces and lands on the bald man's face. And then another gunshot, this one from the gun I'm fighting over. The jolt of the trigger being pulled loosens the grip this fucker has on it.

The bullet flies through the air and strikes me in my upper forearm. Fuck! I curse under my breath. In and out in the blink of an eye. I feel the urge to reach up and grab the wound, but I can't. I won't let it stop me from strengthening my hold on the gun. Nothing will stop me.

"Lilly!" I call for her. I can't hear her. "Lilly!"

My fingertips slip against the gun as the bastard kicks me in the gut. Both of us are wrestling on the ground, trying to rip the gun out from each other's grip. The pain from the shot in my arm shoots up and down my shoulder. I ignore it, merely clenching my teeth from the screaming pain as I continue to fight.

His head is close to the thick front leg of the foyer table. I could take a risk and stop fighting for the gun, going for his chin instead and try to slam his head into the hardwood. But that would mean letting go of the gun that I almost have a grip on. His fingertips fumble at the trigger again, a bullet whizzing through the air and landing into the plaster wall. He flinches from the sudden shot.

I take advantage of the moment, hurling my body upward. Using my forearm instead of my hand, I smash the back of his head against the leg of the table. It doesn't do any real damage, but it makes him close his eyes. I'm able to jump forward and sink my teeth into his forearm and grab the gun the second he loosens his grip on it. In a swift moment, the gun is in my hands and I don't hesitate to put a bullet through his skull. *Bang!*

My heart races as I quickly raise the gun in my hands and

prepare to shoot the other bastard. But instead I find Lilly, staring at the man lying still on the floor. Three gunshot wounds are visible from the blood staining his shirt.

Lilly doesn't look at me when I call her name, still gripping the gun in both of her hands. She's shaking.

I stand slowly with my hands up, looking between the two men dead on the floor. There's blood spilling from their open wounds and pooling on the marble floor beside them. At least it happened out here, where I can easily clean up this mess.

I can hardly look at Lilly. I'm full of shame. It's because of me that she had to fight for her life. I couldn't protect her. I brought this pain to her. It's my fault.

She drops the gun to the ground, and it hits the marble hard with a loud thud as she collapses into my open arms. The moment I close my arms around her, she sobs into my chest, trembling uncontrollably. As if my touch broke the trance.

I've put up with my brother and father for years. But they brought Lilly into this, and that firms my resolve.

I kiss Lilly's hair softly, rubbing soothing circles on her back. But I stare straight ahead at the blank wall, knowing I need to kill them. Tonight.

Chapter 27

Lily

I'm a ball of nerves as I sit in Madam Lynn's office, my mind on what just happened.

I killed a man.

I still can't believe it. It's nearly impossible for me to process. I keep thinking that I'm going to wake up and find out this was all some horrible nightmare. I pull my legs up into the chair, wrapping my arms tightly around my knees.

But it's too fucking real.

Never in a million years would I have thought I'd wind up in a situation like this. It's like a real life action movie. Hell, it's even like one of my romance novels. Except there might not be a happy ending for this one.

The thought chills my blood.

Even worse, I thought Joseph was going to die. I saw him die. I know I did. I couldn't pull the trigger as the man came after me. But I saw Joseph. I saw the bullet. My chest tightens as I remember the gun pointed at his head. God, I can hardly breathe remembering it. My heart felt like it was ripped from my chest. Even now I get cold sweats thinking about it. He was so close to death.

Had I not walked in right at that moment, he would've died. They were going to kill him.

I'm glad I shot that asshole. I'm glad he's dead. I'll never tell a soul. But I don't regret it. Not for a single moment.

And now I'm here. Stranded in an office in Club X. Joseph left me here, shoving cash into my purse and telling me that they'd protect me.

He pushed me away. He told me they would protect me, literally pushing me into the arms of people I don't even know.

And now I'm ready to leave. I rest my face on my knees. My eyes feel hot against my cool skin. I just want to get the fuck out.

I'm tired of being in this office. I either want to be with him, or I want to go home.

I'm tired of being a prisoner.

I know after what happened, he's pushing me away for my safety, trying to figure things out. And he wants me to be where he thinks I'm safe. I understand, I do. But I still don't want to be here. I feel helpless just sitting here and waiting around for I don't know how long.

I look around the office. It's so depressing. Just a medium-size room with a large oak desk littered with papers and not a single window.

Besides the lamplight, it's dark in here. Madam Lynn has been very nice to me and has done her best to make me feel comfortable with what she has to work with, but she hasn't come back in, I glance at the clock above the door, for almost two hours. I haven't seen *anyone* for hours. My heart flickers in my chest. I don't even know if Joseph is still here. I cover my face with my hand.

How could he just leave me here?

I shake my head and put my feet back on the ground. He has to know by now I can't live without him. Isn't it obvious that I love him? He must know.

Restless, I get up from my seat and pace the floor, wondering what the hell I should do. I want to leave, but I'm not sure if I'll be safe. And he told me to stay here. He practically pleaded with me to do as I was told.

The door opens, and I pause mid-stride as Joseph walks into the room. My lips part, and my breath halts.

My heart skips a beat at the sight of him. Dressed in dark slacks, a crisp, black dress shirt and coat, he looks pale and a little rough around the edges with a day's worth of coarse stubble around his jawline, but he's never looked so damn good to me. I'm so relieved to see him after being secluded in this room for hours.

"What's going on?" I ask him, immediately going to him.

He looks at me, holding me as I put my hands on his chest. But he doesn't answer me. My skin pricks with a chill. I know he's hiding a gunshot wound under his shirt. He has to be in pain. But I want to beat the shit out of him. Tell me what's going on!

I cross my arms over my chest, moving away from him and shoving the emotions down.

"You don't need to worry about it," he says finally, walking over to stand in front of Madam Lynn's desk. There's exhaustion in his voice, but he's doing his best to hide it. My eyes feel heavy and raw. I swallow thickly, not knowing what to do or say.

"You owe me more than that," I say warily. "You almost died. I –" I swallow thickly.

And now I'll never be the same. The room is filled with nothing but the sound of my beating heart as he stares back at me, saying nothing. Offering me nothing.

I gesture sharply at him, pointing my finger at my chest. "I deserve to know."

Joseph shakes his head. "You don't need to know anything." His words are hard, but his eyes are soft. "I'm trying to keep you safe."

"Keeping me in the dark is not keeping me safe," I say with every ounce of sincerity I have.

When that doesn't get through to him, I add, "And I

absolutely hate it here." I sound like a petulant child, and I hate it. But I really can't stand it here. I'd almost rather be in my fucking cage. And that's saying something.

His eyes study my face for a moment, and a twinge of hope goes through me. Maybe he'll change his mind. But when he speaks, his voice is firm. "It's the best place for you right now."

I start to argue with him when the door swings open, and in walks a man I met when Joseph brought me in here. Zander.

I turn in his direction, taking in his appearance. With chiseled features and dark blond hair, he's a handsome man, dressed in a black suit with a white dress shirt. Tall and noble-looking, but with eyes like his, he looks like he holds just as many secrets as Joseph does. It makes me wonder if this club is filled with men like them.

I guess it would make sense. Men like these don't become rich and powerful without accumulating secrets.

Joseph turns away from me to meet Zander's gaze. "What did you find out?" he asks him.

Zander glances at me for a moment, as if debating if he should talk in front of me. But Joseph gives him a slight nod to go ahead. The pain in my chest eases slightly at his gesture. At least he trusts me with some things.

"I know for a fact it was your brother," Zander says. Like Joseph, his voice is deep and rich, and it has a kind of calming quality to it. He stares at Joseph as if waiting for a violent reaction. "He set you up."

Joseph's quiet for a moment, and I can only wonder what he's feeling right now. His own brother tried to have him killed? It's not hard for me to comprehend after reading his journal. I know it still hurts him though. It makes my heart ache for him. I couldn't begin to comprehend being in such a position.

There's a coldness in Joseph's eyes that scares me when he answers, "I already know that." It reminds me of death.

"Good, then you'll be taking care of that matter soon?" Zander asks, taking a seat in the corner of the room as if they're talking about a sale on dry cleaning.

My heart skips a beat as I realize what this is about.

I don't even have to hear him say it. I know he's going to kill his own brother. His own flesh and blood. Joseph's answer is short, "Yes."

"When you go," Zander says, crossing his left ankle over his right knee, "check your father's closet." Zander's words are firm as he stares at Joseph with a hard look.

I stand there numb, not believing the casual tone of this conversation.

God, I feel sick. I walk slowly behind Joseph to the far end of the room, wishing I could disappear.

"I will," Joseph replies firmly.

Both men stare at each other for a moment, and then Zander gives Joseph a slight nod before leaving without another word.

As soon as the door clicks shut, I feel Joseph's eyes on me, waiting for my reaction.

"Please don't go," I plead, my voice nearly a croak, "you don't have to do this." My eyes are wide and begging for him to have mercy on me. I can't let him go. I don't know if he'll come back.

Joseph takes me in his arms, but he doesn't answer me. He holds onto me as I feel every last bit of hope slipping away. My nails dig into his shirt. "Please," I whisper. But there is no softening in his position. He's going whether I like it or not.

"I'll have tracking on my phone so you'll be able to see where I am," Joseph says, his voice soft, nearly sympathetic.

"I don't want to have to track you," I cry beneath my breath. "Just don't go! Please. Think about what you're about to do."

Joseph's voice remains firm. "I have. And that's why I have to do this." *Kill them.* The words seem to leap into my mind.

I sag against his firm body, tears burning my eyes. I don't want him to leave. I saw him shot, wounded and about to die. Now he's stepping in the line of danger again.

And it scares me like fuck that he might not come back. I cling onto him harder, feeling desperate and vulnerable and foolish, but I want him to stay. I want him to live. I can't save him if he leaves me.

"Please," I whisper against his hard chest as he tries hopelessly to soothe me. "I'm begging you."

Joseph's silent as he holds me.

"I have to go," Joseph tells me after a while, pulling back

from me. Oh my God. It hurts like hell.

I try to cling to him, but he pries my fingers away from him, pushing me back against Madam Lynn's desk. I instantly feel cold. Abandoned.

"Let me go, Lilly," he says, his voice cold. God, he's breaking my heart. He's ripping it apart.

I shake my head, my throat throbbing from the aching pain. "No, you don't have to go."

"I'm leaving." His words are so cold now that I'm sure this time he means it. I take a step back, wrapping my arms around myself and trying to hold myself together.

He gives me a kiss on the cheek that makes me close my eyes, the hot tears rolling down my cheeks. "I gave myself to you," I speak just above a murmur. He pauses at the door, his hand on the doorknob, and turns to look at me. My skin pricks under his gaze as the tears roll down my face.

I try to say more. I try to explain what I'm feeling. But all I can think about is the first night he took me. I brush away the bastard tears.

Through my hazy vision, I see Joseph staring back at me. He looks like he wants to tell me something. For the first time since he's walked in the room, I see something in his eyes. That same look I saw when he comforted me over Zach's death.

Tell me, I urge him silently. *Tell me that you love me.*

I want him to say it. Because I know I love him.

Say it! my mind screams.

And it looks like he's about to do it.

I part my lips expectantly, ready to say it back.

But then he turns away and walks out, not saying a word as he shuts the door behind him.

It's not till he's gone that I realize I never told him either. I whisper in the empty room. "I love you, Joseph. You better come back to me."

Chapter 28

Joseph

I stalk through the dark hallways of the home I grew up in. If one could call it a home. The memories that haunt my dreams flash before my eyes as my quiet footsteps cause the hardwood floors to creak beneath my boots.

I expected to be nervous. I anticipated my heart beating turbulently with a cold sweat swarming over my body. Instead there's nothing. I hold the handgun in my gloved hand, the silencer pointing down to the floor. As I step closer and closer to the room my brother stays in, I feel resolute.

The Levi household is practically a mansion. A lonely one, full of empty rooms. The screams when I grew up used to fill the halls, I'll never forget that. I know every inch of this place

I also know the escape route and where it leads. I learned

it when I was young, it was something that we all needed to know. My father taught me the layout for my own safety. It's probably the one good thing he ever did for me. And now I'm using it against him.

I used the escape route to come into the kitchen, completely undetected. There are no alarms from there up to here, there's nothing standing in my way of creeping into their bedrooms and killing them in their sleep.

A small part of me wishes I would only kill my brother. My father never came after me. It's all my brother.

At the thought of leaving my father alive, my heart finally races and adrenaline courses through my blood. That's not something I can do. He will come for me. He may not know it was me, but he would come for me anyway. He would come to force me to take over the business. He's getting old, and there needs to be a Levi to carry on the name. But when the night is through, there will be none left.

I'll make sure of that.

I adjust my grip as I approach my brother's door, my heart pounding in my ears. All I need to do is shoot him in his sleep. He's an easy target, a simple kill. He deserves a much worse death. I'd like to wake him; I'd like to beat him into a bloody pulp with my bare hands.

Killing him this way isn't justice, but I can't afford risks.

Not when I have Lilly waiting for me.

I imagined his door will be locked, and testing the

doorknob proves that much true. It doesn't take me long to pick it though. He was in the habit of locking his door when we grew up. He was also in the habit of stealing from me and of hurting women in the middle of the night. The memories flash before my eyes as the lock clicks, and the doorknob turns.

The memories make me sick. Not just because of what I've witnessed, but because of what I allowed to happen. I didn't have to; I could have fought. I would have lost, but I could have at least tried.

I open the door so slowly that it barely makes a sound. But every tiny noise forces my heart to jump in my chest. I know for a fact he'll have a gun near him. We all did growing up. That was the only way to ensure our safety. I can't afford to wake him.

I can barely breathe as I stalk into his room, placing each step as silently as possible. My eyes had already adjusted to the darkness in the hallway, and the faint light from his windows only adds to my ease of seeing in the dark.

The covers are loose around his hips. His body is visible, an easy target. I get closer than I need to, just to get a better look at him as I steal the life from him.

There's no bang to my gun. No sound other than the harsh breeze of the bullet whipping through the air. His body jolts once as the first bullet enters his head, and then another. And then another. I waste three bullets on him, staring at his dead body without feeling as though it's not real. The last two were unnecessary, only a result of my anger. Each time I pulled the trigger, I thought of the look on her face as she stared down at the man who tried to kill her. The man she killed. I put the gun to his head and pull the trigger again.

Looking down at my brother, even dead he looks cruel. There was never any hope for him, no saving him.

My father's next. It's the only thought in my mind, and the only thing that keeps me from putting a fifth bullet into Ricky's skull as I leave my brother's room. My father's suite is at the other end of the hallway. I don't hesitate to go to him next. My brother's death doesn't faze me in the least. If anything, it gives me more strength to put my father into the ground next to him. That's where they belong.

My heart stops when I walk into the room. Not needing to pick the lock, it opened easily. My feet halt when the floor creaks beneath my weight. I'm unsteady as I count two bodies in the bed. One is my father, and the closest to me. His breathing is coming in heavy as he faintly snores in his sleep.

The other body is much smaller. A woman. And as the sound of my weight on the floorboards creaks through the night, she turns in her sleep. My heart beats erratically, my body heating and every tiny hair standing upright. I only planned on two deaths tonight. I don't want an innocent life caught in the crossfire. There's no way I can leave without seeing this through though. And I can't leave any witnesses.

I take one more step, pointing my gun at my father. I'm

a few feet away, but all I need to do is put a bullet in his skull and I can leave, leaving the woman unharmed. *She doesn't have to die.*

My heart refuses to beat as the one last step I take is enough to wake the woman. She groans, stretching her arms and sitting up in the bed with a sleepy yawn, her eyes closed tight. Fuck! She rubs the sleep from her eyes as I take two steps forward.

The sound of my jeans scraping against one another fills the room and wakes her further. The silencer points directly at my father's head; I get one bullet off before the woman screams. It's all I need though. My father's head jolts as the bullet leaves a neat hole just to the right of the center of his forehead.

I can't think; I can't breathe. My body feels like it's heating to an unbearable degree. I don't know how I can save her. As I try to think, she does something she should know not to do. She turns her back to me, grabbing the gun off the nightstand. She grips it with both hands, turning toward me, ready to shoot me.

And for a split second I consider letting her.

What good have I done the world? Killing my father and brother were the last good things I could ever do. The best things I've done with my life. I've lived with no purpose for years.

The sound of her pulling the hammer back, the cold steel shaking in her trembling hands, loading the barrel of the gun with the bullet she intends to kill me with, triggers the memory of her, Lilly. Of my flower.

I need to live for her.

Without another thought, I pull the trigger. The bullet whizzes through the air, hitting her in her throat. She falls off the bed, the gun leaving her hand and falling with a thump onto the padded carpet.

I'm quick to go to her side, now that she's unarmed. I kick the gun to the side as both of her hands press against her throat, trying to stop the blood. My initial reaction is to save her. I kneel on the ground; she looks at me with wide eyes filled with fear. I press my palm to the wound in her neck even as she tries to helplessly push me away. The woman has fight, but there's too much blood. It pains my heart. I didn't want this.

"I'm sorry," I barely get the words out as her hot blood covers both of my gloved hands and soaks into the cream carpet.

I stare down at the dying woman. Her innocent blood is on my hands as I try to stop the wound from gushing blood. The pumps of hot liquid become weaker and weaker as her heart slows, and the life falls from her eyes. One deep breath leaves her, and she's gone. Another victim. I don't know who she is, but her death is on my hands.

The sick fuck that my father is, he had to tie me to a chair before he did it. I struggle against the binds at my wrists, but it's useless. My ankles are bound, and my thighs are strapped to the chair beneath me. So is my chest. I scream until my throat is raw and hoarse. For the first time in my life, my cheeks are wet with tears.

He's punishing me for not doing his will. For disobeying an order. I was trying to do what was right. I was trying to save the woman he wanted me to torture. And now I have no choice but to watch as he beats my mother in front of me. I look up at my brother, pleading with him to help.

"He's killing her!" I scream at him. Mother isn't even crying anymore. At first, she tried not to scream. She didn't want to see me upset. She told me it was okay. She told me she loved me. Even as my father slapped her across the face with the butt of the gun. But as he continued, his brutal hits coming with more force, she couldn't hold it back any longer. She begged him, just as I am now.

My brother looks back at me with the same look that my father's always had. Eyes filled with malice. The breath leaves my lungs, and my voice is lost as a shrill bang echoes in the small room. I hang my head low.

I was only twelve, and that was the last time anyone called me little sparrow. And the last time anyone told me they loved me.

I look down at the woman one last time, wiping her blood on the sheets as I stand, towering over her and glancing back at my father. Her eyes are closed, and she's covered in blood. My father's eyes are open and cold and that's how they always were, staring at nothing. Beneath him blood pools into the mattress. The sheet soaks up the dark red liquid.

She may have died because I came tonight. To finish this.

I almost leave without heeding Zander's words, that I need to check the closet. My eyes dart to the double doors, and I take cautious steps to see what lies behind them. My body heats, knowing I'm trusting him. A man I don't know.

The door squeaks open slowly, the only sound in the room other than my own shallow breathing. The blood rushes in my ears, drowning out all other sounds as I stare at the monitors and video recordings of every inch of this house. Some areas I don't recognize. The screens flicker and move to rooms I've never seen before. It's surveillance, of this house and of somewhere else.

I watch them for a moment, each second passing, my body chills and my heart pounds. I remove the tapes, one by one. There are eight of them, and I stop the recordings before leaving. Had Zander not told me, there's no doubt in my mind I would've gone away for murder this time. The hard evidence is undeniable.

I walk to the door, stepping over the poor woman's dead body and turning my back to my father.

It's over now.

And not another body will be put in the ground because of that man. I close the door behind me and leave the way I came.

Chapter 29

Lily

I've been tossing and turning all night. The back of my eyes is throbbing from a terrible headache, brought on by a lack of sleep. I think I've been up for over twenty-four hours, running on fumes.

I'm in a private room at Club X. The bed I'm lying on, a king-size plush pillow top mattress, is soft and comfortable. It practically begs me to go to sleep. But I can't. It's nice and all, but I prefer my room back at Joseph's house. Or his room, as long as he's next to me.

I can't stop thinking about him. I don't know if he's okay, or if he's even alive.

I swallow thickly as I see the dim light of morning peeking around the luxury curtains and then glance at the phone he left me.

The little dot that tracks his location is in the same spot. It makes me feel sick, like something's terribly wrong. The fucking dot won't move. I wish I could talk to someone--Joseph, or one of his associates, and be assured that he's okay. Anyone!

I called his phone at least a dozen times, but he hasn't answered. I knew he wouldn't in the beginning, but by now he should've.

My throat constricts and I roll over in bed, hating to think about it. Hating time for going so slowly.

Just come back to me.

A knock on the door brings me to my feet faster than I would have thought possible, my heart pounding in my chest.

I'm just at the door when Madam Lynn walks in.

She looks sharp as usual, dressed in a black dress that has ruffles at the bottom and black glossy heels, her hair pulled up into an elegant bun while wispy bangs frame her face. She looks perfectly fine. As though her friend isn't out killing his father and brother this very second.

Her face is solemn as she steps into the room and stops a few feet away from me.

"I'm here to tell you that you can go home now," Madam Lynn says softly. "Isaac set up a security system around your townhouse. You don't need it," she shakes her head gently, her eyes rolling as she adds, "He's peculiar about safety."

I part my lips to ask her about Joseph when there's a

knock at the door.

Isaac sticks his head through the doorway, glances between the both of us, and then steps inside the room. Though I'm filled with anxiety, I can't help but notice the authority Isaac radiates. It reminds me of Joseph. Those chiseled features, the power and ruthlessness behind his eyes are familiar to me.

"It's done," Isaac tells Madam Lynn. "I've made sure that no one will gain access."

The look that passes across Madam Lynn's face as she glances at Isaac is one of extreme gratitude.

"But what about Joseph?" I ask. The hell with my safety, I want to know what's going on.

Madam Lynn exchanges a glance with Isaac and something seems to silently pass between them. My heart pounds harder in my chest.

I look back and forth between the both of them. "Where is he?" My body trembles with anxiety. Someone tell me something!

Madam Lynn is silent, and the look of sadness she throws my way makes my stomach churn.

"Please tell me what's going on!" I cry.

"You're better off without him," Isaac says finally, firmly. At the frown that crumples my face, he adds, "I'm sorry if it's not what you want to hear, but he's no good for you, Lilly."

"Isaac!" Madam Lynn snaps, and she looks pissed. And Isaac's shocked.

"If he really wanted you, he'd be here. Not leaving you to wonder where he's at," Isaac says.

"That's not true. You don't know him!" I cry out.

"Get out, Isaac," Madam Lynn says in a low voice. "I told you, you don't know him." Her voice is full of hurt. And from the look that flashes in his eyes, he seems genuinely sorry.

"Out," Madam Lynn says in a bit of a brighter tone, shooing him away.

Isaac stands there for a moment waiting for her to look at him again, but she doesn't. He looks like he wants to tell me something. But again... nothing.

He presses his lips into a straight line and nods before leaving the room. At the door, he stops to tell me, "My team and I will be waiting to escort you home, Ms. Wade. Just come to us when you're ready."

I don't answer him. Fuck him for saying that. It hurts. I'm already hurting, and what he said was only salt in the wound. The only words I can get out are, "You don't know him."

The second the door closes, Madam Lynn says, "I was really pissed at Joseph." She clears her throat, taking the seat in the far corner of the room. The chair is a pale pink, and studded nails line the smooth leather. She runs her hands down the edge and it suits her. She looks like she belongs there.

"He's okay," she says and I stare at her with wide eyes. "Joseph is." My body sags with relief. "He called a few hours ago. It's over with."

A few hours ago? Her words hit me like a knife to my back

"I'm sorry about Isaac. He doesn't know Joseph well." I can tell she's trying to change the subject, but I don't let her.

"Hours?" I ask her. Her expression tells me that she knows how I feel.

"He's safe. And he knows you're safe." I'm quiet as I sit on the edge of the bed, overwhelmed by so many emotions.

"He'll come for you. I'm sure he will." Her eyes are so full of sincerity, that I believe her. I believe that she truly thinks he will.

But her words don't give me the confidence I need. I want him here now. I want to watch that stupid dot on the phone coming closer and closer to me. Bringing him back to me.

But then I think back to the last look he gave me, and my doubts fall away.

I know what I saw in his eyes. And that wasn't a lie.

He loves me. And he's going to come for me.

And if he doesn't, then I'll go to him.

Chapter 30

Joseph

The trunk closes at the foot of my bed with a loud clack. All the memories of my past have been placed inside, including my journal. I have no need for it anymore, no desire to write another word.

It's over.

There's not a single target on my back with both my father and my brother gone. Zander's assured me he'll keep his ear low to the ground. His finger's on the pulse of what's going on behind closed doors. I'm not sure what he wants from me, he's yet to ask. I don't like owing a debt to anyone if I can help it, but still I'm grateful.

Because of Lilly.

I want her back. I want her here, in my house and in my

bed, just like I did that first night I saw her. She belongs to me now. So any protection I can take, I will. Even if that means making a deal with Zander.

As I grab my keys, they clink off the foyer table. The sound echoes with me as I realized the only reason I'll be coming home without her is if she doesn't want me. My hand hesitates on the doorknob, my mind replaying all the moments we've had in the past month.

We've grown together. I've been there for her, and she's been there for me. At least in my mind, that's what happened. I know these past two weeks she's been a prisoner, unable to go as she pleases. It was for her own safety, her own good. As I close the front door behind me, my body heats as I remember her in the cage staring at me with daggers in her eyes.

She could leave me now. She could walk away from me forever, and there's nothing I can do. I never locked the cage, and I never will.

The thought chills me along with the bitter cold February air. I forgot my coat. I don't give a fuck; I'm not going back. Not until I have her in my arms.

My strides quicken, and I hit the clicker to unlock my car. The faint *beep beep* rings out in the cold.

I'll be coming back with my flower. I know I will.

Just as I open my driver door, I see a car coming up the long winding drive. There's a dusting of snow over the clearing, and as the old red Honda takes the bend, the car drifts slightly.

My heart races in my chest, and I drop the keys onto the ground.

Lilly.

She regains control and takes it slower up the drive. I swear to God if she kills herself finding her way back to me, I'll never forgive her.

I leave the keys where they are as small specks of snow float down from the sky and Lilly parks her car in the driveway. She looks up through the windshield, hesitation clear on her face, that gorgeous vulnerability shining in her doe eyes.

My flower.

I try not to assume that she's come for me. That once again we desire the same thing. A harsh lump forms in my throat, the spikes threatening to suffocate me. My hands clench and unclench as the chill of the air starts to affect me.

I ignore all of it, walking to her driver door and opening it. She looks up at me warily as I offer her my hand. *Please don't deny me, my flower.* Be here for me. Please.

Her hand feels so small, so warm in mine. I've always known we were different, but I've grown to love how she complements me. She brings out a side to me that I don't want to lose.

We share a look, I'm not sure what mine reflects to her, but hers undeniably sends a chill through my body. She's looking at me as though she doesn't know what I'm thinking. I've seen it on her face a dozen times or more.

She should know what she means to me. And the fact

that she doesn't makes me nervous. I'm not a man who likes to be nervous. It's not a comfortable feeling.

My hand splays on the small of her back, but I'm quick to pull her in close, wrapping my arm around her waist and holding her small body into mine as I lead her inside.

When I peek down at her, lowering myself to the ground to pick up my keys that are now freezing and coated with a thin layer of snow, I see a small smile on her lips. Nothing in my life has made me feel better. She makes me feel secure and wanted. I'll never let her go. Never. When you find someone who makes you feel like this, there's no reason to ever give her a reason to walk away.

She shivers in the doorway as I unlock the door, opening it and allowing the warmth of my home to spread through us both. Her heels click in the foyer as she continues walking without me. I close the door with my back to her, taking a deep breath. She came back to me. I can't let her leave. I close my eyes at that thought, realizing that's not what she needs. I need to give her a reason to stay of her own free will. I can't keep her here, but knowing that she's come here has to mean something.

I turn slowly to face her, her ankles cross slightly and she sways, standing there in the middle of the open doorway, her hands clasped and her coat hanging in the crook of her arm. She looks just as nervous as I feel. The sight of her reminds me of the first day I had her here. The same uncertainty, and just like before I know I'll soothe her worries. If only she lets me.

"I want you to stay for another month," I offer her, my voice echoes off the empty walls, walking to her and standing just inches in front of her. Technically our contract isn't over yet; Valentine's Day is tomorrow. But I want to bind her with the contract if I can. I don't want the days to pass and have no claim to her.

"Just a month?" she asks, a look flashing in her eyes. I like hearing the words "Yes, Sir" from her lips. But this may be even better.

"You want more, my flower?" I hope she says yes. Whatever she tells me she wants, I'll give her. I just need her to tell me.

I finally feel like I have a reason to live. And a future to look forward to with Lilly. I can give her whatever she needs. Whatever she asks for, I would happily provide her with. I'm sure she's realized that by now. Without her with me, I was clinging to the past just to feel. I don't want that anymore. I want her; all of her.

"I care for you Lilly," I stare into her eyes as I tell her, for the first time I think in my entire life making my feelings known for someone else. I feel vulnerable in this moment, and she looks back at me, not answering. She could reject me. It would crush me if she did.

My thumb rubs along her cheek as I cup her chin in my hand. Her hands gently wrap around my wrists as she leans into my touch. Her eyes close, and a look of pure happiness is on her face. It soothes the worry in me, but still I need her to tell me that she feels the same. I know the way we started wasn't what she wanted. It was a game of fools thinking we each knew what we wanted, when we knew nothing. But now I know. And I'm ready to fight for her.

"You can say you love me. I know you do," Lilly says teasingly.

Finally opening her pale blue eyes, it's as though she's looking straight into my soul. The look in her eyes doesn't match the tone of her voice. She needs me to tell her. I'm not sure if I'd recognize the emotion love. It's not something I grew up with, nothing I've ever felt before. But there's something different between the two of us. Something that drew me to her that first day. And something that fuels me to move mountains to be with her. To never let her go.

"I love you, Lilly." My lips brush against hers as I whisper the words. It must be love. "I love you."

"I love you, Sir."

Her wrists are bound by the thin rope, the end looped over the cast-iron loop above the headboard. She's bound to my bed where she belongs. Her movements are easy. The only reason the ropes are even there is to prevent her from spearing her fingers in my hair as I continue to lick between her legs. Her arousal is so sweet, so delicious. And all mine.

I crawl up her body, kissing my way as I go. Her thighs wrap around my shoulders and then down my sides to my waist. I've given her as much control as she can manage for this session. No holding still. No asking permission. All she has to do is feel and react. Although I did bind her wrists… she's greedy.

My fingers are wrapped around her throat as I settle my hips between her thighs, spreading her even more. My hard dick nestles between her sweet pussy. I kiss her lips with the intense passion I feel. I'm grateful for every moment with her. I'll never let her go. I need her too much.

"Who do you belong to?" I ask her.

"You, Sir, only you." I love how lust coats her voice.

"Only me for always," I tell her before slamming into her, all the way to the hilt, capturing her cries of pleasure with my lips. The headboard knocks against the wall with each hard thrust. It only fuels me to take her harder.

She is my one and only. And I'm hers.

Epilogue

Lily

"Not this bullshit again!" I slam the book that I'm reading, *Don't Stop,* shut with a frustrated growl. How in the hell did I manage to find another book that pisses me off so much that I want to throw it across the room? And after I took every precaution to make sure I didn't?

This one was even worse than the last. The hero and heroine, Randy and Ada, made it through so many trials and tribulations that I was rooting for them like crazy toward the end.

I got really excited, turning the pages with bated breath. And it looked like their path was on its way to glory, only to find out that Ada was hiding a secret baby from Randy. A baby that was sure to cause major scandal between their families. The book cut off right there.

Ugh. It makes me so mad!

Like, who the fuck does that?

I can't say it enough.

I. Detest. Cliffhangers.

But even after all that, I'm dying to know what happened.

A thousand poxes on the author for doing this to me and making me wait! ...I know I'll end up buying the next one though. I blow a strand of hair out of my face as I toss the book onto the ottoman. I guess I'm a glutton for punishment.

I stretch out before grabbing my laptop and opening up my manuscript.

Last night I rewarded myself with writing a chapter of my new novel when I was finally finished my grueling lesson plans.

I'm excited about *both* the classes and my book.

The words for the novel are flowing easily. And I know with all the inspiration that I have, and the support of my awesome beta reader Jenna, I'll be able to do the book justice.

But it's my hobby. Not my job. I chew my bottom lip, holding back my smile. I got my old job back before the semester even started. Some anonymous donor came through and funded the *Children in Need Foundation*.

Anonymous. Joseph actually started to tell me it wasn't him when I pried. He didn't want me to feel like I owed him. He has no idea how much I owe him. But not in the way he thinks.

I can't believe how much he's helped me in the short time we've been together. How much we've helped each other.

And lately, I've been able to have both sides to him, the Master and the gentleman.

A soft sigh escapes my lips at the thought.

Just thinking about it, I can't imagine my life getting any better.

The sound of heavy footsteps in the doorway causes me to look up, and my heart skips a beat at the dangerously sexy man who's standing there.

"Reading something?" his deep masculine voice asks.

Wearing dark grey dress pants and a white Henley open at the chest, his hair slicked to the side, Joseph looks like an absolute vision as he leans against the doorway with a grin on his face.

"Sir," I practically purr as he pulls away from the door and walks into the room.

I slip out of my chair and onto my knees, getting down on all floors and crawling forward like a vixen.

Joseph chuckles playfully at the sight. He's told me to do this when I want to play with him, and I take full advantage.

"Up," he orders me.

I rise to my feet and look him in the eye. Up close, I'm enveloped by that masculine scent that I love so much, and I inhale deeply, sucking in as much of him as I can.

Grinning, he wraps my arms around his waist and pulls me in close, delivering a soft kiss to my lips.

"I was," I reply to his earlier question when he pulls back, leaving me breathless.

He chuckles again. "I know. I could hear you yelling from across the house."

My cheeks turn red with embarrassment. I hadn't realized I'd been yelling like a maniac. But I guess that's what happens when you get smacked in the face with a cliffhanger.

"Sorry," I mutter.

Joseph quirks an amused eyebrow. "What happened in it that got you so worked up?"

"You don't want to know," I growl.

Joseph pouts. "That's not fair."

Neither was that ending. I still want to beat that author's ass like they're a Submissive from Club X. I don't bother saying it though.

"Life isn't fair," I say, giving him another kiss on the lips.

Joseph grins at me.

We stare at each other for a moment, and my heart feels full. I can't believe how lucky that I am to have this man.

"What?" I ask, breaking out of my thoughts to see Joseph gazing at me with a mischievous smile.

"I've got something for you."

My heart stalling in my chest, I watch as he produces a large, black velvet box. For a moment, I think it might be an engagement ring, but the box is far too big.

A faint smile spreads across my face and I shake my head at my eagerness. It's too soon to be expecting something like that. But I do want it. I want everyone to know that he's mine, and I'm his.

It will happen, I tell myself. *Eventually.*

I clear my throat, reaching out for it, and our fingers brush against one another and I feel that same spark I felt so long ago. Maybe not that long ago, but it feels like it with everything we've been through.

"Open it," he prods softly, pushing the box into my hands.

I keep the smile on my face although my throat closes, and I do as he says. My heart jumps when I see what's inside, my knees going weak.

"Joseph," I gasp, my eyes filling with tears, the air being pulled from my lungs. *Oh my God, oh my God,* I repeat in my mind over and over.

It's a collar, a beautiful one, black and silver, encrusted with sparkling diamonds. But it isn't the first thing that caught my eye.

There's a ring in there, too. I choke on my words for a moment, in shock but mostly just overwhelmed with so much happiness.

"What's this?" I somehow manage, my voice a breathless whisper, though I know exactly what it is. Staring at the ring, a platinum band with a large, sparkling diamond atop of it, it's suddenly very hard to breathe.

I imagined it moments before, but this doesn't seem real.

Joseph sinks to his knee in front of me, his heart in his eyes. My heart skips a beat and my skin pricks as reality sets in. The room spins around me as I stare down at him, and I feel like passing out.

"Lilly Marie Wade, my flower," he says, his voice aching with emotion, "Will you marry me?"

I stare at him in disbelief, my throat so tight with emotion I'm barely able to fill my lungs. I can't find the words to answer. I'm stunned.

The silence stretches on for several long moments as I try to get over my shock. My chest heaves as I struggle to draw in breaths, my legs feeling like jello. Through it all, Joseph waits patiently, staying on one knee.

Say yes, you idiot!

"Yes!" I'm finally able to croak when I find my voice, leaning down to wrap my arms around his neck and bury his face with tearful kisses, my heart pounding like a battering ram. "Yes, yes, yes! I'll marry you, Joseph!"

"Good." Joseph pulls me down into his arms, delivering a deep solid kiss to my lips. "Because I love you, Lilly. And I'm never letting you go."

I smile up at him through my tears, my heart aching from the unbelievable joy that fills my body and the happiness I see reflected in his eyes.

Delivering another kiss to his lips, I breathe out through aching lungs, "I love you too, Joseph."

About the Authors

Thank you so much for reading our co-written novel. We hope you loved reading it as much as we loved writing it!

For more information on the books we have published, bonus scenes and more visit our websites.

More by Willow Winters
www.willowwinterswrites.com/books

More by Lauren Landish
www.laurenlandish.com

Printed in the USA
CPSIA information can be obtained
at www.ICGtesting.com
JSHW080002130124
55289JS00002B/9